Night has a
Thousand Eyes

Also by Cornell Woolrich
and available from Pegasus Books

Manhattan Love Song

Night has a Thousand Eyes

Cornell Woolrich

PEGASUS BOOKS
NEW YORK

NIGHT HAS A THOUSAND EYES

Pegasus Books LLC
45 Wall Street, Suite 1021
New York, NY 10005

Copyright © 1945 by Cornell Woolrich

Introduction copyright © 2007 by Francis M. Nevins, Jr.

First Pegasus Books edition 2007

Interior design by Maria Fernandez

Library of Congress Cataloging-in-Publication Data is available.

ISBN: 978-1-933648-27-9

10 9 8 7 6 5 4 3 2 1

Printed in the United States of America
Distributed by Consortium

"Thus death is nothing terrible; . . .
But the opinion we have of death, that
it is terrible, that is wherein the terror lieth."
　　　　　　　　—Encheiridion of Epictetus
　　　　　　　　(T. W. Rolleston's translation)

Contents

Introduction

Francis M. Nevins

Noir.

Any French dictionary will tell you that the word's primary meaning is black, dark or gloomy. But since the mid-1940s and when used with the nouns *roman* (novel) or *film*, the adjective has developed a specialized meaning, referring to the kind of bleak, disillusioned study in the poetry of terror that flourished in American mystery fiction during the 1930s and forties and in American crime movies during the forties and fifties. The hallmarks of the *noir* style are fear, guilt and loneliness, breakdown and despair, sexual obsession and social corruption, a sense that the world is controlled by malignant forces preying on us, a rejection of happy endings and a preference for resolutions heavy with doom, but always redeemed by a breathtakingly vivid poetry of word (if the work was a novel or story) or image (if it was a movie).

During the 1940s many American books of this sort were published in French translation in a long-running series called the *Serie Noire,* and at the end of World War II, when French film enthusiasts were exposed for the first time to Hollywood's cinematic analogue of those books, they coined the term *film noir* as a phrase to describe the genre. What Americans of those years tended to dismiss as rather tawdry commercial entertainments the French saw as profound explorations of the heart of darkness, largely because *noir* was so intimately related to the themes of French existentialist writers like Jean-Paul Sartre and Albert Camus, and because the bleak world of *noir* spoke to the despair which so many in Europe were experiencing after the nightmare years of war and occupation and genocide. By the early 1960s cinephiles in the United States had virtually made an American phrase out of *film noir* and had acclaimed this type of movie as one of the most fascinating genres to emerge from Hollywood. *Noir* directors—not only the giants like Alfred Hitchcock (in certain moods) and Fritz Lang but relative unknowns like Edgar G. Ulmer, Jacques Tourneur, Robert Siodmak, Joseph H. Lewis and Anthony Mann—were hailed as visual poets whose cinematic style made the bleakness of their films not only palatable but fantastically exciting.

Foster Hirsch's *The Dark Side of the Screen: Film Noir* (1981) and several other books on this genre have been published in the United States and one can attend courses on *film noir* at any number of colleges. But there has not yet developed the same degree of interest in the doom-haunted novels and tales of suspense in which *film noir* had its roots. Although Raymond Chandler, the poet of big-city corruption, and James M. Cain, the chronicler of sexual obsession, have received the fame they deserve, the names of countless other *noir* writers are known mainly to specialists.

I have three names for one of those writers. He was the Poe of the twentieth century, the poet of its shadows, the Hitchcock of the written word. His name was Cornell Woolrich.

He was born in New York City on December 4, 1903 to parents whose marriage collapsed in his youth. Much of his childhood was spent in Mexico with his father Genaro Hopley-Woolrich, a civil engineer. At age eight the experience of seeing a traveling French company perform Puccini's *Madama Butterfly* in Mexico City gave Woolrich a sudden sharp insight into color and drama and his first sense of tragedy. Three years later he understood fully that someday like Cio-Cio-San he too would have to die, and from then on he was haunted by a sense of doom that never left him. *I had that trapped feeling, like some sort of a poor insect that you've put inside a downturned glass, and it tries to climb up the sides, and it can't, and it can't, and it can't.*

During adolescence he returned to Manhattan and lived in an opulent house on 113th Street with his mother and her socially prominent family. In 1921 he entered Columbia College, a short walk from home. He began writing fiction during an illness in his junior year and quit school soon afterward to pursue his dream of becoming another F. Scott Fitzgerald. His first novel, *Cover Charge* (1926), chronicled the lives and loves of the Jazz Age's gilded youth in the manner of his own and his whole generation's literary idol. This debut was followed by *Children of the Ritz* (1927), a frothy concoction about a spoiled heiress' marriage to her chauffeur, which won him a $10,000 prize contest and a contract from First National Pictures for the movie rights. Woolrich was invited to Hollywood to help with the adaptation and stayed on as a staff writer. Besides his movie chores and an occasional story or article for magazines like *College Humor* and *Smart Set*, he completed three more novels during these years. In December 1930 he entered a brief and inexplicable marriage with a producer's daughter—inexplicable because for several years he had been homosexual. After the marriage he continued his secret life, prowling the waterfront at night in search of partners, and after the inevitable breakup Woolrich fled back to Manhattan and his mother. The two of them traveled extensively in Europe during the early 1930s. His only novel of that period was *Manhattan Love Song* (1932), which anticipates the motifs of his later suspense fiction with its tale of a love-struck young couple cursed by a malignant fate which leaves one dead and the other desolate. But over the next two years he sold almost nothing and was soon deep in debt, reduced to sneaking into movie houses by the fire doors for his entertainment.

In 1934 Woolrich decided to abandon the *literary* world and concentrate on mystery-suspense fiction. He sold three stories to pulp magazines that year, ten more in 1935, and was soon an established professional whose name was a fixture on the covers of *Black Mask, Detective Fiction Weekly, Dime Detective* and countless other pulps. For the next quarter century he lived with his mother in a succession of residential hotels, going out only when it was absolutely essential, trapped in a bizarre love-hate relationship that dominated his external world just as the inner world of his later fiction reflects in its tortured patterns the strangler grip in which his mother and his own inability to love a woman held him.

The more than 100 stories and novelettes Woolrich sold to the pulps before the end of the thirties are richly varied in type and include quasi police procedurals, rapid-action whizbangs and encounters with the occult. But the best and best-known of them are the tales of pure edge-of-the-seat suspense, and even their titles reflect the bleakness and despair of their themes. *I Wouldn't Be in Your Shoes, Speak to Me of Death, All at Once, No Alice, Dusk to Dawn, Men Must Die, If I Should Die Before I Wake, The Living Lie Down with the Dead, Charlie Won't Be Home Tonight, You'll Never See Me Again*—these and dozens of other

Woolrich suspense stories evoke with awesome power the desperation of those who walk the city's darkened streets and the terror that lurks at noonday in commonplace settings. In his hands even such cliched storylines as the race to save the innocent man from the electric chair and the amnesiac hunting his lost self resonate with human anguish. Woolrich's world is a feverish place where the prevailing emotions are loneliness and fear and the prevailing action a race against time and death. His most characteristic detective stories end with the discovery that no rational account of events is possible and his suspense stories tend to close not with the dissipation of terror but with its omnipresence.

In 1940 Woolrich joined the migration of pulp mystery writers from lurid-covered magazines to hardcover books and, beginning with *The Bride Wore Black* (1940), launched his so-called Black Series of suspense novels—which appeared in France as part of the *Serie Noire* and led the French to acclaim him as a master of bleak poetic vision. Much of his reputation still rests on those novels and on the other suspense classics originally published under his pseudonyms William Irish and George Hopley. Throughout the forties and fifties Woolrich's publishers issued numerous hardcover and paperback collections of his short stories. Many of his novels and tales were adapted into movies, including such fine *films noirs* as Jacques Tourneur's *The Leopard Man* (1943), Robert Siodmak's *Phantom Lady* (1944), Roy William Neill's *Black Angel* (1946), Maxwell Shane's *Fear in the Night* (1947) and, most famous of all, Hitchcock's *Rear Window* (1954). Even more of Woolrich's work was turned into radio and later into television drama. He made a great deal of money from his novels and stories but lived a Spartan and isolated life and never seemed to enjoy a moment of his time on earth. Seeing the world as he did, how could he?

The typical Woolrich settings are the seedy hotel, the cheap dance hall, the rundown movie house and the precinct station backroom. The dominant reality in his world, at least during the thirties, is the Depression, and Woolrich has no peers when it comes to putting us inside the life of a frightened little guy in a tiny apartment with no money, no job, a hungry wife and children, and anxiety consuming him like a cancer. If a Woolrich protagonist is in love, the beloved is likely to vanish in such a way that the protagonist not only can't find her but can't convince anyone she ever existed. Or, in another classic Woolrich situation, the protagonist comes to after a blackout—caused by amnesia, drugs, hypnosis or whatever—and little by little becomes convinced that he committed a murder or other crime while out of himself. The police are rarely sympathetic, for they are the earthly counterparts of the malignant powers above and their main function is to torment the helpless.

All we can do about this nightmare world is to create, if we can, a few islands of love and trust to sustain us and help us forget. But love dies while the lovers go on living, and Woolrich is a master at portraying the corrosion of a relationship. Although he often wrote about the horrors both love and lovelessness can inspire, there are very few irredeemably evil characters in his stories. For if one loves or needs love, or is at the brink of destruction, Woolrich identifies with that person no matter how dark his or her dark side. Technically many of Woolrich's novels and stories are awful, but like the playwrights of the Absurd, Woolrich often uses a senseless tale to hold the mirror to a senseless universe. Some of his tales indeed end quite happily—usually thanks to outlandish coincidence—but there are no series characters in his work and therefore the reader can never know in advance whether a particular Woolrich story will be light or dark, *allegre* or *noir;* whether a particular protagonist will end triumphant or dismembered. This is one of the reasons why so much of his work remains so hauntingly suspenseful.

Including *Night Has A Thousand Eyes.*

Of all Woolrich's novels this is the one most completely dominated by death and fate, the one in which he pulls out all the stops to make the reader feel like an insect trapped in an inverted glass, the way he had experienced the human condition since early adolescence when he understood his own inevitable death. A simpleminded recluse with apparently uncanny powers predicts that millionaire Harlan Reid will die in three weeks, precisely at midnight, by the jaws of a lion, and the tension rises to unbearable pitch as the doomed man and his daughter Jean and the sympathetic young homicide detective Tom Shawn struggle to avert a destiny which they at first suspect and soon come to pray was conceived by a merely human power. Here is the kind of waking nightmare that lies at the heart of *noir,* and Woolrich makes us live the emotional torment and suspense of the situation until we are literally shivering in our seats.

The specifics of this novel may have been suggested to him by a long-forgotten B movie, *On Probation* (Peerless Pictures, 1935), which was directed by silent serial daredevil Charles Hutchison and starred Monte Blue, William Bakewell and Lucile Browne. Whether or not Woolrich happened to see this film, within a year of its release he used the mystic prediction of death at the lion's jaws as the leitmotif of one of his most terrifying suspense novelettes, *Speak to Me of Death* (*Argosy,* February 1937; collected in *The Fantastic Stories of Cornell Woolrich,* 1981). Eight years after its magazine appearance the tale became the nucleus of *Night Has A Thousand Eyes.*

The novel was published in 1945, not as an entry in the Black

Series under Woolrich's own name nor as a William Irish title but with a byline composed of the author's two middle names, George Hopley, and under the imprint of a publishing house (Rinehart) which had never handled him before. It seems to have been intended as a breakthrough novel, designed to introduce Woolrich to a larger audience, and was recognized early on as a major work even by those who didn't recognize Woolrich as its author. Long and sometimes perceptive reviews appeared in several major publications. *The pace never slackens,* said James MacBride in the *New York Times, from the superb cinematic opening . . . to the gelid pay-off. . . . Leave the night-light burning if you insist on finishing this one in bed.*

Perhaps the novel was *too* intense, *too* suspenseful. Although Paramount Pictures bought movie rights almost as soon as the first copies hit the bookstores, the only reprint edition published in the United States during the 1940s was the Grosset & Dunlap hardcover reissue, timed to coincide with release of the film version in 1948. In the fifties it was reprinted only once (Dell pb #679, 1953), not as by Hopley but under the much better known William Irish byline. In the last full year of Woolrich's life it came out again in softcover (Paperback Library pb #54-438, 1967), this time as by Woolrich himself. I predicted years ago that the then-most recent paperback (Ballantine pb #30667, 1983) would not be the last, and it's a pleasure to be proved right.

The movie *Night Has A Thousand Eyes* (Paramount, 1948), was directed by John Farrow from a screenplay by Barre Lyndon and hardboiled mystery writer Jonathan Latimer. The film kept Woolrich's title but had little connection with the novel and almost none of its power and terror. Edward G. Robinson starred as carnival mind-reader John Triton, the cinematic stand-in for Woolrich's haunted prophet Jeremiah Tompkins, with Gail Russell as Jean Courtland (Jean Reid in the novel), John Lund as her boyfriend Elliott Carson (who doesn't exist in the novel), and William Demarest as a skeptical and middle-aged Lt. Shawn. The picture opens with a striking scene vaguely like the beginning of the novel as Russell, pursued by Lund, wanders in a trance through a railroad yard to a high bridge from which she feels compelled to leap to her death. Lund saves her and brings her back to the coffee shop where Robinson is waiting. In a flashback sequence that's exceptionally long even for *film noir*, Robinson tells the young couple how years ago, while working as a phony vaudeville mind-reader, he suddenly found himself endowed with what he claims is true clairvoyant power—primarily the power to foresee deaths and disasters. He correctly predicted the death of Russell's father in a plane crash and in due course he reveals his prevision that she will die at the feet of a lion at precisely 11:00 PM. The film then mutates into a standard whodunit padded with discussions about whether there's a scientific basis for ESP. Finally Robinson convinces the police that his powers are real, rushes to save Russell from an idiotic plot by one of her father's business associates to kill her, and is mistakenly shot to death by the detectives who were her bodyguards. In his pocket the police find a note in which he predicted his own death that night.

What I hoped to establish, Jonathan Latimer said in an interview near the end of his life, *was a real sense of terror that these things were coming true.* This is precisely what Woolrich wanted too but that hope was frustrated by the film-makers' radical alterations in the storyline, which left a silly and unsuspenseful plot that depended on several interlocked ridiculous contrivances. The film's strong points are Farrow's stylish direction and Robinson's fine performance as a sort of Woolrich surrogate, a man whose gift has turned him into a half-crazed recluse obsessed by the inevitability of death. But one senses the hand of the devoutly Catholic Farrow in the climax where Robinson becomes a sort of Jesus figure, choosing to go to his own death so that his quasi-daughter might live. Less than a year after its release Farrow hosted a thirty-minute radio version of the movie on NBC's *Screen Directors' Playhouse,* with Robinson and Demarest reprising their movie roles, and in the summer of 1953 the *Philip Morris Playhouse on Broadway* offered a different thirty-minute radio adaptation of the movie with Peter Lorre in Robinson's role.

Woolrich knew overwhelming financial and critical success but his life remained a wretched mess, and when his mother died in 1957 he cracked. From then until his own death eleven years later he lived alone, his last year spent in a wheelchair after the amputation of a gangrenous leg, thin as a rail, white as a ghost, wracked by diabetes and alcoholism and self-contempt. But the best of his final *tales of love and despair* are still gifted with the magic touch that chills the heart. He died of a stroke on September 25, 1968, leaving no survivors. Only a tiny handful of people attended his funeral. His estate was left in trust to Columbia University where his literary career had begun, to establish a scholarship fund for students of creative writing. The fund is named for Woolrich's mother. He left behind four unfinished books—two novels, a collection of short stories and a fragmentary autobiography—plus a list of titles for stories he'd never even begun. In one of these he captured the essence of his world and the world of *noir* in just six words.

First you dream, then you die.

In a fragment found among his papers after he was gone, Woolrich explained why he wrote as he did. *I was only trying to cheat death,* he said. *I was only trying to surmount for a little while the darkness that all my life I surely knew was going to come rolling in on me some day and obliterate me.* In the end of course he had to die as we all do. But as long as there are readers to be haunted by the fruit of his life, by the way he took his wretched psychological environment and his sense of entrapment and loneliness and turned them into poetry of the shadows, the world Woolrich imagined lives.

PART ONE

1
The Meeting

EVERY NIGHT HE WALKED ALONG the river, going home. Every night, about one. You do that when you're young; walk along beside the river, looking at the water, looking at the stars. Sometimes you do that even when you're a detective, and strictly speaking, have nothing to do with stars.

He could have taken a bus, ridden home as all the others did, when he came off duty. It wasn't even the shortest route to where he lived, this walk beside the river. It took him out of his way a little. He didn't mind that. It sounded better when you whistled, with the water there beside you. It made the stars seem brighter, and it made you want to look at them more, when the water was there below them to catch them upside down. It made you dream better; those dreams you have in your head in your twenties. You can't dream in a bus, with your fellows all around you.

And so—every night he walked along the river, going home. Every night, about one, a little after.

Anything you keep doing like that, if you keep on doing it long enough, suddenly one time something happens. Something that counts, something that matters, something that changes the whole rest of your life. And you forget all the other times that went before it, and just remember that once.

Shawn was his name. The others couldn't figure him out. But then who can ever figure anyone else out? They didn't try very hard; they didn't have the time. They just mentioned it once in a while, going off duty.

"Hey, Shawn, you coming this way?"

"No, I guess I'll walk home along the river."

Then they'd go their way and he'd go his, and somebody would say it. Not hostilely, though.

"I can't figure him out."

"Sort of a dreamer, I guess."

Heads would nod, but only in mild disapproval. As over some minor defect, easily forgiven, certainly not enough to strain their group loyalty. Then they wouldn't refer to it again for another two months. Because it wasn't a very glaring difference. Just a shading of character.

So now the river, and him, and a night like the many others.

His whistle went along a little ahead of him, before there was anyone there, and then he followed in due course, at an easy-moving stride. Not a very loud whistle. Cheerful and low and not even very good. Usually the same thing every night, almost always the same thing. *Show Me the Way to Go Home.* That's a good tune to have for company beside the river when you're twenty-eight.

Peaceful along there. No one else around. Just him and the stars. He'd look up at them every once in a while. There were myriads of them tonight. They must have brought out the reserves. He'd never seen so many of them before. They were almost woven together in places, like a gleaming fish-scale fabric.

It was high along there, good and high, a sort of bluff. And then it made a slow turn around and went into a bridge. His side was the town, the opposite shore was country. You could see the lights of some boulevard strung along the summit over there, much like a string of beads, where there are too few beads on the string and a lot of empty string stretches between. Once in a while a moving light would crawl from one bead to the next, and that was a car going along at good speed, though from where he was it seemed to creep.

On his side there were the brick ramparts of the town, set back at a good distance from where he ambled along, with a punch-hole of orange let into them here and there at irregular intervals and levels. One o'clock and most of them had been plugged up by now, by sleep. Then there were two or three lanes of traffic out before these battlements, like a concrete moat. And then a wide strip with trees in young June leaf, an occasional lamppost set into their midst making an explosion of vivid apple green in the canopy of their otherwise dark foliage. And then the paved walk he was striding along, alternate blue-black and silver with these same lights, for they bordered it. Then a stone coping about waist-high, and then the drop down to the water.

That was the setting for his whistling and his stargazing and his dreaming, if any. And probably there was some; who hasn't at least one dream to light up and smoke, on his homeward way at twenty-eight?

As he followed the zebra-striped walk, now light, now dark, now light again, his glance hit the ground at the onset of one of the light patches, and he had that illusory impression everyone has had at one time or another that there was money lying there at his feet. He didn't give in to it for a moment, let his legs carry him onward a pace or two. Too good to be true, and it never *was* money when you stopped and made a fool out of yourself by picking it up.

Then his whistle checked itself, and he stooped and turned and went back the pace or two. And he stopped and did pick it up. And this was the one time that it was just what it had looked like. It was money. A five-dollar bill.

He gave another sort of whistle, without tune, just of the breath, and looked the bill over, and started it toward his trouser pocket.

There was a little wind blowing. It was coming toward him, in the direction he'd been going. Before he'd even finished putting the money away, he saw something scuttling toward him erratically. Stopping, then sidling on, stopping, then sneaking on some more. He stopped it with his foot. It was another bill, this one a single dollar.

He craned his neck and looked down the vista of lighted and shadowed strips that were like alternate railroad ties of black and white, until they turned and made for the bridge. There was no one in sight. Nothing.

He went on quickly. He kept the two bills in his hand now. He didn't whistle any more. He stopped, went on. He had three now. He went on quicker than ever. He stopped again. He had three in one hand, one in his other hand now. Sixteen dollars. It was like picking up leaves off the ground.

He was making the turn and there was the bridge entrance ahead of him. The paved walk he was on went on, but over water. The coping beside it went on, but with no earth at its base, only empty space that curved around underneath it. The trees stopped. There were more lights here, ornamental candelabra lampposts, standing one on each side of the way at the approach to the bridge. Then the bridge itself was dark again, like a tunnel running under interlaced girders.

The bridge wasn't his way. He usually skirted it and went on again, still on the town side of the promontory it jutted from. But he usually didn't pick up money with his two hands.

Something winked, as though one of the stars had become embedded in the pavement. He pinched at the little spark, and came up holding a diamond ring in his hand. It bore a single stone, and large, and of good water.

He looked around him carefully. Still no one, nothing. Then he saw that something was breaking the evenness, the flatness of line of the parapet top. Some inanimate something, some black lump. He headed for it. It was close up under one of the ornamental lampposts.

When he reached it he saw that he had the source, the carrier it had all come out of, the ownerless money and the ring alike. It was a woman's black handbag, of some soft substance, probably suede. He didn't know much about those things, but it looked expensive. It had on it an ornamental monogram, of a glittering material that he was to know later, but didn't as yet, as marcasite.

It hadn't been dropped there unintentionally or lost there, for then it would have been down below, at foot level, on the ground itself. It wasn't. It was atop the parapet. It was upside down, and open, balancing crumpled on its own mouth. It was as though it had been held aloft, reversed, by its owner. Up at shoulder height or face height. Then deliberately opened in that position, reversed, so that everything fell out of it, scattered all around. Then, when it was emptied, crushed down atop its own recent contents, still open, still reversed, and left that way in token of renunciation.

Immediately under and around it lay many of the things that, according to his lights, a woman should have held dear to her

7

heart. A wafer of metal that held powder; a crystal rod, the vial of perfume that had sheathed it fractured into bits and still tincturing the air with an elusive sweetness even in its shattered state. He was no expert in women's ways, God knows, but it seemed to him they never threw such things away. This must be meant as some final parting. Close beside, but fallen clear in the overturn, lay the wadded nucleus of paper currency that the erosive breeze had only just begun to disintegrate as he came along. He trapped it under his hand, and thrust it back within the purse.

At a greater distance lay another small object. But this could not have fallen out, it lay too far from the rest. It was a small black silk cord, or two of them rather, and between them a thumbnail's span of diamonds circling a microscopic dial, complete with hands and numerals. A wrist watch. Its position told its story, to anyone who could read such things. It clung to the inside lip of the parapet; one cord, and the watch itself, were topside on it, the second cord hung vertically down the edge. Moreover, when he picked it up, its crystal remained behind on the stone in powdery residue. Its owner, then, had detached it from her wrist, swung it sharply downward by the loose end of one cord, to shatter and to halt it. Then she had left it dangling there. He held it close and squinted at it in the pale reflected light. It marked 1:08. It wasn't going any more. He looked at his own, and that said 1:12. Four minutes ago. Time had stopped for someone.

Then he saw her.

She was not on the pedestrian walk of the bridge, for that stretched vacant to his eye as far as he could see from where he stood. She was up on the parapet, full height, and yet even so she was concealed from him. She was sheltered behind one of the massive stone plinths or abutments that rose far overhead at regularly spaced intervals, to support the steel girders that formed so large a part of the superstructure.

The wind caught at the edge of her skirt and flirted it a little, and the bit of motion caught his eye just as it wandered down the vacant vista. She did not see him at all, for she was on the opposite side, looking downriver, and her back was to him.

She seemed to be doing something with her foot. He received the impression that one leg was bent upon itself, and caught in her own grasp. There was the smothered clap of a shoe to pavement, and the leg had straightened. Then its opposite bent, and a second shoe dropped. They made scarcely a tick, but it was so silent that they had the breathless hush all to themselves to imprint themselves on.

A red spark suddenly struck out behind her, in a sharp downward diagonal, hit the walk and expired, as a cigarette was thrown away, curtly backhand. And this was to be her last disinheritance, her last bequest. There was nothing left now, after this, to abandon.

But he was already running, bent low and with urgent stealth. He had been for the past several seconds already, ever since that revelatory flirt of her skirt. He kept his heels up, to avoid giving her warning; raced with a hissing swiftness on the toes alone. He was frightened. He hadn't been so frightened in the last ten years. Frightened in a peculiar, choking sort of way that had nothing to do with self or self-danger, that was worse than the other kind. His instinct told him that to cry out in advance would be to speed her up, to send her over even faster; to get there too late and find the parapet already empty.

She couldn't have heard him; the tempo of her self-appointed act remained unchanged.

As he swept past the obstructive masonry that had walled her in on the shoreward side, the side he was coming from, her figure came into full-dimensional view. Her head was tilted slightly upward, not downward. She was covering her eyes, as if the stars blinded her. It was against them that her hand was backed in shelter, and not against the water below. For the screen it made was left slightly open at the bottom; it was at the top, along her brow, that it was pressed defensively tight.

He struck the stone bulwark, and at the same time his arms laced around her, in a spiral, one higher than the other; as if the blow against him was what had locked them, automatically.

One held her at the rearward hollow of the knees, fusing her legs together into sudden immobility. The other, higher, soldered itself across her waist, restricting her ability to bend, to fling herself forward, to just her head and shoulders and her upper body.

She swayed drunkenly, like something set into a socket, held constricted below, volatile only above. More with the momentum of his own impetus, transferred to her, than through any active effort of her own. Or so it seemed, by the limp defeated way she danced lightly against the stars. Arms dropping futilely down her sides, head going still farther back, until her throat was arched taut against them, as if they were twinkling knife points and it was their collective target.

This tableau, of arrest, of submission, held for an instant, no more. There were no thoughts in his brain; there were probably none in hers.

Then he had her down beside him, in two or three awkward motions that blended too quickly into one another to be detected separately. First drawing her back, so that she seemed to sit poised on his shoulder for an instant, though she wasn't; she was just held aloft against him. Then allowing her unresistant body to slide down his own, until the ground had stopped it. Then loosing his lower arm, and holding her at full height, against him and supported by him, by the arm that had never left her waist.

It was over, it was done. He had kept her in life.

His breath was coming fast from the run across the bridge apron. Hers only less fast, from the shock of a suddenly dissolved climax, never allowed to reach fulfillment. He could hear it close beside his ear; waited, let it slacken, taper off.

It had ebbed to normality, finally, and his own along with it.

Her hand had gone back to her brow again, but no longer screening her eyes. It was loosely curled at her temple now, in a sort of half fist, pointed outward as if warding off something.

There was a strange absence of speech between them. She didn't rail, berate him, go into the usual dramatics, he noticed. For his part he didn't know what to say. He didn't know what you said to people right after you stopped them from doing such a thing.

Someone had to begin. They couldn't stand there all night like that, in sodden posed conjunction.

He thought: I could offer her a cigarette. But he didn't. If they didn't want the whole world, they didn't want a cigarette either. That was one of the smallest parts of the world.

She still kept holding her head so that her eyes were turned away from the stars, with that loosely adhering hand giving them shade.

It had been going on for only a second or two, most likely, but it felt as if it had been going on forever, this muteness on both their parts.

He spoke finally; anticlimactically, as he might have known he would. As matter-of-factly as if she had just stubbed her toe, or something like that. "What's the matter?" he asked, on a descending inflection.

"Let me get away from them."

"Who?"

She turned her face still farther inward toward his own, away from those points of brilliance lavished all over the sky, thus giving him the answer.

"You should have let me get away from them. I wanted to go down deep, where I can't see them shining, and they can't see me."

There was something the matter with her, of course; there must be. No one felt that way about *them*. They were beautiful things. They were— You wanted to look at them. They were the most beautiful things there were.

"Come over here in the light, where I can see you. Let me get a look at you."

Some poor little drab, he supposed. Crossed up in love. Or something even worse: a night-lady, sick of her lot.

He stooped for something. "Here, don't you want these?" Held her shoes toward her, dangling from their straps.

There was the gentlest of rebukes in her answer. "You make me walk again. I guess I'll have to have them."

She set them back upon the ground, felt for them with her feet, bent within the curve of his arm to fasten the quick strap that was all they seemed to require. He kept his precautionary half embrace about her waist as she did so.

They walked forward a little, to where the nearest of the lights was waiting, scalping a circular bald spot in the gloom of the pavement.

They walked slowly, and not side by side, though linked by his persuading arm. She lagged a step behind him, and moved with reluctance.

It seemed as though, having once begun, she couldn't stop dwelling on it. "You mean to be kind, but you're not. Don't. Ah, don't. Oh, let me get away from them. Let me shut them out. Must they always shine? Won't they ever stop?"

He shook his head slightly, didn't answer.

He had reached the perimeter of radiance. The arc light gave him a drenching flash of surprise, as it tore the darkness apart and she stepped through the rent into full view.

His arm dropped as the first token of it.

"Why—why, look at you!" he stammered. "I thought you were some broken-down— You're young; you're good-looking; you're dressed in expensive clothes. You've got everything! Now, what do you want to do a thing like that for?"

He didn't do her justice. He wasn't adroit with words at any time, and now less so than ever. He'd flung at her the first ones he could lay his mind on in his sincerity, but they fell short of what was required.

She was no more than twenty. She was beautiful, but not in a cloying, simpering way of pouting lips and wheel-spoke lashes. The beauty in her face was expressed in its proportions, in the width of her brow, in the wide spacing of her eyes, in their limpid candor, in the honesty and character already fully expressed in her chin. In all the things that would never leave her, she was beautiful. She was still pale, the shock had not yet left her. There was no paint or other markings on her face, to make it seem anything than what it was. Her hair, which was of the shade where dark blonde meets light brown, fell in soft disorder, no less attractive now than it could have been at the height of full-dressed artifice. She had on a dress of dark cloth, without a single ornament, without so much as a button to distinguish it, yet somehow in the way it fell revealing the fact that it had been made to her order.

He asked it again, overawed at the values he dimly perceived in her. Even he, with his untutored eyes. "What did you want to do a thing like that for? You, a girl like you?"

And again he got that same answer. "Make them stop shining. Make them." Her eyes were fierce with intensity.

He didn't know how to cope with it. "But they're not there to hurt you. They're—they're just there. They always are, they'll always be."

"Then I don't want to be."

He tried to get in past whatever it was, get in to the other side of it, where it was soft. "Look, I'm here with you now. *I'm* not going to hurt you, am I? You don't think I am, do you?"

She touched him on the arm. Suddenly her touch became a convulsive grip. "No, *you* won't. People don't. Men don't. People have hearts. You can reach them. You can say to them, 'Let me alone'—"

"Well, I'm right here with you. Then it's all right. Hold me like that, if you want to. Go ahead, grab me tight. Both hands, that's it, go ahead."

She shuddered. "You'll leave me in a little while, and then I'll be alone with them again."

He put his arm around her again. This time at the shoulder. He managed to make something impersonal out of it, protectively impersonal; a man clasping a child who tells him she is lost. They walked, in this new posture, a few paces. Into the gloom past the first revelatory light; then into a new light radius, then into new gloom beyond that.

He wondered what to do with her. He couldn't just tip his hat, now that he had her off the bridge, and walk away. Go home with her, deposit her there? Home wouldn't do her very much good; she must have come from there, not long before she'd tried—it. Call an ambulance, have her taken to an observation ward? That would only frighten her, and she was frightened enough already.

They'd come to where the bag was, and the litter of belongings, by unnoticeable stages; making little walks, and stops.

She made no move to reclaim it. He was the one who had to stand there and conscientiously put back, one by one, all the things that had come out of it. He stopped when he'd come to the shivered perfume vial, said to her questioningly, "Not this, of course?" and pushed it over the parapet.

She didn't answer. She didn't seem to know what it was. Or if she did, to care.

He remembered the errant bills he'd accumulated along the pavement as he approached the first time, took them out of his pocket, added them to the rest.

The shattered wrist watch, because it was apart, he handed to her direct.

She looked at it with a sort of dull satisfaction. "At least I made this stop," she breathed. Then her lashes dropped, meaning, inversely, she must have checked an impulse to look upward at the sky. "But *they* keep right on."

She handed it back to him, dispassionately as though it belonged to someone else and she had been asked just to look at it. He let it fall out of the hollow of his hand into the bag, and it spilled with a little liquid flash of diamonds.

He had everything in now. He closed the bag, offered it to her.

She didn't take it for a minute. Her original impulse toward disencumbrance must have been still alive within her, even this long after.

"You want it back, don't you?" he had to urge.

"No," she answered with gentle simplicity. "But you want me to, so I'll have to have it, I guess."

She tucked it under her arm the way he'd seen many carry such things.

He asked her a question, and immediately after he had, regretted it, wished he hadn't. It sounded like the devil. It was even more anticlimactic, more fatuous, than his first question back there on the bridge. "Got everything, now?" It sounded as though he were helping her aboard a bus or train or something.

Well, maybe that was what life was; and he was putting her back on, after she'd got off at the wrong station.

"Yes," she said, "everything. My watch, my purse, my life, my hell."

He felt the sting of that, but he didn't answer it. She couldn't make it seem that the right thing for him to have done would have been to let her jump in, no matter what she said.

"Shall we go over this way?" he said.

He led her out toward the traffic lanes, to cut across them and get back to where the city lay, on the other side. He had her hand in the crook of his arm, holding it lightly in place with his other hand. Not tightly, as a prisoner is gripped, but in a sort of sustaining guidance that scarcely made itself felt.

She didn't balk, but presently, at the lip of the first curb, she asked, "Where are you taking me?"

"Just somewhere to sit and talk it over for a while, maybe."

She read his mind accurately. "Away from the river."

"Well," he said defensively, "there are cheerier places."

She didn't answer. He read hers: But it brings you peace.

"I have a car over there," she said after a moment, as though she'd only just then recalled that.

"Oh, why didn't you tell me sooner?" he said briskly. He stopped at once, and turned aside with her, and they went in the new direction. It was up the other way, above the bridge approach. "We'll go over and get in, shall we?"

It was blotted out under the trees, almost invisible from where he'd first been, when he'd looked around immediately before sighting her herself. Then as they came nearer it became a silhouette against the drizzle of light farther down the roadway. Silhouette of a low-slung, custom-built roadster, licorice-glossy. A coin or two of arc light, no more, fell through the layers of leaves that bowered it and made sequinlike disks upon it, one over the hood, one over the rear guard, one over the bulge of the rumble.

He gave a short whistle. "This yours?" He tried to rally her, in a clumsy well-meaning way. "And you were going to leave *this?* How could you have the heart?"

She didn't answer, he noticed; as though she couldn't understand what was of value about it.

He got in under the wheel. "Got the keys?"

"I left them sticking in it, I guess."

He found them fallen down by his feet. "Funny, isn't it?" he philosophized. "If you'd wanted it again, and done that, it probably would have been gone by the time you got back. But because you didn't want it again, it's still here."

He touched something, and a fuming torrent of platinum shot up the roadway ahead of them, making noon under the trees. Then he tempered it to a more moderate glow.

"What a job!" he said, running his hand across the top of the slanted windshield.

"Father had it made up for me when we were on the other side, gave it to me for my eighteenth birthday."

He might as well find out something else while he was about it. "How long have you had it?" he asked, fiddling with the ignition.

"A little over two years now."

Twenty was right, then.

She'd remained there standing by the door, as though now that his arm had been taken away she no longer had any volition toward motion of her own. He wanted her to get in and sit beside him. He made her the offer he'd originally intended to make on the bridge, as a means of drawing her nearer, drawing her in next to him. Offered her his cigarettes, without extending his hand very far toward her. "Would you care for one of these now?"

She entered the car and sank down beside him. She didn't

17

know she was doing it, he could tell. He held a match for her with one hand and with the other, reaching across her, slapped the door safely shut.

Then he watched her for a while, turned toward her, elbow to seat-back.

"We're going to talk about it now. Do you mind?"

He saw her head give a slight shake. He couldn't tell if that meant she didn't mind, or that there was no good talking about it.

She looked so licked, he thought, so baffled. It made you want to tighten your arm around her and— He took hold of his own wrist, made a bracelet around it, a handcuff, with his opposite hand, and held it there fast, slanting down the seat-back.

She kept looking down, into the little boxed floor of the car at their feet. He knew why. To keep from looking up; she was afraid of them, they were still bothering her.

"Who is he?"

She smiled. "I've never been in love."

He thought of the handbag, the bills fluttering along the sidewalk. "It isn't money."

The smile became a laugh. A rueful one, not gay. She answered it with a single word in kind. "Money." The way you speak of dust. Or something that's always there, that you can't help having underfoot a lot, but that you don't dignify by discussing as a rule.

He answered his own question. "I figured it wasn't."

He traced the outline of the wheel rim with one hand, speculatively. "Not love, not money. Is it something the doctors have told you? Something like that? Sometimes they're wrong, they don't always know."

"I haven't been to a doctor since I was twelve. There's never been anything the matter. There isn't now. I've never had an ill day in my life."

18

He couldn't think of anything else. He ducked his chin to the wheel. "I'm only trying to help."

"You're so young, and they're so old. You're just one—and there are so many of them."

She had them on the brain bad, he thought. A thing like that will take weeks to get it out of her. It'll take one of these special kinds of doctors—what do you call them? He couldn't think of the word.

She was starting to shiver, he noticed. And the night was warm. It was stifling under the trees. Maybe the aftereffects of the emotional somersault she'd experienced on the bridge. You couldn't key yourself up taut to a thing like that without having all your cords jangle loosely for a while afterwards.

"Excuse me," he said, and reached out and touched the back of her hand. It was like ice.

He started the engine. "Shall we get out of here?"

"Take me in some place where I can't see them. In away from the open sky. Glaring—a thousand eyes—"

They glided into motion. He drove down the riverside lane for a while, he had to, until there was an opening he could take to turn off. She rode with her head bowed, looking down at her hands. Turning them over from time to time, to refresh the monotony of staring at them fixedly like that. All to avoid looking up.

It was hideous to go through life like that. Half the world, at all times, was sky. Half of the time, that half was dark and lit with stars. One quarter of the world around you, one quarter of your entire life, barred from you, a forbidden zone, a danger zone, something not to be looked at. He still would not have undone what he'd done; but he wondered now, for the first time, which of them had been the wiser on that bridge, he or she? Maybe she'd known what she was doing.

This wasn't just an incident in the course of an evening, he could see that now. A single act that had already concluded. He said to himself, I've got work ahead of me, a job ahead of me. This is going to take time, and it's going to be a hard pull. I just saved her pretty little skin, back there. Now I've got to finish it, and save *her*.

They were coursing through a thoroughfare freckled with electric lights now, away from the river. It was a little better for her along here. The glow and pollenlike haze of the various signs and illuminated tubes, rising to a certain distance, combated and dimmed those other, more lasting sparks in the sky.

They passed a taproom or two, smoky, sullen with subdued light, but those weren't the sort of places for him to take her, anyone like her. Even apart from tonight's circumstances, any man could see that just by looking at her. She was in trouble, and it would only have heightened it to submit her to the stares of semidrunks and the clatter of cheap conviviality. Besides, this wasn't a social occasion, this was a mild form of first aid. He eschewed several eating places they came upon as being unsuitable too. They were just counters, frequented by cab drivers and night truckmen and that sort.

He had a certain place in mind. It was an all-night restaurant, an anachronism in their day and age in that it offered no entertainment or distraction of any kind, simply food. It was very old and musty, and what kept it going he had never been able to determine, unless it was the lifelong habit of its owners, which they found themselves unable to break.

He drew up before its quiet entrance and they went in. It was practically empty. It always was, at any time he'd ever seen it. Two men were sitting at a table, lost in a conversation that had been going on for hours. A man and a girl were sitting at another, lost in a lovelorn silence that had been going on for hours. A single waiter, very tired, very uncomplaining, stood about doing nothing.

He led her first to a table in a forward corner, drew back a chair. "This all right?"

She sat down, then got up again with an odd little twist of aversion. "No, this is too near the window. They're out there. If I turn my head, I can still see them. I'd keep— They're sort of spying over my shoulder."

He noticed an alcove or indentation at the rear. They went all the way back to it. "How about this?"

She sat down, this time, and remained seated.

When he saw that she intended to, he sat down in turn.

"Waiter, pull those drapes closed on the side window there. Block off the—view."

"Pardon me, sir, but that way you can see all the—"

"I said closed."

"Shut them out," she said when he'd gone. "Cover me up. Pull a thousand curtains across. But their rays are still coming through. There isn't any place in the world, or deep down under it, that their rays aren't still coming through."

"Whew!" Shawn said softly to himself.

He tried to smile at her. "How are you now? Let me feel your hand a minute."

It was still cold.

"A little whisky, maybe?"

"What good will it do? I would have drowned myself in it by now—"

The waiter came back again. "Coffee for the lady. Black coffee. Good and hot."

He lit another cigarette while they were waiting, more to give himself something to do than because he wanted it.

"Do you want to tell me your name?" he asked her solicitously. "You don't have to, of course, if you—"

"Jean Reid," she interrupted.

"Thank you, Miss Reid."

"You can call me Jean, if you like." He wondered what she was looking at. There wasn't anything there on the table between them, where her eyes were fixed immovably.

He had to keep talking for the two of them. "Would you care to know who I am?"

She kept looking at that spot on the table, where there was nothing.

"You're a man. You came along. You've made me keep on looking at them long after I would have stopped, if it hadn't been for you. I don't know if you say thanks for a thing like that or not."

He blinked that by, looking down himself now. "I'm Tom Shawn," he said. "I'm—I'm a member of the Police Department. I'm a detective in the Homicide Bureau. If there's anything I can do to—"

"Police. A detective." She began to laugh.

He waited for her to get through.

She didn't get through. It seemed to feed on itself. It wasn't raucous or shrill, it didn't even attract the attention of the other two pairs in the room outside. It was well-bred, like everything about her. But she couldn't seem to stop it.

Weeping is nothing. There is nothing more terrible than having to sit and listen to a person laugh, endlessly, without joy, without mockery, without hope. He clenched his fist down under the table where she couldn't see it, and pressed down hard with it on his knee.

He wondered how to stop her.

He'd heard that if you slapped them, that stopped them. He couldn't have done that if he'd tried.

He'd heard that if you dashed a glass of water full in their faces, that stopped them. He couldn't have done that either. That was just as bad. He wished it had been a man he'd saved on the bridge; then he could have hung one on his jaw without any compunction.

She perked a thumb backward across her shoulder. "Arrest those stars out there, officer. Put handcuffs on them. Hit them with a blackjack."

He had a certain native dignity, this Shawn. He'd meant to help her. He got up, put his chair carefully back into place, started to walk away without a word.

The laughter had stopped, suddenly. He looked back, from across the room, and her head was down, her arm coiled tight around it. She was mute.

He stood there undecided. Then he turned and walked back toward her again, as slowly as he'd walked away. He drew out the same chair he'd just now left and sat down again without a word. When she looked up at last he was sitting there before her again, patiently waiting. He was trying to show her, in the only way he knew, that he wanted to help her.

The underlids of her eyes were heavy with hoarded moisture. She looked at him, and pushed her hair back a little.

"Now do you want to tell me?"

"I can't."

"Why can't you?"

"I don't know how."

"Just let it out, that's all. You've got it all choked up inside of you. Just—just let it come."

"It won't go into words. It can't be passed on to anyone secondhand. You have to live it. You can't be told it."

"There isn't anything you can't be told. I've listened to some of the strangest stories—"

"This is just a lot of little things, like grains of sand or drops of water. You can't *tell* about grains of sand or drops of water; it doesn't sound like anything. They don't know what you mean."

"Maybe if I help you. Maybe if I get you started. Try to forget I'm sitting here in front of you. Tell it as if you were telling it to yourself, out loud, with no one else around."

She couldn't even do it that way, she couldn't get started.

He waited. Then, patiently, "You're afraid tonight. Right?"

She took a deep, shuddering breath. "Yes, I'm afraid tonight."

"There was a time you weren't afraid."

"There was a time I wasn't afraid."

"Well, begin there. Tell it that way. Tell it from then."

He watched her eyes slowly change; film, not with present substance, but with retrospect; stray past him, down the night, beyond it, into distant vistas of the past.

"There was a time I wasn't afraid—"

2
The Telling

IT BEGAN IN SUCH A little way. A drop. Yes, that was it, a drop. But not of water. A drop of hot consommé on a white evening frock, worn for the first time. There is no littler way in which a thing can begin than that.

A drop of spilled consommé. A parenthetic look of reproof, a sideglance, between two phrases of the conversation in progress at the moment. Signs of distress on a face glimpsed at one's shoulder. Distress because of that one spilled drop, most likely. The face withdraws. The drop evaporates. The conversation goes on. But something has begun.

Death has begun. Darkness has begun, there in the full jonquil-blaze of the dinner-table candles. Darkness. A spot no bigger at first than that spilled drop of consommé. Growing, steadily growing, by the days, by the weeks, by the months, until it has blotted out everything else. Until all is darkness. Until there is nothing *but* darkness. Darkness and fear and pain, doom and death.

I am Jean Reid, as I told you, and Harlan Reid is my father. God put it into our hearts that we should love our fathers, and God put it stronger into the hearts of daughters than of sons. But then God forgot to give us anything that would take away the pain that love can sometimes bring. Above all, God permits us to look backward, but God has forbidden us to look forward. And if we do, we do so at our own risk. There is no opiate that can precede the pain; only one that can follow, called time.

I lost my mother when I was two, and so I really never knew her. It was always just my father, my father and I. Sometimes I think that is the strongest of all loves; the full strength of natal love, to which has been added all the aspects of romantic love but a forbidden few. That is the way it has always been with us, and maybe it is not good, but still we should not have been punished this way.

I first found out when I was eight or nine that there was something different about me. About us. Until then I hadn't known. Children don't know those things, if they're left to themselves. It might have been a bad thing for me. My father saw to it that it wasn't. Just as—well, as when you fall and skin your knee or bark your shin on the sidewalk, and go to your father about it, he puts you on his knee and in his superior wisdom dabs something on it that prevents it from festering. So he did with this thing I found out. Cauterized it. Sterilized it. Made sure it would leave no mark or mar.

A little girl planted herself before me in the playground at school, looked at me wide-eyed, cocked her head a little, and said, "You're beastly rich, aren't you?"

I backed away a little, defensively. "No, I'm not," I said, not sure of my ground. It sounded like being accused of swimming around in some sort of greasy, unpalatable gravy.

"Yes, you are," she insisted. "You're rich. They told me so. You're rich."

When she wasn't looking, I stole a glance down at my own frock. It looked clean and neat enough, I seemed to be all right. But I was troubled.

I went home that night and I said, "What does it mean, when you're rich?"

He spoke slowly, and a little sadly, and very wisely. "Listen close. And tomorrow don't remember this. But remember it some other day, when you're eighteen or you're twenty. You'll need it more then. It means you'll have a hard time of it. It means you'll always be a little lonely. Reaching out, with no one there to clasp your hand. It means no one will ever love you. And if they do, you won't be able to tell if it's meant for you alone. It means you'll have to be careful. There will be traps laid."

"What do I have to do?" I asked, sucking in my breath.

"There is only one thing you can do. Act as though you didn't know. Act—and live, and think—as though you weren't rich. And then maybe the world will let you forget it."

The next day I'd forgotten. Or surely, the day after. And then it came back again, years after, when I needed it more, as he'd said I would. Like something you throw into the water. That stays down at first, for a long time, then finally shows up again at the top. He gave me it for a creed. And I've lived by it ever since.

I don't remember much about the days immediately before this little, this single drop, fell on me and started darkness. I had my little missions and my errands and my interests. Life was sheltered, life was safe. I had few friends my own age, because I didn't share their interests. I was a funny, retiring sort. I didn't like parties, and clothes didn't interest me much. I liked to read a good deal. I liked to walk alone, bareheaded, in the rain, hands deep in my pockets, and turn my face up and feel the drops come down. But at least there wasn't fear in the world yet.

And then one night at dinner—this must have been a day or two before the drop fell—my father mentioned quite casually: "Jean, it looks as though I'll have to go to San Francisco Friday."

"For long?" I asked. He'd made these business trips before. He was always making them.

"Two or three days," he said. "Just out and back." And then something about a consignment of silk from Japan being in difficulties.

I cocked an inattentively warning finger at him and went ahead spooning my dessert. "You'd better make it Monday instead. You know what Friday is? The thirteenth."

He gave a comfortable little chuckle, which was all that I'd hoped to elicit by the remark in the first place, and we went on to talk of something else, and the maid stood pouring our coffee over at the buffet.

Then a night or two after—and that would bring it to Thursday, the night before—we had some people in, as I remember. The candles of state were lit, and we dined a little more formally. Which meant, as far as he and I were concerned, a little less comfortably. We'd confessed that to each other long ago. But it was a thing you had to endure every so often. I had this new white dress on, and there was everything about it I didn't like. First, it was new; secondly, it was white; thirdly— well, yes, the fact that it was a dress at all. I hated that dressed-up feeling, with one end low and the other end long, and a lot of material following you around wherever you went. I liked the comfort of jumpers and tweeds. But that too was a thing you had to endure every so often. I kept it down to a minimum.

Tonight I sat in trappings of grandeur, and talked with people

28

I didn't care about, of things I wasn't interested in. I think it was an opera singer, at the moment, who was to be put up for private display.

"Then you must come," the dowager with the overabundance of diamonds who was sitting opposite me was saying. "We're counting on you. Tomorrow evening."

"Oh, wait; tomorrow did you say?" I remembered something with a secret and vast sense of relief. "We can't come then. Father told me he expects to fly out to Frisco."

I turned and looked up the table toward him for confirmation. Abetment might be a better word.

There was a soup plate descending in front of me at the moment, and the hand that held it seemed to give this slight hitch. A drop jumped out and fell on my dress, and I could feel the sting of it for an instant through the gauzy material.

There was my parenthetic look of reproof, and there was the appropriate expression of distress on the face of the maid, lowered close to mine by the act of serving. Or perhaps over-appropriate; it would have been more tactful to ignore the trivial mishap, as I was prepared to do.

The conversation had rolled along without me and I hurried to overtake it. "No, it isn't a very propitious date for a plane trip," I agreed. "But then, is it any the better a one for an aria?"

"I'm sorry, miss," a voice breathed close beside my ear.

This time I didn't turn to look. "It's quite all right," I said briefly. And then went on: "Father pretends he detests these little jaunts of his, but I think he secretly likes them."

"Oh, yes," he said with mock ruefulness. "There is nothing I enjoy more than trying to shave over an air pocket. It's quite exhilarating. I mean, you leave the razor up *here* and your face has suddenly gone down to *here.*"

And so on. The stain the drop had made was already drying.

I doubt I would have remembered it an hour later. But it was brought back before me again. Printed on my awareness, so to speak.

I went up the moment they'd gone, and got out of harness. I was sprawling in a woolly robe, browsing through a book, when there was a knock on the door, and the maid looked in.

It almost took me a moment to remember where I'd seen her before; and she was now in a plaid blanket coat and pulled-down little hat for the street.

"Yes? What is it?"

"Could I speak to you a minute, miss?"

"Why, yes, of course. But how is it you're still here? I thought you'd gone home long ago. Why, it's almost twelve."

"I know, miss. I waited purposely, so I could tell you how sorry I am." She went over to the dress, which was still blanketing a chair—I never hang things up properly—and pretended to look it over to see if she could find where the damage was. "I hope you'll excuse it, miss. I can't forgive myself."

I can overlook having things spilled on me, even a great quantity at a time, but I detest having anyone brush at me or clean me off afterwards. And it seemed to me that was what she was trying to do, even if only verbally.

"It's no great tragedy, Eileen," I said. "Don't lose any sleep over it. I look like a charlotte russe that's burst out of its container in that particular dress, anyway. A little wetting down might help it, for all I know."

She came away from it, then, but she still didn't leave. My hand was getting tired holding the same place in Hemingway.

"But, Miss Jean, it isn't that. It's what caused it. My hand is usually so steady."

"Well, then, for a moment it wasn't. That's what caused it. And now are we through discussing it?"

We weren't. There's nothing more terrible than the persistence of the meek. Or shall I say of the seemingly meek?

"It's that airplane trip."

"What airplane trip?"

"Of Mr. Reid's, miss. I heard him say he was going tomorrow. I was right there behind your chair, you see."

I didn't quite get it for a minute. I closed the book, looked at her puzzled. "Oh, the thirteenth. Is that it? Good God, Eileen, grow up."

She shook her head. "No, miss. A date by itself can't hurt you. It's just a number."

"I'm glad you told me," I said ironically.

"But it's that p'tickler plane that leaves, out there, that—" She saw me looking at her. "I know it isn't up to me to—"

"No, go ahead," I consented evenly. "I want to hear this."

She wrung her hands surreptitiously, as though it were from them she were squeezing out the reluctant words. "It's not good for him to take that plane. If—if he'd go later, he'd come back later."

"Oh, I see," I said dryly. "You know ahead of time?"

"It's not good," she repeated defensively. "Don't let him, Miss Jean. It's not good. If he leaves tomorrow—"

"Yes?"

"That means he's going to take the night plane back from there Monday night."

"That's the schedule, yes. What about it?"

She blurted out with a sort of desperation, as though afraid to say it, but at the same time even more afraid not to: "*That's* the one. The eastbound one. Something's going to happen to it."

"Oh, something is?" I queried. "These things are known before they happen?"

"No, miss, they're not," she said reproachfully. "You know they're not."

"Look, Eileen. I don't mind your having a drink or two downstairs, but I do object to your coming up here and giving me the dubious benefits of it."

"I don't drink, miss," she murmured almost inaudibly.

I could tell by looking at her she didn't. She had a wan, peaked face, and a thin, scrawny body, and one good drink would have floored her.

"Did you ever hear of Cassandra, Eileen?" I said, a little more kindly. "I don't imagine she was very well liked. You don't want to be like that, now, do you? Going around casting a damper on people. They'll start to avoid you, you know."

She seemed properly penitent. "I'm sorry, miss," she said. "I didn't mean to annoy you—" And then, on her way toward the door, "It's not me, miss. It's a friend of mine."

"I see. In the fortunetelling business, is she. Well, thank her for me, and tell her I don't need any assistance along those lines."

Her eyes opened as though I'd uttered a sacrilege. "Oh, no, miss. I wasn't supposed to tell you a word—"

"Well, now you have." I was getting a little tired by this time. "Good night, Eileen."

She swallowed the dismissal. It made a lump going down her scrawny throat. "Good night, miss," and closed the door.

I went back to Hemingway, and read him with a smile on my face along a place that wasn't supposed to be funny.

II

I drove with my father to the airport the next day. I took a snapshot of him on the way, with my mind I mean. We were talking as we rode along, and I turned and glanced at him—oh, not for any reason, with no thought in mind of cataloguing or perpetuating him as he was at that moment—but simply as you turn and glance at anyone when the two of you are sitting side by side in a car and talking as you skim along. And out of it came this print.

I still have it, in my mind, that snapshot; fresh and clear as of today. It's lasted, just as a real snapshot would, printed on paper. It's of something that's gone now.

He looked so virile and so handsome, sitting there beside me. Perhaps it was that his almost-glistening white hair acted as a sort of counterpoint to all the other things that were so youthful about him, setting them off all the more by contrast; that I don't know. But I do know that he gave an impression of far greater spruceness, haleness, clean-cutness, virility, call it what you will, than almost any dark-haired man you see about you, once past twenty-five. His complexion had always been high, ruddy, full-blooded, and against this was set the shocking whiteness of his hair, brushed so trim, scissored so immaculately at all times at the back and sides of the head, the way young men wear theirs. Looking at him, seeing what it did to him, I could understand only too well why the young in the eighteenth century, both men and women alike, had powdered theirs white.

He had a magnificent jawline, you could see the clean line of the bones, none of these drooping, puffy jowls. And when he talked it moved, you could see it move under the copper-pink skin of his cheeks, and you thought of strength. You thought of strength—perhaps even a dash of stubbornness too, but that didn't dominate—and of common sense; and above all, oh, above all else, of sincerity. I don't know why, I don't know what sincerity has to do with the jaw, it should be of the eyes rather, but you thought of it when you saw that clean jawline, at rest or in motion.

The eyes were clear, crystalline with unabated life, the eyes of youth that never grew weary of looking, that never grew tired of what they saw. They were of a blue that was almost gray at times. They were full of kindness and gentleness, and the little crinkles about them, when they came into play, expressed more than anything else a perfect understanding. At least for me they did, but then, you see, I did not see them when they looked at others, only when they looked at me, so I cannot press this point.

He had the collar of his camel's-hair coat upended at the nape of his neck; he always wore his coats that way, just as the younger men do. He was sitting so effortlessly, just as he moved; all his joints fluid, relaxed, not rusted with age. He was holding a brief case on his lap, looking in to make sure it had all the right papers in it, as we went along and as he talked with me. I can see it now; creamy-smooth pigskin, with a tartan-plaid lining. I'd given it to him myself a year or two before.

He had one glove left on and one taken off, because he was smoking a cigarette on the way. His fingers were strong and compact, the way a man's should be; none of these tapering, spindly things. He had a green-gold signet ring on one finger. It was the only piece of jewelry he'd ever owned or worn, since I could remember.

He was through shuffling through the papers in the brief case. He brought the flap back upon it, and his thumb went down and pressed upon the little chromium latch shield, fastening it. It was oblong, and bright as a mirror. I remember noticing how it clouded, as his thumb left it, to clear again, as a mirror does when you breathe upon it. Sometimes I think that's all the impress we make upon life, a misted, evanescent finger mark like that, that evaporates again even as our touch is removed from it.

So that is the snapshot I still hold of him, arresting him for an instant as he was, holding him complete to view. A snapshot of something that's gone now.

We had a minute or two when we got there. We sat in the car, out in front of the administration building, in pale watered sun-wash. I didn't even turn the motor off, I remember, because this was just a brief stop. I was going on again. It never occurred to either of us that I should get out and go in with him. What for? This was nothing. He'd done this so many times, it was just like taking a taxi to go downtown.

"Are you going over to the Ainsleys' tonight?" he asked humorously.

"God, no!" I grimaced. "I'm glad of the excuse to get out of it."

"Oh, by the way," he said, "if Ben Harris phones, tell him I'll play him a week from Sunday. He should get the same fellows we had last time, if he can. I liked them."

I touched a finger to my forehead, then out.

"Well, I guess I'll get in." He got out, swung the door, and kissed me over the top of it.

"Fix your tie," I said petulantly. "Can't you ever get the knot centered right?" And did it for him.

"Is there some law about that?" he wanted to know dryly.

Suddenly I smiled in recollection. I'd only just remembered it. "Oh, here's something I forgot to tell you. One of the maids came upstairs to me last night—you know, that Eileen McGuire—and tried to tell me that you shouldn't come back on the Monday plane. Some friend of a friend of a friend of hers read the tea leaves—I wish you could have seen how she took on, she practically got the carpet damp in places."

He couldn't even place her for a minute. Well, after all, that was Mrs. Hutchins' job, not his. "McGuire? Which one is that?"

"The new one."

"What's supposed to happen?" he grinned.

I snapped my fingers. "I forgot to ask her that."

He laughed. I laughed with him. There wasn't any more time now for conversational stopgaps.

"See you Tuesday morning," he said cheerily, and turned away with his brief case.

" 'Bye, pops."

I threw the clutch and sidled off without waiting even to see him get to the entrance doors. It was nothing. He'd gone on many such little whippersnapper trips before. Besides, I had an appointment, with my hairdresser, I think it was, and I didn't want to be late.

She waited on me at dinner that night. I ate alone.

She didn't say anything, but her face was grave, and each time our eyes happened to cross paths, she lowered hers troubledly. I hadn't thought of it until I saw her again, but now that I saw her again, I thought of it.

I could sense that she was aching to have me broach the topic of my own accord, in order to give her an opening, and I was determined not to. Why should I encourage her in her nonsensical ideas?

But those commiserating, downcast eyes finally got the better of me. If she'd only kept them down. Or kept them up. But the way they dropped each time, as though afraid to look at me.

"Look, Eileen, do you mind not creating quite so soupy an atmosphere in here with me? I'm trying to have my dinner, you know."

She retreated submissively to the pantry door. But then she couldn't hold it back any longer.

"He left, miss?"

I flung my hand impatiently toward his chair. "You don't see him, do you? Then naturally he left."

She was going to withdraw, now that she'd unearthed the subject once more. She had the typical stab-and-run courage of the craven. But I held her a moment, to scotch the thing once and for all. "Eileen, that wasn't even amusing the last time.

Tonight I'm not in the mood in the slightest. Just coffee, please, and then that will be all."

"I'm sorry, miss," she mumbled, and the hinged door effaced her.

I shook my head, in a sort of incomprehension, and lit a cigarette.

I ate dinner alone Saturday night too. Again the troubled face. Again the downcast eyes. Again the eloquent silence.

I pushed a plate back from in front of me a violent inch, swung half around in my chair.

"Eileen, I'm sorry to say it, but you're getting on my nerves."

"I haven't said anything, miss."

That was true, she hadn't. Only "Good evening," in a tearful sort of way, when I first entered the room.

"You don't have to. You keep looking at me. It's the same thing."

"I have to look at you sometimes, miss, to see where I'm going, to watch what I'm about—"

It would have been splitting hairs too fine to follow the thing out any further. I had a dissatisfied feeling of having been worsted, in a contest I hadn't even known I was in. You can't order people not to look at you. You can't order people not to *think*.

But she kept reminding me, reminding me. She'd planted something. All I had to do was look at her, have her about me now, to remember the thing. Belief, credulity, had nothing to do with it; it was just awareness, but that was annoying in itself.

I got up and left the room without waiting for my coffee.

I called Mrs. Hutchins to me in the upstairs hall, well out of earshot. She'd been housekeeper for us for fifteen years. She'd started to tack on "miss" before my name about the time I was sixteen, and I'd stopped it again almost as soon as it had begun. She had none of the earmarks of a professional housekeeper, which perhaps was why she was so excellent at it. She always reminded me of someone's gentle, elderly, slightly faded aunt, a band of black velvet ribbon around her throat, speaking low, never raising her voice, nothing tyrannical or domineering in her makeup. You scarcely ever saw her about, and yet the house ran itself like clockwork, not a grain of sand clogged its works. It was an art. I couldn't have done it.

"Enjoy your dinner, Jean dear?" she asked me.

"Grace, will you do something for me, please—" I started out volubly. And then I stopped. And didn't know how to go ahead. What could I say? What could I have her do about it? "Make that maid stop being so ominous"? It didn't sound right. It just wouldn't work.

"I—I—Oh, never mind, forget about it, I've changed my mind," I said lamely, and abruptly turned away and left her.

The next was the Sunday night meal. In the mornings I just took a cup of coffee in my room, and there was someone else who brought it. And at midday, almost always, I was out in the car. So the evening meal was the only time I encountered her.

I came into the room telling myself firmly, Now, we're not going to have any of that stuff. I'm almost as much to blame as she is; I'm playing it back to her all the time. If I stop doing that, then it'll stop by itself. It takes two to create that sort of tension.

I said to her with almost militant cheerfulness as she drew my chair out for me, "Good evening, Eileen. Some day, wasn't it?"

"Oh, lovely, miss," she said fervently. "Did you enjoy your drive?"

"Very much. You should see the flowers I brought back."

She went out, brought in something, went out again.

She came back again, after due pause. She began speaking, with a sort of forced garrulity, almost from the pantry doorsill, before she had reached the table. "I never saw such a grand day in my life. The sun was just pouring down the whole time—"

"We already agreed about that," I said mildly. I was going to add, Just wait on me, you don't have to entertain me, but it seemed too cutting.

She set a plate down before me, and it vibrated the whole way down, though it wasn't very heavy or very hot.

I took it from her before it had reached the tabletop, and set it down unaided, so that it would come to rest gently and not the way it had threatened.

"Your hand is shaking so," I said quietly. "You mustn't let it shake so."

It was almost as though Mrs. Hutchins had read my mind, and dropped a word to her that she must be cheerful when waiting on me. The pendulum had swung to the other extreme. She was keyed up, overanxious lest she fall into a silence, and I wasn't sure but that this was the worse of the two.

"And it's so seldom that you get days like this, this time of the year. If it was that nice around here, imagine what it must have been like on the links; just the right kind of a day for your—"

She stopped short, almost with a body lurch, that threw her whole frame violently like a hiccup. As though that weren't enough, her hand had flown up, palm to mouth, before she could stop it, and pressed tight there. Her eyes rolled quickly sideward in the direction of his chair, then she quickly curbed them. She dropped her hand again, trying to undo what she had done, but now nothing would come, she had throttled herself into numbed silence. She began to falter away from me, a backward step at a time. Her face was aghast.

I could feel a constriction in my own throat, but of another kind. Of anger. I didn't let it creep into my voice; I made that very steady, very quiet-spoken.

"My father is not dead. There is no reason why you should not refer to him, without going through a shocked pantomime."

I sighed and distanced my chair from the table. I'd never fired anyone yet in my life.

I said, "Get out of here. I can't stand it any more. Do me a favor and get out of here. Take a month's wages from Mrs. Hutchins and—and please go."

I saw tears gloss her eyes. Her lips trembled. "I haven't done anything, miss. You're not being fair."

I looked the other way.

"I'm sorry. You've started something that—that I can't seem to control any more. I'm not angry at you, if that'll do you any good. I'm not blaming you. It's just that—it's better for the two of us if you go."

She ducked her head sharply, I suppose to keep me from seeing the red, weeping scowl beginning to form. Then with her head already bent, she turned around. Not in one place, but in a circular little track, that carried her forward and around while she turned, the way you turn a small wheeled vehicle. Then she ran out of the room on little shuddering chop-steps, the way Japanese women are conventionally supposed to run.

It was the most ludicrous little exit I've ever seen. And it made me feel cheap and mean and heartless. But yet I'd acted according to the way I'd felt, and what else is there you can do if you're to be honest with yourself?

I dismissed her from my mind as I'd dismissed her from the room and from the house. She went from all alike, and I thought that was the end of it.

Monday came, and glowed to its noon, and waned toward its appointed night. Security, safety, confidence, are habits not quickly broken; it takes time to break any habit, good or bad, and their hold was still strong on me. There was no fear in the world, no such thing as fright. The car rode smooth, and the sun was warm on the shoulders of my loose cashmere coat, and the little breeze I made for myself was cool in my face. I stopped for gas, and I gave the chap who waited on me fifty cents for a tip because his eyes smiled back at me in such a friendly way. It was the reflection of my own I was looking at, most likely, but that didn't matter.

"That's some boat," he said admiringly.

"She's a good girl," I admitted. "Never talks back to me."

A little girl waved to me from a village crossroads as I skimmed by, and I threw up my arm full length and waved back. I'd liked to wave to moving things like that too when I was a little girl, I remembered, and I'd felt bad when I didn't get any answer. I didn't want her to feel bad.

I looked at my watch, and it was nearing six. "I'd better turn and go back," I said to myself. "No point in getting in too late and giving them trouble in the kitchen."

I thought of him for the first time all day. Nearing six, our time. That meant it was nearing three Pacific Coast Time. Three hours difference. He still had six hours in San Francisco. Take-off was at nine, their time.

And then I thought of her; or—shall I say it?—what she'd been trying to say. The smile came, and then it went again, and she was still there, knocking at the door of my mind. I wouldn't open it and let her in. But once at the threshold, neither would she go away again and let me be.

The sun was lower now, and it was no longer warm on my skin; but that was due to the lateness of the hour and not my own thoughts. I drew my coat a little closer around me, and snuggled a little lower in the seat, to expose less body surface to the new sharpness of the wind.

I passed a Western Union office, and for a moment watched it recede in my rear-sight mirror. Then suddenly I had slanted in to roadside, and gone into reverse, and was trundling along backwards to recover the ground I had just discarded.

41

I stopped and got out and went in. I had no conscious thoughts at the moment, I am sure of it. Such as: I am going in here. I am going in here to do such and such. I just went in.

I sat down at a desk, and drew out a pad of blanks, and took up one of their chained pencils and began to print:

HARLAN REID
C/O REID & SEWELL
MARKET STREET, SAN FRANCISCO
COME BACK BY TRAIN INST—

Then I slackened, and I stopped, and I looked around me. Without thought of the things I was looking at. The large, milk-white light bowl in the ceiling, already lighted though it was still daylight out. The undersized messenger, he looked about twelve but must have been older, in the olive-drab uniform, sitting dangling his legs from a bench over at the side, waiting for the next message to go out. The man standing behind the counter, pecking away at a message with the point of his pencil, automatically counting the words without reading them. The bulky cube of white tabs on the wall, forming a leaf-by-leaf calendar, the topmost one with a beetling black "16" on it.

I looked down again and crumpled up the message and dropped it in the basket, and started over.

HARLAN REID
C/O REID & SEWELL
MARKET STREET, SAN FRANCISCO
TAKE TUESDAY DAY PLANE INSTEAD OF TON—

That was even worse.

I said to myself, What am I doing this for? and I couldn't find any answer. Am I uneasy? No, of course not. Am I afraid? No, of course not. Do I *really* believe that twaddle? Don't be absurd! Well, then, what other reason is there for doing this?

You know what *he'd* say, don't you? He'd only laugh. He'd be the first to laugh. He'd never quit kidding you about it afterwards.

No, you'd better not.

I chucked the pencil back, and the little beaded chain that secured it formed an intricate Arabic tracery as it fell to the glass slab.

I got up and went toward the door. Came back and peeled off the uncompleted message, so that the address shouldn't fall into the hands of any unauthorized person; crumpled it and threw it after the first one, then went out for good.

The drive back was chill. The sun was gone, and the road was dusky, and the wind had teeth; I was glad when I'd got back. And that was a frame of mind I seldom concluded my solitary drives in.

Mrs. Hutchins had a buxom, friendly Swedish girl to wait on table tonight, and she seemed to warm up the room every time she came into it, even though, being new, she was all thumbs. I wondered why I should be conscious that the room lacked warmth. There must be that same atmosphere in it. And since the other one had gone, and it was I who remained, it must be emanating from me. I must be at fault this time.

I said, "What did you say your name was?"

"Signe, miss."

"Would you go over there and throw that switch? The one by the door. That's it."

"Throw it, miss?" she said, nonplussed, with her hand out to it. I suppose she thought I meant pluck it bodily out of the wall and fling it away.

I smiled a little, but not as broadly as I would have at another time. "Tip it up with your finger, that's what I mean. That's it."

The room was suddenly bright, and I leaned forward and blew out the damned candles. I'd never realized until just now that I didn't like candles. And perhaps I hadn't, for all I knew. I wondered why I should suddenly begin to dislike them now, in the middle of their burning, in the middle of a meal.

She nodded approvingly. "Is better so. Is gude for churches, them little t'ings, not for house. Make too gloomy."

The rest of the evening comes back to me now in vignettes. Each one separate, yet all of them linked together to form the strip of film, the continuity, that was the evening. I see myself sprawled back against a puffy overstuffed chair in the living room, in a posture of outrageous indolence, such as I would never have dared assume had any second person—any second person but him—been in the room with me. The greater part of my body a cantilever between chair seat and floor, I was so far down in it. My shoulders almost down to the seat level, my head very little above it. My clasped hands a cushion behind it. My crossed feet, far out from the chair, bucking up and down as one single limb, beating time against the floor on the heel of the undermost one. To percussion music stifled behind a lighted gash across the face of a hardwood cabinet there to one side of me. My shoes standing off by themselves, like a pair of little boats drawn up on a beach after their occupants have left them. A cigarette speared into the break in the rolled-up brim of a little crystal saucer at chair side, and sending up a tenuous unbroken skein that looked like an unraveling thread of very fine gray cotton, sometimes one-ply, sometimes two, to a vast height above itself.

Just an evening at home, like hundreds of others there had been before, like hundreds of others there would be to come. Contentment, vacuity; nothing that can be described, a mood, a state of being, rather than an active happening.

When you're at peace you sing. When there's music there already, you join it. I've never had a voice. When I bring it out at ordinary speaking pitch or over, it becomes musically unmanageable. But if I hum below that, I can stay on key. And there was no one in the room anyway. I joined the man who was singing, matching him word for word.

And then suddenly, a quick spring out of the chair. The shoes stayed where they were. The wispy gray thread bent way over flat for a minute, and only slowly got back to where it had been, and started upwards once more. I flicked something, and the livid crescent in the cabinet went out, and it was just a piece of furniture, dark and silent once again.

I looked back to where I'd just been, and drew my hand across my forehead lightly. Was that I? Did I move so fast then? What for, what was it, what was the matter?

I didn't go back to the chair again. Something had gone out of the room, leaving it emptier and bigger than before. Some atmosphere, it must have been, some inner lining, for none of its physical contents had moved. The lights were all still on as they had been, but they seemed to have lost some of their heat and glow; it was as though they had been tempered, watered down. It was a very large room to be alone in. There was too much space all around me. And it was night, it was dark out. I hadn't been thinking of these things a moment ago.

I'd suddenly discovered I didn't like the music—at least not that particular selection they'd just been playing—just as I'd suddenly discovered I didn't like the candles at the table.

I picked up my shoes by their straps and padded out in my stocking feet. And when I put the lights out, I did it backhand, without looking behind me. The vignette ends.

Then another, briefer. I was sitting on the little silk-padded bench, upstairs, before the mirror, in my room. Completely faceless, a bared neck at the back, a downfalling mane of hair at the front that covered me like a curtain, running a brush down it in rhythmic regularity. And then suddenly the brush stopped, poised. Through a cleft in the hair I had just caught sight of the little tent-shaped folding clock there on the dressing table. Eleven-thirty. Just a good time to go to bed, my usual time when I wasn't being kept out against my will at some dreary function. But then I didn't have to stop like that, just to certify the time.

I kept looking at it. I parted the cleft, made it wider, let some of my face show through. Then I turned and looked around over my shoulder toward the bed. Not at the bed, but at the stand beside it, with a telephone standing on it.

Then I turned back again and looked at the slanted-back dial some more. Eleven-thirty. Eight-thirty. I put the brush down definitely. I flung my head back, and the whole curtain of hair went up and over, and fell back to the rear where it belonged.

I went over and sat down on the edge of the bed and picked up the phone. "Give me Long Distance, please. I want to make a person-to-person call. This is Jean Reid. I want to speak to Harlan Reid, at the Palace Hotel, San Francisco, California."

I gave my number and hung up, and immediately I was stricken. Now what did I do that for? What's the matter with me tonight? *Him*, of all people. I'll never be able to say anything to him. Why, he'll roar right in my face. I'd better cancel it, before it goes through.

My hand crept out a little way toward it, then stopped, slunk back again. My hand couldn't seem to make up its mind, any more than my head could.

I got up and went back to the mirror, and sat down by that. I picked up things one by one, things I didn't intend to use, and didn't use. And set them down again. As though I were taking a sort of digital inventory.

Then suddenly there was that flutelike little trill I knew so well. And my whole body gave a start. I'd never been startled before by the ring of a telephone. I was now. There are so many firsts, when your path has entered the twilight regions of fear.

I ran to it fast, and held it to me with a sort of convulsive embrace. I knew as I got to it that I was going to tell him now, plead with him; that I *believed*, if only for this single passing moment—

"Miss Reid?"

"This is Miss Reid."

"I'm sorry, we cannot connect you with your party. The Palace Hotel, San Francisco, informs us that Mr. Harlan Reid left just a few minutes ago."

I hung up, all crumpled.

Courage came creeping back. Courage was the craven quality, cowardice had been the brave one. Courage was tinctured with the sourness of the grape: Well, all right. That takes care of that. It's out of your hands, and it's all for the best. You knew all along you shouldn't have tried to do that, and you've been kept from making a sniveling little fool of yourself. You should be grateful.

I went over and put out the lights, all but the one beside the bed that I intended to read by. A tarnished-gold subglow was all that was left in the room, such as a low-burning fireplace might radiate.

I picked up the clock and wound it, and brought it over to the stand, beneath the lamp. I brought over the book I'd chosen, too, and carried upstairs from the library before.

I unwound the cord about my waist and dropped off the white toweling robe. An upper triangle of the covers was turned back; I peeled it back farther and got into bed.

"He'll be back tomorrow. You'll see him then, and you'll tell him what you almost did tonight. But that will be different, somehow. You'll be telling him afterward, instead of doing it at the time. You'll both laugh about it."

I clicked my lighter to a cigarette, and took up the book, and leaned back within the ostrich-egg nimbus of the lamp.

> *"Ah! Manon, Manon, repris-je avec un soupir, il est bien tard de me donner des larmes lorsque vous avez causé ma mart."*

My eyes left the page. Ten minutes to twelve. Just about getting there. He never got there any sooner than he had to. They dropped back again.

> *". . . il est bien tard—vous avez causé ma mort."*

I had to start over.

> *". . . il est bien tard—"*

It wouldn't work, it wouldn't make sense. The book slid down a little farther on the covers, still open. I pried up the phone.

"Long Distance again. Please hurry. Jean Reid at this number. Person-to-person. Harlan Reid. San Francisco airport, Transcontinental and Western, Administration Building. He's booked on the nine o'clock eastbound plane. Oh, don't repeat it after me. Please hurry, it's urgent."

I hung up.

I thought it would never ring. It was so hard, leaning there on my elbow, crouched forward, hovering over it. My fingers drummed soundlessly on the covers. Then they pleated a short line in them, a fold, a tuck, running back and forth over it again and again. Then they rose to my hair, which was back already, to make sure it was back, to feel if it was back. Childish things came and went in my mind. Maybe by leaning over it so close you're stifling it, you're keeping it from— Get back away from it, give it room to sound in.

I put my hand on it, waiting. I took it off again, snapped my fingers at it twice, the way you would a dog to quicken it.

Then suddenly that trill, as close as though it were inside my own chest.

"Miss Reid?"

"Yes! Yes!"

"I'm sorry, the airport has been unable to contact Mr. Harlan Reid for us. The nine o'clock eastbound plane has already taken off."

My own clock was still only four to twelve.

My voice was a little dry, I had to force it. "What is the correct time now, operator?"

"The correct time is now one minute after twelve, Eastern Standard Time."

Ten minutes later I moved again. I had the testimony of the clock itself for that, so I knew ten minutes had gone by. It was six after on its face. I reached for it, and took it up, and turned it forward to eleven after. Then I set the alarm for seven-thirty, and put it back where it had been. In those ten minutes I must have just sat there quiescent in the lamplight; I couldn't remember having done anything. I must have just sat looking— but not at anything on the outside.

I put out the lamp, and the ectoplasm-like puddle of light it had cast over the pillows shriveled into nothingness. After a while, in the darkness, the music came back, the music I had heard earlier in the evening, at first faint and uncertain, then stronger, like a radio warming up, until at last it was boiling-loud inside my head.

I threshed around violently in the dark; I took the pillow by its two ends with my two hands, and curled it up tight against the sides of my head, pressing it convulsively over my ears. But that didn't still the music. It was already on the inside, so how could that keep it out? Unnoticeably it changed it, however. The words and the melody dimmed and left it. Only the rhythm remained, growing more even as it grew fainter, until it had altered into the drone and throb of a plane's heavy engines whirring aloft in the sky. That familiar sound we have all heard so often, as one passes overhead. Then that too receded, drew away, diminished, into irretrievable distance, beyond power of recall. And at the heartbreaking point at which it vanished into silence, uneasy sleep began.

A moment later the clock cymbaled, and it was day, and he was almost here, he was coming in, it was time to go and meet him.

I flung up the blinds, and the sun was like a chunk of copper ore from its recent mining. Strange thoughts and fears that came at night had gone away again. There wasn't any corner of the mind that sun couldn't reach into and cleanse of the soot and dregs of night. The law of the senses came back into full sway: only what you could see and touch and hear, that alone was real, that alone was true.

I stepped under the shower in its ice-cold, unmixed state, and took the pride I'd always taken in not flinching, not even by so much as the twitch of a shoulder, at its stinging bite. And later, as soon as my lips were dry enough, I whistled as I toweled and dressed.

They gave me a cup of coffee downstairs. I took it with my coat on and standing up at the table. I refused everything else, told them I'd have breakfast with him when the two of us had come back together.

I drove too fast because I felt so good, and wouldn't have

minded if some cop had chased me, just for the fun of it, but no one did. Then when I got in closer, I tapered off, so I wouldn't hit something or hurt someone. When I came out of the city at the other end, I opened up again. The wind felt good, it pulled my hair straight out behind me in an even line, almost took the curl out of it.

I got there five minutes before time, and parked, and then walked back and went into the waiting room. They had it on the board, marked for arrival at 8:30. I bought a pack of cigarettes at the counter, and then ambled around aimlessly. I stood for a minute at a swiveling rack, leafing the corners of magazines that I didn't seriously intend to buy. Then I let them be, and went over and sat down, and smoked in blissful contentment for a moment or two, and looked at my face in my pocket mirror to see if I looked as all right as I wanted to look.

I glanced up suddenly, and a man had come out and climbed up on a portable step arrangement, and was withdrawing one of the stenciled plaques from the adjustable schedule board. The one that said "San Francisco—8:30 A.M." It remained blank where he had taken it out.

I got up and went over and stopped him, on his way in with it under his arm. "That should be in any minute now, shouldn't it? I have twenty-nine after—"

He looked at me and shook his head briefly. "It's overdue," he said reticently, and tried to go on his way again.

I stopped him a second time. "Well, how late will it be, can you give me any idea? I came all the way out here specially to meet it."

"Hard to say," he said charily.

"Well, find out for me—please. Ask them in there. They must know in there."

He went into the office and closed the door. I waited there, where I'd accosted him. Then he came out again and said: "We don't know when to expect it. No use your waiting around for it. The best thing might be for you to go home, and then call us up later in the morning. We might have some more definite—"

"But you *must* know," I persisted. "What's the last stop before here—Pittsburgh? What time did it leave Pittsburgh? Can I go in there a minute?"

"I'm sorry, miss, the public isn't allowed in there. Just a minute." He went in again himself. Then another man came out.

He was somewhat absent of mien, I noticed, as though his thoughts were elsewhere even while he was addressing me, and I didn't like that. "If you'd care to leave your number here at the airport," he said, "I'll see that you're called as soon as—"

"What time did it leave Pittsburgh?" I repeated. He looked at me first for a moment, as though he weren't going to answer. Then he said, "It didn't arrive at Pittsburgh."

"Well, has there been trouble? Did something happen? When did it leave Chicago?"

He looked at the other man. He said something under his breath about "She's entitled to the information; it'll be made public in a short while, anyway." Then he turned around and went in again.

"It hasn't been reported since eleven o'clock last night, Pacific Time, two hours after leaving San Francisco."

The man went on talking to me, but I scarcely heard what he was saying. I suppose trying to ease me, telling me not to worry, that it would be all right, that they hadn't had any definite bad news, just no news at all. He walked with me part of the way back toward the car, as far as the doors of the waiting room; as much as anything else, I suppose, to get me off the premises, started on my way. That was congenial to me; I was as glad to have his brief escort terminate as he must have been glad to terminate it.

Then I was outside again in the open. The same biscuit-colored sunlight tincturing everything; the same crisp dark-blue shadows where you walked about under it; the same mirrorlike blue sky, with just two or three flecks of cloud, like blobs of shampoo lather, thrown up against it as if somebody had been careless with a sponge. Everything had such a clean, washed look.

I got back in the car, started it, and then I sat there for several moments. I knew I had to press my foot down on the accelerator if I expected it to move, but I didn't, it seemed too much trouble.

I think I would have sat there longer than I did, but one of the parking-lot attendants finally came over, trying to be helpful. He could hear the engine turning, but no motion resulted.

"Are you having any trouble, miss? Something go wrong?"

"No," I said dully. "No, it goes all right, when you want it to." And I pushed my foot down, and showed him, and went away from there.

I drove slowly on the homeward way. I crawled along. I kept forgetting to keep at it, and the car would taper almost to a full stop. Then I would remember I must keep applying myself, and I would send it forward again.

I was dulled, and glazed with shock. And I knew that this was not bad; what would come after this, once it had worn off, was what would be bad.

The city, when I coursed through it on my way out at the other end to get to our place, had that sparkling, bustling, vivacious look that a clear day can give a city. The store windows blazed and sent gleams into your eyes, like mirrors backing the sun. The limestone and the granite façades rearing sharply upward here and there against the sky all looked as though they had been newly chipped and scoured, they were so spotless. The people moved about in droves, each one dipped into his own little pool of dark-blue ink that followed him wherever he went. Even the very sidewalks twinkled, with minute particles of mica embedded in them.

I stopped for a light, and it occurred to me he should have been there in the seat beside me, in that floppy coat with the collar turned up at the back, and with his brief case on his knees; that we should have been jabbering away, the two of us, instead of my sitting in the car alone like this, and in silence. I turned and looked at the empty seat beside me, and my hand strayed out and lightly touched it, with a sort of mute longing. Then came back again to take up the wheel rim once more.

A little farther on I saw a news truck backed up to a news-stand in one of the squares, unloading a new edition, and I drew up and motioned the concessionnaire to bring over a copy to the car, almost before he had finished severing the rope that bound them into a great square block.

It was in the papers already. But little or nothing that I already didn't know. It just had the finality of print now, than which there is nothing more awful and more doomingly final. "Plane reported missing with fourteen aboard. Last heard from some-where over the Rockies. Searching parties being organized—"

More pain welled in. It was beginning to pour in now through the crevices. I twisted the paper into a misshapen bowknot, and let it drop to the running board, and from there fall off to the street. I glided out from the curb again.

They had already heard at the house, I could tell by their faces. And the fact that they didn't say anything, didn't ask me why he wasn't in the seat beside me, told better than anything. They thought by not speaking of it they were being tactful. Per-haps they were; it would have hurt either way, anything would have hurt.

I wanted to get to a room and be by myself, but I had to pass them first.

I saw Mrs. Hutchins looking at me. "I had the trip for nothing," I said, and gave her a steel-rimmed smile.

I made the mistake of stepping into the dining room for a moment, and caught them off guard, before they were able to efface the traces of the home-coming breakfast.

"You can clear those things away," I said, and turned my head sharply.

"Just a coop of coffee, miss?" Signe pleaded.

"No, thank you. You can give me a drink of brandy. I'll take it up to my room with me."

When she came out with it, she had to go looking for me. She found me standing by the radio. I knew they'd had it on before I got there, I could tell because the little glass shield over the scimitar of dial was still lukewarm to the touch.

"Did anything come over this yet?"

"No, miss. Mrs. Hootchins try. Only comes how to bake a cake."

"There's news every hour on the hour, on this station here, the one at the end. Keep it on that. One of you keep listening. I'll be upstairs, call me if—if anything comes in."

She squatted down then and there, made a great big puddle of her skirts on the floor in front of it. She looked grotesquely funny. But I didn't laugh. I suppose she thought by being that close to it, she could hasten it. Her eyes were steamy with unshed tears, they were only awaiting my permission to overflow. She was the sort ready to cry with anyone and everyone.

I didn't want her to cry for me. I went upstairs to do my own crying.

Every hour on the hour. That phrase took on a special meaning it had never had before; not in all the thousands of times I'd heedlessly heard it parroted, intruding on something else. Something to be obliviously tuned out of the way, until it was over and the basic program had resumed its flow. One thing I knew was sure: I'd never again be able to hear that stencil, that catch phrase, without a shudder running through me, without the memory of pain awaking again and aching again. It would mean, for all time to come, these hours of this day. Slowly, so slowly, passing one by one.

I think noon was the first time, after my return from the airport. They sent someone up to knock on my door and summon me, but I met the envoy on the stairs, on my way down. I'd been marking the time up there as closely as they.

I came into the living room, and they were all gathered there ahead of me, motionless, silent, in a tableau of breathless attention. Mrs. Hutchins standing by the cabinet itself, with her hand out touching a corner of it, as though fearful that if she raised that hand the flow of revelation about to come would automatically cease. The Swedish girl Signe again crouched low on the floor before it; and for all I know she had remained there that whole time. Another of the maids standing midway along the wall, between entrance and radio cabinet, pressed self-effacingly back against it, her hands hidden behind her. The chauffeur just outside the room entrance, as befitted one whose duties were not supposed to bring him within doors unless summoned. And the cook still farther back, peeping arrestedly out of the door that led into her domain, head inclined in taut listening. And Weeks, the butler.

I came unobtrusively into their midst. I saw them all trying not to stare at me, to avoid incommoding me. Somebody shifted a chair a trifle, in unspoken offer, but I shook my head and continued on over to the window, and stood there with my back to them.

"Every hour on the hour, the latest news bulletins. There has been no further word of the transcontinental air liner missing since eleven o'clock last night. Fourteen passengers were aboard, and the plane is believed to have been forced down somewhere in the region of the Rocky Mountains—"

I took a deep breath, to see me back upstairs again, past all of them. I turned, and the room was empty. They had all gone, they had all slipped out tactfully, most likely at some unobtrusive signal from Mrs. Hutchins.

I moved away from the window. It was still going on, in a sort of horrid parody of itself. "For those of you who tuned in late, we repeat: There has been no further word of the transcontinental—" I stepped quickly over to it and switched it off. Then I went upstairs, up the empty staircase, past the considerately closed doors.

I didn't cry; I cried scarcely at all. Crying was for little woes, not for this. I endured this seated at the dressing table for the greater part of the time, my forehead resting upon it, arms folded back over the top of my head. Quiet like that, unmoving like that. A little cut-glass bottle had fallen over close beside me; I saw it there, but I let it be.

At one I went down again, and then at two; at three, and then again at four, to these séances of communal misery and anguish. "Every hour on the hour, the latest news bulletins. Every hour on the hour, the latest news bulletins." And then nothing else. Until I thought I would go mad. Until it caught on inside my head, as well as on the outside, and there was no longer any way of stopping it, the turning off of the dial was no longer enough. "Every hour on the hour, the latest news bulletins. Every hour on the hour—"

Around half past four or so, one time there was a timid knock outside the room door, and for an instant a solitary flame-tongue of hope shot upward through me, sudden and flaring and quickly checked. It was gone before I had even moved to look toward the door, or risen to go to it. For the knock was too timid and uncertain to be the harbinger of any sort of news, whether bad or good.

I opened the door and Signe was standing there, holding a steaming cup of coffee on a small tray, and with a mutely pleading expression on her face. She was afraid even to ask me to accept it, just held it gingerly toward me, ready to withdraw it again at the first sign of refusal, lest she trespass on my misery. Which, to tell the truth, was what she was doing.

I took it from her, as a quicker way of having done with her presence, and particularly that look on her face, than to refuse it and entail the consequence of having her linger on there and importune me. I closed the door and set the cup down some-where and didn't touch it thereafter. The steam slowly spent itself and left it, and it stayed there, still and darkling.

I recognized that the focus of this pall of fear and grief that hung over me was not the catastrophe itself or even the loss that it had wrought; it was the fact of having been forewarned against it. There was a curious sort of clammy terror in that, there was horror, there was—I don't know what. There was a nightmare feeling heavy upon me, and not even the fact that the destructive climax was already past and no longer still ahead, could lessen it any. Without this, I would still have been stricken, yes, at such news. But I would have been stricken in the full of daylight. Now I was stricken down in a night of my own making, a night of the mind.

I screamed in the turmoil of my mind: Those things *aren't* known ahead! They can't be! It isn't true, it isn't true!

And lo, the answer would come back each time: But it is. You know it is. Don't let your heart lie to you. It was told to you, and you knew it. She came to you and told you. She came to you and wept. She risked dismissal—and she finally provoked it—solely to tell you.

It isn't so! It isn't true, I tell you (and over goes the chair, and down goes the little scent flask that was already overturned)! I won't have it! I won't believe it! A plane engine goes wrong, and the plane crashes into flames against the midnight mountainside. But only a minute before, thirty seconds before, until that engine developed trouble, the pilot himself, sitting before it, did not know what was going to happen. Not a living soul on that plane knew what was going to happen. That is the way things are. That is the way God in his goodness orders things to happen. And yet you are trying to tell yourself that a girl three thousand miles away from there, here in the East, two whole days, three whole days before, *knew* it was going to happen that way? A little chambermaid, a little drudge, a little what not—

But— And so low and quiet the answer, yet so implacably inescapable, like a whisper close beside the ear:

Here, look over this way, toward the door. About where that chaise is. She stood in this very room, on that very spot you're looking at now, that night. Didn't she come up here? Didn't she twist her hands about like this, trying to find the words for it? Open the closet. Look in there, under that cellophane wrapper, toward the left. That flowing white dress. If you take it out, there'll be a spot on it; a spot that her foreknowledge and fear caused her to make.

Jean, drink some brandy. Don't let those thoughts in. Keep drinking it until you've drowned them, burned them out, every one. Reel around and fall down, if you must, but keep those thoughts out. There's madness at the end of them.

They knocked to find out what was the matter, I was overturning so many chairs and things, stumbling around, already more intoxicated with fear and my own groping for an answer than I could have been with any brandy.

"No, I'm all right; don't notice," I called out. "Bring me up some brandy. Bring me up the whole decanter, and put it down outside the door."

There was no whisper of knowledge ahead? You yourself had no inkling, even if secondhand, transmitted from her? Liar. Cowardly liar. Then why did you stop your car, and leave it, and go in and all but send a telegram, last night at six? Then why did you pick up the phone, in this very room, before twelve, and call his hotel? Why did you pick it up a second time, at twelve itself, and call the very airport, as a last resort?

Do you deny you did those things? You admit it. Then if you admit doing them, do you deny you had a premonition? You admit having it. Then if you admit having it, do you deny that she was the source of it? You admit she was the source of it. Then if you admit she was the source of it, do you deny that *she,* at least, had forewarning, and tried to transmit it to you?

Brandy, quick, brandy! All the brandy you can swallow.

It didn't help, it didn't do much good. Thoughts are stronger than alcohol. It burned swiftly downward, like a flame in reverse, as when that knock had come on the door before, and then it flickered bluely, and went out again almost at once.

Your hands are cold, and you're shaking. You spill more than you can get to your lips. When you were four or five, and you went to Sunday school for the first time, they told you all about God. You'd never heard of Him before. But you weren't frightened. Because that was positive. That was walls about you. That was a roof over your head. Now you're twenty. And now you're frightened, frightened sick. Because this is negative. This takes the walls away, and takes the roof from over your head. You're alone now and naked and very small against the night wind.

They don't know. They *can't* know.

They did. Someone did.

Someone came running, and knocked on the door, and this time called through it without waiting.

"There's some news on, Miss Reid. You'd better come down quick."

I flung the door back, and brushed by them, and ran all the way down the stairs, the robe I had on streaming out from my shoulders like a pennant, the forgotten decanter still grasped in my hand.

I'd already missed it. "—since eleven o'clock last night." But it would be repeated, the newscaster was still on. It couldn't have been good; I noticed they didn't try to tell me what it was, any of them. They sidled out of the room, and only Mrs. Hutchins was left, lingering there over by the door, as if to see whether she could be of some help to me in the moment that was about to come.

I saw that I was holding the decanter in my hand, and I set it down absently. The opening of the newscast came around again, and I held my head bent very low and stood very still.

"For those of you who tuned in late, we repeat. The transcontinental air liner that has been missing with fourteen passengers aboard, was sighted about an hour ago by rescue planes. It came down in deep snow on the side of a mountain, in a remote inaccessible spot. They report there were no signs of life, and it is considered unlikely that there are any survivors. It may take some time for rescue parties on the ground to reach the spot. Nothing had been heard from the plane since eleven o'clock last night."

I reached out and turned it off.

Mrs. Hutchins took a half step to come back to me.

I warded her off slightly with my hand. "It's all right," I said quietly. "I'm going up to my room again."

She made a choked sound in her throat, and disappeared.

Then presently I was back within my own room again. I suppose I'd walked up the stairs. The house was quiet, the house was in mourning. It was still bright out, and the brightness came through the windows in talcumlike effusion, but it was that transitory brightness that precedes extinction, that overreaches itself and then dies. Just as a match flame will flare wide again an instant before it is gone.

I'd put on my dress, I saw. I was taking down a coat from the closet, removing a hat from the little wooden stand it was pegged on. I was moving about, imminent to departure. I caught my own reflection passing back and forth in the glass several times, and that showed me what I was doing.

I'm not sure that I knew what I meant to do, where I was going, at first. Or perhaps I did. The mind is not a printed page that can be referred back to once a particular passage has gone by.

I came out and closed the door of my room, coat slung over my arm, hat slung heedlessly onto my head. I plumbed the depths of my bag for my car keys, made sure they were there. And by now I knew what I was going to do, but not why, nor what it would gain me.

I went rearward along the upper hall, instead of down the stairs, and when I'd reached the door of Mrs. Hutchins' room, I dabbed at it twice with one fingernail. It made a small ticking sound, but she must have heard it. She said, "Come in," and I opened it and went inside.

She had been sitting in a rocking chair close by the window, looking out. Her attitude, before she had seen me and destroyed it by moving from it, suggested melancholy affliction. A sense of loss that, if not as acute as my own, was at least fully as sincere. For her head had been tilted considerably sideward, as if she were looking slantwise out the window at an acute angle of perspective close to the outer wall of the house—though she obviously was not looking at anything out there at all—and the flat of her hand supported that overturned side of her face, covering it, almost as though she had a toothache and was trying to relieve it by pressing intensely upon it. A small handkerchief lay untended in her lap, as if left there after recent use.

Then she moved at my entrance, and showed nothing. Which was her nature. To feel, perhaps, but never to display.

She rose and stood inquiringly before the chair, which simmered slightly with its loss of weight.

"Grace, have you the address of that girl that was here? Could you let me have it if you do?"

"Eileen?" she said. "Eileen McGuire? Yes, I have it." Her face showed nothing. She went to her desk and opened it. She was an orderly and systematic person. She seemed to have a card-index filing system for all those who had worked for us, past and present. I had never inquired into her habits of management before. In a moment she was holding a withdrawn card in her hand.

"Shall I give it to you, or do you want me to get in touch with her for you?"

"No," I said, "I want to go there myself."

"It's in the city." She read the street and number from the card. "She's at one-twelve Holden Street."

"Thank you. I'll remember that."

She put the card away. She gave me a look that was so articulate it held me for a moment as I was about to turn through the doorway.

"Did you want to say something to me?"

She spoke so low I barely caught it. "Don't go there, Jean. It may not be good for you to do that."

I saw that she knew the reason for the dismissal. I hadn't known until now whether any of them did or not.

"I have to go somewhere," I said. "There isn't any other place that I can go."

I closed the door after me, and went downstairs through the

tactfully hushed house, and out into the tarnishing gold of the evening. I got the car out, and started back upon the long road to the city.

I hadn't known there was such a street until now. There were so many things I hadn't known until now. I wouldn't have known where to find it unaided. I coasted up alongside the traffic patrolman on duty in the main square, and leaned out.

"I'm looking for a Holden Street. Can you tell me how to get there?"

"Och, that's way over in the back part of town," he said thickly. He glanced at the car, and he glanced at me, as though trying to link us up with such a destination. He waved those behind me on their way around the momentary impediment I made. "Tell you what you do, you keep following Third Street straight along. You'll be able to pick it up out along there, when you're getting toward the end of it."

I drove along this wide, ugly channel for what seemed like endless miles, past brick brewery chimneys and coalyards and dully glistening gas tanks sheathed with mesh wiring. The lights came on suddenly, but they only emphasized its barren width and drab dinginess; they were set so far apart and they stretched in two such long lines into the distance that they only made it seem lonelier and more forlorn.

The day was dead, and this section was its cemetery. An ugly yellow murk hung low across the western sky, where elsewhere it was gold, and the rest was a sooty wash, like smudged charcoal drawings of houses and street vistas thumbed out of all clarity.

I asked again, of the attendant of an ice truck that was standing before a plant for loading, and he told me where to turn off, and how to go thenceforth, to reach this Holden Street. In a little while after that, I was in it. The beams of my lights made a great scar down it that brightened its surface more than it could ever have been brightened before.

It wasn't what I'd expected, after the section I'd just come through. It was poor, yes; threadbare-poor. But it wasn't derelict, nor slatternly, nor a slum. It was genteel, sedate in its poverty.

It was a row of flats, all of one height, one shape, one size. You couldn't tell where one ended and another began, save that there was a doorway breaking into them every so often. Each with the same short flight of iron-railed steps marking it. The windows, where there were lights behind them to give them depth, were neatly curtained, and the glass was unobtrusive in its cleanliness, and more than one had boxes of earth with geraniums planted in them standing on their ledges. Anyone with a penchant for exact social stratification would have classified it at the level where upper lower class meets lower middle class.

I found the number of the house I wanted, and I stopped, and turned off my lights, and sat still for a moment, arm dangling full length down the outside of the car.

A little girl came spilling out of the next-closest doorway and shrilled into the gloom: "Tiny! Mamma says you should come up now or she's going to give it to you for making her send down special!"

A second figure joined her, there was a brief ear-splitting wrangle, and then they both disappeared inside once more. It became as quiet again as it had been before.

A man came shuffling up the street, tired from his work, and glanced at me and the motionless car with a sort of passive curiosity, and went in the doorway I sat keeping my vigil before.

My downfallen hand struck the side of the car door. I thought, It isn't from here—it isn't from any of these houses—that knowledge of that could have come ahead of time. No, I must be mistaken, I must be in the wrong place!

And yet the plane was down, and a girl who came from this street had told me it would be, before it ever left.

I got out and stood irresolute. What do I want of her? I wondered. What shall I say to her?

I saw that I was clinging to the rim of the car door with both hands. I pushed myself away from it, and the unnoticeable propulsion seemed to send me across the sidewalk and up the few iron-railed steps, and into the common doorway.

It was lighted in there, poorly but enough to distinguish the push buttons. They had names below them, for the most part, and one of them was McGuire. It was the second one in from the street, so I took that to mean that the flat was on the second floor.

I tried the door without pushing at the button, and I saw that it opened. I went in without further ado, and up the hare-lipped stairs, run over by years of usage. I think I must have been afraid I wouldn't be admitted if I announced myself from below. I wasn't conscious of such a thought, but something kept me from pushing the button down there in the street entry.

I gained the little oblong that broke the stairs and stopped before the upstairs door. I was terrified of going further, I was determined against going back. I could hear muted sounds of occupancy, sometimes coming close, sometimes receding into depths of background that deadened them. But they were commonplace sounds, not strident nor acute nor dramatic.

I knocked suddenly, before I had even expected myself to, as if a spasmodic impulse had carried to my hand.

A woman's voice said, "Go see who that is."

The door opened rather violently, and a girl of eleven or twelve stood there, blocking the gap with her entire figure and looking up at me.

"It's a lady, all dressed up," she reported, without taking her eyes off me.

A large hand suddenly found her shoulder, flung her aside, impatiently but not abusively, and a stout woman in her forties had supplanted her, with the rather abrupt disconnectedness of a change of slides on a magic lantern screen.

She began to wipe her hands on her apron front, more as a gesture of amenity, I imagined, than because she felt they required it.

"Does Eileen McGuire live here?" I said.

"Yes, miss, she does." She bethought herself of her hair, and wove back a wisp of it, with a sort of nervous rapidity that betokened an overanxiety to please.

"May I speak with her a moment, please?"

"She hasn't come back yet," she said. "She should be here any minute." With that same rapid anxiety she had shown about her hair. Trying to mollify me over the disappointment by her haste of speech. She even called loudly over her shoulder, as an added sop: "Cath-reen! What time is it on the clock?" Then, apologetically, without waiting for the answer, "She's a little late. Maybe she had to wait for her bus." She widened the door hospitably. "Would you care to come in and sit down?"

The background view its swinging-away offered me was so perfectly in character, with herself, and with the building in general — or perhaps I should say with my impressions of both—that paradoxically enough it almost seemed artificially contrived; designed intentionally to point up, to label, a whole mode of life so that there could be no mistaking it, at sight through an open doorway. I do not know what other aspect it could very well have presented, given the milieu, but I do know that it was so pat it struck me almost as strange. You expect deviation; this was the uttermost norm.

The walls had been painted a light, watery green. On the section directly in view hung a massive square frame of gilded wood, intricately scrolled and tortured into complex design. Within this stretched a mat of cherry plush, with an oval opening left in its center. Within this, in turn, peered a bridal photograph of a man and woman, in faded sepia; the man seated, the woman standing.

A center table projected fractionally beyond the door frame as it limited my gaze; on this, halved with almost mathematical precision by the same constricting frame, stood a remarkable lamp. It was a dome of frosted glass, ribbed like an open umbrella, which indeed it vaguely resembled in miniature. From its bottom rim dangled long pendants of glass. A length of mottled, encased wire escaped from under it, and then ran upward in a straight line to a socket overhead in the ceiling.

Before it, chin to tabletop, sat a small boy, smaller even than the girl who had opened the door, staring round-eyed at me, to the willing neglect of what was evidently school homework; for there was a disintegrating book open before him, a sheet of yellow paper spread out, and a pencil stub protruding vertically and point in air from one tightly closed fist. It had made marks all over his upper lip: I think it was that, although it might have been something else.

In the instant or two that was all that elapsed between the woman's invitation and my refusal, there was a violent interruption at the table, which had nothing to do with me. A layer of folded sleazy white stuff landed soundlessly on it, at the upper end, just out of my sight, protruding no more than a tongue or two to where I could see, but giving vent to an air current that stirred the small boy's hair and lifted the sheet of paper before him. I heard the girl order him sharply: "You got to move away from there now. I got to set the table for Momma."

The cascade of white flooded across the table, inundating it and submerging paper and book and almost their user's whole head as well in its erratic flurries. He withdrew from under it, retrieving the articles that had been before him with a great deal of ballooning of the cloth, and finally nearly pulling it off after him as he suddenly dropped to floor level and became even shorter than he had been before. He struck twice, open-handed, at someone just out of sight, and a hand came back from that direction and struck once at him, also open-handed. All three blows missed by a wide margin. They were delivered with a sort of dutiful retaliation, rather than viciousness.

But meanwhile I had answered the mother. "Thank you, no. I'll wait for her downstairs."

"You're perfectly welcome to come in."

"I'll wait for her by the door."

She wondered who I was, but didn't know how to bring it out. "Who—who shall I say was asking for her, if you don't mind?"

"Miss Reid," I said. "Jean Reid."

I saw her face change. The door opener's beam slipped from it, and it sobered. No actual ill will came into it, but rather a sort of rueful remonstrance.

I wondered if she would speak of it, and while I was wondering, she already had. She was no hypocrite, at least. "Miss Reid, why did you have to turn my girl out like that?" she said with a reproving, sad-miened air. "I'm sure she was doing her best to please you, from what she tells me."

It seemed she didn't know the cause, then, only the effect.

I didn't answer.

"Oh, she's found something else to do," she said. "But she took it hard."

"I'm sorry," I said quietly. "I'll wait downstairs." I turned away.

The light from within, back of where she was standing, made a pale fan beside me on the wall as I went down. This narrowed, as though the wielder were slowly closing the fan, until the two end-sticks had folded together and there was no more fan to see.

I went down slowly, trailing my hand along the aged rail, where so many hands must have trailed before mine. I came out of the street doorway and went over to my car. I just stood beside it, without opening and re-entering it. I stood looking into it, instead of down or up the street. My back was to the house. I thought perhaps, above, there might be two small faces peering down at me out of the lighted window. She'd filch a quick glance herself, most likely, to see if I were waiting; but then she'd drive her youngsters back and tell them not to peep, it wasn't proper.

But I didn't turn to look up and see if I was right or not. Let the whole world stare at me, I didn't care.

I saw her figure coming from down the street, and I knew it must be she, though I hadn't seen her walk—at a distance— often enough to know her step, and it was too dark by now to make out her features from that far away. But it was a woman, a very thin woman, and alone, and hurrying to get home; walking fast, and yet dejected with weariness from long work even as she drove herself forward, her upper body at a slight inclination from its rightful center of gravity, without being actually stooped; so I knew by all this it must be she.

I turned sharply outward from the car, almost pivoted on the space of one heel, and then stood there where I had before, facing her approach now, rigid, taut, and with a curious quickening sensation in my breast that must have been accelerated heartbeat, though I didn't stop to analyze what it was.

She came closer. Light found her at last. The neutral blue of night-distance left her, washed away by her approach, and the tints of the familiar plaid blanket coat that I had seen once before settled on her figure. And then the knitted cap came into focus; it was like a stocking cap, or the sort of cap boys used to wear for skating on the ice; it had nothing to do with style, it covered the whole head, fitted it tight, and on the top there was a little round ball of wool, the only break in its functionalism.

And then her face, last of all; the wan, anemic, pinched face I remembered. The sort of face that is ageless, for even now in her youth it looked peaked, and so it had little change to make later. And now it looked very tired and drawn, even worse than when she was working in my house. The mouth drooped and the lips were colorless; she had been too tired and too anxious to get home even to redden them.

She noted the car first, as she came up to the doorway, and strangely enough her look passed over me without recognition for a moment. Nor was this artifice, I could tell; no one was of any interest to her, she was too drained of energy to pay heed to figures about her on the street. All she wanted was to get into that doorway and get upstairs, to where she lived.

I wasn't sure my voice would serve me; my throat felt too constricted. "Eileen," I called low.

She seemed not to have heard. She went up the three or four low threshold steps.

"Eileen! Wait."

She stopped and turned, and looked at me. And then she recognized me.

The blankness of questioning became a sulking expression, and she was about to reverse the turn she had just made, and go on again.

I had a feeling of prying myself from a fixed spot to which I had become fast, there beside the car. I lurched over to the foot of the steps, as when you summon too much energy to make a move and therefore project yourself too violently, and caught the handrail with my one hand, and half raised the other upward toward her. She was above me, because of the difference the steps made.

Then I dropped it again, without knowing what its purpose had been. Perhaps just to stay her; perhaps a stifled sort of appeal.

"Don't you know me? I'm Jean Reid."

"I know you, Miss Reid." She spoke with injured coldness.

Then nothing more, for agonizing seconds. I looked up at her; she looked down at me. As though we were mutually hypnotized by each other.

"It—it happened," I stammered. "I don't know if you know— Did you know? But it happened."

I heard her breath go in, with the softness of hisses. "I didn't—know," I heard her say. "I didn't bother picking up a paper—I'm so worn out. My father used to be the one who brought it home, but since he's gone—"

I heard her saying this, but I couldn't see her say it. Something happened to my sight. Her image dissolved, broke up into shards like the image of the moon on water, and floated off into the corners of my eyes out of focus. I felt my head go down as though a hand had suddenly bent it with full strength, and my forehead came to rest against the iron handrail, and stayed like that, just rolling slightly from side to side, from temple to temple, as if to relieve an intolerable pressure within my skull by the grateful touch of the cold smooth iron.

I felt her hand touch lightly at my head, as if trying to alleviate me, and then withdraw again, frightened at its own presumption.

I looked up. Her face coalesced again, became a round whole. I could see then, in that one look, that unmistakably there was no evil there, no rancor, vindictiveness, gloating at my pain. It would have shown if there had been, it could not have kept itself hidden. That insight, gained in an instant, stayed with me from then on.

There was no enmity there.

Her face was twisted in sympathy with mine. There was fear there, at least equal to my own. There was helplessness there too, perhaps greater even than any I felt. There was weakness, vast weakness; muted, passive, floundering. Her whole personality was weakness incarnate, buffeted about. But there was no ill will there. There was no sense of personal gain, expressed in grim satisfaction. Of that I could be surer, in that moment I looked at her, than I had ever been sure of anything before.

"Eileen, I should have listened—" I whispered.

"I don't blame you. Anything you do, you have to do—there isn't any way of changing—"

She let her arms, which had been held short at waist height, fall down passive full length at her sides. Even sway a little with their own drop, they were so unresistant. There was a brown paper sack in one of them, I remember, and that swayed too, down lower still.

"Is he—? Was he—?"

"I don't know," I said numbly. "I haven't been able to hear— All day I've been waiting— He was on it, he must have been. I tried to reach him last night, just before it left, and I was too late—"

"It wouldn't have been any use. Anything you do, you have to do, and there's no getting out of it."

The night seemed darker than it was; the darkness was on the inside, not the out; I could barely see her face, there before me. Will, volition, was like a flickering candle flame going out in all that darkness, going lower, lower, lower, guttering to an end. Leaving the eternal, rayless night of fatalism, of predestination, to suffocate us, herself and me alike.

Then I fought and struck out against it, and coaxed the dimming flame up a little higher. No! No! No! There *was* will. There *was* mastery of course. There *was* improvisation. Things weren't fated to happen; they just happened, spontaneously. And until they did, they weren't known, they weren't waiting, they *weren't*. They came into being only as they happened.

She saw me shaking with a curious passion of revolt, and I know she didn't know what it was, thought it was fear or the tragedy of loss. But it wasn't; this was another battle entirely. This was battle of the spirit; this was reason fighting its last-ditch stand against the forces of darkness, there on the outer steps of this commonplace brick flat.

"Come up a while to my house," she said pityingly. "You're ill, you're tired—"

I shook my head and held my ground. The flame was sinking again, I could feel it. It had nothing to feed on.

"If only he hadn't gone just now. If only he'd waited until next week—"

"He had to go," she said softly. "Just like you had to fire me. And just like you had to miss him on the phone. That's why it was so foolish of me to try to say anything. But it's hard to learn, you keep forgetting—"

I pressed my hands with sudden violence to my ears, trying to shut her out, and shook my head from side to side. "No! No! That isn't true! I won't listen to it! He *didn't* have to go. Anything could have stopped him, the slightest little thing, a straw blowing in the wind—"

"Nothing could have stopped him. The only thing is, you don't know, you don't believe that. It took me a long time too. You saw what I did, I tried to tell you— As if that could have stopped him."

My hands had dropped again, freeing my ears. She didn't know what it was that had just happened. I'm not sure I knew myself. The flame had just gone out. It was very still and very dark, inside of me, and outside, and in the world all around me. There was nothing to fight for, or against, any more.

She stood there watching me, not guessing. Her own soul, perhaps, had been simpler; she hadn't struggled.

"I wish— If I could only help you—" she said at last.

I looked up at her, and reached, and took the overlap of her coat. "This friend, this person—Eileen, take me to her. Let me find out. Were they all— Won't there be anybody? Out of fourteen like that? That's why I came over here to see you. Eileen, I've got to know. I can't stand it any more, waiting like this, not knowing— It's like an ax, ready to fall and it never falls—"

I saw her bite her lip, as if in doubt.

I tightened my grip on her coat, pulling it convulsively. "Eileen, at least let me go with you— Let me find out— You said it was some friend—"

"It is." Then she said, "He doesn't like to be asked questions, like that. He wouldn't like it if he knew I'd told you. He doesn't like others—well, strangers, you know—to know about him."

So for the first time I learned it was a man.

I could tell by her face she was relenting. She stirred a little in uncertainty; looked behind her into the doorway, then back to me again. Then she twisted her head, glanced upward along the outside face of the house. Toward the windows of her own flat, I surmised, although this was only my own supposition; it could just as well have been some other window her abstract inquiry sought. Then back to me again once more.

I pressed the plea home. "Just at least to know, to be told— It's this waiting, not knowing, I can't stand—Eileen, I'll go mad. Help me. Look, I'm begging of you, if you have any compassion at all—"

She must have read the thought of my intention; seen the little dip my body had begun to make, to bring itself down to its knees before her, there on the grimy doorstep of her shabby house. She quickly caught me, held me as I was, in a little spasm of pitying inflexibility; that was a flash of unwonted firmness, brief as it was, for a character such as hers. Then it was gone again, like a gleaming morsel of mica in soft, shapeless sand.

"Wait," she said, "I'll—" And looked behind her, like a child contemplating doing something she is not sure is permissible. "Wait down here, I'll try to find out—I'll see if I can talk to him— He doesn't like it if he thinks you're asking him direct questions; but maybe I can find out something for you—" Then she quickly added, "You're sure you're not afraid? You're sure you want me to?"

"Yes," I panted, "yes. The worst. Anything, I don't care, as long as I don't have to go through any more of this—"

"Then you wait for me out here. It's better if he doesn't know that I'm trying to find out for someone else. He lives right in the same house here—" And she gave me a little consolatory clasp on each of the upper arms with her two hands at once.

"Try to tell me if there's any chance—" I begged. "If they've all been lost—"

"I'll be down as soon as I can," she whispered. And she turned from me and went in, and I was alone in that brooding doorway of the oracle.

I heard her step going up inside, thinning until it had faded out. I said to myself, Do you hear that? That is just the tread of a tired girl, a drudge, working somewhere in a factory or shop, going up inside a tenement house; nothing more. Why have you come here? Why do you stand here waiting, for her to bring you down knowledge that no one in this place can possibly have, that no one in this city can possibly have yet tonight? You fool, fool, why do you strain your ears to catch it to its last? That is not a step going up into rarefied regions of prescience, that is just a shoddy step upon a crumbling stair within a moldering building, a sound such as the inmates make all the time, coming and going, night and day. Why do you hang upon it so?

I was left alone there a long time. I could see, all right, and know the things about me. My car was there at the curb, glistening in the dark, with a thin ripple of wet orange paint running down its hood in one place where the light from the doorway struck out at it. A ripple that never moved, and yet was warped and liquid as running ripples are. I even shifted once, from where she had left me standing, and moved over to it, and stood up close beside it, my hands pressing down tight upon the top of the door, as if I were unsteady and needed something to cling to in order to remain upright. My head inclined, as if peering intently at the upholstery of the seat backs.

Yes, the car was real, it was there. My hands could feel it, my eyes could see it, I had but to touch a button to make light shoot out of it, light that no shadows could withstand; but yet the shadows had the best of it, it was powerless to rive this pall that blanketed the eyes that looked at it, the mind that considered it. It could not take me out of the shade, it was I who had brought it into the shade with me; its powers of contrast were lost, it became one with the other Gothic shadows about me. For the shadows came from within, and so anything they fell upon was shadowed. Just as if you front your eyes with a piece of smoked glass, the most sparkling sunlight will become somber.

Each unto himself has his own world that he looks out upon, and though someone else were to stand on the very selfsame inch of ground your feet were placed upon, guided by chalk marks, he would not see the same things you did. There would have been two different views there, not just one. Or is there any world at all, I wondered, *out there* before us as we look upon it; may it not be inside, behind the eyes, and out front nothing, just a blank infinite? But madness lurked along that trail, and I quickly turned aside.

A little ownerless dog came along the quiet emptiness of the street, on soundless trotting paws, and veered over toward me when he saw me standing there, and sniffed sketchily toward my shoe. I looked down at him, and his eyes found mine and looked straight into them for a moment, from that low level. He moved his tail once, in memory of some past friendliness, and then he turned and trotted away. His light-colored body blurred into the shadows and spiraled to extinction with a sort of optical swirl, that left nothing as it closed up at its center.

You are trapped too, I thought; just as trapped as I am. You had to come along at this precise moment and through this exact street. You could not come at any other moment, nor through any other street. That halt you made, that sniff you gave, that single tail wag, all those things it was ordered that you do, it was written for you to do, hundreds of hours ago, or per- haps hundreds of years ago, I don't know which. They lay waiting for you to do, there was no escape from them, no turning aside, until you had arrived at them.

Yes, we are trapped, you and I; but I am even more trapped than you, for you at least did not know you had to do those things, but I—now—know that you did have to.

I raised my shuddering face from the squared frame of my arms upon the car doortop as I heard her step coming slowly down the stairs again, inside there in the house. The sound seemed to enlarge, as if it were an empty shell or husk that sur- rounded her, so that I could catch it even outside there where I was, and yet it wasn't a very heavy tread nor a very sharp one. More like a dried leaf whispering and scratching as it idly rolled from step to step.

I stood motionless a moment, unable to release the car, unable to order my body about. The leafy patter had reached bottom, had stopped. Then when I turned, she was already in the doorway, immobile herself, leaning against the side of it, inert, looking over at me, with her head propped over to the brick facing as if it were loose upon her shoulders.

He's gone! flashed in me. Every limp line of her body expresses—

The intervening sidewalk seemed to give a tug under me, as when someone bodily pulls a rug you are standing on, and I was up on the doorstep close beside her.

"It frightens me," she moaned, "whenever I hear him do it. I can't stand it—" She pressed both hands against herself. "My stomach gets all cold—"

I could see that her teeth must be chattering; her lips were pulsing, without speech, so it must have been that.

"He knows—He knew—" she whimpered. "Before I even had gotten up the courage to say anything— Maybe he could tell by the look on my face. But that always scares me too. He must've known you were right down here. 'Go down and tell her—' he said."

"Maybe he saw the car from the window." I wasn't aware I'd said it aloud, but I must have, for I heard her answer me.

"His room's in the back of the house."

That flicked by unnoticed, a twig carried past on the dark stream lashing about me, threatening to break over my head. I held onto her, as one would who was literally in danger of being engulfed and swept away; my hands clung to the front edges of her coat and pulled them out toward me.

"What?" I breathed. "Eileen, what?"

"They're all dead. All fourteen. No one was left alive in it."

I could feel darkness, like a cold whiplash, coil close about my throat, about to be pulled tight.

Her voice came from far away, it seemed to have to travel a long distance before it could reach me. She was holding me now, and not I her. And we were close; yet her voice seemed to come from far off. "Then he said, 'But tell her she'll see her father again.' Do you hear me, Miss Reid? Can you understand what I'm saying? He said, 'Tell her to go home, she'll have word.' "

"But he was on it. I know, because I phoned a moment too late, and it had already taken off, and he was on it. And if there was no one left alive in it—"

"Here, let me help you over to your car. Do as he says. Go home—"

I was in the car now. She stood there watching me. I could see her face blurredly.

"Are you all right? Shall I get you something? Are you able to drive?"

"I guess so," I said vaguely. "You don't have to do much. You just push your foot down a little, and keep the wheel steady—"

Her face slipped slowly backward in the darkness, and I must have been driving.

I'd see him again. Oh, yes, I supposed I would; but how? As a dead body on a stretcher, being taken out of a plane a few days from now?

The two things contradicted each other. If they were all dead on that plane, then he was too. If I would see him again alive, then they were not all dead on that plane. And of the two, I believed the first.

Once a red light stopped me at a busy intersection. I would not have stopped for the light itself, but there was a car in front of me, and that did, and I stopped for that, gently nosing into it until I remembered to brake. Some other car came up alongside me, on the outside lane, and stopped abreast. I think it was a taxi, I don't know. The monotonous, staccato running account of a prizefight was blaring from its radio, driver and two back-seat passengers alike huddled forward to catch every word.

And then suddenly there was a break, an instant's silence,

and a voice said with knell-like clarity: "We interrupt this broadcast to bring you a news flash just received. Ground parties have now reached the scene of the transcontinental air liner that crashed. It has now been definitely established that there are no survivors. The bodies of all those who were on the plane when it took off from its last stopping place have now been accounted for. Some of them were found at a distance of as much as—"

Horns were honking angrily behind me. The red light was gone long ago, and the car ahead of me was gone, and the taxi alongside was gone. My own car was standing there in mid-roadway, damming up the flow of traffic.

It was easy; there wasn't much to remember. You just put your foot down lightly, like that, and kept the wheel from swinging too much. And you waited to cry until you got home. You kept your face numb and stony like that.

You weren't sure that it was home, even when you'd driven up before it. Your hands on the wheel seemed to have guided you without your knowledge, and they had no eyes, only memories. You looked twice to make sure, and even then you weren't sure. But then the door opened, and they were standing there in it, waiting to admit you, so you knew you had come back to the right place after all.

They were all standing around in the entrance hall waiting for me, when I came in. They were all looking at me in that mute, helpless way people have, when they want to tell you something and don't know how to go about it.

"I know about it," I said quietly. "I heard it on the street just now."

Somebody's arm came tentatively toward me, and I said, "No, I can get to the stairs all right. Just let me through, just make way—"

Somebody sobbed surreptitiously behind me, and was hushed

peremptorily by someone else, in an undertone. I suppose it was Mrs. Hutchins.

If only they wouldn't stand there ranged about watching me go up, I knew I could go up quite steadily. Five steps already, without a fluctuation, and with just one hand to the rail.

"Miss Reid," somebody said timidly from their midst.

I turned my head inquiringly, and it was Signe. I wouldn't have known, but Mrs. Hutchins' angry little slash of the hand, in an effort to silence her that came too late, pointed her out to me.

"Yes?"

"And then this come, too."

I saw where their eyes all turned to look, afraid to touch it. It was a maize envelope on the edge of a table, one corner stabbing out over the rim.

The death-telegram. The official notification.

"Give it to me," I said. "I'll take it up with me."

Mrs. Hutchins snatched at it and hurried up the three or four steps after me to hand it to me herself.

I turned away, and went up another step. And then still a step more. It was harder now. The telegram seemed to weigh so much.

I stopped again. There was a ripping sound, and my finger had burst through its flap. The envelope fell away over the banister.

The violet ink had blurred; the capitals were all out of focus. But then as I stared, it coalesced again into clean, thin lines of print.

> JUST HEARD. DON'T WORRY, UNHARMED. STAYED
> OVER FOR BUSINESS. ARRIVING DAY AFTER
> TOMORROW BY TRAIN.
>
> FATHER.

I heard Mrs. Hutchins' voice again. It seemed to come up

toward me from the telegram, as though the message itself were speaking. But that might have been because the telegram, and I as well, were going effortlessly down toward her on the lower steps where she stood.

"Quick! Help me with her, one of you! Can't you see she's falling into a dead faint?"

At the station waiting for the train, I thought at first that I was going to tell him right away, that it would be the first thing to pass my lips. And then when I saw him coming through the gate, saw that blur of tan camel's-hair coat that I had already detected through the transverse lattices, chopped up into segments, cohere into his single form and come toward me through the funneling-out crowd; and when I ran to him and crushed myself against him and held still, I couldn't say a word. Nothing would come; neither that nor anything else. Just being up against him, just feeling him hold me to him, was enough. It was so warm there and so safe, against his coat. There was no night there, against his coat. There were no stars looking down at you. Just his face, just the warmth of his breath was all that was over you.

We stood there, riveted, until the disgorging crowd had thinned to a trickle, and then the last laggards had filed through and dispersed, and we were alone there, in the middle of that vast, gloomy floor space. Oblivious in our motionless embrace, conspicuous. The way a submerged piling or rock formation stands out when the water level has dropped all around it.

"It did something to you," he said compassionately.

He tried to take my chin and turn my face more fully so he could see it. I held it back from him.

"Don't let's stand here any more," I said muffledly. "Let's go outside and get away from here."

We started walking out of the station, still clinging together.

"Have you been waiting long?" he asked.

"Since daylight."

I felt a momentary hitch snarl the evenness of his pace beside me.

"But this is a nine-o'clock train; I thought you always knew that."

"I know. But I *had* to go part of the way to meet it, even if it was only up to the outside of the gate. That seemed to be the only way to bring it in quicker."

"Poor kid," he said under his breath.

He hadn't seen my face clearly until now; only a quick flash as we rushed together in the gloom back there. He saw it now, in the little channel of clear daylight that was all there was between the cavernous station mouth and the car. He didn't say anything. He stopped short in his tracks, and a flicker passed across his own face, and then he went on again. We went on together, for our arms were still interlocked behind our backs, mine on the inside of his loose-hanging coat.

"Drive?" he said, when I'd closed the door after us.

"Yes, go ahead."

Our hands touched on the wheel rim.

"Your hands are cold."

"They've been cold for three days straight." I blew on them. "They'll be all right now." I ran one in under his arm, and the other one around on the outside, and linked them there.

"It gave you the works," he said huskily, scowling at the traffic up ahead.

He didn't say anything more until we'd lost most of it again and were in the clear, near home.

"How long were you like that? I tried to get word to you fast as I could. Was there much of a time lag between the news and my wire?"

"That wasn't it," I said briefly. I changed the tense. "It isn't that. Not the smashup."

He thought that over for a while, and I saw that he couldn't make it out.

"Jean," he said concernedly, "you're a different girl. All the fuzz is off, and— I don't know, it's as though I'd been away ten years."

I felt like saying, I'm not a different girl. It's just that the world I'm in is a different world.

They were all glad to see him; they said so in a word or two, in varying stages of intensity. But the difference was, it was over for them, they were back again where they'd been before it came along. I wasn't; I never could be again.

Weeks took his hat and coat in a special way, folded the coat downward over his arm, almost caressingly, as though it were very fragile, very precious. That was his way of showing it. Cook said, "I've made some molasses muffins for you, sir," with her eyes a little moister than molasses muffins would seem to warrant. Mrs. Hutchins gave the rest of them a lot of crackling, unnecessary orders, sent them scattering in all directions with good-natured severity.

But they were lucky, all of them. For them it was over.

Presently we went in and sat down together at the breakfast table. He said, "Ah, this is nice!" and planed his hands together briskly. The sunlight was like jonquil pollen, lying all over the tablecloth, and even streaking his shoulder and the edge of his sleeve. And the glassware sparkled, and there was a swollen little face leering back at mine from the nearest facet of the mirrored percolator. He shuffled through the accumulation of mail, without opening any of it.

I waited. But it had to come out sooner or later. It was there, it had to come out. Sunlight couldn't dissolve it. The fact that he was back couldn't dissolve it. It was like a cake of ice formed around my heart. It needed a pick and tongs to pry it away.

"Jean," he said, "what is it? What's been done to you?"

We both slowed up in our eating. Then we both stopped eating entirely, before we'd reached the point at which we were through. The little scattered noises of our cups and plates stopped, and we were quiet, and we were just looking at each other.

"Look," I said abruptly. "I've got to talk about it. I've got to talk about it to you. It's no good trying not to. I'm thinking of it every minute of the time, by day, by night. It's got to come out. It's got to!" I banged my fist down on the table, once and twice and again, each time more lightly than the time before.

He jumped up and came around the table to my side, and standing beside my chair, held my head and shoulders pressed against him. And I clung to him like that, and turned my face inward against him.

"But it's over, Jean. It's over. Just think of it that way."

"I tried to tell you outside in the car. It's not the smashup, not the close shave."

"Then what? What's done this to you?"

"It's that I was told it was coming *before* it came. There's a man here in this city that said it would happen. And it did."

"Oh, no, Jean," he drawled comfortingly. "That story of the maid's that you mentioned? I remember that now. No, dear, no. You're too sensible, too intell—"

"And then that night I went there. And *that* part of it was told me. That you'd be all right. And I came back, and your wire was here. You were." I shuddered a little.

He didn't answer this time. One of his hands left me, and although I didn't look up to trace it, I knew somehow it was pensively stroking the underturn of his face.

"How did you happen to stay off?" I said after a while.

He gave a slight start. Not a violent one; the start of a person whose thoughts have strayed.

"I got a telegram at the last minute, just as I was about to board the plane. In fact I think my bags were already on, when I heard them calling my name over the amplifier—"

Fear was like a knife. It had a sharp point. And it went in, and turned around in you. Then withdrew again. But it still hurt where it had been.

I'd started to send one. I'd drafted form after form. But I'd never put it through.

"Oh, my God!" I said in a sickened voice, and banked my wrist limply against my forehead.

"Why do you say that?"

"I thought I hadn't filed it—I *know* I hadn't—"

He held my shoulders in a reassuring vise. "It wasn't from you."

I felt my head go over limply, like an overripe melon on a vine. I could hear my own breath being blown out exhaustedly.

His voice tightened up a little. I heard him say, "I don't like whoever did this to you. I'm going to show him up. I don't like them monkeying around with my little girl—"

Then, as if remembering that I was there and could overhear his spoken thoughts, he stroked my hair back once or twice.

"It'll be all right," he said softly. "We'll go there, and— I'll show you, you'll see; it isn't anything."

She was frightened, I could see. Not of us, but of what she knew we were about to ask her, of what she knew we must have come there for. She fell back from the door, at sight of us. Not violently, but in a sort of shrinking way.

She stammered, "How do you do, miss? How do you do, sir?" and caught at her own upper arms, with opposite hands, and looked about her helplessly, looked behind her, as if trying to draw support from someone else who might be in the place with her.

I said, "May we come in, Eileen?"

She said, "Yes—yes, do," and moved a chair by its arm, but not enough to make it more accessible.

My father, trying to put her at ease, smiled and said, "How are you, Eileen? How have you been?"

"Oh, fine," she said breathlessly, "oh very well, sir," and again touched the same chair arm, this time to move it back again to where it had been before.

Then she sort of cowered over it, leaned a trifle over it, herself, as if her balance were untrue and her own legs were insufficient to support her. The way a child does when it is stricken with mental uncertainty.

I looked at him and he looked at me. The kindest thing, I saw, was to have it out at once, and over. "May we see him?" I asked. "May we speak with him? You know, that friend of yours." And lowered my own voice a little, as I asked it, perhaps thinking I could inspire more confidence in her in that way.

She gnawed at her underlip for a moment, the way you do when you wince with pain. Then she released it, and darted between the two of us, and over to the door, almost with relief, as if knowing beforehand that her errand was to be footless. "I'll see if he's in yet," she offered. "I'll go up there and knock. I haven't heard him go by, so I don't think he's home yet."

She ran out and left the door open behind her on a narrow gap. We could hear her soles hastily sandpapering up the outside stairs.

Her mother came to the inner opening between the rooms and looked out at us. She was holding a plate in her hands and slowly wheeling it about between the folds of a dishtowel.

She said, "Good evening," grudgingly. The rotating of the plate stopped, while she eyed us, and then it went on again.

My father nodded pleasantly, and I answered her in kind.

The door ebbed back, and Eileen had returned. She was more composed than when she had left. To the timid, postponement is succor. "He didn't answer," she said. "He can't be back yet."

The older woman grunted through the opening to her, "What, are ye taking them up to make a spectacle of his gift? Ye shouldn't do that. Ye know he doesn't like it."

"It's not Eileen's fault," I interceded. "We asked to meet him."

"I'd like to know him," my father said with an easy amiability that pretended to take no note of their halfheartedness. "I'd like to have a talk with him. Surely there's no harm in that, is there?" He looked about and selected a chair. "May we sit down and wait?"

"Yes, do," Eileen faltered. But the act had preceded the permission. And as a last attempt at discouragement, she wound her hands harassedly around one another and murmured, "I hope he doesn't take too long. He may not be back right away."

"We're in no hurry," he answered. "I feel he's really worth speaking to." He began stripping the cellophane from a cigar and studying it as he did so, with that deliberation and ease of manner he could assume when he chose, that made an impregnable defense against outward currents of opposition. I had seen even more sophisticated people rendered helpless against it, by its seeming obliviousness, which was probably wholly artifice.

"Do you mind if I smoke here in your parlor?" he said, holding the stripped cigar poised.

"Oh, no, sir, not at all!" Eileen exclaimed hastily. "Go right ahead." Here, at least, she was on different ground: the obligations of hospitality. She hurried over to place a receptacle beside him, then stood back again, breathless with her own eagerness.

Looking at him, I wondered how many years it was since he had last been in some place where he was unwelcome, and determined to stay there in spite of it. A very great many, probably. Perhaps when he was a young man he had sat in one or two business offices like this, persisting in remaining, ignoring the lack of cordiality, until he had accomplished his purpose, concluded the transaction he had determined to conclude. But not since then, surely. Not in all the years since those early, beginning days. And yet he hadn't lost the knack, it sat on him well.

I perched on the arm of the same chair he was in, and rested my hand on his shoulder, to add what I could of informality and friendliness to our being there.

The mother turned and disappeared from the room opening, giving her consent to our remaining by default rather than spoken permission. Eileen remained for a minute or two erect against the wall, as though propped there, as though forced back against it by our being in the room. Then, sensing her own awkwardness of posture, aggravated rather than ameliorated it by sidling downward into the nearest armless chair and perched stiffly on that, too far out from the back of it and too rigidly erect to be either rested or restful to others.

Silence descended on the room; there was no conversation.

The mother's step sounded, and she reappeared, this time entering the room full-depth. She carried with her a stack of dishes. She set them down on the table. Then she opened the wings of a small china cabinet set back against the wall, and began to transfer them to it one at a time, building up various sizes, shapes, and uses.

"I did everything but the cutlery," she remarked to Eileen.

The latter jumped from her chair with an alacrity that was motivated by her own eagerness to escape from us and from the room, and not by any imperativeness or rebuke in the remark itself, for there had been none.

"I'll finish that for you," she offered, and fled outside.

The mother continued putting the plates in one at a time, in silence, ignoring us.

"Do you believe in his gift, Mrs. McGuire?" I asked her suddenly.

"It's there." She didn't turn to look at me.

"Have you known him long?"

"Long, yes," she said briefly.

I didn't think she was going ahead, her attitude had been so forbidding. She took up a plate and wiped it around the edge with her apron. Then suddenly she spoke again, as if there had been no interruption.

"We were children together, him and my husband and me. We used to play together. We came from the same place." Then again she stopped.

It had to be asked. If my father hadn't asked it, I would have.

"Did he have it then?"

"Yes, I guess so. He's always had it."

"Did you notice it then?"

"How should we? Children don't think of things like that."

"There must have been a first time, though, when you did?" he persisted gently.

"There was. One day when he was about twelve, we were playing up on a hillside, the three of us. You could see the farm below, his people's farm. Spread out below us like on a table-cloth. Suddenly he broke off playing and said, 'I've got to get down there. Our barn's on fire.' We turned and looked, Frank and me. You could see it plain in the sun. It was a clear day."

I was holding my head slightly inclined, looking not at her but down at the floor. He'd stopped smoking. We were both afraid she would stop.

" 'No, it isn't,' we said. The air was spotless above it, there wasn't a speck of smoke.

"He went off at a run, so we picked up and ran after him. Until we got down there, not a sign. And then just as we came up to it, the first white wisps crept out from under the barn door, and in a minute it was all riddled with it, it was leaking smoke at every seam.

"They came running from the house and from the fields, and we all helped and we put it out. Well, we saved it, and then afterwards, I remember, we were lying there resting, and Frank said to him, 'You must have awfully good eyes. There wasn't anything to see, from way up there.'

"And he kept nibbling away at a piece of straw, and he said, 'I didn't see it. I knew it was going to burn, that was all.'

"We didn't laugh at him, because he'd been right. We asked him how he'd known. He said he didn't know how he'd known, himself. We saw him trying to think about it, squinting up at the sun. Then he said, and these were his own words, I've never forgotten them: 'I happened to think about it, on the way up there. Every time you think of anything, there's a picture goes with it, comes before you, of what you're thinking about. If you think of a tree, you see a picture of a tree for a minute. If you think of a house, you see a picture of a house for a minute. I happened to think about our barn. And all of a sudden my mind got awfully white and clear, like there was a strong light on it. And I saw a picture of the barn burning. A picture of it, burning, came into my mind, awfully strong. I looked, and I saw it wasn't burning yet, so I knew that must mean it was going to.' "

There was no sound from either one of us. He'd caught ashes from his cigar in the hollow of his hand, and he held them that way for a moment or two, not moving. Neither one of us stirring. Then he thrust out his hand at last and allowed them to trickle into the receptacle meant for them.

I kept looking down at the floor. She'd told it so simply, how could it have been anything but the utter truth, I said to myself. How could there have been any artifice, any pretense, in such an account as she had just given us?

She'd finished putting away the last plate now. She closed the wings of the closet, and then she lingered by it, dusting off the little glass knob with her apron, past all need to do so, over and over, as though unaware herself she was continuing to do so, with her thoughts elsewhere.

In the silence a chink of silverware sounded, from Eileen, at her duties, in the distance. Sounding strangely on another plane.

She continued to knead the knob, and to look off, across the room, into the past, toward the remembrance of the things she was telling us of.

"There were many things like that, afterwards," she said quietly. "None of them, maybe, quite as sharp, quite as noticeable. But that was the first time of all. That was the first time it happened. There's no need to tell you of the rest."

"And did other people learn of it?" my father asked.

"A few of them, yes. Not many. Word slowly spread around the countryside, among those that knew him and us."

"How did they feel about it?"

She shrugged. "I don't know. Like us, I suppose. They were people like us, they were our own kind. It was something we couldn't understand. We allowed he had some sort of a gift that others didn't, but outside of that, we didn't feel that he was any different from anyone else. There wasn't anything about him to make us feel that way. His father cuffed him many a time, like other fathers do their growing sons, after that day. No more, no less."

"Well, didn't people try to make use, to take advantage, of this—this gift of his, as you call it?"

"At first, a few of them did, yes. Women who were expecting

would come, now and then, to seek to learn if they would bear a son or daughter. A neighbor would ask what success he would have with his crops. Things like that he didn't mind, if they were sincerely put to him. But when people came out of idle curiosity, just to test him for the sport of it—that he couldn't stand, that gave him some kind of pain and shame, I don't know what it was; like being exposed to view. He ran away from some of them, one day, and tried to hang himself. Frank found him in the barn, and cut him down just in time. So after that we spared him. We wouldn't speak of it to outsiders any more, and we let him be."

"Is he alone here?"

"He'd always be alone, a man like that. Frank and I came to the city within a year after our marriage, and he followed us not long after. His parents died, he sold their place, and we were the only friends he had. Where else should he go? What else should he do?"

My father said, slowly, thoughtfully, "But he could have all sorts of power, with a thing like that. He could have wealth, and—" He turned to look at her helplessly. "Why?"

"He's a good man," she said devoutly. "He takes what God has given. He doesn't ask for more."

We didn't speak again for a while. He watched her while she left the knob her hands had been busy with for so long, and moved across the room, and stood finally beside the table, bent slightly and looking down at it, as if scanning her own reflection within its polished surface.

"What is it, Mrs. McGuire? What would you say it was?"

"It's not for me to say," she answered. "It's not for me to question it. I didn't question it when I was young, and I'll not question it now that I'm old. He's never done a harm to me with it, nor to anyone else that I know of. It's God's will, and other than that, I don't want to know what it is."

Eileen came into the room and said to her, "I've finished."

Her mother said, "Thank you, darlin'," with an absent sigh, as though it were she who had performed the task.

"I hope we haven't put you out any," I felt called upon to say.

"No, not at all," they both assured me, their protests as insincere as my apology.

My father took no part in this typically feminine tithe paid to the amenities, men being less responsible in that respect.

"You'd better tell Cathreen and Danny to come up now," the older woman suggested. "It's time they were in bed." And then, partially for our benefit, "Them kids would stay down on the street all night if they wasn't called."

Eileen moved toward the window, evidently about to raise it and shout down to them from where she was, in the immemorial custom of these parts of town.

But then she suddenly stopped, and listened, and we heard it too.

There was a slow step coming up the stairs out in the hall. We could hear it without difficulty in there where we were. It was tired and soggy, and somehow you could tell, by the very sound of it, that its owner had an arm out, clutching at the stair rail for exhausted support, moving progressively along with his footfalls, step over step. It was the sort of step that leaned flaggingly against the rail.

It was strange to be so close to him, and yet not see him. Just outside the thin partition that encased us, going slantingly up one side of it, from bottommost corner to the opposite upper one, *chup, chup, chup, chup,* but very slowly, very wilted, very meek—and yet not see him. Just hear the sound of someone passing, through the plaster and the laths. There should have been fanfares, there should have been a glow of light coming through the crevices of the door. There was nothing; just a flat, deflated, shoddy trudge upon worn stairs.

And yet we were breathing quicker. I know I was. And my

father had straightened attentively in his chair, was no longer supine there, his shoulder beneath my hand.

"There he is now," Eileen said. We knew already.

I suddenly left the chair arm, and turned, and took a step toward the door.

Mrs. McGuire's hand jabbed out. "Wait, don't open the door and look out at him. Let him go by in peace. Ye can go up there with Eileen in a few minutes' time—if ye must." Her disapproval of the whole intrusion was strong on her face. She got up and left the room without addressing us further.

We waited in silence. I wondered what my father was thinking. I couldn't tell by his face. Skepticism, determined to vindicate itself? Eileen was sitting at the table now, elbows close together on it, head averted to one side of her intertwined hands, almost shrinking away from us, cringing, in her reluctance to carry out the errand thrust upon her, yet equally helpless to escape from our unspoken demand. Her whole life must have been a series of these agonies of indecision, I reflected pityingly, for where there is no inner will strong enough to repel, to strike a balance, there is a continual teetering before any slightest outward compulsion. The will power is a weather vane, spinning to whoever blows upon it. And if two currents cross, then it fluctuates helplessly. It must have been that way with her, I reasoned, when she had first tried to tell me about the plane.

Overhead, the slight sounds coming down to us through the ceiling had dwindled and at last stopped altogether; he had settled himself in his room.

My father rose to his feet. "Shall we go up now?" he said.

I saw Eileen looking at me, looking at my apparel, and suddenly she said to me, "Not that way."

She beckoned me inside after her, into her diminutive bedroom, and gently eased the fur scarf from my shoulders and dropped it onto the bed. Then she detached a diamond clip my father had given me, from the neck of my dress, and put it into my hand, and I in turn opened my handbag and dropped it in there, out of sight. I saw her hands make a hesitant half start toward my hat, so I removed that of my own accord and placed it on the bed.

She opened a cupboard door and took down a drab coat of her own, and offered it to me. "Put this on instead. He—he'll be more at ease with you." She handed me a shapeless, worn beret. "And this." Again she gestured helplessly. "And—and—" I drew a tissue from my bag and passed it across my lips and paled them.

We went back to the front room again, and my father glanced at me with raised brows. I heard him murmur something half inaudibly that sounded like "class consciousness" with a question mark after it.

We opened the door and the three of us went out to the stairs, one after the other, she in the lead.

Going up he turned his head and said to me surreptitiously out of the corner of his mouth, "There's a contradiction in this somewhere. He's all-seeing, but we can fool him by putting on a different pair of overcoats."

We came to his door, on the floor above. It was quiet behind it: you would not have thought anyone was in there. When you looked close, though, at the bottom seam, there was a hairline of livid yellow lurking back of it.

We had stopped, stood huddled there in a small group now. Eileen was suffocating with fright. I felt a certain breathless tension that was akin to fear. I couldn't tell what my father felt. He stood there staring intently at the door, as though trying to read something on it or by it, in itself.

I touched her, for encouragement, and her hand went up in answer as though I had pulled a guide string controlling a puppet.

She knocked, and a man's voice said on the inside, "Come in."

It was deep and slow. It suggested a huge, heavily bearded, patriarchal man.

And then she had swung the door back and we saw him.

He was thin and scrawny, almost to the point of emaciation. His cheeks were gaunt, his neck was like a gnarled stem supporting his head, his bared arms were bony and whipcorded by their own leanness.

I looked at his face. It was commonplace, flat with lack of any strong characteristic, whether for good or ill. His eyes were blue, and dull. There was no drama in them, no piercing quality whatever. They expressed mildness, that was their main attribute. Over them were sandy brows, incapable of etching any very great expression upon his face, perhaps because of their coloring. They might frown, but it would not be a very dark frown. They could not express derision or disdain. They could crook querulously, perhaps, that was the most. Bland eyes, and meek brows.

His hair was a reddish gold, and very fine, and growing thin. The scalp was showing through at the crown of his head, with only a light glint still masking it. Only at the sides was there enough of it for its protective coloring still to be emphasized in full tones.

His mouth and chin were good, they were the best part of his face. They were not weak or slack. They were not strong in a brutal, overbearing sense of aggressive determination, but rather, taut and stubborn, wiry, as if resistant under some inner compulsion fortified by knowledge of self-righteousness.

He sat in a soiled shirt, with patches of damp at the armholes, and his braces over his shoulders. He had taken his shoes off, and his white, blue-veined feet were thrust into shapeless carpet slippers. He sat at a table, under the light, with the parts of a pipe strewn on a newspaper spread before him. He was cleaning the inner stem with a piece of rag, and from time to time I saw him wipe it on the thigh of his trouser.

And thus, for the first time, we saw him.

It was like a curtain rising upon a stage, after a great fanfare and flourish and expectant tempering of lights, to reveal— nothing; a barren scene, an overlooked stage carpenter tinkering with a nail or piece of wood.

The drama had exploded into vacuity after its long buildup.

He had looked up at us for a moment. Now he was looking down at his pipe once more.

Eileen faltered, "Jerry, I—I wanted you to meet two friends of mine."

He didn't answer; the pipe stem had his attention.

"This is Mr. Reid, and this is his daughter, Miss Reid."

He looked up at her, rather than at us.

"Are these the people you used to work for?"

She completed the introduction, almost in desperation. "This is Mr. Tompkins, an old friend of ours."

Somebody had to say something. I did, at last. "May we sit down?"

He took his time. He looked up first, then down at his task again. "Help yourselves," he said grudgingly.

Eileen said, "I—I think I hear my mother calling me. I'd better see what she wants. I—I'll be right back." And fled from the room.

We were left alone with him. I opened my mouth to speak. I caught my father's eye. I checked myself. He wanted Tompkins to be compelled to speak first. We were in his room, after all. He wanted to gain that gossamer psychological advantage, for what it was worth.

There was silence for long minutes, while Tompkins put the

pipe together again. Then when he did speak, it was with almost shattering abruptness, though without any heightening of his voice.

"Have you your fill of looking at me?"

I took a quickly concealed breath. "I didn't mean to stare."

"Have you come in friendliness, or have you come out of unhealthy curiosity? If I had a withered arm, or a clubfoot, would you stare?"

"I apologize if we seemed to stare," my father said with manly dignity.

"We've come here to thank you—" I murmured tactfully.

He continued addressing my father. "You've come here to laugh at me. You've come here to show me up, to teach your daughter a lesson. So that she'll stop thinking on it."

"I can assure you that my father has no such—" I began plaintively.

"He hasn't said a word to you, maybe. But it's in his mind."

My father colored with a sudden violence. There was the answer there.

He went ahead looking stonily at my father. "You think you'll put me to a little test. Well, I refuse your test. I'll match no wits with you. I'm not on trial."

"No one said you were," my father murmured deprecatingly.

"They sent an agent to me once. He said he'd heard about me from someone. He was all excited. He offered me money, a fat living, if I'd go on the stage. Just sit down on a chair three times a day in front of an audience and tell people what they had in their pockets. He wanted to test me too, like you do now, and I let him. I wanted to be rid of him, and it was the quickest way. He held up a cigarette case in front of me and asked me how many cigarettes were in it. I could have told him there were none, that he used it to carry around aspirin tablets, but I told him there were three.

Then he opened it and showed me there were aspirin tablets. He asked me what the inscription on the inside of the lid of his pocket watch said. I could have told him there was no inscription, only a horseshoe traced with diamond chips, with the end one on the left missing. I told him it said, 'To So-and-so, from his loving wife,' and used the name he'd already given me, which wasn't his own rightful one, incidentally. He opened it and showed me there was no inscription at all, only a horseshoe traced with diamond chips and with the end one on the left missing.

"He asked me who the letter was from, in the envelope he carried in his inside coat pocket, and showed me the edge of it, with the red stamp and the cancellation mark. I could have told him there was no letter in the envelope at all, he was using it to hold betting slips on a horse race. I told him the letter was from a woman. He took out the envelope and showed me, and there was no letter in it at all, he was using the discarded envelope to hold betting slips on a horse race. And even the address on the outside, he pointed out, originally had been written in a man's hand.

"He muttered something about getting even with someone, and he went out curling his lip at me, and that was the way I wanted it."

We didn't say anything, either one of us.

Then suddenly he brought his fist down on the table in unmistakable rage, and the area of his mouth paled and tautened with it.

"But you're a cleverer man than he was by far!" he shouted bitterly. "And you've turned the thing around on me so that now you've just got me to tell you out of my own mouth the very thing I didn't want to tell you!"

I looked at my father quickly, in innocent surprise, and I saw the tiny quotation marks of a smirk at each corner of his mouth. And there was the answer there.

"I didn't put the words into your mouth," he said gently.

"Well, make the most of it. Go back now and tell all your friends, so that they'll come over here in droves and torment me. I've been tormented before." His stress and emotion seemed genuine. He was trying to light his pipe, and his hand shook so with the match that he barely could succeed.

"Go now, if you please," he said thickly. "You've seen your freak. You've had your curiosity satisfied. There's nothing to keep you."

My father stood up abruptly, as though the barbed insult had caught him off his guard, had jabbed him instinctively to his feet before he could command himself. But then he moved quietly aside, and stood for a moment as if in deep thought beside a rickety chest of drawers, with his back to our host, and I saw him idly fingering a tobacco jar and a number of other articles, as if contemplating what to say next.

He turned to him at last. "I'm sorry if we've trodden on your toes," he said mildly. "We didn't come here to test you nor to tease you. We came here to show you our appreciation, to offer our thanks."

"You're not beholden to me," Tompkins said sullenly. "I've done nothing." He smoked his pipe and kept his eyes surlily fixed along its hypothetical trajectory, away from the two of us.

"We feel we are," my father said. "And as for telling our friends, I can assure you, if that's your wish, we won't say a word about this to anybody. I know I can speak for my daughter as well as myself, in that respect."

He came over close to him and offered him his hand.

"If there's anything I can do for you, if I can be of help in any way—"

"There's nothing," Tompkins said stolidly. "There's nothing I want from anybody. There's nothing I ask of anybody, only to be left alone."

I wondered if he was going to take the offered hand. He did finally, but in a rather grudging, graceless way, and was quick to release it again.

It occurred to me for an instant, as I watched, that he must be innately small in spirit, petty in spirit, no matter what powers he had or had not; it showed itself in this trifling incident. Better not to have taken that hand at all, than to have taken it in such a miserly way. Just a farm boy, a lifelong misfit, embittered by the burden of something he wasn't equipped to cope with.

I saw him look at my father's hand for a minute, as he released it, and I recalled what he'd once told Eileen's mother, as a boy, and that she'd repeated to us downstairs just now: "Every time you think of anything, there's a picture comes before you of what you're thinking about."

"We have nothing in common, you and I," he said caustically. "I didn't ask you to come here in the first place. But now that you have, let well enough alone, make that the last of it. You'll only be getting me in a lot of trouble some day, if you come here any more. Go back now. Go back to your own kind of life, and leave me to mine. Go back to your fine house, and your dinner guests with diamond watches at their knees, and your broker, and your buying of shares. And try not to run down any little girls getting there."

"Come on, Jean," my father said briefly, and held the door back for me.

I saw him turn and look in at Tompkins before closing it. I couldn't see what was in the look, for his face was from me, but I could tell by the stiff way in which his head was held that it conveyed unspoken rebuke for his gratuitous discourtesy.

I had one last glimpse of the man we had come to see, centered in a narrowing panel as the door swung around. Sitting there behind the table, pipe held to mouth, head sloped downward, mild blue eyes fixed upon us from under those sandy brows. Drab, he seemed, in the tawny electric light, inconsequential, commonplace. There was no grandeur anywhere about him, outwardly nor within. Just a lump of figure in a tawdry room. And I almost wondered what we had been doing there.

Then the door came around, and he was gone, and my father was ushering me down the stairs.

We didn't speak. We passed the McGuires' door by with common consent, and went on down to the street, and got into the car.

"I'll take the wheel," he murmured. "You must be tired."

It was the first thing we had said since we had come out of there.

The air felt good against my face, and I lit a cigarette, and that felt good too.

I knew we'd have to speak of it sooner or later, and I thought, We may as well begin here, before too much of the impression is erased. So I began.

"You don't believe?"

"That was a pretty good act. A perfect act." I thought he said it a little uneasily. I wasn't sure.

I thought of the plane. Of the telegram. I wanted so hard not to believe, myself. I wanted him to help me not believe. I was fiercely glad he didn't believe. I only wished that he didn't believe more tenaciously. I wanted to stay out in the sun with him. The sun of skepticism. My marrow was still chilled from the gloom.

"It set our intelligence high," he went on. "And it shot up at it. No superstitious little Irish housemaid now."

"In what way? The whole burden of his contention seemed to be to deny—"

"Exactly. But the denial was the affirmation. Don't you see

how he worked it? A trick within a trick within a trick. Like those labels they used to have on cans of baking powder. A circle, with a picture of another can within it. And on that, a circle with picture of another can within it. And on that, a circle with a picture of another can within it. Until it becomes too small for the eye to follow. He said I was clever, and turned the thing inside out, so that he told me out of his own mouth the very thing he didn't want to. But maybe he was cleverer still than I, and within the inside-out, turned it outside-in again, so that what seemed to be the thing he didn't want to tell me, was after all the thing he wanted to tell me most."

"You can't follow it. The thing becomes a maze."

"You tire, and drop off, and he has remained safely one con-volution ahead of you."

"But then what has he got to gain, by letting us seem to have convinced ourselves against his own opposition?"

"What has anyone got to gain in this world? What is gain? What is the meaning of the word itself?"

"Money? But then you asked him if there was anything you could do for him."

"I expected him to refuse or ignore that. I knew he would before I'd ever set eyes on him."

"How?"

"When she arrayed you in her threadbare coat, before she took us up there to see him. I knew then. The technique became typically that of the holy man to whom emoluments are anathema—"

I glanced down at myself in sudden discovery. "I'm still wearing it. I left my own things back there!"

He slowed the car a little, questioningly.

"Not tonight," I said. "I couldn't."

"Meaning you'll have to go back again some other time for

them. Though he ordered us not to come near him again. More of that inverted technique. Perhaps that was the whole idea in getting you to change in the first place."

"But that's insane, to hold up every little thing and look on the reverse side!" I protested, shielding my eyes. "How could they know ahead of time that I'd forget?"

"You did, didn't you?" was all he answered.

I dropped my hand again, limply.

"To get back to what I was saying just then," he went on. "I set a trap for him. He doesn't want to be helped. He doesn't want anything from us. Did you see that tobacco jar, standing there on a chest by the wall?"

"I think I noticed one."

"I left five hundred dollars in cash under there."

I turned and looked at him. "And if he tacitly accepts it—?"

He shrugged slightly. "You asked me before what he hoped to gain by letting us, shall I say, convince ourselves of his powers."

"But if he refuses it, that will make you more willing to believe—"

He shook his head. "I don't believe, either way," he said flatly. "He can see pictures in his mind, by thinking of a thing. But he couldn't see that five hundred dollars under that tobacco jar, two or three yards away from him."

"Perhaps because he didn't happen to be thinking of the tobacco jar, while we were in the room with him."

He gave a sarcastic snicker.

He isn't detached about it, I said to myself. He must be fighting off belief hard. He's emotionally involved. Or is he doing it just for me? Am I the one he wants to convince against believing, and not himself?

"Aren't you dealing them to him from a cold deck, though, in doing that?" I remarked after a moment. "Five hundred dollars isn't carfare. I saw a newspaper there in the room with him, with the help wanted columns folded outward."

"I saw that too," he said gruffly. "And perhaps it was left just that way, intended for us to see."

Every last thing had two sides to it. And there was never any hard and fast label to say "This is the right side" and "This is the wrong." I sighed a little, and mourned for the old two-dimensional world before this.

His hand reached out and pressed mine. "I don't believe," he said with a sort of rough gentleness, "and I don't want you to either!"

The car gave a sudden swerve and I was thrown against him. Then it straightened course again, and I heard him swearing softly under his breath.

"What was that? What happened?"

I saw him turn to look back, so I turned too.

A small figure was crouched on one knee, in the roadway behind us, as though it had jumped aside suddenly just now and overbalanced in the act. It picked itself up unhurt, and the white of a pinafore fluttered about it as distance whisked it back away from us into the gloom. It was a little girl. She looked after us in pert indignation for a moment, then she turned and scampered offside to the roadway.

The car coasted idly to a belated halt moments later, not because of what had so nearly happened—for that was already over and done with by then—but because of its implications, as they slowly filtered into our minds. And, I suppose, unconsciously he braked, as one punctuates a sentence by putting a period at the end of it.

We sat looking forward. And we didn't turn to meet each other's glance. I think that was what we both wanted to avoid more than anything else. Behind us in the darkness there was no longer anything to see; the ghost-child had vanished.

We didn't speak of it; we didn't need to. Our words were dinning in each other's ears without that. And each would only have been saying to the other what the other was already saying to himself.

I thought, Here at last is the incident impossible to reverse, with only one side to it. Here is the thing I wanted a moment ago, with the label stark and unmistakable: "This is the right side; there is no other." But this is not the way in which I wanted it.

I was conscious of him sitting there beside me, and I thought poignantly, Where is all your logic now? Where are all your arguments now? Poor darling.

"Come on, father, let's go home," I said in a small, stifled voice.

The car glided forward again.

"Shall I take the wheel for you?" I offered.

"No," he said, "it gives me something to do; it's better than—"

I knew what he meant. He kept squinting forward, but he wasn't seeing the road so much. I opened my bag, and took out a morsel of handkerchief. "Father, your face is all moist up there." I dabbed at his forehead with it. "She gave you a bad fright, that brat."

"Here," he said, "try one of these while we're getting there." I had my own cigarettes, but he took his out of his pocket and handed them to me.

I think we were both trying to be very gallant and considerate of each other. I think we both knew we were lying our heads off to each other, without a word of it being said.

We were near home now. "Jean," he blurted out. "We've never been hypocrites, you and I. We've always been frank with each other. Don't let's start changing that now. It's on both our minds. Don't let's take it into the house with us. Let's get it out and over with here and now."

I nodded, waited.

"That was a coincidence, back there just then." His voice rose, almost to a shout. "I don't care what the odds were against it, fifty-fifty, eighty-twenty, or a hundred to one; that was a coincidence, I tell you!"

"Is that what you want to think?"

He hit the wheel rim. "It's what I want both of us to think! It's what it has to be! Nothing else will do. Jean, I've never tried to control your thinking, and I'm not going to begin now. Every time anyone's out driving a car, such a thing might happen. He happened to drop a sarcastic remark at random, because he begrudges anyone the use of a car, he's envious of those who own one. And the incident just happened to match up with it. The streets are always full of children. And any time you're driving, you're likely to have such a thing happen."

But it had never happened, with either one of us at the wheel, until tonight. And this was a little girl. I didn't say that to him aloud.

Faith, they say, is a stubborn flame that can't be quenched, that will not die. But so is skepticism. It's just as hard to put out. I could sense that it was flaring up in him again, brighter, more defiant than ever.

"It's just a coincidence," he said, and his jaw locked tight. "A shot in the dark that hit its mark." He turned and winked at me jauntily. "Now let's get back to our 'dinner guests,' shall we?"

"We're not having anyone for dinner," I said. "Just the two of us, you and I."

"I know that as well as you. And even if we were, do you know of anyone who wears a diamond watch at her knee?"

I laughed that out of the side of the car.

He was smiling now in a steely sort of way. You can disbelieve, and smile that way, but you can't be detached, uninvolved emotionally, and still smile that way. "Just a freak of coincidence," he slurred. "A lot of bunk."

I turned and squeezed his arm with almost convulsive appreciation. "I'm *glad* you feel that way about it!" I said fervently. "If you only knew how *glad* I am!"

And I meant every word of it, although I couldn't join him in it myself.

III

I thought the living-room windows looked unusually bright, as we got out of the car and went into the house. We'd been away, they should have been dark.

He noticed it too. "One of the servants must have forgotten to turn out the lights in there after her," he remarked casually.

"Probably that new girl. She doesn't know how to work switches."

It wasn't an important infraction, after all.

The place seemed to be full of voices as we opened the door. Laughter drifted toward us, and the buzz of modulated conversation.

The butler came hastening toward us from the back of the hall to apprise us. "Mr. and Miss Ordway are here, sir. And another lady. They said they'd wait for you to return."

There wasn't anything presumptuous in that. They were brother and sister, friends of his of forty years standing, honorary "aunt" and "uncle" to me in my own childhood.

We went in and the buzz rose to a crescendo for a minute. Louise Ordway rushed forward to kiss me, as was her immemorial prerogative. Then to him: "Harlan, you're not annoyed with us for doing this, are you? We were on our way to . . . and when I saw how close we were, I said we simply mustn't pass by without dropping in to see Jean and Harlan . . . after all, I don't care how late we get there, I'd just as soon not get there at all. And Maria has been hearing so much about the two of you from us, for years past . . ."

She was one of those people who speak without punctuation. I had at one time thought she must have modeled herself after those characters you see in drawing-room comedies, but later in fairness I was more inclined to believe it was the other way around.

"I would have been annoyed if you hadn't," my father said.

The other person was a statuesque blonde, in her late thirties or early forties; a Continental type, who spoke with a spice of accent. She wore a clinging sheath of black dinner gown which emphasized her graceful stature; they were all three in evening clothes.

"Maria Lisetta," Louise whispered to me on the side, in postscript to the more formalized introductions, "of the Rumanian State Theatre in Bucharest. We've known her for years in Paris. It's her first trip over, she's staying with us. Did you ever see her over there? She's my standing rebuttal to those people who keep insisting women aren't as brainy as men. Eight languages, my dear . . ."

"Louise is being my press agent again." The celebrity smiled from the other side of the room. "I can tell by that animated look her face takes."

She was almost pulsingly charming. You succumbed, or at least became aware of it, from the moment your eyes first rested on her. Expressed baldly like that, it should have been a quality in her disfavor; I dislike arduously exercised charm. But this was unforced and unsynthetic, an innate attribute that could be no more held against her than her height or the coloring of her eyes. It was just a certain personality pattern that happened to fall into pleasing form to the greatest possible number of people.

Weeks was lingering unobtrusively just beyond the doorway, waiting until he'd caught my father's eye.

"About dinner, sir?"

"Oh, yes," my father said. "For five, of course."

What else could he have said—could anyone have said, even though his very life were at stake?

Then he turned, and found me looking at him, and our eyes met in unspoken but devastating understanding.

We had dinner guests, after all. And who could have known a short while before that we would have?

"I think," he said brittlely, moving toward the shaker, "that I'll have one of these Martinis the rest of you are having. But double."

And I understood.

Louise remarked discerningly, "Are you sure we're not infringing on anything? You both look a little worn and—well, on edge."

"We had rather a long drive in the car just now," I said.

"And where did you get that odd-looking coat, my dear?"

I looked down at it and swallowed, and didn't know what to answer for a moment.

My father came to the rescue. "Borrowed it," he said quickly. "It was chilly in the car."

"I think I'll go up and change," I said. "Would you care to come up and powder, mademoiselle? Louise?"

"At my age very little improvement is possible," Louise answered, "and the potential returns are practically nil. You two run along."

As soon as we were up there, Lisetta turned to me confidentially. "I am so glad you ask me to come up. You—how you say it? —save my life. You have one of these—" she circled one finger helplessly in the air "—I could borrow? That is one English word I do not know yet. I have an accident in the car. I do not care to mention it in front of Tony—"

She thrust one exquisitely molded leg out before her, and drew up the clinging black sheath nearly to her hip on that side.

112

"Oh, a garter," I said quickly.

"Elastique," she nodded. "I have to do what I can until I find first aid. I am *ingénieuse.*"

Just below the dimpled knee a diamond-outlined wrist-sized watch twinkled exotically, like a rosette at the side of her calf; the black silk cord it was attached to stretched to its uttermost limits of expansion to support her silk stocking in unfurrowed smoothness.

"I take it off here, put it on there. But if someone have asked me the time in the meantime—" She shrugged in humorous dismay.

Then suddenly the hem of her dress had dropped to the floor again, she straightened, took a quick step toward me in unfeigned concern.

"What is the matter, Mademoiselle Jean? You look so white, so—You are feeling ill? Shall I ring for someone?"

"No," I said weakly, "I'll be all right—"

"Here, come, sit here for a moment." She put her arm solicitously around me and led me to a chair. "You have some cologne? I freshen your forehead with it."

"No, thank you, I'll be all right." I smiled gratefully at her. "I'm glad you came up here with me, though." I looked around, a little uncertainly. "Doesn't this room frighten you a little? Isn't there something about it—?"

"It is a lovely room," she said quietly, and stroked my hair reassuringly once or twice.

"I'll hurry up and change," I said, bending to my shoe. "We mustn't keep them waiting." I knew she was standing there looking down at me without saying anything, though I didn't raise my eyes. "Talk to me, mademoiselle," I pleaded. "Talk to me while I'm changing. Talk to me about Bucharest or Paris or the theater or yourself. Talk loud, and fast. Oh, won't you please keep talking!" And suddenly I turned and buried my face and burst into wild sobs for a moment or two like a frightened child.

We were a little late getting down to the others.

"Did you have your double drink?" I accosted my father. "Well, now I'm going to have one of my own. A triple one."

When they left we saw them to the door together, and watched them get into their car and go away, standing there in the doorway, he on one side of it, I on the other. We kept looking out until the big oblong patch of night it gave us was empty. Empty, with just stars. Then we closed the door, and we were alone together. No, not alone; if we only had been alone, but we weren't; this thing was in there with us.

We walked back toward the stairs together, still a door's width apart, he on one side of the hall, I on the other. I don't know why; it was as if we were afraid to come together.

I went up without saying anything, and he went inside, to where the liquor cabinet was, and I heard him open it.

Then a few moments later I heard him come up in turn, and go into his room, and close the door.

Then later still I came out of mine, and went over there, and knocked.

"Come in, Jean; come in," I heard him say in a flat, forlorn sort of way.

He was in robe and pajamas, sitting on the edge of his bed. The far edge, with his back to me. There was a bottle of brandy on the small table there, and a little pony of it riding the flat of his hand, unsupported, as though he were testing it for weight. Or perhaps it was efficacy.

He didn't turn; he said, with the back of his head still toward me, "Are you pretty badly shaken up?" Then without waiting for my answer, "I know; so am I."

I sat down on the other side of the bed from him, but slant-wise, looking toward him. "She even had the watch on her knee; that Rumanian friend of Lou's." I already couldn't remember her name, it had gone out the door with her.

He swallowed the brandy quickly, as though forestalling someone who had been about to take it away from him. "Done up brown," he said, with a little inward cough. "Every *t* crossed and every *i* dotted."

I smoothed the patch of counterpane nearest my hand. "Everything but the broker."

The pony held brandy in it again. "You have to allow a slight margin of error. I don't hear from Walt for months at a time any more, these days. My stock-dabbling days are years behind me. But who's to know that but you and I? Or am I taking away the last slim straw you might—?"

"You're taking away nothing, because I have nothing."

"But that diamond leg watch, Jean," he went ahead in a smothered voice.

Again someone tried to take his brandy from him, and again he warded them off and got it down.

"Who was to know that, *even* you and I?" I said softly. "Even Louise, in the same car with her, didn't know it."

He didn't answer. I was sorry for a moment I'd said it. Yet, if I hadn't, he would have thought it anyway, so what difference did it make?

The back of his head made a quick little move again. Like a nod toward the ceiling.

"It's the shaking up it gives you. It's like everything suddenly taking a half turn around on its pivot, so that you have to learn to walk on your ear. I like my universe nice and level, not on the bias."

The cork clucked.

"I'm going to do something I haven't done in twenty years; I'm going to drink myself into bed and drink myself asleep."

I reached out and patted him understandingly on the back. Then I got to my feet. "I guess I'd better go along. I can't stay here in your room all night."

"Will you be all right in there?" he said.

"In there or in here," I said. "It goes with you. It has nothing to do with places."

"You're right. The ones that have to do with places are the easier things to duck."

I went over to the door and opened it.

He didn't look around, still sat there shoulders sloped. "Well, we'll get used to it," he said. "You can get used to darn near everything, even ground glass nudging into your backbone. We'll work out some way of living with it."

He raised his pony, looked at it.

"But tonight it's not much fun, is it?"

"Tonight it's not much fun," I assented wryly, and I closed the door.

He was down ahead of me in the morning. I still carried the night under my eyes, in graduated shading. But otherwise it was morning, and the sun was cauterizing everything. Especially those twinkling motes in the sky.

His melon was standing there waiting for him on a bed of shaved ice, with his letters beside it, but he wasn't at the table. I found him in the other room, holding the telephone to the side of his head.

He must have been listening, he wasn't saying a word.

He turned and saw me, and as I started to go out again he beckoned me over to him with his head.

"The one remaining thing came out too," he said to me quietly.

116

"This is Walt Myers on the line now. His call. . . . No, Walt, go ahead; I was just saying something to Jean."

The sun cooled off a little; if there's such a thing as chilly sunshine, that was it over there, forming a livid gangplank from the window sills to the floor.

He saw me start to turn away again, and his free hand quickly reached for me and held me there, with a sort of pleading urgency. "No, wait; don't go. I want you to stay here by me."

There was something infinitely poignant about the little abortive gesture that struck straight into my heart; *his* wanting *me* to stand there by him; an instinctive cry of loneliness, of helplessness, of bafflement, from him of all people. Yes, the axis of our world was on the bias, all right.

I stood there by him, and he put his free arm about my shoulders and held me that way. And as I stood against him, I could feel his heart going a little faster than it should have. Not because of what Myers was saying to him. But because it *was* Myers.

"My Consolidated shares," he breathed to me in an aside. "I didn't even remember I had any—"

Then he listened again.

Then he said, "Something's happened since closing time yesterday; he doesn't know what it is himself. They've hit the chutes, they're tobogganing—"

He listened some more.

"He wants to know if he should dump fast, while there's still any profit left in it."

He kept looking at me. I knew he wasn't thinking of me, though, as he looked. I knew he wasn't thinking of what Myers was saying, much, either. I knew what he was thinking of. He had a sort of distant, half-apprehensive, half-querulous look. He couldn't understand; he couldn't understand how this man should be on the phone like this, at just this time.

"Well, is it very important—?" I asked.

"It doesn't matter when you own them in the hundreds. But when they're up in the five and ten thousands, every quarter of a point can—"

Then he stopped, and said, "Too late. The profit just left it. It's underwater now, under our buying mark."

Myers must have been screaming at the top of his voice; the receiver was giving filelike rasps.

"He wants to know if we should salvage what we still can, take a loss and get out. And he wants to know bad." He said into the phone, "I hear you, Walt, I hear you. I understand what you're saying. Not necessary to repeat. That isn't it." Then to me once more, "And all I can think of is that I was told yesterday evening this phone call was coming, before he knew he was going to make it himself."

That was all I could think of too. "You'd better tell him something," I said helplessly.

He went on talking to me. "What was it he said? What were his exact words?" Then he repeated them himself. " 'Go back to your broker and your buying of shares' . . . 'Your broker and your *buying* of shares.' "

Suddenly his arm had left my shoulders. He was speaking into the phone, brisk, clear, taut.

"How much have I got now of that stuff, Walt? No, in shares." He took a pencil out of his inner pocket and jotted down a numeral on the margin of a discarded newspaper that was at hand there by the phone; a four-digit numeral. "All right. Double it. Buy me an equal amount. Buy me another—"

The phone gave a sudden sharp snap. It must have been a high-pitched yell at the far end.

"*Buy*, I said. *Buy*. Now *you're* the one not hearing *me* right. Bee-you-wy. Buy."

The phone was sputtering now, in jangled discord.

"Buy," he repeated inflexibly. "Those are my orders." And he hung up.

He wasn't smiling, and he wasn't very happy. "It would be worth the additional loss," he said, "just to prove the damn thing wrong. I hope it goes down to five. I hope it goes down to zero. I hope it explodes right in our faces."

"Your melon's waiting," I said.

We went in and we sat down at the table. The place was brilliant with sunlight, but I wished I had worn something warmer; I drew my cardigan more snugly around my shoulders.

We both put our spoons in, and then left them sticking there, as though they'd become caught fast. He began opening his letters, and I just sat there working the handle of my spoon back and forth, as though I were trying to pry it out.

"Look," he said. "Look at this."

The address was poorly written, in ink. It even had our name spelled wrong, the *e* was where the *i* should have been. And up in the left-hand corner, equally laboriously, "J. Tompkins."

It had nothing in it, no writing, no paper. Just currency. Five bank notes. He held the slit envelope up on end and shook it, and they came sluicing out onto the tabletop.

I didn't touch them. I even drew a little farther away from them, as though they frightened me. They did.

"What I left behind under the tobacco jar," he said. "The postmark is midnight. He must have dropped it in the mail almost as soon as he found it."

"And he'd been looking at the want ads before we came into the room."

He saw that they were frightening me by lying there. He picked them up and put them carelessly away in his wallet. He seemed to be careless about it; his hand, though, was a little maladroit, fumbled slightly, as though it weren't perfectly steady.

"The trap didn't work," I said. "He's not out for that. He's not to be bought."

He motioned with the envelope. "That's the message that we were supposed to get in here," he agreed.

He crumpled it with one hand and threw it away.

"Or maybe he's smarter than five hundred dollars' worth of trap," he said, giving me a steady look. "Maybe his smartness is the long-term kind, that doesn't believe in cashing in too soon, that lets its dividends accumulate." He drummed on the table. "When five hundred is accepted, what need is there to offer a thousand? But when five hundred is refused, what else *can* you do but offer a thousand? And so on up the line. I'm just speaking figuratively now."

But he didn't believe that any more, himself, and I could see it; I could tell just by looking at him, just by listening to the way he said it. He was saying it just for me. Or maybe just for himself. But I know neither one of us believed it, even as he said it.

Myers called back in midafternoon, and Father wasn't there. I told him I'd have him call him back as soon as he came in. At his own home, if he was no longer in his office. He wanted to give me the message, but I wouldn't take it. I was afraid to hear what it was; I quickly hung up before he could get started. He'd sounded almost incoherent, under great stress.

Then he rang back three times more, anyway, without waiting, at fifteen-minute intervals, and I let the servants answer the calls. I knew he wouldn't give the message to them.

Then he quit. The market had closed by that time, anyway.

When my father came in, toward dinner, I told him how frantically Myers had been trying to reach him. "He tried right and left, all over town. You weren't anywhere that he could locate you, he said."

"I know. I purposely stayed out of reach all day. I wanted to give it all the rope it needed."

"Are you going to call him back, now that you're here?" I asked.

"No," he said. "I haven't got the courage, I'm afraid to." And I knew he didn't mean the money, or the loss or gain.

Then, as we stood there, it started to ring suddenly, and we both jumped, as though an electric current had passed through us.

"There he is now," he said. Our eyes sought one another. "This is hell," he said, "I can't stand much more of this."

He went in to answer it, and I went the other way, to where I couldn't hear anything. As far the other way as I could.

I waited as long as I could, but he didn't call me or come to me, and finally I couldn't stand it; I went back to where he was.

It was over. He was bending slightly, pouring himself another brandy, the way he'd been doing in his room the night before. His face looked very white; it was almost chalky. He seemed to have a hard time straightening up again, a hard time letting go of the corner of the cabinet.

"It went down an additional quarter of a point after he put my order in," he said. "And then it stopped, and hesitated for a while, and finally started up again. Maybe *because* my order was put in, I don't know. Ever since it's been going up steadily, and faster and faster. Half an hour before closing time it had reached the point from which it had first started to drop. At three o'clock, when the exchange closed, it was already two and an eighth above it, and there's every indication that tomorrow it'll do still better."

He gulped his brandy and coughed, but his face still stayed white.

"We've made twenty-two thousand dollars, as of three o'clock today. And tomorrow it may run up to forty, or even fifty."

But his face still stayed white.

"Here," he said, "do you want one of these?"

So mine must have been too.

Maybe this is the trap, now, I thought fearfully. And not a five-hundred-dollar tip hidden under a tobacco jar.

But if it is, the cheese is on the other side of it. The mouse and the bait have changed places.

Eileen came two or three days later. Signe said there was someone waiting to speak to me in the downstairs hall, and not being very exacting in matters of that sort, I went down without inquiring any more closely than that into who it was. I would have gone down in any case, even had I known, but I would have spared myself the slight quiver the unexpected sight of her gave me. It wasn't because of her, herself; it was because of where she came from, because of whom she had to do with, because of the association in my mind that now linked her indissolubly with that matter, whether justly or unjustly.

At any rate, I found her standing sheepishly against the wall down there—she always seemed to cling to walls, rather than dare the open center of a space, in any given interview—beside a small settee, but too timid to have sat upon it while waiting for me to come down, though that was its exact purpose in being there. Over her arm she held a fur scarf I recognized as mine, and in her hand a paper bag enclosed a small rounded form that by its shape must have been a hat.

I said from mid-stair, "Oh, it's Eileen; hello, Eileen," and went on from the brief stop the first sight of her had brought me to.

"I didn't mean to trouble you, Miss Jean," she quavered. "I didn't know if I should just leave these here for you, or—"

Well, then, why hadn't she? I wondered parenthetically.

"You left these at our place the other night, and—and if I might I'd like to have my own back."

I'd forgotten; I did have them. But did she actually require them, or was that just the excuse for seeing me again face to face? Again one of those two-sided labels; and which was the wrong side, which was the right? Any slightest thing now that had to do with these people— It was unendurable; he was right, it was hell.

"I would have brought them down with me just now, if I'd known." Then I asked her what it was really on my mind to ask: "Did you tell Signe who you were just now?"

"No," she admitted embarrassedly, "I just asked to speak with you. I was afraid you—you mightn't want to see me. And I did want those things back—"

"But they would have given them to you just the same."

"I didn't know that, Miss Jean," she said humbly. "I thought they'd perhaps have to have your permission. Or maybe not know just which things I meant. They might have given me something *good*, of yours, by mistake."

Which was the wrong side? Which was the right?

But all right, then. Say she had maneuvered to see me face to face again. Now she was seeing me face to face again. What for? What did she want? The motive should reveal itself, or else the happening *was* innocent, uncontrived.

I sent a girl up for the things, giving her their description and explicit instructions as to where to find them.

There was a game-legged wait, and neither one of us spoke.

Then the girl came down again, bringing the flaccid coat and beret, and with her nose turned up at them for Eileen's benefit. She handed them over to her with an arching of her upper body, as though trying not to come too close to them. It was one of the most expressive little cameos of snobbishness I'd ever seen, and I didn't like her much for it. After all, I'd *worn* those things on my own body, without feeling that way about it myself. Superstitious fear was what I felt, but not that.

I waited until we were by ourselves again. "Look," I said, "do you like that hat? That fur piece? Would you like to keep them for yourself? I don't want them back."

She put them both down hastily, on the settee. You couldn't even offer her anything, it seemed, without frightening her. "Oh, no, miss, I— Thank you very much, I appreciate it, but—I couldn't—I couldn't do that."

"Why?" I pressed her. "Why not? Why couldn't you?"

"Oh, I don't know, miss . . ." She backed away a step, to match her recessive excuse.

"But you must know," I persisted. "Look, I'll never wear them again myself." I couldn't, I wouldn't be able to. They were steeped in fear, they were dyed with it, tinctured with it, redolent of it. I'd never be able to look at them again. "Then why don't you take them?"

"I couldn't." She backed away some more. "It'd be too much like trading on someone's—" Then she didn't finish it.

"Someone's what?"

I couldn't get it out of her. But I didn't need to; it was fairly easy to supply it myself. Not gratitude; gratitude offered favors, and there was no compunction about accepting them, it was the expected thing. It was something that did not ordinarily bestow rewards; that it was shameful to derive them from. Unhappiness, misfortune, distress, trouble; one of those words was the missing one. One of those words was the right one.

I went with her toward the door. She stopped short there and turned to me, as though driven at last to say what she had wanted to say all along, but had lacked the courage to say, until now that there was no more time.

The motive. The motive for the visit was coming.

"Well, good-bye, Miss Jean. And—and I wish you well."

Phrased like a final parting? Why?

She wanted to say something more than that. I almost labored with her, to bring it forth, but I gave no sign.

At last she whispered in hurried daring, "Don't come over there any more, miss. Try not to." And took an added little step away in trepidation immediately afterwards, as though in imminent danger of rebuke.

"Oh?" was all I said.

"For your own selves, you and Mr. Reid—" she whimpered lugubriously.

I didn't say anything this time.

"It can only have a bad ending," she murmured poignantly.

She wasn't there immediately before me in the door any more, so I had to close it. She was hurrying down the steps to gain the walk.

There was the motive. And again two sides. Which was the right one? Which the wrong? Artifice or sincerity? Was that a lure in reverse, meant to entice us all the more by seeming to discourage us? Or was that an honest plea, given out of the simplicity of her heart? Or was she simply the honest, unguessing medium for an artfully contrived lure, stemming from someone else entirely but passed on to us through her?

I stood there and I held my head pressed between my two hands, as tightly as though I wanted to crush it out of shape. This was unendurable, it made life an agonizing maze; fear, fear, all over and all around you, fear. And the outlets were in reality barriers, and the barriers were in reality the outlets, and you didn't know which to take, and you wandered around helpless, until you dropped, all spent.

The maid had been spying on me, from up the hall.

"Did she give you a headache, miss?"

"All over me," I said, "from head to foot."

I passed the things she'd left lying on the settee. "Take these," I said, "and give them away, get rid of them, get them out of my sight."

She pounced on them greedily, and, whisk, they were gone.

Now it's over, I said to myself. Now it's done, finished. Now the connecting thread has been broken. Now there's nothing to take us to them any more, nothing to bring them to us. Nothing but our own folly.

And, oh, what fools we two would be—!

I found him in the car, waiting for me at the door, a few days later. I don't know how many, I don't know how few. Enough, I suppose, to have struggled, to have held out against it. Eight or ten or twelve, or maybe two full weeks.

I could tell he was waiting for me, by two things. Because he was in the seat alongside the driver's, and not at the wheel himself. And because of the way he'd been looking toward the door as I came out.

I wondered why he sat facing me so expectantly all the way down the steps and out.

I came up beside the car and stood there.

He wasn't evasive. "Jean," he said abruptly, "I'm going there."

"There" didn't have to be amplified, I knew where it was.

"Do you want to come over with me?"

"They've even taken that one excuse away. She brought back my things only a day or two later, you know she did."

"I know, but, Jean, we're human beings. I'm going without an excuse, I have none."

"Just—just idle curiosity? Just to try him out some more?" For one of the few times in my entire life, I was disappointed in him for a moment or two.

"Oh, I have a valid business reason," he went on.

"Then you do have an excuse—"

"It isn't the same thing. I'm not being honest with myself, if I say that. If I were going to him for some flimsy pretended reason, that I didn't believe in myself, just to try him out, then I could say that I was using an excuse. But I'm going to him about something that's of vital importance to me, I'm not using it as an excuse. It's the reason that's important to me in this case, and not him; not what he can or can't do about it. I don't know if you can follow me or not."

"I think I see what you mean," I said. And then I added sadly, "But you *are* going."

"Jean, I'm at my wits' end. I don't know what else to do about it. I don't know whom else to turn to."

"I thought you acted a little worried at dinner tonight."

"Tonight? It's been going on for days and days—"

I opened the car door. "I'll drive you over," I said.

"You don't have to go there with me if you don't want to."

"I don't want to go there," I said, getting in. "But I want to go anywhere that you go. And if that's where you're going, then I want to go there with you."

I closed the door and turned on the ignition.

"It's going to be harder," I said, "not to go, after you've gone this time, than it was not to go, after you'd gone the last time."

"I know, Jean," he said despondently, "I know."

We drove a while.

"Not stocks again, is it?"

"No, that would be a cheap stunt." He didn't say any more for a while. Then, when we were near there, "There's been a strike, you know, on the Coast."

"I know."

"I've got a consignment of raw silk, worth thousands; it's been stuck in Honolulu for months. Can't unload it in Frisco. I've had an offer from a dealer on the Islands, considerably below its original value, let alone any profit. It looks like a case of take what I can get or lose the whole thing. This deadlock will go on forever. I've already drafted the cable accepting the offer, I have it in my pocket right now."

I braked, and we were there.

He got out.

"Do you think I'm being childish, Jean?"

"You're only being very human," I said, "and that's all any of us can be."

He went in.

I sat there in the car.

He came out again.

We drove off. I didn't ask him anything. After a while he took the cable blank out of his pocket, and turned it over on its reverse side, and penciled a new message to his Honolulu agent. I couldn't help seeing the six words; they were printed capitals: "Tell him to go to hell."

The Chief Executive himself intervened unexpectedly less than twenty-four hours later and the whole thing was arbitrated and called off between sunup and sundown. Loading and unloading recommenced for the first time in six months. His own closest advisers hadn't known what his intentions were, the papers said.

Our consignment beat every other into San Francisco; by getting there first it turned into a windfall. He got exactly double what it would have brought originally. A short drive to a shabby furnished-rooming house, a climb of the stairs, had turned a profit of two hundred thousand dollars. He told me those were the exact figures.

I sat there waiting for him, cigarette in my hand, light-blue swagger coat loose over my shoulders. I never went up any more. I don't know why. I never asked him any more. I don't know why. He'd come down again, and he'd tell me little things, each time. I always wished he hadn't. My heart would cringe.

"He knew my mother died when I was fourteen."

I hadn't known how old he'd been myself.

"He knew that it was the sight of the beautiful silk kimonos and wrappers she wore that really made me go into the silk export and import business later on."

"Was it?"

"Yes, but I hadn't remembered that myself until now."

My heart cringed and curled up all around its edges.

I sat there waiting for him, rust-colored swagger coat loose over my shoulders. I never went up any more. I never asked him any more. He'd tell me little things. I always wished he hadn't.

"Do you remember that night we all went to the Embassy Club to celebrate Louise Ordway's birthday? Very much against our wills, I might add. And your shoes were new and they burned you after dancing, so you took them off under the table to rest your feet? And the other dancers kicked them around the floor, you never got them back again, and Tony had to carry you out to the car in your stocking feet?"

"He—he knows about that?"

"They're in the window of a rummage shop over in the pawn-shop district, one-twenty Norfolk. They can't be seen from the street. They're behind a very large secondhand banjo."

I drove by there the next day, and got out. I could only see the banjo, nothing else.

I went inside.

"You have a pair of gold kid evening sandals in your window. Could I see them, please?"

"No, miss, not that I know of. I think you must be mistaken."
He went to the window and looked, from the inside; and I at his
shoulder.

You couldn't see them from the inside either. Just the back of
the banjo, and a welter of rag, tag, and bobtail. I felt good.

He plunged his hand in and disemboweled the welter, just so
as not to lose a possible sale, and they came up.

He scratched his head, open-mouthed. "I didn't know I had
them myself," he gaped.

I sat down and tried them on. Quadruple A heels on a double
A last, size three; feet so damnably small, mine were, they
belonged in Mandarin China. They went on like a glove.

I kicked them off so agitatedly they looped in the air, and ran
out of there for my life.

I sat there waiting for him, plum swagger coat over my shoulders. I never went up any more. I never asked him—

"Do you remember that bundle of love letters I wrote your
mother when I was courting her—no, you wouldn't."

"You've told me about them, though. When she was in school
in Switzerland. She always kept them, tied in ribbon, even after
she married you. So you kept them yourself, after she was gone—"

"I wasn't sure where they were. It's so many years now. We
were—talking about her, I don't know how it came about. He
told me they're in our safe-deposit box at the National Security
Bank. I must have put them in there seventeen years ago. He
told me the ribbon is blue. He told me there are forty-eight of
them. She was away nearly a year, and I wrote her once a week—
I must go there and look—"

I put my hands to my ears for a moment. He was at the
wheel, so the car kept straight.

"A diamond and ruby necklace I once gave her, it's in there

too. I remember it now. Ten diamonds, he said, but only nine rubies. One ruby was lost, and we never replaced it—I must go over there," he said again.

What for? The ribbon will be blue, I thought. There will be forty-eight letters. One ruby will be missing.

"Do you know what the number of our safe-deposit box is?"

I thought he was asking me in ordinary conversational inquiry.

"No, do you?"

"No," he said.

Then he said, "He says it's 1805."

I phoned the custodian of the vaults at the bank, in the morning.

"This is Jean Reid. Could you give me the number of our safe-deposit box, please?"

"I'm sorry, Miss Reid," the custodian said. "I'll have to call you back, for identification purposes, at the residence listed here before I can give out any such information."

I waited, and he did, but it took some time.

"Just a safeguard," he said. "The number that you asked me for is 1805, one-eight-oh-five."

I sat there waiting for him, fawn swagger coat over my shoulders. I never went up, I never asked. He didn't tell me any more. I was glad he didn't—

I sat there waiting for him, green swagger coat over my shoulders—

I sat there waiting for him, black swagger coat over my shoulders, as I'd already sat waiting so many times before. So many times that I'd lost count of them by now. Before that same doorway, before that same house. The street stretching away in front of me, two narrowing lines slanting together. The houses lining it shortening until they seemed to sink into the ground. Everything seen darkly, as though a puff of charcoal dust had been blown over it and then softly rubbed in.

Overhead, stars; seeming to contract and expand, like peculiar living pores in the sky. They were a part of it. They came to mean *it*.

Down below, me; alone in a car, sitting very still. I didn't move for minutes at a time. Once in a while I'd see a little smoke drift over the top of the windshield and float away into the dark on the other side. And that was from me. And once, I think, I turned my wrist over and glanced at it, holding it close to the dashboard, but I don't remember now what time it was. And I don't think I knew even then; I did it just from habit.

But other than that, I didn't move at all. I sat there waiting, very still.

Then suddenly I saw him in the doorway, and he must have already been there a minute or two before I caught sight of him. For he was standing immobile, he hadn't just come to a halt. The outlines of his body were stale from purposeless standing, as though if you stood too long in one place, in this element called night, you began to be absorbed by it, worn away around the edges.

I pushed the car door open for him, to save him the trouble of doing it for himself. He didn't seem to see me do it, or if he did, he didn't seem to know what it was for. He didn't come any closer.

He took a groping step at last. And it was the wrong way, it would have led him away from me, had he followed it out.

"Father," I said. "I'm over here. Here I am."

For a moment I almost thought there was something the matter with his eyes. Either that it had been so dark in there he couldn't get used to the street or—

Then he turned waveringly and came my way. And I saw that it wasn't his eyes. It was his face there was something the matter with. His whole face. It was as though there had been an explosion directly in front of it a minute ago, and the concussive recession, the flattening out, the stunned bleach it had received, hadn't worn off yet. Or almost as though the thing were still lighting it up; there was a phosphorescent pallor to it, like one of those watery reflections of light cast by a mirror.

He couldn't find the door gap. I saw him feel for it along the top frame of the door with dancing hands, and miss. And it was right there before him.

"You're sick, you're ill," I said. "What's the matter?"

"Help me in," he said.

I pulled him in, and he sat down heavily beside me. The whole chassis rocked a little, it was so final, so definitive, so expiring a descent.

I saw him fumble toward his collar, so I quickly opened it for him and drew his tie down out of the way.

"Be all right," he whispered with difficulty. "Don't pay any attention."

I took out his own handkerchief, and held it to his forehead, for a moment at a time, now here, now there, now in another place.

"You're like a ghost," I said.

"I am," he breathed. "I am one."

Suddenly he let his face topple forward, over the wheel. He was sitting by the wheel, for I'd moved over to let him in beside me. It came to rest in the space between the spokes, and it was as though he were staring downward through it to the floor of the car. His hands came down inertly on the wheel rim, on either side of it, and it was as though he were driving, guiding the car, all sodden and slumped over like that, and peering downward at the floor.

His body shook once or twice, but no sound came from him and no tears fell. It must have been so long since he had cried, he couldn't express weeping any more.

My arm went around him, and I clung to his shoulders for a moment. The two of us inclined forward like that now, not one.

"Nothing," he said. "Don't take any notice."

He straightened back again into sitting position.

"Was it something he said?"

He shook his head. Then he said, "No," but far too long afterwards. It was the disjointed segments of a lie.

"It must have been. You were all right when you went in there. You don't have things like this happen to you."

I could feel hysteria rising in me. A fevered fright, kindled from him.

"What's he done to you? Tell me what!"

I caught him by the coat lapels and began to shake him like an importunate child. I began to cry a little, with baffled anger at not knowing.

"Tell me. You've got to tell me. I have a right to know."

"No." Then he said, "Not this."

"I have. I'm Jean— Look at me. Answer. What did he say to you, to make you look like this, and act like this?"

"No," he said exhaustedly. "I can't tell you. I won't." He let his head go back on the top of the seat and stared upward, bereft.

"Then I'm going up and ask him myself! I'm going to make him tell me, if you won't!"

The car door cracked to and fro, and I was out.

He raised his head violently from its sloped position. And then in sudden fright that only spurred me on the faster, he cried out sharply after me, "No, Jean, no! Don't go near him! For God's sake, don't go up there—I don't want you to know, I don't want you to know!"

I darted inside the doorway. I ran sobbing up the stairs, my sobs keeping time with my staccato steps; sobbing in indignation and protective defiance of whatever it was that had done this to him. All fear forgotten, rushing to meet fear and grapple with it.

I came to the door, that door, and I beat shatteringly at it, and then I seized the knob and opened it for myself, before he could tell me yes or no, or come or stay. I wasn't waiting, I wasn't asking permission to come in; I was taking it.

He raised his head slowly to look at me, and that was the only move he made. That slight upward move of his head. So little did he move otherwise that the hand that had been clamped like a bracket to the side of his head, to the temple, as if in pensive melancholy, remained there erect in position, still curved to the shape his head had given it, but holding nothing now but space.

He didn't speak. The shadow of his uptilted hand fell glancingly across the lower part of his face, creating an irregular patch of dimness, as if just in that place he hadn't shaved.

"What've you done to my father?" I flared. "What've you said to him?"

He didn't speak.

I closed the door behind me. "What happened up here just now?"

His hand dropped at last, and the patch of shadow swept from his face.

"Don't ask me that. Go on your way. Go with him. Go home with him now." He said it soothingly, the way you speak to a fretful child.

My voice became shriller. "I can't. I can't live with him like that. You've done something to him up here. You have to tell me, have to tell me, have to tell."

He'd risen from the chair, but whether in defensive timidity at my outburst or in obstinate hint to me to go, I couldn't tell. "I've done nothing to him."

"You have. It must be you. Who else? He wasn't that way before he came into this room, and now that he's come out—"

He didn't speak, just stood behind the chair now, clutching at the top of it.

"I'm his daughter. I have a right to know. How can you look at me and see me standing like this before you? What kind of man are you?"

He didn't speak.

I dropped down suddenly before him and caught at his coat.

"Get up. Get up off your knees, child."

"Just this one thing. Just this one thing more. I can't stand to see him like that."

He tried to pry my hands away, but without embittered violence. *"You don't know what you're asking."*

I wouldn't rise, he couldn't get me to. His hands played uselessly about my shoulders.

"Until I've told you, you don't know how better it is not to know."

I tugged at his coat, and could feel my face writhe in supplication.

"I begged you. I told you both not to come back here. From the first—"

"That doesn't matter. I don't want to hear it. He came." My voice was hoarse. "Now speak. Tell me. What was it?"

He sighed in capitulation. I felt myself rise to my feet, guided unobtrusively by him. We were standing now, face to face.

"He came here to ask me a question. And I answered it."

"That isn't— That can't be all," I faltered.

Then he added, "More fully than I meant to."

He moved sideward a little, as if to withdraw from me. I moved sideward in turn, to face him once again.

"What? What was it?"

"A question about business, such as all his other questions have been."

"I know that. He told me when he left. But that's not enough. What was the question? What was the answer?"

"He asked me about some long-term transaction that he had under contemplation. He asked me whether it would be to his advantage to pursue it or to let it lapse."

He stopped.

If my hands didn't reach out physically to clutch at him, he must have felt the mental gesture as powerfully. I did myself.

His voice went lower. "I saw the picture—of the undertaking. I told him it didn't matter, one way or the other. He asked how that could be. He wouldn't be content with that, he pressed me. I told him again to let me be, not to ask any further about it. He wouldn't heed me, he persisted. He's a cleverer man than I am, by far. When he wants something, he knows how to get it. He got me to tell him over again, and in telling him over, I told too much, I told the part I hadn't wanted to tell."

He sighed wearily.

"Then tell me too, just as you told him. You can't stop now. You've gone too far."

"He said, 'But it has two possible conclusions, this transaction?' I said unguardedly, 'It has. Six months from now.' He nodded. 'It will take at least that long to pay off. I know, I realize that. But then, which will be the one more favorable to me? That is what I want to know.' "

He breathed deeply again. I didn't breathe at all.

"I said, 'Neither.'

"He said, 'That can't be so. If there are two possible conclusions, they can't be both alike. One must be to my advantage, one not.'

"I said, 'Neither.'

"He said, 'If both are to my advantage, one must be at least more so than the other. If both are to my disadvantage, one must be at least less so. If only by a hairbreadth. Tell me which.'

"I said, 'Neither. Not even by a hairbreadth. There is no other answer.' He caught me gruffly to him, and he shook me, and the words that his prying had already loosened, slipped out. 'It will take six months to reach a conclusion. And you will not be here.' "

He shut his eyes for a moment.

"And then when he understood, I saw the look on his face that I see on yours now. A look that I've never seen before, and that I hope never to have to see again. The look of a death that has come too soon, before the body is ready for it. And then he began to bargain with me, as if for something over which I had some say.

" 'Five ?' he said. 'Five months from now?'

"He read my silence.

" 'Four?'

"I didn't answer.

" 'Three?'

"He saw my eyes.

" 'Two?'

"I shook my head.

" 'One, then. One, at least!'

"He was pleading for something it was not in my power to give him.

" 'When, then? When?'

"And anything was better than to see him slowly die before me, of not knowing. Anything was better than that strangled pain. I'm only a man, I'm not a thing of stone. 'In three weeks from now,' I said. 'On the seam between the fourteenth and the fifteenth of June. At midnight on the stroke.' "

"He had one word left, that he could use. 'How?' he asked.

" 'You will meet your death at the jaws of a lion.' "

And suddenly it was so quiet in that room, where there had been such a clamor of our voices only a few moments ago. It was as though a blanket had suddenly dropped over it, deadening everything.

The silence went on and on, until I thought it would never end. Then a small voice, so weak, so faint, so thin, that I didn't know where it came from, yet it couldn't have come from him, for I didn't see his lips move, whimpered, "No." And waited. Then, "No" again. And waited. Then, "No" a third time. Then there was silence again.

I was seated now. He must have guided me to a chair. His hands were lingering at my shoulders, seeking some way in which to aid me. They were clumsy, lumpy hands; they couldn't find a way. I wouldn't have been able to show them one, myself, had I wanted to. They fell away finally.

"You shouldn't have come. You shouldn't have asked."

I looked at him without seeing, and I heard him without hearing. Vaguely, as if in dim recollection of present surroundings, I thought, What am I doing here? Why do I sit here, why do I stay on here?

I rose to my feet, clinging to the chair back, and I turned blindly, this way and that, looking for the way out that was there around me somewhere, I knew.

"He's waiting for me downstairs," I mumbled. "I'd better go back to him. He's alone."

"We're all alone," he answered softly. "Every one of us."

He helped me to the door, his hand again unobtrusively hovering at my shoulders. I couldn't feel it actually touch me, so it must have been held off from me, in readiness lest I sway and stumble.

Then he opened the door, and I moved on through the space it presented, and his enfolding hand was left empty, poised in midair at the height my shoulders had been before they drew away.

It seemed to me that it was dark, but whether it was my own darkness brimming outward or an outer darkness bearing inward, I couldn't tell. I moved through it slowly, paying out the wall lengths at my side with my two hands, one over the other, like a sideward swimmer on a slanted sea.

"Can you see your way down?"

"No," I said softly. "But I don't know what my way is, so it doesn't matter."

Then presently, from farther back, he spoke again.

"Don't fight, poor heart. There isn't anything that can be changed."

I heard his voice behind me, but it was dark. Dark before, and dark behind, and dark on every side.

One of us moved after a while, in the car. I forget which one.

But it was I who spoke. I looked about me dully, as if my eyes had been closed until then, and I said, "Have we been sitting here long?"

"I don't know, Jean," he said.

I looked up, overhead, and I winced. "It's still night," I said. "The stars—I can tell it's still night. Is it the same night we came here?"

"I don't know, Jean," he said, with a strange new docility that was in his answers now; as of a small boy, who is on his best behavior, who speaks only when spoken to, and waits for his elders' guidance in all the things he cannot understand.

"I feel so lightheaded," I said. "They swim around, when you look up at them, and blend into streaked circles, like the jeweled movements of a watch, and your head swims with them."

I could feel my upturned chin describing a little oval in time with those flashing, whirring, interlocked wheels I thought I saw, and I quickly dropped my head again, and let it dangle inert, looking downward where they weren't.

"I think we'd better go home, to our house," he said. "I don't feel anything, but I think we'd better go home. People come along and stop a minute and look at us so funny. I don't like them to do that."

"I don't either," I said, without moving my averted head.

"I think we'd better go home, to our house."

"It's so far away from here, from where we are now."

"But we have to go back there, we live there."

"I don't think I can remember the way right now. I can't think very clearly."

"Can you drive?" he asked, looking helplessly at the dashboard.

"I don't think so. I'll try, if you want me to, but I don't think I can."

"People keep looking at us so funny," he whimpered. "Look, how they stand and look at us, and won't move on."

"They think we're drunk," I said. "We're so huddled together."

I tried to take the wheel rim with one hand. I tried to turn the key in the ignition with the other. The key fell out, and down to the floor. My hand fell off the wheel rim. I couldn't get it to stay on there, it wouldn't close right.

"I can't," I whispered to him. "I can't. I don't know what's the matter with me. Just let me think quietly for a minute. I'll try again."

"I'll help you," he said. He put his own hand on the wheel rim. I brought mine back to it. Then we added our other two. We were gripping it with four hands now, two on each side. We tried to shake it a little, between us. Then we both slumped back from it, frustrated, and let it be.

"We'd better get into a taxi and leave the car here."

"Can you get out and get one?"

Then I stopped him quickly. "No, I don't want you to. I'm afraid you won't come back. Ask that man looking at us."

"Mister," he said in a feeble voice, "will you get us a taxi? Will you bring one back here to us?"

"What's the matter, can't you get one for yourselves?" the man jeered.

Nobody can help you when you're dying, I thought resignedly.

"We're not well. We can't get out of this car."

It was there only waiting to be seen, and once it had been pointed out to him, instantly he could see it himself. His face changed to contrition. "Oh, sure I will. Excuse me."

He turned and went down the corner, and around it, and we couldn't see him any more. But distantly we heard his abortive hail on the night air once or twice, and then finally a shrill lip-formed whistle, as piercing as a metallic one.

"She looks all white," a woman standing by said. And then coming in closer, she spoke to us directly. "What's the matter, did you have an accident?"

They were dotted here and there, not many of them, three or four, for it was late and it was dark, and there was nothing to see, only the fact that one or two others had stopped and were looking at the nothing there was to see.

"Let them alone," a man standing a few paces off said in gruff pity.

I looked up into her face. "Yes, let us alone, please," I begged abjectly.

She withdrew to where she had been before, unresentful.

A taxi came up on the outside and stopped even with us. The man who'd found it had coasted back on the running board, one leg trailing off in air. He dropped down and helped us by opening the two doors, the cab door and our own. They almost met, and formed a little sealed-off causeway for us to step down from one and up again into the other. He helped us with that too, helping me first by the arm, and then the two of us, he and I, helped my father, this time by both arms, he from the ground, and I from within the cab.

Then I had him beside me on the seat, and the driver thrust his arm back and closed the door for us.

We stood a moment longer, and I wondered why we didn't go. Then I remembered I hadn't told the driver where. I leaned forward, and when he heard me fumble with the glass slide behind his back, he turned and opened that for me, and I told him where our home was.

He hadn't been struck down as we had; he could still drive. We glided off and left that place behind where our car was and where we'd sat so long.

You couldn't see the stars now any more. The cab ceiling was over us, and if you stayed close in toward the middle of the seat, you couldn't even see them out at the sides, the buildings running along beside us blocked them out.

Once we stopped and stood for a minute, and I said, "Do you want a drink—on the way, until we get home? There's a bar over there. The driver can bring it over to us."

"No, I'm afraid to—now. It was different the first time, when it was just a little thing. I thought it would help then. But I'm afraid to—now."

I was holding him to me, with both my arms in a tight circle about his curved form, and his head was under mine, hanging downward over my lap.

"Is it wrong to be so afraid, Jean?" he murmured.

I don't know what my lips said, but my heart said to him, It's human not to be able to bear knowing when you are to die.

143

The cab stopped, and curved away again behind us, and we stood there alone in the dark, out in the countryside now.

We felt our way forward, toward the lighted windows we saw ahead. "Lean on me a little," I said. "These are just our own steps."

We finished them at last, and stood before the door. They beat upon our backs from up above, they pelted us like silver rain, and we were afraid to turn and look, but in a moment we'd have the door open, we'd be in where they couldn't follow, couldn't see us. And as we stood there close together, summoning the last remaining strength that it took to lift an arm and knock, he breathed, "We got home, Jean."

"We got home, Father."

3
End of the Telling: Beginning of the Wait

IT WAS LIGHT NOW OUTSIDE the little restaurant, and the night was over, and the stars were gone. And inside, Shawn noticed that the lights on the walls had waged a losing battle against the brightening day. They dulled to globes of muddy yellow, self-contained, without any outward radiation. When they went out at last, all at one time, touched off by some master switch, the difference was unnoticeable.

The light outside kept getting stronger. The blue started to seep out of it, and more and more white to ooze in. Then the white began turning a warm yellow, and that was daytime on, full strength. The occasional figures passing by outside the window cases became more numerous and more distinctly outlined. From blurred, anonymous silhouettes, they changed to three-dimensional pedestrians, complete and rounded, with separate shadows of their own that glided across the glass after them. Even the reversed lettering on the glass had a shadow of its own now, far behind it on the floor inside: CAFÉ.

A bus meshed gears, and the sound traveled into the stillness inside. A moment later you could hear the clang of its register as a coin was slotted in. Then it glided by with a whir and disappeared. The waiter was outside sweeping the street, and you could hear the scratchy hiss of his broom against the sidewalk, heavy on the outstroke, lifted clear on the instroke. Someone disengaged an awning over a stall or shop window, and it came down with a rubbery thud.

The unappreciated, disregarded miracle had happened once more; it was day again.

Unappreciated, except by one out of all those hundreds and thousands of beneficiaries.

They were both motionless. The man, the girl. It was as though they'd both fallen asleep there at the table, but he sitting upright at it, she slumped over on it, head down.

His eyes were open, though. Hers couldn't be seen; they were hidden behind her enfolding arm, that curled around her head like a rampart.

They were both motionless. The only thing that moved at all, at that little table where so much had been said, where so little had been solved, was not animate, it was a substance. Smoke from a cigarette put down long before by one of them, by him probably, stubbornly continued to baste the air with zigzag white stitches that ran up into nothingness.

That moved, and nothing else.

He kept looking at her. Her hair was so young, even fear couldn't dull it or mar its soft smoothness. The part was so straight, so white; so clear and decisive; seeming to run up perpendicularly, from where he sat.

Kept looking at her. One arm lay out along the table, toward him, almost as if unconsciously reaching out to him in plea for help, though it had fallen that way inadvertently. The fingers were but an inch or two short of touching him, as if she could reach only so far and no farther, and the help she sought to attain must come toward her the rest of the way of its own impetus. Fingers that were so smooth, so unknotted; so fragile-looking and so helpless to fight against menace. They looked as if he could have snapped off each one short, simply by bending it acutely enough in one hand of his own. No dye on the nails, just the rosy coral of nature, polished by a buffer and carefully shaped, their perfect edges unbroken for years past, probably since she'd stopped childhood play. And they had to fight for a life! Two lives.

Kept looking. Down by the floor, and a little out to one side of the table, her two feet were side by side, toes pointed backward to even the bodily balance as her head and shoulders went forward on the tabletop. So small, so seeming unsubstantial to trust support to. With heels like the spikes driven into a railroad-track crosstie. How could they carry her forward against the buffetings of doom?

The clenched fingers of her hand, on the arm coiled tight around her head, loosened a little, then contracted again. He could see her side, where her figure was bent over the table edge, rise and fall a little with each deep, hidden breath.

His eyes were narrow with a stern, dour pity as they coursed over her. Sternness for the cause, pity for the result. There was hatred latent in them too, but hatred of a helpless sort, without anything to focus on that he could see. There was bafflement, bewilderment, an honest striving to understand that missed its footing and slipped back again each time, and shot out little furrows in all directions. And there was one more thing, too, above and over all the rest. A thin, cold glaze of horror, as when one has been the unwilling witness to a mutilation.

He reached out and he touched her. Lightly on the hand, first, the one that was close before him.

"It's light," he said softly. "They've gone now. Look. They aren't out there any more."

She didn't move. He touched her higher on the arm, on the bulge before the elbow, and left his hand there for a moment, in gentle insistence.

"Lift your head. Look up. They're gone. Don't you believe me? Don't you trust me?"

She didn't seem to hear. He gave up waiting, he didn't think she was going to move any more. He took his hand away at last.

There was a wait. Then slowly her head came up, from behind the protective rampart. Her face revealed itself to him, feature by feature, in slow ascension. The white forehead, with so much pain packed in it. Then the brows, unridged, even, straight-lined with patient endurance. And then the eyes.

She was speaking now, without a sound. It was the first time he'd seen her eyes in the daylight. They almost made him wince as they first revealed themselves to him. God, he thought, those eyes! Can't I help them? How can anyone stand it, reading what they're trying to say?

She turned her head and looked wonderingly around her. Out that way, up that way, more than any other. Where the danger lay, and where her fears came from.

He put his hand back on her arm, reassuringly.

"It's the sun. That's all it is. See it? It's even coming in on the carpet. Over there, in a yellow puddle, as if they spilled something. See it? Spreading, spreading—"

She seemed dazed.

"Is this the place we first came in so long ago?"

"A few hours," he said.

She passed her hand before her eyes. "I lived it all over again."

"I know. I'm sorry. That was the only way."

"Did it do any good to tell you?"

"If I have my way—"

She shook her head. "The night'll come back again, and where will you be?"

He looked down and didn't answer.

"You can't stop it from coming back again. It's on its way even now. It goes around on a curve. The farther it gets, the nearer it gets. It'll come back. And you'll be gone. I'll be alone in the middle of it again."

"What can I promise you?" he said almost inaudibly, drawing in his underlip shiveringly.

She clasped her hands together on the table, and then did nothing more, sat there looking down at them.

"Won't you let me take you home now? Don't you want me to go with you and see that you—"

"Home?" Her hands flew open again. "Death is waiting there. Death that hasn't died yet, and that death is the worst of all. Death is in bed there, in the room that used to belong to my father, with the covers up to its chin. And it hasn't moved all night, but still it hasn't slept, it's lain there awake, staring out before it. I know. I go in that room every morning. It'll turn that helpless look, those eyes, my way when I go in the door, saying, Help me, help me. I saw your face just now when you saw my eyes. You didn't think I did, but it was so clear to read. Such pain, such pity. And you're just a stranger I met last night. Then how do you think I feel, seeing those other eyes?"

"Do you want to leave him alone now, stay away? You know that isn't it."

"I tried in my own way. And you wouldn't let me. Now we're past that point."

"Well, then—?"

"You go. You don't have to sit here. You shouldn't. You have your own life, your own job. You've given me a night."

He shook his head. Slowly, but for a long time. "I'm not going to leave you. I mean, I'm not going to leave this thing that's happening to you, ever again. I'm in it now. You caught it from him, and now I've caught it from you. I'd never be able to sleep very well again. A year or two from now I'd still be waking up at times saying, What was it? What *was* that, anyway? Why did I leave her and go on about my business? Why didn't I wait to find out? It would do that to me, I know it. I'm that way."

She quirked her upper lip in deprecation. "It won't be for very much longer, anyway. Only three more days. Two more nights. Two whole ones, and then a half one, ending at mid—"

He reached over and backed the joint of one finger lightly against her lips, and broke the word in the middle.

A customer came in and sat down, near the door so that he wouldn't have to take up too much time walking to and from his table. Instantly he began to read his morning paper propped against a sugar bowl, and as he read, without taking his eyes from his reading, he rapped against the table's edge with a spoon or something, to hasten service.

The noise reached her and she looked over there for a moment. Shawn could all but read her thoughts, they were so evident in her half-wistful, half-reproachful expression. That man has so much more time than I, and yet he's in such a hurry. He has a whole lifetime ahead of him, and yet he can't wait five minutes for his food. I have three days until the darkness comes, and yet I sit here, limply waiting.

He said to her, "If you won't let me take you home, will you come some place else with me, then? Some place where—I have a couple of friends, someone who may be able to help us?"

"Where?" she said listlessly.

"You won't be frightened? Now don't be frightened, I don't mean to frighten you."

She looked at him steadily. "The police," she said. "That's what you want to do, isn't it?"

He watched her carefully a minute, to see how she'd take it.

"Isn't it?" she repeated.

He fooled around with the dish holding ashes, turning it a little, as if it were a dial attached to the tabletop, and watching it as he did so. "We don't have to use *that* word," he said placatingly. "That's just a name for them that doesn't have to enter into it in your case. Look, let's put it like this. I'm a businessman, let's say, any kind at all, a salesman, it doesn't matter what it is. I work for somebody who's smarter than I am, who knows more than I do. That's why I'm working for him, instead of him for me. I came along last night and—did what I did. Now I want to take you to my boss, McManus, the man I work for, talk it over with him, that's all it is. Nothing in that to frighten you. He's a wiser man than I am, and he's older, more experienced. He's kind, he's considerate, he's understanding. Not with people that are punishable, maybe, but that's a different thing. That hasn't anything to do with this. He wouldn't do anything to harm or frighten you—"

"You like your boss, don't you?"

"I think he's swell," he said simply. Then he quickly went ahead with his persuasive efforts, as if to allow them to slacken for a single moment was to risk losing her. "He's got a kid of his own, a daugher. She's not as old as you are yet; fourteen, I think, or fifteen. He shows you her picture, if you—if you get him talking about her. That kind of man, I mean. We'll go and talk to him a little while; we'll just talk it over, the three of us. It'll be like talking to your own—" He quickly checked that word as he saw her face shadow. "He may be able to help us, he may be able to give us some good advice. At least we don't *lose* anything, do we?"

He palmed one hand toward her, left it there suspended for a while, in unspoken continuation of the argument.

Then he allowed it to drop at last, uncertainly, as he saw her withdraw her own hands and rest them on the table's edge, in some preparatory gesture.

She stood up slowly before him. He remained seated, face tilted, watching her anxiously.

"I have no other place that I can go," she murmured.

He straightened alertly. "You mean—"

"I'll go with you, Shawn, to the man you work for."

PART TWO

4

Beginning of Police Procedure

AFTER McMANUS HAD PICKED SEVEN of them, he sent the rest back. He closed the door of his office, and went back behind his desk, and sat down. The seven he'd picked remained standing in line there, out before him, with the gaps still between them where the nonselectees had been until just now. He motioned desultorily with his hand, and they closed up. They were almost like soldiers at attention on a parade ground, though not quite as rigid. Their arms, for one thing, were held in varying positions; one held his clasped behind him, another held his folded before his chest, another's were at rest at his sides, still another's were gripped to the lapels of his coat and hung from there. None at least were in pockets.

All eyes were on him, with an unwavering intentness that almost created a tension in the room. They didn't blink. They didn't move. You couldn't even hear them breathe at all, though there were that many of them gathered that close together. A water pipe somewhere would occasionally gurgle or whine a little in the stillness.

He took so long before beginning to speak that it almost seemed as if he didn't intend to begin to speak.

He had taken up a pencil, an ordinary yellow desk pencil, and he kept tripping this as he spoke, bouncing it lightly now on its point, now on its other end, now on its point again. That too made a faint sound, a very small tap or tick each time. He was obviously unaware that he was doing it, for his eyes were on them.

He said, speaking slowly and quietly, "This thing I have on my hands is confidential. It's got to stay confidential, by its very nature. It's not to be discussed within-precincts any more than it would be on the outside. It's not to be discussed with the other men, who haven't been selected. As well as being confidential, you might say that it's unofficial. It's something that I'm doing on my own responsibility, without any official directives from above. In view of that fact, I can't *order* you to take on the various assignments I have in mind. You're at liberty to refuse, to ask to be excused. But only *now*. Not once the thing is under way. Once you accept, you're under orders just as strictly as if the job was regulation. Is that clear?"

He waited.

"Now I'm going to give it to you in a nutshell. In capsule form. A man's death has been predicted by another man. It's supposed to happen three days from now, day after tomorrow night at midnight. There isn't anything we can get him on, the second man, the forecaster, ahead of time. No law has been broken, no threat made. There's an ordinance against telling fortunes, but we can't even get him on that; the statement was simply made verbally, as a piece of conversation, and there's freedom of speech in this country.

"I don't believe in predictions, but that's neither here nor there.

I do believe that this prediction *is* going to happen, unless something's done to stop it. But *not* because it's a prediction; no, but because either the predicter himself or somebody working with the predicter is going to see that it happens, is going to carry it out.

"Now the big prediction has come as the climax to a lot of little ones. There's been a slow build-up toward it, over a period of weeks and months. Each little preliminary prediction paid off, came true. Until now, of course, the victim is convinced the final big one will come true too. Why shouldn't he? That was the main idea.

"And that's where we come in. The way to tackle the final prediction is to hit the little ones first, break them wide open, find out what made them tick. The big one hasn't happened yet, so we can't go after that. The little ones have, so we *can* go after them. They'll tell us about the big one—what's behind it, who's behind it, what direction it's coming from, what it's all about. Explain the little ones, and you've explained the big one.

"By doing that, we'll be saving this guy in two ways. We'll be saving him from the pay-off itself. And we'll be saving him from his own belief in the pay-off. Which is doing him just as much or even more harm; which is killing him just as surely.

"Now, have you men got the idea?"

They gave him the answer by indirection, by continuing to stand there without moving.

"Now, if anybody wants to check out, there's the door."

One of them glanced around at it, as if he'd forgotten about its being there; other than that they didn't move.

"All right," he said briskly. "You're under orders from now on. You men are volunteers. And you're getting assignments that no detective's had before, ever. I'm not sending you out to track down murderers. I'm not sending you out to trace missing jewels. I'm sending you out to track down *prophecies*. Yes, that's what I said. I'm giving you *prophecies* to work on. Your job is to break them down into the practical, the—" He scoured his chin. "Well, what word'll I use?—the understandable; to find a plausible explanation for them. How they were engineered, how they were rigged up. How they came to click, to latch on.

"Now here we go. These are your assignments.

"Archer: a telegram that reached the San Francisco airport fifty-five seconds before plane time on the night Harlan Reid was coming back. And kept him off it so that the postscript to the original prediction about the plane crashing—that is, that his own life wouldn't be lost—rang the bell. His daughter didn't send it. Find out who did. Find out why. And don't let whoever did find out you're finding out. Got it?"

"I've got it," Archer breathed softly, "but, boy, could I use a ouija board!"

"And, by the way, you haven't three days to do it in. We need that information now, if we're to make any use of it."

The door closed, and there were six of them left.

"Dominguez: you're on a pair of shoes. A pair of women's shoes that disappeared from the Embassy night club. That turned up in a pawnshop—or rather a rummage shop—all the way across town. Find out how they made that trip from the nightclub floor to the rummage-shop window. Find out who helped them make it, and why. And again I say, don't let whoever did that know you're finding out while you're finding out. And you have the same time limit. Here's the address."

The door closed, and there were five of them.

"And you, Bradley. Find out how the number of Harlan Reid's safe-deposit box, one-eight-oh-five, got into Tompkins's head. And find out how the *contents* of the box got into Tompkins's head. And don't go near Tompkins, he's another guy's; work from the opposite end."

"Is that an assignment!" the unlucky Bradley moaned.

"Don't be frightened, Brad," McManus reassured him. "It didn't get into his head by short wave. It got in it some way that can be seen or heard or felt or smelled. That's for you. You see or hear or feel or smell it."

The door closed, and there were four.

"And now we come to the easier ones. That's enough for the prophecies or whatever you'd care to call them. I'm just picking the high spots. I've left out a lot. I haven't men enough, and I haven't time enough. But that's not wholly the real reason, either. I'm almost afraid to monkey with some of them, myself. They'd be too hard to get our teeth into. The Rumanian actress that ran a diamond bracelet up her gam. The little girl that just missed being run down. The stocks that went up and down, almost to order.

"The ones I've picked will do. If we can hang plausibility on those three pegs, we've saved a man's mind from dying. I'm not worried about his body. Shawn is going to save that.

"Schaefer, you're on a girl named Eileen McGuire. And when I say *on*, I mean on. You're the slip she wears. You're whatever it is they wear under their slips. You're the skin on her. You don't leave her any more than that does."

The door closed, and there were three.

"Molloy, you're on lions."

The man gulped. "On what?"

"Lions. Find out what zoos there are within a five-hundred-mile radius of here. Check with every one of them and find out if they keep lions. If they do, keep your eyes open to make sure none escapes or is swiped—"

"Swipe a lion?" breathed the detective.

"Warn the keepers at all of them to keep extra close watch over their lion cages, the next two or three days. Especially at nights. And don't overlook any traveling circuses or animal acts or what not that may come into your territory, while you're at it. Anything on lions, report to me immediately."

Molloy went out furtively touching a handkerchief to his forehead.

"And now I'm going to pair two of you off. We've come to the king pin. And if the old saying about two heads being better than one has anything to it, I'd really need the whole squad, just to break even. They say he knows what you're thinking. *I* say: act like he does. Then you'll be safe, then you can't go wrong. Jeremiah Tompkins is his name, and he lives at—this place, here's the address. He doesn't look like much, but don't kid yourselves by the way he looks that he's no great shakes of a guy. Men before you have made that mistake, and lived to regret it. Don't let him out of your sight if you can help it; but if you *must* let him out of your sight for a moment or two at a time, at least make sure that you don't let him out of your hearing. Dictaphones and all the tricks of the trade."

Sokolsky looked at Dobbs. "And he's supposed to *know* what we're doing, while we're doing it?" he quavered in an apprehensive voice.

All McManus said to that was "How old are you, Sokolsky?" And then ran on without waiting for the answer.

"Be ready to pinch at a moment's notice. Wait, if you can, until you've got something on him. But whether you've got something on him or not, he's got to be in custody before midnight of tomorrow night, one full day before the deadline of the final prophecy. Now take it away!"

The door opened, and a mumbled voice could be overheard complaining in departure: "How d'ya keep from thinking so you don't give away what you're thinking—?"

Then it closed, and McManus turned to Shawn.

"And now we come to you. You're right in at dead center. You're covering the target."

He stroked his chin reflectively.

"Are you afraid of lions, Shawn?" he queried.

"I never thought about 'em much," Shawn admitted frankly. "I wouldn't exactly—go to bed with one, if I had any choice in the matter. But—up to this point in my life, anyway—I haven't had much truck with them. They've minded their business, and I've minded mine."

"Well, from now on," McManus told him dryly, "I'm afraid you're going to have to mess around with them a little. Needless to say, you don't have to take me too literally. This 'lion' that I'm matching you against might take almost any kind of shape. It might be a bullet, it might be a tight cord around the neck, it might be a poisoned cup of coffee. Then, again, it just *might* be a life-sized, honest-to-goodness lion. We don't know. All we do know is the time set for it: midnight day after tomorrow. And that's something. In fact that's a whole lot.

"Your job is to keep him alive. I could fill that house up with fellows like you, send six of them, a dozen. Then the 'lion' would smell them, only defer its visit, come around some other time when it wasn't expected any more. I don't want that to happen. I want it to come when it was said it would come"— he banged his fist down peremptorily—"so that, by Jesus, it'll never come again!

"So I'm sending you out there alone. You go into the back room where she's resting, and wait'll the matron says she's feeling a little better. As soon as she is, you go home with her. You're her house guest, her boy friend—I don't care what you are.

"*But see that that man stays alive past midnight, day after tomorrow night!* Beyond that, you're on your own."

Shawn wheeled and went out without a word.

McManus was left there alone, with just his desk and his pencil. And the thing had begun.

5
The Wait: Bodyguard Against Planets

THE WHEELS LOCKED AND THEY had halted in front of the place. She keyed off the ignition. "There it is." She tilted her chin over at it.

Shawn looked at it. Looked at it good, with eyes starting from scratch, seeing it for the first time. He had heard somewhere that a detective must look at a thing many times, to begin to understand it; that the more he looked, the better, learning a little more each time. That that was the whole warp and woof of being a detective, to look and look until at last you knew everything that the thing in itself could tell you. He'd never agreed with that; it wasn't for him. That was all right for small things, for pieces of evidence; things that were to be detached from their surroundings and taken up for examination by themselves. But for things in the aggregate, the panorama, the scene in toto, the general setup, call it what you will, he liked the first look, with fresh unspoiled eyes. Nothing that came later could ever improve on it. The later looks simply blurred the clarity of the first impression. It was like trying to print more than one picture on the same strip of film. In the end you had neither a good first impression nor a good later one; you had simply a hash.

That didn't mean he was so omniscient that all he had to do was look at a scene or situation and he knew all about it. But it did mean that whatever his impression of that scene was at first sight, it was likely to be closer to the truth than at second sight or third. He had good imaginative instinct, and he was weak on logical build-up. That may have been why they called him a dreamer.

And so he saw this big chunk of countryside, all included in their private estate, with the house itself simply a fractional part of it. Dead center only because they had happened to stop in that perspective to it. Otherwise it would have been little more than a gray-white marker half lost in the rolling green sweep it was set into. This rose gently to the rearward, and its final outline was blurred with a heavy feathering of trees. Birches they were, judging by their white bark. There were too many of them, and they straggled down too close, forming a phalanx of potential danger. For you couldn't look under them, after your eyes had penetrated past the outermost two or three layers. Shadow set in, and inscrutability. Something could have crept down through them, and remained undiscovered until almost the last moment.

The house itself he didn't like. What its style was, he could not have told, he was no architect. It was of light-colored stone, and it was low and spreading. Though it was of two-story height, it tricked the eye into taking it for one story only; for almost all the windows on the lower floor, particularly in the front, were of the elongated type that open like doors, and they took up so great a proportion of the façade that only a small strip along the top was left for the upper-story windows, and these were small inconspicuous squares by comparison.

It was not gloomy looking nor sinister in any respect. And yet it was too massive, too classically formal in design, to be exactly prepossessing or to appear livable. It had somewhat the neuter characteristics of a public building. It should have been an art gallery or a library or some sort of community center. Then you would have wanted to go in and roam around with enjoyment. But you wouldn't have wanted to sleep in it. It didn't give that kind of urge.

"How long have you lived in it?"

"All my life."

"Then you don't mind it, I guess," he said softly, reflectively.

They got out and went up the short paved approach to the front entrance. At the base of the steps, as a sort of permanent cachet of proprietorship, there was a bronze wreath embedded in the pavement, circling the letters W. R., also in bronze. Small, but ineradicable.

"I thought your father's name was—"

"That was Father's father," she said. "He built this place. You had to come all the way out here by carriage in those days. And if you started the first thing in the morning, you could make it by dusk." She stroked the initials with her foot. "He made all the money in the family. I never knew him, but I sort of envy him."

"Why, because he made all the money in the family?"

"Oh, no; because he had about twenty years of his own *before* he started to make it. Neither Father nor I ever had that, ourselves."

There were two marble lions couchant on slabs, one on each side of the steps. Or lionesses, perhaps, for they lacked manes. Rather small, somewhat less than life size. The marble was streaked and yellowed in places from the elements. He palmed the head of one as they went up the steps.

"These are a little unfortunate, don't you think? They must meet his eye every time he goes in or out."

"I thought of having them removed, back in the beginning, but then I never did anything about it. I've watched him, and they don't seem to have any meaning to him when he goes by them. He's so used to them, I don't think they register on his eyes any more. They're stone, and he doesn't think of what they were originally intended to represent, they're just part of the doorway now. It's the—real ones he's afraid of."

A butler had the door open for them by the time they were ready to enter. Evidently having seen them alight, he had been at hand waiting to perform this duty ever since. He was a rather wholesome-looking man in his late forties or early fifties; certainly there was nothing of the decrepit family retainer about him.

If, on his part, he was surprised to see her return after an overnight absence, and accompanied by someone never seen before, he didn't show it. He glanced at Shawn with respectful brevity, no more.

"This is Mr. Shawn, Weeks; a friend of mine. He has a bag in the back of the car. And, oh—the room opposite Father's, the one across the hall."

Shawn looked around him with amiable vacuity, such as a random guest might show. "Well, it was very nice of you to have me, Jean."

"Father hasn't been feeling himself lately. We don't exactly know what's the matter with him. Do we, Weeks?"

She fixed a discretionary eye on the man, that, while it pretended to include him and exclude Shawn from its confidence, in actuality included Shawn and excluded the butler.

"No, we don't, miss," the man answered docilely.

She dropped her voice a trifle. "How is he, Weeks?"

"The same, miss."

He went out to bring in Shawn's prop bag.

"I'll show you around, before I take you up to him," she offered. She led him off the entrance hall, to the left, through a large, nearly ceiling-high door. "This is the drawing room." He went in and moved around, leaving her there by the threshold.

He was there on a job. A specialized job. He wasn't there as a guest, nor as an appraiser of antiques. He was conscientious about what he was there for. He showed this plainly. He glanced at the room as a whole first, from mid-center. Then he moved about it marginally, testing whatever outward openings there were. The windows; tried them for fastness, opened them, looked out, closed them, tried them once more for fastness.

She moved on. "This is where we dine."

He examined whatever inward openings there were, closets, passage doors, alcoves.

She noted that. Once she smiled very faintly at it, unseen, unguessed by him.

"This is Father's study."

He tilted over a book or two, as if to make their titles more easily decipherable. Or perhaps it was to see what substance there was backing the shelves.

And when they came to a marble fireplace in one of the rooms, he even crouched down and looked upward into it, to see whether it was an open or an artificial one.

"It's real," she murmured.

He turned and caught her expression.

"I know," he said. "But my assignment is to keep physical harm from him. Without knowing what form it may take, nor which direction it may come from."

She led the way out again.

"And that's the conservatory, that end room down there."

She answered the unspoken question she detected on his face.

"I'm not sure myself what a conservatory is. We use it once in a while when we have to endure someone's singing or someone's recital on the piano."

On each side of it a ceiling-high stained glass window was set into the blank wall.

"Those are fake," she admitted as he started over. "There's no outlet behind them. Wait, I'll show you; you can't get the full effect this way."

She touched an electric switch and lights hidden behind them glowed on, to throw them into relief. They gleamed out in tones of ruby, emerald, sapphire and amber, like the stained windows of a medieval cathedral. In the center panel of each was a full-length religious figure. Each leaded subdivision surrounding it bore the head of some mythological or heraldic animal—a unicorn, a griffin, a wild boar, a lion, a phoenix.

"They came from England," she said dully. "Some royal abbey or other. Time of the Plantagenets. More of Grandfather's work. Transplanted bodily. You know, in those days wealthy Americans went over and transported whole castles intact. He was modest, he was satisfied with just two windows." She turned the switch again, and they faded.

It occurred to him that, judging by the number of decorative animals around, the seeds of the prophecy might very well have been originally implanted right here in the house, in someone's evil, too-fertile imagination; but he didn't tell her so.

A woman was coming down the stairs just as they returned to the hall.

"Jean," she said breathlessly, and almost ran the remainder of the way.

"Oh, Grace. This is Mrs. Hutchins, Mr. Shawn. A friend of mine, Grace."

Her face acknowledged him with a nod, but her eyes, her anxiety, never left the girl.

"Jean," she said again reproachfully. "Jean dear."

"Were you frightened about me? I'm sorry. We sat up talking all night in a restaurant. It really helped. It took my mind off myself."

Shawn said, "I didn't mean to keep Miss Reid out like that."

Again she acknowledged him, at best, with a parenthetic nod.

"You didn't tell Father?" Jean said.

"How could I? Nor anybody else. But I couldn't close my eyes until seven. I called the Gilberts. I called Louise Ordway. Not to ask about you," she added hastily. "I made up something, to see if you were there."

"I wouldn't have been with them—" Jean started to say deprecatingly, then didn't continue. "I'm sorry I frightened you, Grace. You shouldn't worry about me. I'm a big girl now."

The housekeeper said, "The west bedroom for Mr. Shawn, I believe I heard Weeks say. I must run up and see to things a minute; you didn't warn us, you know."

"She doesn't believe us," Jean murmured, watching her reascend the stairs. "About you, I mean. I saw the way she looked at you. How could she? She knows all my friends and she never heard your name until just now."

"You're young enough yet to continue making friends," he suggested. "It's not a process that stops automatically."

"But so suddenly, out of nowhere. Let's go up, shall we?"

In the upper hall they stopped again, and he stood waiting expectantly. She was, he could tell, bracing herself mentally. "There, that door," she said, and then they still stood where they were.

Mrs. Hutchins reappeared, coming out of the door of the room that was to be his, opposite to the one Jean had indicated; tactfully closing it after her, passing them with a wordless smile, and continuing down the stairs.

"I'll take you in to see him now. Get yourself ready. This is going to be a little hard on both of us."

"I'm not a person, in a case like this, Miss Reid. I'm a protective agent assigned to this household, and to be here is my detail."

She put her hand to the knob, and then still waited. "I have to brace myself all over again each time I go in to see him. Even if I left him only a short time before. You see, I remember him as he was—before this."

She raised her hand to knock.

"Oh, one more thing. There'll be a number of clocks in there, he can't surround himself with enough of them. He'll ask you the time. Take a minute or two off whatever your watch says, make it slow, to match the others. I always turn them back a little, at the start of the day, when he's not watching. That gives him a minute or two extra, a little borrowed time. It's the best I can do to ease him. We put them all ahead again when he's asleep at night, and that starts them off accurate for the new day."

"He shouldn't have them in there with him."

"He's more frightened without them. He's afraid it's going faster, slipping away from him. The imagination, you know, is always more terrible than the reality."

Her arrested hand at last sounded against the door. "It's Jean, dear," she called. "I have someone with me." And turned the knob and opened without waiting for the formality of consent to be given.

Shawn's mind ordered his faculties: "Now, get this good. Don't miss a thing. Now you're at home plate."

The man was sitting in the middle of the big room, in an easy chair. It was impossible to tell how old he was, for death has no age. And he was as dead as anything that still moves can ever be. He was basically dressed, but a dressing robe was over his shrunken frame and his feet were in soft leather slippers. A rug or blanket had been walled protectively about his legs by someone.

His hair was a clean white, and still copious enough. And whereas, Shawn could guess, a few short weeks ago its color had been the only telltale sign of age about him, that shock of white over a youthful, warm-blooded face, now its role had reversed, now it was the only remaining sign of continuing vitality about him, that shock of clean, healthful white over a collapsed football bladder of a wizened, leathery face. His neck was like a slim sheaf of wires, and their rubbery insulation collapsed in circular folds about them—and very little current still passed through. His eyes were like rivets burning at white heat, eating their way inward through his skull, and deepening the holes they left behind.

There were four timepieces gathered about him. A shelf clock standing on a dresser by the wall, a small upright clock on the table beside him, a wafer-thin pocket watch placed face upward beside that, and an oblong gold one looping from his attenuated wrist on a leather strap whose innermost hole was no longer close enough to buckle it tight. It swung like a bracelet.

Their conglomerate ticking was like the faint chirping of mechanical birds about him.

He addressed Shawn at sight, before she had had a chance to introduce him. "An outsider! I can check now. Have you got one? What have you got? What does yours say?"

Shawn upped his wrist, shielded it with the turn of a hand. He subtracted a minute from the already-slow timepieces in open sight. "Twenty-nine past," he said, and let his hand drop and the cuff slide concealingly over it again.

Reid's face lit up joyously.

"Oh, Jean!" he cried. "Jean, do you hear that? That gives me a minute more! Just think, a minute more! Put them back—"

"And I'm even fast, I think," Shawn added, with a throat-constricting compassion. He thought, For what he's done to him already, Tompkins deserves the chair—whether he intends

170

doing anything more or not. Slow, with not enough current to kill, the first two shocks!

"Father," she said, going over to him and reversing a down-fallen plait of hair with softly tender hands, "I want you to know Tom Shawn."

His burst of enthusiasm began to dampen, as though this wasn't the first misleading approach that had been made. "Another doctor? Another psychiatrist?"

"No, dear, no." She built up an elaborate genealogy that was all Greek to Shawn. "You remember Tad Billings. Marie Gordon's fiancé. The boy that was killed in Florida when his car turned over a couple years ago. We had him here a couple of times. Well, Tom is a—was a classmate of his. I met him at —at one of Marie's parties at that time."

"I never knew you went to any," he said listlessly, as though the subject was too remote to him now to arouse interest any longer.

"Well, anyway, here he is, bag and baggage. I've asked him to stay."

"Don't you think he should be told what's going to— Or have you already?"

Shawn sliced his offered hand through her perceptible confusion, extending it toward the older man. "How do you do, sir?" he said heartily.

It was like clasping twigs. He could feel every separate bone. He almost expected them to shatter, they were so brittle, so unclothed.

"You're a little early, young man—" Reid said wanly. "But welcome to our home all the same."

"A little early?" Shawn repeated cheerfully. "I didn't know you were expecting me at any particular—"

"You're a little early for the funeral."

• • •

At eleven she rose from her chair. They had been in the drawing room, the three of them.

"I think I'll go up now. I didn't—have any too much sleep last night." Her eyes met Shawn's in a brief glance of shared understanding.

She went over to the huddled figure in the other chair.

"Good night, Father."

He didn't move. He didn't seem to hear her. His eyes never left the clock, that was like a pale moon against the wall, with a golden satellite twitching endlessly back and forth far down below it.

"Good night, Father," she said again. "Good night, dear."

It was like talking to the dead.

Shawn felt a curious sense of irritability. He realized his nerves must be on edge. He wanted to bang his fist down suddenly, or raise his voice to the rapt man and shout, She's talking to you; don't you hear her? Anything to jolt him out of his hypnotic reverie. He controlled the impulse; got up slowly and needled his upper lip with the edge of his teeth.

He put a hand to Reid's shoulder to attract his attention. Reid tore his eyes from the clock, looked around blankly. He had to look at the hand first to see what it was that had touched him; then at their faces, to see who it was that was with him.

She bent and kissed him lightly on the forehead.

"Until tomorrow."

"Until—" He didn't finish it. Stopped, as though the omitted word bore intrinsic pain.

Shawn went with her as far as the outer side of the doorway. She turned there, and pressed his hand with sudden, unexpected fervency. "Thank you."

"For what?"

"For being here. For *my* being here." She veiled her eyes momentarily. "Last night at about this same time, I was getting into the car, alone, out there in front of the door—"

He passed over that. "Try to get some sleep."

"I will. Tonight I'll be able to." She glanced past him into the room she had just left. Reid was looking at the clock again. That was the only thing there was in the whole world, for him. "Talk to him," she said in an undertone. "That's why I'm going up ahead. Two men, when they're left alone, sometimes can manage to—The heart opens to its own kind. Even a daughter is on the other side of the fence." She released his hand with a final pressure of entreaty. "Talk to him, see what you can do— Keep him alive. As you kept me alive. Good night and God bless you."

"Sleep sound," he said after her.

He watched her midway up the stairs. Then when the ceiling-tilt had shorn her head off, he quietly closed the door.

"Mr. Reid."

His heart must have been beating in time with that clop-clop, swish-swish, clop-clop, up there; he couldn't hear anything else.

"Mr. Reid, don't. Don't do that so much."

He made noises with a bottle and glasses, purposely.

"How about a nightcap?"

He was talking to himself, in an empty room.

"Here, take this."

He had to take up the hand, and bring it around, and pry the fingers back; then shape them closed again about the glass.

The glass slowly tilted, the level of its contents slid toward the downward rim, flushed over, began to run down.

"Raise it. Raise it with me."

He had to take Reid's head and turn it toward himself, to break the electric voltage of that steady stare. Only then did the eyes forgo the clock, because their sockets had been drawn around out of range.

Shawn raised his glass. He kicked it off against the other one with force enough almost to drive it out of Reid's insensate grasp. "Here's to crime," he said with husky-throated defiance.

He gulped it, and then he winked at Reid. And somehow, it wasn't a friendly or a playful wink; it was hard and brittle and steely.

Reid looked at him with wan curiosity, as though he were seeing him now for the first time. "What are you, son?" he asked suddenly.

Shawn's eyes flickered, as though he were recharging the batteries behind them. "I don't know how to answer that. I'm a fellow. My name's Shawn. I'm twenty-eight. What else is there to say, when you ask me what am I like that?"

"Never mind, I know what you are. I learned to know men while I was still alive. I used to be good at it too; I had fifty years to learn it in. You're a detective. Either a private one or a municipal one."

"I am, am I?" Shawn said lamely.

"I'll tell you more. You're honest. Look at your face, watch it. Lies slip off it like drops of sweat." If he'd been able to smile any more, what there was on his face would have been a smile. As it was, there was just a parting of the lips, a contraction of the eyelids.

"I'm a detective," Shawn said quietly, looking down into his empty glass, as though he were reading the words from there. "I haven't liked lying to you, passing myself off for something I'm not. That was—"

"Can you save me, son?" Reid cut him short.

"From what?" Shawn answered almost inaudibly. "From words? From—"

Reid wasn't listening to him. "Lift me up. My back pocket. Reach in. Pull that out. Now that pen you've got in your pocket, give it to me a minute—" He scribbled hastily across his knee, there was a rending of perforated paper, and he'd handed him a check, filled in save for the amount. "Fill that in. Write your own figure in here. Any amount, I don't care! Only—save me, save me."

Shawn's fist tightened, and his face tightened to match it. He was getting sore again. He crumpled the check, swept it behind him. "How many of these have you given to Tompkins? How many like this?"

"We're not talking about that now. We're talking about you saving me." His hands climbed up Shawn's coat sleeve, one over the other, until they got nearly to the top. "Can you, son? Can you?"

Shawn brushed them off like caterpillars. "You can save yourself, Mr. Reid."

They dropped down, dead. "That comes into it again," Reid said.

Shawn's under jaw was tight; it wouldn't move easily to let him talk. "Why don't you get yourself a little courage? You're not only doing this to yourself, you're doing it to others."

"It's so easy to be brave, when you've got a slack of forty years. Try it when you've got less than forty-nine hours," Reid said hostilely.

He turned away as though he'd lost all further interest in him. His eyes sought the clock again, clove to it, stayed there.

The drink was aggravating Shawn's temper.

"Don't, will you? *Don't* keep looking at that thing. It's beginning to get me myself. It does something to me."

He wasn't in the room with Reid any more, as far as the latter was concerned.

"Cut it out!" he said on a rising inflection.

He felt that same irritability as before surge through him, this time with a rush. She wasn't in the room with them now, to force him to curb it.

He felt an equal hatred of Reid and of the clock, they were both acting like irritants upon his already jangled nerves. His voice was getting hoarser by the minute. "Look *away* from it for a change. Look over this way for once!"

"You can be extravagant with your minutes," Reid answered dully. "I have to watch mine. I'm down to my last forty-eight hours' worth." His eyes wouldn't leave it. "My life span isn't written on your face. My life span is written on this other one here—"

Shawn succeeded in deflecting his sudden hot spurt of anger, when it came, away from Reid and against the clock; and that was about all.

He'd drawn his gun before he realized it. "I'll fix that God-damned thing! I'll show you it's nothing! You won't have to look at it!" He closed in, went at it with the gun butt, infuriated. Thick glass dribbled off. The hands dented in in the center where they joined. He struck at it again and again and again.

"Take a look at it now! Take a look! Ask it to tell you something now!"

Something happened to it. There was a violent whirring sound somewhere within the damaged mechanism. The hands began to fluctuate like a pair of compass needles. The minute hand fast, the hour hand more slowly. They telescoped, jammed together, blended in a straight line pointing upward to the top of the dial. They stayed that way. The whirring sound ceased. The apparatus went dead. Time had stopped.

Reid's hand rose with the slowness of expiring motion. He pointed a bloodless finger at the omen.

There was silence in the room for minutes that the clock could no longer record.

Then Shawn's overheated voice broke it, coming from somewhere behind him now. "And I say it was just a coincidence!" he barked pugnaciously. "You say it too! Say it, d'you hear me? That happened to be the nearest place on the dial where they both met exactly. And I'd bent them so they couldn't pass each other. They got stuck there, that's all. Say it, I tell you! Say it over and over! It was just a coincidence!"

Reid must have heard the charge of water hit the glass, must have heard the strangled gulp. He didn't look around. He kept staring at the ravaged clock. There was no satisfaction on his face, no triumph. There was only a brooding confirmation on it.

"Who needs the drink now, son, you or I?" he mused sadly.

Shawn stepped to the nearest French window and whipped back the enshrouding drapery, as if he couldn't get enough air.

Outside it, a tell slender panel of stars suddenly leaped into being.

There was derision in their beaded brightness, their rippling, regimented, pin-pointed expanding and contracting, all at one time all over the sky.

6
Police Procedure:
Dobbs and Sokolsky

SOKOLSKY WAS CARRYING THE SAMPLE case. They turned the corner, suddenly appearing as if from nowhere, and came down the street together. They were not in a hurry. Dobbs had a newspaper folded over and thrust into his outside coat pocket lengthwise, the way one carries a newspaper that is to be taken out and consulted at frequent intervals. It was two in the afternoon.

They walked in silence for the first third of the block.

"Over there," Sokolsky said abruptly, and slanted toward the curb to cross over to the opposite side.

Dobbs changed direction and accompanied him. "That isn't it."

"I know, but there's a vacancy sign there, don't you see it? If we're looking for a room, we don't pass that by and go on to inquire at a place that *hasn't* got one."

"Aren't we being too elaborate?"

"There's no such thing in this business. One little oversight like that can give away the whole show."

They were on the opposite sidewalk now. Dobbs sighed. "If he can read our minds, what chance have we got anyway?"

"He can read minds—*maybe*—only when he's aware of them being there. If he doesn't *know* our minds are anywhere around, how's he going to read them? It won't occur to him."

Dobbs gave his shoulders an uncomfortable quirk. "It makes you kind of afraid to think too hard."

"Is that anything *new?*" Sokolsky wanted to know sarcastically. "All right, in character now. I'll be in favor. You knock it. You talk me out of it."

They went in. They rang one of the street bells. The door opened. A woman was standing peering out at one of the inside doors by the time they had entered.

"Yes?"

"We're looking for a room. We seen your sign."

Her face dropped. "Oh, two of you? I'm only looking for one roomer. Two is too many to take care of."

"We're not dirty," Dobbs said aggressively.

"All right, Eddie," Sokolsky silenced him.

"I'd have to charge you double," the woman said.

"Well, how much is double?"

"Ten; five apiece," the woman said, a little unsurely.

"Forget it," Dobbs said. "Come on, Bill."

The woman was giving ground. "Well, don't you want to look at it, at least?"

"Yeah, let's look at it, long as we're here," Sokolsky urged. "Maybe we can come to some agreement."

They looked at it.

"Well, what would you be willing to pay?" the woman said. "I'm trying to be reasonable."

"Kind of small," Dobbs said, looking around discontentedly.

"All right, nine then, for the two of you."

"It's a single bed," Dobbs said.

"There's a cot in the basement. I could have it brought up."

"That would mean me again," Dobbs protested shrilly. "Oh, no, nothing doing, no cots!"

The woman's patience was running out. "What do you expect, twin beds for nine a week? That means double linens and double work. You won't find a room at such a price anywhere else in the city."

"Come on, Bill," Dobbs said.

"I'm sorry," Sokolsky said diplomatically. "Do you know of any other vacancies available along the block here?"

The woman had accompanied them to the door. Her eyes snapped. "Listen, I'm trying to rent my own room. I'm not an information bureau." The door closed vigorously.

Outside on the street, Sokolsky pointed rather obviously. "Let's try our luck up this way." They trudged on. The window curtain behind them gave an angry fillip.

"For McManus you have to be an actor as well as a plain-clothes man," Dobbs said in an undertone.

"It doesn't hurt any," his partner assured him.

They stopped again presently, as if at random.

"This is it," Sokolsky murmured.

They went in and rang for the janitress.

"Under or over is what we want."

"We'll never make it," Dobbs said with a pessimistic shake.

"If we can get in the building at all, that'll be the first step."

The janitress appeared wearing a coat sweater over some more indeterminate garments, of which she seemed to be wearing several layers.

"We're looking for a room," Sokolsky said.

"No separate rooms in this house, only flats. I don't handle that; you'd have to see some of the tenants themselves."

"Know of anyone in the house that has a room they'd be willing to rent out? We've been tramping the streets since eleven this morning." Dobbs took the newspaper out of his pocket and flashed it at her. A line of artfully penciled checks ran down the entire margin of the rooms-to-let column, as though indicating offerings that had already been inspected and rejected.

"Have you tried two-fourteen down the block?"

"We just came from there. She wanted to soak us."

The janitress curled her lip. "She ought to get wise to herself. She's had that room on her hands for eight months straight."

"How about this house, though?" Sokolsky persisted.

She shrugged. "Try your luck, if you want, but I've got my doubts. Maybe Tomazzo, on the second floor back, would be willing to rent out a room to you; they've got one over. The eldest daughter got married on 'em last month."

They went up the stairs, unaccompanied.

"No good; second floor back," Sokolsky breathed. He continued on upward. Dobbs followed him acquiescently.

He spoke again, in a whisper, as they rounded the fourth-floor landing. "That's it. The one on your left. Got it placed?"

Dobbs averted his head slightly, and probably without being aware of it himself, as they sidled by; apparently to keep his thoughts from bearing too directly upon the inanimate woodwork.

They went up one more flight.

"This is the matching one," Sokolsky said. He rapped with the back of his hand three times in a row.

They waited.

"Nobody in," Dobbs said.

Sokolsky held him where he was with a hitch of the head. "I heard something."

The door opened abruptly, as though somebody had been listening from the inside. A woman with a hard, lined face was looking out at them. Her hair was a lush terra-cotta color. "What do you two want?" she asked surlily.

"We're looking for a room. The janitress said maybe you might be willing to—"

Her features scarcely stirred. "Beat it," she said.

"But the janitress said—"

"Tell her to keep her big yap shut or I'll go down there and shut it for her." Her features were those of a graven image. Graven stone. "Through?" she added.

She answered the question herself.

"Yes, you are."

The door closed.

"Gravel Gertie," Sokolsky murmured.

They stood a moment. Then they turned and backtracked down the stairs.

"Did you get her number?" Dobbs remarked.

"No. What d'you mean?"

"She hustles."

"She didn't just hatch," Sokolsky told him doubtfully.

"If she don't now any more, if she's retired and living on what she earned, then she used to hustle. Nobody could get that sandblasted except cruising sidewalks."

They accosted the janitress once more. "What's that dame's name, top rear?"

"Elsie Moore." She spaced it. "She says."

They went out on the street.

"What do we do?"

"Phone McManus."

They went around and did it.

Dobbs came out of the booth, perspiring. "He said, 'I'll give you an hour to get into that flat. And I don't mean get in with her in it. I mean get in it with her out of it. I want you in there by three.' He's checking to see if she has a record. And he's sending two guys over to help us."

"Help us do what?" Sokolsky wanted to know blankly. "Does it take four of us?"

"I don't know. That's how he said it."

They waited where they were for them, and they came around in about twenty minutes.

"I'm Elliot of the Vice Squad," one said. "This is my partner. You the guys?"

Sokolsky moved back a little, like a Brahman from an untouchable.

"Sixteen pinches," Elliot said. "She used the name Elsie Moore the first time, then dropped it, so it's probably her right one. The last one was six years ago. She's gone straight since then."

"She's taking a dive today," Dobbs said grimly.

"It's a dirty trick," Sokolsky put in.

"Once more won't hurt her. McManus wants this job done; she's blocking traffic."

They went back to the house and posted themselves out of sight. Elliot went in and conferred with the janitress.

He came out again, said, "We won't have to go up. She's got one of these floor-mop dogs she airs every day about this time. She's due out here any minute."

"You going to do it in broad daylight, right out in the open street?" Sokolsky gasped.

"When they've got a record, they've got three strikes on them. They don't have a chance. I could do it right outside a church door and it would stick."

They waited; she came out.

"Take her," Elliot said remorselessly.

The second man broke cover, went straight after her. He didn't attempt to conceal his approach or maneuver around. She glanced back at him suspiciously, continued on her way. He reached into his pocket, took out a spongy bill.

"Hey!" he called after her curtly.

She stopped and turned.

"Did you drop this?"

"No." She got a look at it, became more uncertain. "I don't think I did. I'll take a look and see, if you want me to—" She thought she was getting away with something.

"You must have," he told her. "I just saw it fall." He pressed it into her hand. "Better put it away."

She succumbed; the temptation was too great. She opened her handbag, harpooned her hand into it.

Her hand couldn't come out again, nor let go of the money. Elliot was holding onto her wrist.

"Did you just give this woman money?"

"Yes, I did."

Elliot wrenched out her hand, with the money still in it.

"You're under arrest," he told her.

She began screaming, "What'd I do? Take your hands off me!" and the dog began yipping in reedy tone.

"For soliciting on the public street. Take her away. And turn the dog over to the janitress."

"She'll show in night court," Elliot said, taking leave of them. "It'll be good for thirty days."

She could be heard screaming and railing at them all the way to the corner and around it. She didn't struggle bodily against them—not unduly. It must have been a trip she'd made more than once. A large crowd escorted the party as far as the turn, then melted away. Not a voice was raised in protest. The men smirked sheepishly, the women nodded in frowning approval. A ghost of some previous reputation must have been hovering over her for six years past, waiting to alight in confirmation.

The janitress grinned demoniacally and made a dive for the ownerless dog. "I been waiting a long time to get my hands on this hairy pest!" she gloated. "Giving me extra work on the stairs all week long!"

They stood a moment, watching the street quiet down.

"It's still a dirty trick," ruminated Sokolsky.

"It's nothing more than poetic justice," Dobbs answered. "For one time she didn't and got pinched for it, I bet there was a dozen times she did and never got touched for it. Besides, what does it cost her? She saves on her food and light for thirty days. And reputation she's got none to lose.

"Come on," he added. "He said we gotta be up there by three. And it's twenty-to now. It took us forty minutes to gain occupancy."

7
The Wait:
Flight of the Faithful

WHEN A MAN SLEEPS IN a strange room, in a strange house, nothing familiar about him to meet his eyes when he first opens them, often he cannot remember where he is nor how he came to be there. A detective is only a man, after all. When he sleeps, he sleeps just as dead and his mind goes just as dead. So put a detective in that situation, and he's just as likely to have it happen to him as the next man.

Shawn opened his eyes and drew a blank.

The things that always greeted him weren't there any more. That familiar crack running down the plaster on the wall beside his bed; long and spidery, and opening up in one place in a walnut-sized abrasure to show a brief glimpse of the fill. Then wriggling some more, and finally petering out, as though it couldn't quite make the floor. That pivot glass above the dresser, that was always slumped over at an angle and that reflected things through slantwise strokes of static black rain due to the wearing out of its quicksilver backing. And then the inter-locking-window outlook, on a straight line beyond the foot of the bed. That is to say, two windows fitted one within the other with mathematical evenness. The nearer and the outer one his own; the farther and the smaller one the one facing it across the cramped shaft. There was always a bottle of milk on the ledge of it. It was always on the left-hand side of the ledge of it, never the right. It had always been opened and about one glassful taken by the time he saw it; then the rest put outside there until evening. The milk line was always at the same height, just where the neck widened into the body. If he kept his head low in his own bed and stared straight at the bottle down his chest, he could lose the base of it, make it appear to be standing on his own window ledge and not the far one. Several times, when it had been cold out and he'd hated to get up, he'd wished it were. So that he could just open the window, haul it in, and have an effortless hoist at it direct from the bottle. There was always a rumpled tawny shade down full length behind it. He'd never seen it go up, or even ripple. He didn't know who lived there. He'd never seen anyone. Never even seen the hand that set the milk bottle out. He didn't particularly want to.

All of this was gone. But the recollection of it still was traced on the scene around him. It was like a double exposure. The walls had receded, doubling the space around him. The windows had tripled, and they were all in the wrong places. Instead of the gray, brick-seamed pattern of the shaft, there was almost a dizzying amount of openness, you could see way out to nowhere. The strip of rag rug, that invariably skidded and bunched when he first put foot to it, had spread out all over the floor, bloomed into Persian tracery.

Even when he sat up and looked bewilderedly down at himself, he couldn't place those broad blue and white stripes. He was *dressed in pajamas, in bed!* The height of time-wasting formality.

He got to the floor. Where am I? sputtered through his disconnected mind. How'd I get in here? He couldn't find the right place to plug it in.

He went over to his clothes and anxiously fumbled for something. As though instinctively knowing the compass, the one thing, that could unerringly right him. And with the touch of the gun to his hand, it came back.

Oh—their place. I'm here to—help them. And then with a cynical twist of the mouth, Big help I'd be; can't even remember where I'm at.

He was on the lace of his last shoe when he heard voices somewhere outside. Beyond the windows. They weren't very near, but they carried, because it was so still around.

He went over and looked, finishing wrangling with his tie.

At the foot of the entrance walk, where the driveway stemmed it, one of McManus's operatives was standing talking with a woman. Someone he didn't recognize immediately; garbed and hatted as though she had just arrived. A valise stood beside them on the ground. They were arguing. Twice she reached down for it, and twice she desisted, to answer more fully something he said.

Shawn hoisted the window, looked out.

"What's matter, Gleason?"

"She wants to go. And I've got no orders to let anyone through."

"Whaddo I care what orders you've got!" the woman said sharply. "I'm *going!*"

Shawn placed her as her face came more fully his way, in the act of hoisting the valise. This time to completion. The Reids' cook.

"Wait a minute, I'll be right down."

The altercation had evidently continued unabated the whole time he was on his way down the inside stairs. He opened the front door and came out on the walk in time to overhear Gleason insisting, "—nobody goes in or out, they told me."

To which the woman rejoined with asperity. "They didn't say out, they said in!"

"Oh, *you know!*" the plain-clothes man said with ponderous sarcasm. "You're going to tell *me* what I was told!"

Shawn drew up before them, gave them a minute to calm down. "Now, why? Why do you want to go?"

"Why?" she echoed scornfully. "Everyone knows."

"Everyone knows what?" he fenced, giving the other man a quick look of mutual understanding.

"Listen, mister," she said sturdily, "you're not fooling anyone. I didn't close my eyes all night long. Look at me, I'm shaking now." She held out one hand toward him to show him. Her voice rose a little, excitedly. "I'm going to get *out* of here, d'you understand, *out* of here. I've got a family of my own. I've got a husband and two kids of my own."

"Nothing's going to happen."

Her voice rose still further. "Listen, mister, I'm not going to argue that with you. Even if nothing does, I still don't want to *be* here when it doesn't. Can't you get that through your head? I just want to get *away from this house,* for good and for all!"

She was already in a state of semihysteria, he could see that; unanswerable to reason. "Does Miss Reid know?"

"I spoke to her on the way out just now. Now give me my valise and let me go. You can't hold me here against my will, and neither can this other man."

Shawn let his foot drop from it. "Those your own things in there?"

"Own!" she flamed. "I'll open it and show you right here and now, if you want me to!" She began grappling hectically with the latches.

He fanned her back. "If I let you go," he told her, "it's only because I don't want you around here acting the way you are now, frightening those two people more than they are already. I'm trying to help them, and you're no help this way."

He stepped back disgustedly. "All right, Gleason, let her go."

She snatched the valise and ran down the curving driveway toward the estate entrance in the distance. She grew smaller as she ran, but the driveway was so lengthy and its curve so gradual, she seemed not to move much, simply to shrink to doll-like size while maintaining her same distance between the two points. She cast frightened backward looks from time to time as she bobbed along. Not at the two of them; up over them at the house itself.

"I never saw such a frightened skirt in my life before," Gleason commented. "Of nothing."

I have, thought Shawn, unspoken. Only not a girl, a man of years. And who is to say if it's nothing, or if it's something?

The door suddenly clipped open behind them, and the Swedish girl Signe was standing there, agitatedly tightening a wool scarf about her throat, a bulging carpetbag with double grips laced over her arm. She ignored them completely. Her eyes sought and found the distant fleeing figure.

She emitted a high-pitched wail of feared abandonment that went winging down the sloping ground after its objective. "Anna! Wait! I come too! I come with!"

They didn't try to stop her. They parted and she went rushing through between them, as obliviously as if they were trees or stone entrance flanges like the lions farther up from them.

The first figure had halted, was hooking an arm toward her repeatedly, to spur her to even greater haste. As if even to stand still for that little was dangerous.

They joined. They hurried on together without a moment's delay.

"I always knew panic was contagious," Shawn remarked. "But this is the first time I ever saw it catch on with my own eyes."

The figure of a man suddenly materialized at the distant driveway entrance. He hadn't been in sight a moment before. The two women stopped before him. Gleason raised one arm high, executed a slow overhead sweep with it. The two women hurried on again, unhindered. The man wasn't there any more. Even if you'd been looking right at him, it was impossible to tell where he'd gone to.

Shawn and Gleason turned again, simultaneously. Weeks came running out, his feet agilely taking the steps like water spilling over their edges. "—'d they go yet? —'d they leave yet?"

Gleason backed a thumb over his shoulder. "Hit it, you rat," he said scathingly. "Maybe you can beat them out if you run fast enough."

He skittered edgewise around them, and both their heads turned in unison, moving with him in wordless contempt as he went. He'd been engaged in cramming something into his side trouser pocket when he first emerged, and he continued as he ran by. Then in withdrawing his hand, he lost it; it fell out. A mangled check, newly received. He stopped, skidded back to it, swerved for it, crammed it in a second time, and ran on.

"And when you do that with your pay check, you're frightened," Gleason said. He spat offside to the grass.

They didn't stand and follow his course to its completion, as they had the first two.

"I'm going in," Shawn said.

She was standing there in the hall, Jean, with the remaining one of the two maids. Not a girl, this one, a sensible-looking middle-aged woman. She saw him enter, but she didn't say anything to him.

"Eight years is a long time," she said gently. "I'm grateful to you for staying."

The woman didn't answer. She nodded in embarrassment, looked down at the scanty floor between them.

Shawn didn't know whether to approach them or not. He could tell by Jean's face that she was badly hurt by the flight of the others.

The woman turned toward the kitchen. "It's that Anna," she mumbled. "Before I knew it she had the others all steamed up and everything—"

"I know," Jean murmured as the woman went out.

Shawn moved over to where she was standing, beside the library entrance.

She tried smiling.

"It hurts a little, you can't help it. Are people always that way, when their own skins get in the way of—?"

"No," he said, "not all."

"She's the only one left—she and Mrs. Hutchins," she said wistfully. "Mrs. Hutchins would never leave me, *she'd* never go. She's been like a second mother to me, ever since I was a little gi—"

They both turned at the soft sound of the slowly descending steps on the stairs. The plane of the hall ceiling beneath which they stood hid the maker until her gradually lengthening figure had descended under its level. Gray silk stockings, prim black skirt bottom, step by unwilling step. Then above, at last, the face of Mrs. Hutchins. She twisted a handkerchief she had in her hands. Shawn held his breath.

Jean turned aside to go into the library, with a deft little movement of avoidance. Not wanting to know.

Shawn caught at her hand and pressed it briefly in surreptitious consolation as she went by. Then he turned to the woman on the stairs.

"You too?" he said acidly.

"No," she said, almost inaudibly. "I'm staying. I don't want to, but I am. I've been here too long. I couldn't leave her."

8
Police Procedure: Schaefer

"SCHAEFER, LIEUTENANT. I'M SORRY, SIR, but I have to report I've lost Eileen McGuire; you know, the Reids' former maid."

"You've lost her! What d'you mean? Didn't I tell you to stay with her night and day, to keep her in front of you every minute of the time? Didn't I tell all you men not to lose sight of your objectives no matter what—? How did she manage to get away from you?"

"It isn't that, sir. I know where she is. She's right here with me—"

"Then if she's right there with you— Can she see you?"

"No, sir."

"Does she know you're tailing her?"

"Not any more, sir."

"Then she did know, is that it?"

"I don't know, sir. I don't know if she did or not, lieutenant. You see—"

The entrance to the old-fashioned seven-story factory building was recessed, set back in an indentation from the outer building line. Though open to the street, it was roofed over by the upper part of the building itself, supported by two grubby stone columns, and offered if nothing else a windbreak from the needling little flurries of air that scampered along footloose over the sidewalk. At the back of this enclave were swing doors giving into the interior of the building, and through them could be glimpsed a shabby tiled corridor and a lattice-guarded elevator bank with the cables left exposed to view. An open platform would descend, sallow light would peer through the lattices which would be pleated aside, and sheaves of tightly bunched legs would disintegrate and obliterate the corridor flooring, swarming over it on their way out. No one was going up any more, everyone was coming down. Over the swing doors, facing outward, was a stone peristyle. Within this was set a yellowed clock face, and on this the hands were minutes away from five.

On both sides of the outer vestibule were affixed shingles in a perpendicular line of black sandpaper, bearing in gilt lettering the names of the various tenants. The third one from the bottom, on the left-hand side, was inscribed: "Art-Craft Novelty Company, Artificial Flowers."

There were five men waiting around the shallow setback, two on one side of the way, three on the other. One of the latter, as a matter of fact, was rather more on the streetward side than within, lingering inconspicuously around the bulky turn of the supporting column, so that he was not vis-à-vis to those leaving the building. Each was intent on his own concerns; though they were at one another's elbows at times in their shifting about, they all refrained from noticing one another. Once one asked his immediate neighbor for a light; it was given and accepted in wary taciturnity, no further amenity followed, and a moment later the two were as unaware of each other as before.

The lift reached bottom and a bunched-up knot of girls disgorged. They spread a little as the corridor offered its width, but they still came out en masse. The entryway was suddenly raucous with their strident voices.

They were all young. Few were pretty, or even passable. They were all tired-looking, sallow-faced from confinement, yet effervescently animated by their release.

The men looked at them, and they looked at the men. There wasn't one pair of eyes among them that failed to glance with almost suctionlike propulsion at the heavy, unreceptive masculine faces. There was almost a ferocity in the glances. No second look was given, however. That was because no first look had been returned.

They dispersed. Silence fell in the entryway.

Again the five were alone. Again each one was alone, insulated from the others.

One glanced at the clock, and then a moment after spat to the ground a little to one side of where he stood. It was impossible to determine whether there was any connection between the two acts.

Again the elevator grounded. Again a knot of girls disgorged. Again they streamed out, replicas of the first. Again their eyes accosted the waiters', primitively avid, but didn't linger when no spark was struck.

"She'll be down in a minute," a high-pitched voice called out ribaldly in passing. It was impossible to determine whose. It was impossible to determine which one of the men it was addressing. Perhaps no single one, the entire five in a group.

The elevator was making faster trips now. It seemed to go up and down almost like a piston. The building was emptying.

Another group. A girl suddenly went off at a tangent, had clipped herself to one of the men, arm through arm slack.

His eyes didn't lose their dour inscrutability. He didn't smile. He didn't touch his hat.

"Do y'always have to be the last one down?"

"Who asked you to wait?"

There were four men left now. Three within the door gap, the fourth around to the outside of the entrance pilaster.

The elevator was coming incessantly now. It almost seemed to bounce; down-up, down-up, down-up.

Two girls detached themselves this time. They aimed themselves, not at two men but toward a single one. One faltered to stop a step or two short, the other possessively fastened herself to him. Their voices were brassy with the same five-o'clock excitement that possessed all.

"Is that him?"

"Yeah, that's him. How is he?"

An introduction was pattered off with almost unintelligible haste and lack of inclination. The introducer promptly separated its two component parts almost before it could take effect, swinging out into the homeward-bound stream with her escort riveted close to her. By her own effort rather than his.

"C'mon, Sam. See you tomorrow, Helen; we go this way."

Sam looked back over his shoulder. His eyes had a lingering quality. "Pleased to meet you. See you s'more, I hope."

"I always get through work at five; same time every day," was the rejoinder, delivered with alacrity.

He received a violent corrective tug that righted him on his course. "C'mon, Sam," could be heard, in a tone of latent warning.

The discarded member of the trio remained standing where she had been left, facing their way and holding a lipstick poised absently to her lips without doing much with it. She acted as though she were waiting for some unspoken pact or understanding to be sealed.

Pink showed briefly over the man's collar, as his face turned a second time. He looked over the opposite shoulder this time, the one farthest from his escortee.

The girl standing behind gave a slight wave of her fingers, little more than a flicker. She turned away immediately, but she was smiling. The pact had been sealed.

The fast-retreating couple had suddenly severed. They continued on their way parallel to one another, but several yards apart now. The girl was gesturing violently, almost explosively. The man's elbow kicked up once, in her direction, in contemptuous disregard.

Back at the entrance there were only two men left. Another carful had just come down. Half went one way, half the other. A laggard suddenly appeared, finished with bending protectively down over one stocking top in a secluded corner of the inside corridor. She claimed one of the remaining two.

"Got any money?" was his grunted greeting.

"Didn't that horse come in?" was the exasperated answer. "I told you he was no good! Couldn't you pick one once that would come in?"

"That's what I'm trying to do. What do you suppose?"

"Come on. Now we'll have to go home to my place to supper, and have the whole family on top of us the whole evening!"

There was only one man left about the entrance. The one on the outer side of the column. He acted dispirited, he acted dejected. His head was down forlornly, and his hat brim was down over that. He acted like a man who's been stood up, and knows it at long last. He shuffled unobtrusively off, close along the building line, one hand slung limply to pocket. He appeared, metaphorically, to have his tail between his legs. He didn't look up to see where he was going, and he didn't seem to care. His ego was deflated, and it stood out all over him that he wouldn't wait for her any more, ever again.

Ahead of him one of the two groups was rapidly melting away, but still fairly cohesive. There was a girl embedded in it, walking by herself and ignored by the others all around her, who acted as dejected and forlorn as the unnoticed man to the rear. She wore a threadbare plaid coat, and a babushka tied under her chin. She was thin and scrawny, and there was no lilt to her pace.

At the crossing the group thinned still further. They drained off this way and that. They diminished to a few individuals, for the most part no longer together nor acquainted with one another.

The man kept losing ground. The girls all walked faster than he. Even the babushka drew slowly but steadily away from him. He kept going, however, in that same general direction.

She turned in at a bakery.

The man reached its window after a time lag of about two, two and a half minutes. He stopped at the margin of it, looked at some cinnamon buns down there in the corner. Then he moved out a little farther, looked at a cake toward the center of the display.

Through the window could be seen the backs of women, in a double line. A babushka peeped demurely through from the front rank, its wearer otherwise obliterated.

He lost interest in the cake. He turned and sidled back, as inconspicuous as an illusory reflection swimming across the plate glass; back along the way he'd just come. The impulse wasn't very strong; it died and left him motionless two store lengths down, and then he stood there inert, the least noticeable thing on that whole stretch of street. The loiterer, the idler in his shell, a human nonentity, almost an invisibility, so accustomed is the eye to them at every turn.

She came out again, a brown paper bag now in her hand. She advanced only a few more steps in the same general direction she had been pursuing before. Then with no warning she looked back, and the look seemed to flatten the man, like a concussive blast of air grazing past him. He didn't move acutely, and yet he thinned, went back deeper into his surroundings in some way, so that they closed over him. But she was looking back obliquely, toward an oncoming bus, even more distant than he.

She began to run ahead, to meet it at its stop.

The man didn't, but he was walking again now. Toward that same eventual point.

The bus stopped. His timing was beautiful. Beautiful, that is, if for purposes of not losing the bus altogether and yet not being seen to board it by anyone else doing so. For seven people got on, the babushka the second of the seven, and he wasn't even in the group at all, hadn't arrived yet. Then just as the seventh ascended, he joined in at his heels, making an eighth. Only a direct backward look could have shown him to his predecessors, and they were too occupied in depositing their fares and struggling into the crowded interior.

Her struggles carried her to midsection of the bus, then she desisted, stood clinging to a white hoop overhead. He remained a little beyond where he had entered, in spite of the driver's incessant and generally disregarded commands to "Move back, please! Allaway back! Plenny room in the back!" repeated anew at each stop, and which everyone took as being addressed to everyone else but himself.

They stood opposite ways, he looking out one side, she

looking out the other. At his shoulder, however, was the driver's rear-sight mirror, giving a view of the whole center aisle; at hers, nothing.

Someone got up and gave her a seat, and she sank from sight. The standees between swallowed her. His head didn't even move. He could still, in the mirror, see the hole where she had been.

Then presently, as the outflow of passengers accelerated, its retaining walls sundered, so to speak, she came back to view, like something buried, when the earth around it has crumbled away and partially exposes it again.

She was not looking out the window now. She was looking forward, but she saw nothing there was to see ahead of her. Her eyes were open, but they were sightless. She had no surroundings. She was lost in some place into which her mind had strayed.

A stop called Purdue Street came along, and it seemed to bear a certain meaning to him. Once it was past he began, very unnoticeably, to shift into position to descend. He turned frontward, and advanced the short distance to the step beside the driver, and dangled one foot over it in preparation, ready to be the first to leave when the eventual next stop was made. As if to make his departure as inconspicuous as his entry. There was an exit door in the middle, more likely to be used by anyone sitting in midsection.

The driver said, "Holden Street," the bus stopped, both doors opened simultaneously. The man swung down to asphalt with a quick economy of movement meant to carry him from sight as swiftly as possible. He swung his body around, using his grip on the handrail for pivot, as if intending to cross over before the bus and get to the other side of it before it got under way again; keep it between himself and whoever else might have got off at the same time he did. But no one had.

The center and the front doors were closing again on vacancy. He saw that just in time.

He reversed a second time; swung bodily around counter to the way he'd just been about to go, and lodged one buckled leg onto the step again. The door touched it, and sidled back abashed, sensitive to the slightest obstacle. He raised himself aboard again. The door closed unopposed. The bus proceeded.

The driver said, "Make up your mind, mister." But there was a weariness to the rebuke, bred of long tribulation, that took most of the barb out of it.

He didn't seem to hear the driver, though he must have.

She hadn't moved. She was still sitting there like that, entranced. Her eyes were vacant. Her face was worn, but there was more than fatigue on it. It was the wear of a troubled mind; of consuming inner conflict.

The man's own face was a little uneasy now, itself, as one street and then another told off along the bus's right of way. His eyes were steady on the mirror; when they wavered, it was the vibration of the bus across the glass and not they.

She jumped up suddenly, as though someone had stuck a pin in her; plucked at the cord above the window. She hurried to the center door, and stood there, and palmed it fretfully.

The man's face cleared; there was assurance in it again, no longer disquiet. She had forgotten her own stop, that was all.

The two doors opened. The two of them got out. She at the middle, he at the front. He held his face close to the shiny green-painted side of the bus as it flowed by, so close it all but threatened to flatten his nose. That diminished, at least from the back and sides, the area of visibility of his face, even if it risked the wholeness of its skin.

The long green panel passed, and then he turned and looked covertly.

She was walking rapidly away. Hurrying as one does who must make up wasted time. A little, openly running step interlarded at every third or fourth quick walking pace. Already the chill haze of the evening was softening her distinctness of outline, overrunning it, like a sort of corrosive agent.

He began to walk that way. She didn't grow any more blurred, but she didn't regain her former clarity. Conversely, neither did he.

She turned aside into Holden Street. He crossed it to the opposite side, the far, and then their continuity of direction resumed.

She turned aside once more, was swallowed by a doorway, and contact broke.

He passed the doorway without stopping, the street's width over, without looking at it or seeming to notice it in any way. He continued three building lengths, four. Then suddenly he was coming back again. He turned into an entrance beside him. It was still several short of being directly opposite the one she had chosen. It swallowed him, and he was gone as completely as she was.

He fell motionless, framed in coffinlike black. Like someone standing in an upright coffin with the lid left off. All he could see was a slice of the building opposite. And in the middle of that slice, the doorway into which she'd gone.

He gave a sigh. Not of disappointment. Not of frustration. Of endless patience.

Up the face of the building a short way, at the third floor, two windows brightened that had until now been only dimly lighted, as though the occupants had been in some other, deeper room, and this light was only the excess coming from there. As though additional light had been thrown on, immediately behind them, light of their own and not borrowed light of a distance. The shades, already partly down, were adjusted lower still, by some nebulous gray shadow that didn't linger long enough by either one for its outline to be traced as either man or woman, child or grownup.

He waited; breathing, and that was all. Things moved, but not he. Sooty ripples of cloud moved slowly across the already black sky; and yet somehow they could be seen. It could be detected from below that there was motion going on up there. A car would go past once in a while; a dusty, cheap passenger sedan or a bulky, red-beaconed truck, trundling heavily, shaking the whole carcass of the street. A figure would come by afoot now and then. A window would light up that had been dark before; another would go dark that had been light before, as though some mystic equation must be maintained. Those things moved, but not he.

One hour and fifteen minutes passed. The windows on the third went down again. Not out altogether, but down; as though near light had been extinguished.

Four or five more minutes went by after that.

He'd sighed again. Not in relief. Not even in alerted hope. Simply in patience that had known all along.

Then suddenly she'd come out of the doorway, and turned, and was walking up the street, back along the way she'd come one hour and twenty minutes ago.

He stayed where he was, motionless. That same equation, as of the lighted and unlighted windows before, seemed to come into play. For while she was in sight on the street, he wasn't. As she turned the corner and no longer was, he was in sight, moving along the street down that way.

She walked three blocks along the lateral way, the avenue along which the buses ran and there were lighted stores. She went into a drugstore, and for a moment her figure flamed into full color as the revealing swath from its entrance caught her. He came up in turn and passed it, letting it only stripe him for a moment—purple from the urn of colored water at one side of its show window, yellow-white in between, then vivid green from the urn at the other side—then passed on into the comparative darkness beyond.

He stopped there and examined the photographic "still" his mind had printed during its brief passage across the foursquare glass lens that was the drugstore front. Gleaming nickeled surfaces, tall spindle stools, figures on them siphoning straws thrust into cloudy glasses—that was all foreground detail, to be discarded. At the rear end of the enclosure, her back to him, before a counter. Facing her behind it the druggist, holding up a thimble-sized bottle and pointing to it in recommendation. Lingering nearby another customer, a woman, in an attitude suggestive of impatience at the delay in being waited on in turn; fingernails in claw formation to the countertop.

He stood a moment. He stepped back and looked again. There were alterations in the new "still." Small ones, of no great consequence. The two customers were still there at the rearward counter. The druggist no longer was. He must have stepped back behind-scenes to secure something at request. The carriage of the motionless figures subtly revealed a change of role. The impatient one was attentively upright now, no longer tapping. She had gained her way, been waited on. The other figure was now inclined to the counter, uncertain, dilatory, decision postponed.

He withdrew again. A moment or two passed. He could hear the faint tinkle of the cash register, even out where he was. He withdrew still farther, to an unlighted store entrance a short distance away. Both customers came out almost simultaneously. The register had sounded only once. One must have left without buying anything.

She passed him, crossed in front of the place where he was.

The other one had gone the other way. She was holding nothing in her hands. But she had a handbag sheathed under her arm.

He stepped out again in turn. But now he hesitated, turning his head between her receding figure and the lighted drugstore entrance down the other way. He started for that first, as if to go in and inquire what she had purchased, or what she had asked to be shown.

Her figure was already gaining distance. He seemed to measure the relative space between him and it, and between him and the counter far back in the store, and to discard one as impractical. She was nearing a four-directional crossing, well peopled. He let the drugstore entrance alone and hurried after her.

She walked and walked, as though she were never going to get through walking. After a while, with enough of it to sample, he could decipher it to a certain extent. For a walk that continues in one definite direction for a long enough time must have a destination in front of it. And if the region, the locality, the walk progresses through is fairly well known, the destination can be roughly guessed. But her walk didn't continue in one definite direction; it kept altering, canceling itself out, repeating itself unnecessarily. So before long he was able to read into it that it was aimless, a walk without a destination, a walk taken for the mere sake of being able to think something over while walking. Her mind was lost within itself, while her feet continued to carry her on at random.

She came to the entrance to a park, finally, and turned and went in, as though discovering in this an even greater opportunity for remoteness, for removal from outward disturbance. Or perhaps she was becoming conscious of growing tired at last, and had remembered that there were benches provided in parks.

At any rate, as he followed her along the winding, sparingly lighted walk, he saw her sink down upon the first bench she came to, and abruptly he stopped too, and moved offside into the inky shadow of a tree. There was a lamppost not very far from the bench, so that a faint pallor was cast over her. And in this new situation he could watch her more safely than at any preceding time. For he was completely blotted out, and there was no one else in sight to distract his eyes, he had her all to himself.

She didn't move. She sat there with her body turned sideward on the bench, and her back toward the lights and noise of the city.

A policeman came along presently. He turned his head curiously toward her as he passed, but he continued on. Then he looked back, as though uncertain whether she should be allowed to stay there alone like that. But still he continued on a little more. Then he looked back a second time, to see if she was still there. This time he halted. But this time he was close enough to the tree.

A low whistle sounded from under it, and he went over, was lost for a moment in the obscurity. When he emerged, though he couldn't resist glancing back again, this time with doubly sharpened curiosity, he continued definitely on his way.

A young couple came along, their heads resting against each other. They were speaking so low that they could scarcely be heard as they passed the tree. They came to the bench, slowed slightly in indecision, then went on again, looking for a bench they could have all to themselves.

She moved a little; as though belatedly aware someone had gone by, but without having seen them at the time they did go by. He saw her open her handbag, and reach into it, and take something out. He saw her looking at it. He couldn't see what it was. Something small.

Then with some haste she put it away again, as though hearing some sound of imminent interruption that had not yet reached him. It did a moment later. It was coming from the other side of her. A man came along, alone. Not in any impetuous hurry.

Oh-oh, thought the watcher under the tree, warningly.

He passed the bench and looked at her. He didn't glance as the policeman had, he looked hard and long.

He stopped and stood. Then he went over and sat down, the bench length away.

The watcher under the tree began to move toward them, marginally, without revealing himself on the path.

The man was on mid-bench now, he'd halved the distance between them. Her back was still turned; she didn't seem aware he'd joined her.

He must have spoken, in a low voice. She whirled around, blankly. Then she bolted upright, with a half-suppressed scream.

She ran down the path toward the park outlet, passing the hidden watcher.

The man now sitting alone on it upped the palms of his hands philosophically. "You're too thin anyway!" he called after her in belated rancor. "Save your shoe leather. I ain't coming after you!" He crossed his legs and spread his arms comfortably along the bench top, as though now that he was on it he might as well stay there.

She stopped running as soon as she'd safely gained the entrance, and when he came out in turn she was still securely in sight ahead of him, at a walk once more. The incessant cat-and-mouse play resumed.

He thought she'd go home now, after being shaken out of her reverie. She went at first in that general direction, then, diverging suddenly when almost back there, went aside the space of a street or two, until she had come to a church. One that was evidently known to her, for it was small and inconspicuous, and its presence otherwise could not have been guessed from a distance.

She went slowly up the few brief steps, opened the small door set within the massive large one, and disappeared inside.

When he reached it he hesitated only momentarily. He would not have gone in if it had had only the one entrance. But it was on a corner plot, it fronted two ways, and there was a side entrance farther down. Unsure that she was unaware of him, and this was merely a subterfuge to slip out at the side while he waited at the front, he went in himself.

He hadn't been in one since he was a boy. The silence immediately abashed him, though he had been in many silent places since then. But this was silence with a meaning. He couldn't remember any of the proper things to do on entering such a place, or if there were any, except to take his hat off, and he did that.

He crossed the empty vestibule and entered the second door, as she must have before him. He softened its closing with one hand, and stood there by it.

He saw her. She was far down ahead, at the end of the aisle, on her knees before the altar rail. A small huddled shape. The candles were like clusters of white daisies glimmering in a dark-blue meadow. The imaged face of the Mother holding the Child, inclined downward from on high, was palely revealed from below, in a sort of indirect luminousness. Even at the distance at which he stood, its brooding aura of saddened, merciful compassion could be felt, seemed to reach out toward him, as if trying to soften him. In his heart he could almost hear the tender burden of its entreaty: Let her be; let her be.

His hand went to his collar and sought to ease it.

They were alone. There was no hunter and no hunted now. The laws on the outside had stopped short at the door. And if there was a transgressor between the two of them, it was he and not she, that sorrowing face up there seemed to caution. For she had come in trouble, and he had come to inflict it.

He shook his head, as though the impression disconcerted him.

She rose and moved back along the aisle. He stayed there motionless, invisible against the black lining of the door. She entered one of the pews and sank down again, her head scarcely visible against the pallid candle glow beyond it.

He moved aside, entered one of the rearmost pews. He crouched down on one knee, let his hat fall, clasped his hands against the back of the pew before him, inclined his head. He watched her through the seams of his fingers. They were still, the watcher and the watched. There is no time in a church; the minutes and the hours had been left behind at the door.

Her head rose at last, and she came out into the aisle again. She dipped her knee briefly and made the sign of the cross altar-ward, then came up it, past where he knelt, blurred in the dimness. She didn't look at him; his face could have been uncovered, turned her way, and she would not have seen him.

She opened the door and went out.

He made the sign of the cross. He did it in the furtive way of a person ashamed of himself.

He rose and went out after her.

He put his hat on and held his head low for a time, hunched over, as if weighted with an intangible guilt, on the streets outside.

She was becoming aware of him. She stopped twice, but without looking around. Rather in the way of a person listening to, or feeling something, within them.

Then she turned suddenly and started back directly toward him. He had grown careless, the surroundings were unpropitious, and he was badly caught. There was no time to turn back. The duplication of her own turn would have caught her eye, carried its own message, if his presence hadn't already. There was no sideward escape, no doorways to veer off into. They were beside a blank stretch of industrial wall, fencing some sort of yards.

He continued onward; there was nothing else he could do. Their paths would cross, they would reverse themselves, he thought; he go forward of her, she back of him.

Instead she stopped as they reached each other.

"*You're* not following me, are you?" Her voice had in it a forlorn, almost abject plea for reassurance. It wasn't an accusation, it was as though she were baffled and seeking help of the first passer-by she happened to encounter.

"No, miss, I'm not," he said quite simply, though his cheeks tightened a little. "I'm going up this way, you're going down that."

She nodded. "I knew you weren't," she mused sadly. "I knew I was mistaken." She backed her hand distressedly to her forehead. "All day long I've been thinking—"

"I haven't seen you until this minute."

"I know you haven't. And I haven't seen you. I don't know what made me do that." There was something childlike in her helplessness.

He went on.

She went on.

He stopped, looked back, swearing soundlessly between his clenched teeth.

Then he turned, started after her once more, his anonymity riddled. He'd have to be switched, he was no good for his purpose any longer.

The lighted motion-picture marquee threw a yellow glare over her as she drifted under it. She didn't seem to see it until she was already overstepping it at its far side, and darkness had begun to run down her back again like a spreading stain. Then she turned, and looked up overhead to see what it was. Then noting what it was, and as though it hadn't occurred to her until just then that there could be such a place, she opened her bag and plumbed it, as if to see whether she had money. Then she went over to the little glass kiosk and bought admission. Then she rounded it to the back and went in. All this without the barest glance at the advertising so lavishly displayed all about her, in lighted lettering above and in lighted glass-covered panels on both sides of her. As though the fact of gaining entrance, and not the presentation, was the motive of her entering.

A moment later he had bought a ticket in turn. He crossed the empty vestibule, gave the ticket to the taker at the door, plunged into green-tinged darkness, that rippled a little along the walls, as though there were glistening water at hand somewhere nearby.

A pocket light went on, drawing a sort of tracer for him across the gloom, and brass buttons peered dimly just behind it. "Which seat did that girl take who came in just ahead of me? The last one through the door there, just now."

The usherette bridled. "Are you with her?" she asked suspiciously.

"Never mind that, I'm not a masher." He palmed his badge underneath her downpointed torch. "Hurry up. Where'd she go?"

"In there." She pointed toward a door on the opposite side of the foyer from the orchestra seats. It didn't show in the darkness. A lighted indicator of orange glass was the only thing that showed it was there.

"Oh," was all he said, and remained where he was.

Two spectators entered. The usherette left his side, guided them through a gap in the head-high partition backing the rows of seats. The faces of all three of them took on a palely green cast as they turned forward through it and passed from view.

He kept looking at the door.

The usherette returned. It was the back of her head that had the pale-greenish cast now.

"Is there anyone in there?" he asked. "Posted in there, I mean?"

"There's a matron."

"Oh," he said.

Another pair of spectators entered, on a full-voiced wrangling note, quickly quelled as the silencing darkness welled over them.

"—it's already half over."

"—well, you had to stay and wash the dishes; you couldn't do that when we come home."

"Sh," the usherette reminded them tactfully.

She went with them. She came back alone.

A volley of shots rang out from the screen, and he nervously gave a slight jump, then looked back at the door again.

"It's taking her— Go in there a minute. Take a look in there for me."

She obediently started lengthwise along the foyer. She never got to the other side of it. A muffled scream rang out, some-where behind a door. The quavering scream of an elderly woman. Then there was an impact, as though a heavy chair had overturned.

An orange split suddenly ran down under the indicator, as though a hidden spring had been set off freeing the stubbornly closed door. The head of a white-haired woman peered out; a flailing arm accompanied it, turning the usherette around and sending her flying back the other way.

A hoarse whisper slashed after her: "Get the manager! Get the manager! Something's happened in here!"

He sprinted forward, as the usherette passed him, going the opposite way. Even as he ran, he knew there was now no reason to hurry.

9

The Wait: Deeps of Night

REID WAS HASTILY PACKING BELONGINGS into a bloated, sausagelike white shape that resembled a duffel bag.

"Hurry!" she kept whispering fearfully, peering out through hangings that lined the entire inside wall surface of the alcove or chamber they were in. "Hurry!"

They were in the dark, and yet she could see his every movement. It was as though some indirect light were playing upon him from below, or perhaps from above, creating a sort of incandescent twilight effect.

And each time she'd whisper that urgent "Hurry!" he'd whisper back, "I can't go without my muffler" or "I can't go without my tablets," and put something more into the overfilled bag.

Suddenly a man stuck his head in, close to her own face. The hangings seemed to be like ribbons, that could be parted almost at will anywhere. It was Shawn. The suddenness of it didn't frighten her; her fright was for other things, of other things.

"You haven't much time," he warned them ominously. "You'd better be quick."

"Father, do you hear what he says?" she implored.

Reid looked up from the bag. "I can't go without my knitted vest," he said inflexibly.

Shawn's head withdrew as suddenly as it had projected itself. He wasn't out there any more.

She turned and ran to her father and wrung her hands at him. "He won't wait, if you take much longer. He may be gone already. He may throw the assignment over and leave us by ourselves in here."

He was fastening the neck of the bag. "Now! I'm ready," he said at last.

She took him by the hand and they started to tread warily forward toward the hangings, he trailing the duffel bag after him in turn. It held them back, it was like an anchor.

"We'll have to go faster than this, even to get out to the other side of those hangings," she admonished him.

She fumbled with them, the slits, a moment ago so profuse. Now they eluded her.

Suddenly Shawn's head reappeared. But this time behind them, all the way over at the opposite side of the alcove.

"Not that way," he warned tautly. "This way. You can't go out that way any more. There's one of *them* out there, lurking in wait."

They knew what he meant by *them;* a cold thrill ran through her. She and Reid both recoiled violently at the last moment, as though even to have touched the hangings on that side would have been dangerous.

They recrossed to his side. His hand made a part in the

hangings, and they lowered their heads and passed through. She noted a police shield affixed to the palm of it as they went, like a sort of talisman of safety, good, however, only at very close range like that.

But as they came to the outside, he went in through the hangings to the inside, to where they had been before. He and they had changed sides.

"Aren't you coming with us?"

"You go along the outside passage," he said. "I'll keep up with you along the inside, underneath the hangings. If you get frightened along the way, reach in through the openings and you'll be able to touch me, you'll know that I'm there."

The hangings, accordingly, seemed to have altered configuration; they were now no longer arranged foursquare around an enclosed alcove, they ran in a straight line along the passage they were to follow to eventual egress and safety, forming a partition between him and themselves. This insidious change did not frighten her in the least; there was still only one thing that could frighten her.

The passage they had now embarked on was remotely recognizable as one of the familiar halls of the house, but all similarity of proportion, particularly as to length, had disappeared. It was grotto-dim, like the other place had been, and yet every fold in the hangings was visible.

"It's so long," she complained as they strove onward. "It wasn't this long when we came along it earlier today, it's grown longer since."

"That's because we were going the other way then," her father whispered. "It always seems longer when you're going out than when you're coming in."

They advanced for long moments more, and still no end appeared in sight. Her courage began to fail her at last. "Shawn," she called hoarsely. "Shawn. Are you in there? Are you keeping up with us?"

Instantly his hand reached out and took hers, and she could feel the police badge still set into its palm when she clasped it, and she felt better.

Then he let go again and they went on.

The passage had altered again, with that optical fluidity that all her surroundings seemed sensitized to, as if projected through water running down the face of a mirror. There was a turn down at the end now, and too late she became aware of a faint pale-green reflection playing upon the columnar folds and corrugations of the hangings, coming from some cause out of sight beyond that turn. Lethal it was and impalpable, the faintest of luminous traces. Seeing it had brought the menace into being; it was as if had they turned their backs and fled away from it *before* seeing it they would still have retained immunity.

But it was too late now. Awareness had brought the peril to a head. And with continued awareness it elongated, was drawn forth from its anonymous obscurity. The original of the reflected glow came into being. Two livid eyes, drawn into baleful slits, and glowing a rabid green. Set into the spade-shaped cat head. Small pointed ears lying flat with vengeful imminence of attack. Jaws wide and studded with fangs, and a livid red line bordering them, almost like a glowing neon outline.

It was low to the floor, crouched in threat to spring. And behind it came the sinuosity of its body. It was reptilian, almost, rather than leonine. Its head was the only definite attribute of the lion. It was a dragon body, belly-low, swirling concentrically, straddling foreshortened outward-bent legs, tail lashing maniacally back in the infinite distance.

They turned and fled, minds needled, legs leaden and unmanageable. "Let go, let go that bag," she panted. "It's holding us back."

He released it and it rolled backward, as if carried by gravity into that charcoal-glowing maw. Just before it disappeared, it browned over evenly, as if slowly scorching and about to be consumed.

Again the escape passage betrayed them; again a liquefied turn developed in it. Again that pale-green phosphorescence, the first warning, sicklied the hangings. Again the thought was father to the horror, materializing it into the visible and tactile. Again the head slithered forward, bared fangs to floor. But it was not the same one. Behind them there was still the other, sidling after them with undulant implacability.

They were blocked now at both ends.

"Let go of me," her father pleaded. "*I'm* holding you back now."

"No," she gasped, "no!" And pinioned his arm tighter to her by locking her own over it, pressed to her side.

"Shawn?" she cried out desperately. "Shawn!"

His voice sounded, in even-toned remonstrance. "There was a time you weren't afraid," he said, as if instructing her what to say.

She tried to repeat it, but the words wouldn't come. "Shawn!" she screamed.

"Just say it after me. 'There was a time you weren't afraid.' That'll save you."

She plunged her hand between the hangings. There was no answering hand to meet it. He wasn't in there, where he'd said he'd be.

Slowly, like flickering gaslight, that same telltale onset of fetid metamorphosis began to peer through the gap the insertion of her hand had created. A little of it even bathed her wrist. There was one of them in there too, creeping along between the hangings and the wall like some sort of giant vermin.

She whipped her hand out again, as if fearful of having it mauled, as if the advancing light itself could have developed teeth and bitten while it illumined.

She turned in terror to her father. "He's gone! I couldn't say the words he wanted me to!"

He wasn't there either. She'd lost him now. In ghastly, unguessed dismemberment carried out behind her very back. The arm that she clung to, pressed beneath her own, was all that remained. She could see his other hand reach upward in despairing futility far back within the luminous maw behind her. Then it sank downward out of sight.

Her screams came loud and full now, taking on a new quality of voice that rang in her own ears. As if before they had been simply *thought* rather than vocally uttered. She began to beat violently at the hangings on all sides of her, trying to discover Shawn, to go through them to him.

Something like the windshield wiper of a car at work upon the clouded pane through which she, the beholder, gazed began to switch restlessly back and forth, scythelike across the area of vision. Invisible itself, only its effects could be detected. At each stroke it made the lens it acted upon grow clearer, and clearer, and then clearer still. All the dark colors lost body, paled into daylight. As if it were scouring them, rubbing them out.

The sable hangings had bleached to white, had bunched into squared compact masses. Her screams thinned, faded into distances of the soul. "Shawn," she was whimpering under her breath, "Shawn." And pummeling despairingly at her pillows.

She sprang galvanically to a sitting position, and then her eyelids flew open. The greater alteration preceded the lesser, and not the lesser the greater.

The room around her was in darkness, but the touch of her finger to the lamp dispelled that. And now there was the light of reality, and everything was in order, everything was in familiar place.

But terror wasn't less, terror was even greater, for fresh from the dream she was plunged into a milieu that was strange all over again, at least to the present moment, even though it had been familiar before sleep. And terror-laden as she was, the readjustment wouldn't take immediate effect.

The dream-mainspring was still alive within her. To find him, to get to where he was and be safe beside him. She flung herself out of the bed. She knew all the details of everyday action that it was necessary for her to go through, and she went through them. Where her wrap was, and to slip it on, and to put her feet into the mules beside the bed, and to hurry over to the door and fling it open; where his room door was, down the quiet night-laden hall, and that she must go to it and seek him out. All these she knew and carried out, but it was the dream-impulse within her, still all-powerful, that activated her.

She stumbled out into the hall, still sobbing his name, and as she fled for his door, looked back across her shoulder, remembering where that turn had been in it, in her recent tormented imagery, and where that baleful greenish light—and worse—had slowly materialized, stalking her. There was nothing of that there now, it ended clear and straight at the overlip of the stairs, and shaded electric wall candles, a pair bracketed on each side, cast a kindly, sane light, low enough to be lulling, clear enough to be comforting. But memory still possessed her, the afterglow of fright, and she fled to his door, a furtive slim wraith in billowing blue satin, spreading out behind her like a peacock's tail. Then she gathered it close about her, and knocked with vibrant, low importunacy, that didn't break off to wait even for an instant.

His weight made a single thudding sound within, and then the door had slashed open. So that her last knock, unable to desist, fell upon his chest in a sort of mute, clenched appeal, and her hand lay there.

His face was frightened. Not for self, but for her, as if he'd already guessed who it must be at first sound of it, before even opening the door. His arms were behind him, stiffly contorted, the elbows akimbo out of sight. A strip of bisecting robe was hoisted to one shoulder; on the other it hadn't climbed high enough yet. He hitched his backbone, an empty sleeve perked up, and a snub-nosed automatic and a hand came through it, filling it out.

He swept her close to him with his free arm, and she went willingly. Then he looked about, beyond her, scanning the hall.

"What is it? What?"

"A dream, I guess. But I can't come out of it."

"Something in there with you? Want me to look?" And then with briefly narrowed eyes, "You didn't hear anything, did you?"

"No. No. Nothing. Just a dream, I guess."

"Stand here a minute," he said. "Stand inside the door."

He went down to her doorway and disappeared inside.

She stood there peering out close along the wall, like a furtive child. It seemed like a long time he was in there. He must have gone over it thoroughly. She could hear the wood framework of the windows creak slightly as he tested the tightness of their closure with pressure of his hands.

Then finally he came out again, and she was as glad to see him as though he'd been gone an hour.

"Shipshape," he said.

"I don't know why I should run to you."

"I don't know why you shouldn't. That's what I'm here for."

He stood there looking at her, and she thought: I'll have to go in there again. That's what he expects me to do.

"Feel better now?" he asked, watching her closely.

She nodded, and she wondered if the feigned alacrity of the nod fooled him any. Possibly it didn't, for there was a speculative narrowness to his eyes.

"Does this thing frighten you?" He glanced down at the gun still weighting his hand.

"No, I like it. I like you to have it."

"Yeah, but I shouldn't be flourishing it around like in a Western barroom." He put it away.

He looked at her. Then he looked down at the waiting doorway. Then he looked back at her again. As though wondering what the best thing was.

"Want to go back now?" he said tentatively.

"I don't know if I can go in there again. I'll try."

"Want me to walk with you as far as your own door?"

They walked down as slowly, as lingeringly, as if it were an immense distance, instead of a mere few steps.

"Be all right now?"

She turned to go in. The room expanded into view again, tinctured with sediment of the dream. She recoiled involuntarily. He must have noticed that.

"I'll stand out here," he said, "until you're back in bed again. Leave the door the way it is. I won't look in."

He turned his shoulder to the room, and stood there in the open doorway, facing downhall.

She went on, emboldened. She let the robe drop from her, and crept into the bed again, and drew the covers to her.

"All right? All right now?" he queried, without turning his head.

"I can't do it," she said suddenly, wincing. "I can't do it. It's all right while you're there, and I know that you're there, but as soon as I think that you're not—"

He turned and he saw that her arms had stretched out toward him, without her being aware of it herself; for as soon as she saw him turn, they had dropped. She was like a child, the dream had swept away all grown-up attributes.

He strode outright into the room, fanning the door closed backhand as he passed it. "All right," he said. "Fright such as you've got comes first."

He drew a chair over to the bedside, sat down in it.

"See now. Better?"

Her hands moved uneasily, as though she were holding them back. He stretched out one of his own toward them, and instantly they flew toward it, seized it.

A fleeting, wan little smile touched her face. The child and her protector. The child and her big brother. Now I'm safe, you're here. Now I can sleep; you're here. There always should be someone older, wiser, stronger than I am.

Her face turned a little and fell away from him down the pillow. She stared a moment, as if at the security she seemed to see down there along the soft snowy undulations. Her eyelids flickered, fell, rose a last time, then fell for good.

There was silence in the room.

He sat there docilely, leaning forward from the chair, his extended hand given over to the lonely, pleading clasp of both of hers, wound tight around it in confidence that it would not leave her.

Everyone must have something to hang on to.

That smile had come back again to her sleeping face. It stayed there now.

He reached slowly, cautiously aside with his unpossessed hand and plucked the drop chain of the bedside lamp.

His face went out.

10
Police Procedure: Dobbs and Sokolsky

A POLICE ELECTRICIAN CAME IN at seven-thirty—this was seven-thirty of the morning following the requisitioning of the room—bringing the necessary wiring coiled into a thick circle, and then indented in the middle into a bone-shaped oval to take up less room, and then finally wrapped in newspaper as a camouflage. This tucked under one arm. In his other hand he carried a bulky box, resembling a large-size tool kit, containing the receiving end of the apparatus.

He gave a single cryptic knock, as brief as it was secretive, and apparently easily identifiable, for the door opened on the second, and closed again behind him with equal immediacy.

Sokolsky was behind it. Dobbs was crouched knee-high, over in the opposite corner, in what at first glance might have been mistakenly taken for an attitude of the utmost dejection. His face was thrust in toward the joint where the two walls came together, as though he were hiding it. In addition his head was turned sharply downward, almost hidden from sight beneath the curvature of his shoulders. His hands were clasped across the back of his sharply inclined neck, as if to ease the stricture. He was sitting upon his own upthrust heels. A blackened steam or water pipe speared upward before him, disappearing into the ceiling. He was as motionless as an Indian yogi, or holy man, sitting reversed.

Both inmates of the room had taken off their shoes, to make for soundlessness of tread. But nothing else; not even their coats. Sokolsky not even his hat. They were not in here for domestic purposes, after all. A rather generous yellow-white hole blemished the upended heel of one of Dobbs' socks, without in any way impairing his efficiency.

"We can't do anything yet," Sokolsky murmured to the technician. "He's still down there."

"Let me look it over a while," the newcomer said.

Sokolsky pointed to his footgear. "Watch it. It goes right through."

The electrician put his bulky adjuncts down on the bed, removed his shoes. Then he moved softly, and a trifle painfully, about the room, apparently on the lookout for flaws or rents.

He didn't seem to find anything of a suitable nature. He tapped the huddled Dobbs on the back at last, and the latter slowly uncoiled and elongated into the stature of a human being, though a painfully stiff and lame one.

He sought the edge of the bed, and let himself down upon it, and rubbed himself.

"He's getting up," he said. "I just heard the bedsprings sing out. And a turned-on faucet came whining up the pipe."

The electrician was down now in Dobbs' former collapsed

position. He straightened up after a moment and came back to them.

He kicked his thumb backward toward the pipe. "That'll do. It don't fit the hole in the flooring made for it, plenty of slack all around it. I can whittle it out even bigger and drop the wire behind the pipe. It'll look like its shadow when his lights are on."

Sokolsky hooked thumb and forefinger together in unspoken symbol of approval. "I'll give you the go-ahead," he said.

He eased the room door open and went out into the hall, shoeless as he was. He tested the stair rail, apparently for slants of downward perspective, in several places along its length, by leaning over it and then drawing himself up again. He finally found a stance with a satisfactory angle, made a cushion of his own crossed arms on the rail, bedded down on them, and stopped being animate. He gave an impression of being able and willing to remain that way all day, if necessary.

In the room Dobbs, on relief now, continued to massage the calf of his leg. The electrician was straightening the tortured wire out of its circular formation by hand, the rapidly diminishing hoop slung over his arm as he did so. A pair of pliers and a number of other tools had appeared on the outspread newspaper on the bed, arranged in the neat symmetry and precision that always betokens the artisan, the artist who loves his work for its own sake.

Sokolsky jarred slightly, crouched a little lower. The alteration was scarcely noticeable, could have been taken for an illusion created by the dim light that outlined him so uncertainly. Seconds later, however, a door had plucked open, somewhere below, then closed again with somewhat greater distinctness, and springless footfalls began disheartenedly to descend the stairs, with a looseness of grip that was almost like a flapping sound.

They dwindled, petered out, the stair well fell silent.

The electrican had picked up a small, pocket-sized hacksaw and was waiting. He had his wiring arrow-straight now, and paid out in one single length that reached entirely across the room and pointed amputatedly toward the water pipe, ending inches away from this in a small forked tongue that seemed to be trying to fang the slender iron cylinder of its own accord. It lay along the floor, then ran up across the bed, then continued along the floor on the other side. It wasn't meant to stay there; that was just for accessibility. Every move counted, had been done so many times before.

Sokolsky reared, breasted the turn of the rail, and began to descend the stairs. He could be seen going down, but he couldn't be heard. Neither of the other two moved yet. A key picked metallically at a lock, with a deftness that didn't prolong the sound even to their acutely attuned ears. Then there was silence. Whether a door had been opened or not, it traced no sound on the sensitized air.

Moments passed. Suddenly Sokolsky was on the stairs again, coming up them. The other two men had advanced as far as their head, meanwhile, prepared to descend. He signaled them not to by crossing hands in front of his face and then spreading them wide apart.

Nothing was said until the three were joined once more on the upper landing.

"He's coming back again," he whispered. "Get in."

They closed the door, relapsed into immobility. Dobbs was back again at the corner orifice.

Presently he nodded vigorously to the other two, pumped a single finger downward toward the floor a number of times.

They continued to wait.

This time Dobbs cast his thumb over-shoulder in the general direction of the outside hall. Sokolsky cautiously eased open the door. Footsteps were descending below somewhere, in the same slovenly manner as before.

The former procedure repeated itself. Again Sokolsky went first down the stairs, again he went in, again he came out again. This time he snapped his fingers twice. A moment later the other two were down beside him.

They closed the door of the new room, Tompkins' room, after themselves.

"How'd you know he was coming back again?" Dobbs breathed.

"His pipe was on the table. The bowl was still warm when I felt it. Meant he put it down by mistake, didn't leave it behind on purpose."

The electrician worked rapidly. He clamped a small attachment to the steam pipe in the corner of the room, on the side of it facing the wall. It could still be seen if the eye was already directed over at that exact place along the pipe's slenderness. Dissatisfied, he drew it all the way down to floor level without releasing it. There, because of a greater depth of shadow, it passed from view. He lit the room light and tested it. It still remained effaced from view; to an even greater extent now, for the pipe itself cast its own shadow backward upon it.

He went out. There was a slight grating sound at the orifice circling the pipe at ceiling height. It was very sparing, could scarcely be detected. The tip of the saw peered through once or twice, then shyly retired. A few grains of sawdust and plaster spiraled down in a brief spun-sugar trickle. A wire appeared, trailing down beside the pipe; only visible while it continued to move, blending from sight as it stopped.

The electrician came in again. He drew the wire down farther, attached it to what was already in place down at the floor.

"Try it for sound," he said. He went out a second time.

Sokolsky gazed at Dobbs, as though it was Dobbs he was addressing and not the electrician a full floor above. He kept his voice pitched to their own immediate proximity. "Okay? Can you hear me, Graham?" he said quietly.

The pipe sounded off, as though somebody's fingernail had tapped it affirmatively.

They moved across to the other side of the room.

"How about over here?"

The pipe ticked again.

"Now over here. We don't want any dead spots. We're in the corner, left of the door, Graham. Can you get us?"

The pipe ticked.

"No blind spots," Dobbs said.

The electrician reappeared. He took a blotter from his pocket, allowed a few drops of water from the tap to moisten it, and then pressed it to the floor all about the base of the pipe, where the sediment of sawdust and plaster had fallen earlier. Then he folded it over upon itself and carefully thrust it into his pocket.

At the door he stopped long enough to join thumb to finger in a circle of successful completion, fluctuated it at them. "Yours," he said. He left.

They left, but not for an hour and a half after. Dobbs was carefully filing something away in his pocket. "These checks from Reid have to be taken out and photostated, then they have to go right back where I found them, fast."

"Think he knew they were there? What was the idea salting them away? Twelve thousand dollars' worth—"

"He wasn't hiding them. I think they've been left kicking around until he forgot he had them. The places they turned up in showed that. I found one caught between the dresser and the wall, as though it fell down through the back of a drawer.

Another was crumpled and had tobacco smears on the back of it, as though he'd used it to wipe off a pipe cleaner."

"What kind of a guy is he?"

"Either very dumb or very smart. And that's for McManus to decide, not us. I'll take them over, you get on the earmuffs."

At six o'clock the checks were long back, and Dobbs was at the headset, spelling Sokolsky.

All he got was silence, the silence of an empty room.

At 6:27 a door opened—over the wire. It closed. Footfalls shuffled about, expired. There was the spongy slap of discarded cloth striking a chair back.

Nothing moved in the room above, save Dobbs's right hand, penciling shorthand symbols on a pad. And even that was only occasionally; it lay still more than it vibrated.

It got dark outside. A thin crescent of light peered around the pipe, where it fitted into the floor. A fingernail paring, no more. Otherwise the room above stayed dark. They could scarcely see even each other in it. Dobbs's hand traced little curlicues and pothooks in the blackness. He kept his little finger out for a guard, to tell him when he was running off the pad.

At seven a spoon scraped vigorously at the inside of a pot, emptying it. From then until the half hour, crockery occasionally chinked. Then it rattled, as though several pieces were being gathered together, carried for a distance. Water was discharged with sandpapery force, and the rattling was blended and drowned with accompanying splashes and gurgles. Then the crockery gave thuds of finality, piece by piece, one to a piece.

Another period of silence ensued. Dobbs's hand lay fallow, except when he consulted phosphorescent numerals on his wrist.

At 9:12 a man coughed.

At 9:14 a newspaper crackled.

At 9:16 a pipe bowl was tapped out.

At 9:17 a chair creaked in dislodgment.

At 9:19 more water was heard to cascade, this time with greater resonance and at a greater distance. Dobbs's hand went up in the dark and pulled at an imaginary chain. Sokolsky nodded in judicious agreement.

At 9:20 a shoe struck flooring.

At 9:20:15 a second one followed.

At 9:21 the paring of light at the pipe base went out.

At 9:22 bedsprings creaked.

At 9:24 they creaked once more, but far more lightly, in final adjustment.

After that, nothing. The night wore on. At midnight Sokolsky took over the headset and the pencil and the pad.

All he got was silence. The silence of a sleeper's room.

"A full twenty-four hours now, lieutenant. No one's been near him yet. He just comes in, sleeps, goes out, comes in, and sleeps all over again. All we get is background music; we haven't even once heard the sound of his voice. No one's shown up, not a soul."

"Someone will. Someone's got to."

"No room's ever been listened to before like we're listening to this room now. I haven't been out in hours. Dobbs brings in our food when he's taking a relief. I eat right at the set."

"Don't let those ear pieces grow cold. I don't want 'em off your heads. Just listen. Aid if there's nothing to listen to, keep on listening to that nothing. I want every creak of the floorboards. I want every nibble a mouse takes at the molding in the middle of the night!"

"I wish a mouse would. That would break the monotony. We haven't even got them to listen to."

"You'll get your mouse, Sokolsky. But it won't have a long tail."

11
The Wait: Farewell to Sunlight

SHAWN WAS COMING BACK TOWARD the house from a tour of inspection with the man in charge of the detail guarding it. The afternoon light was coppery in the west, igniting the windowpanes on that side of the house, and every tree and every bump, and the men themselves, sent long spindling blue shadows slanting the other way, toward the east. Like direction finders pointing at night.

They stopped just below the entrance lions to part company. "McManus worked it out himself," the man said. "We've got the place completely ringed, in three separate circuits. The road that comes up here is blocked off at both ends. Nothing on wheels is allowed to get by, and there's a car patrolling it. There's a line of men all around the borders of the estate. You can't see them, but all someone has to do is try to trespass, enter the grounds from the public domain on the outside, and he'll find out they're there. Then on the grounds themselves, I have them spotted all over at strategic intervals, wherever there's any cover. Where there are trees, like in back there—"

"Yeah, those trees have been bothering me," Shawn admitted. "They still are."

"You can quit worrying. Nothing can get through them without being seen. Without being stopped. Each man is near enough to be able to see as far as where the next man is. They're all armed, and if anything moves they've got orders to shoot first and then find out what it was they were shooting at later. Then finally, as soon as it's dark, I'm going to have two men pacing the outside of the house all night long, right up against the walls. They'll keep moving in opposite directions, meeting at the front, meeting at the back, reversing each time. So don't try to come out of the door without giving warning, once it's fully dark, or you're liable to get accidentally potted. Is there anything more foolproof than that? Can you think of a thing that's been left out?"

"Not a thing," Shawn agreed. "When McManus does things, he does them right. Don't forget the signal, in case something goes wrong on the inside."

"A light going around in a circle behind one of the windows. Any window at all. We close in on the double, with our guns ready. I'll be down there where I showed you, all night long— Somebody's coming out."

"All right, get back," Shawn said hastily.

A coppery sheen blurred the glass in the front door as it swung outward, and Jean appeared, her arms double-linked to one of her father's, supporting him. She was without a coat, but he had a herringbone topcoat thrown over his shoulders, sleeves dangling empty.

For a moment Shawn thought they were contemplating a flight from the house itself, and he scissored hastily up the steps toward them, arms half extended ready to bar their way and shepherd them back inside again.

"Where are you—?"

"He—he wanted to see the setting sun," she explained.

"To say good-bye," Reid whispered forlornly, "before it goes down."

Shawn glanced aside at it uncomprehendingly for a moment, his face glinting orange as he turned. His recent respite with his fellow police officer, brief as it had been, had restored his own outlook so completely to normal, it took him a second or two to recapture Reid's macabre meaning.

"It'll be back again tomor—"

"But not for me. This is my last look. I'll never see it again."

Shawn's eye caught hers. Let him, she indicated with a pleading little quirk of her head.

"All right, come on out here," he acquiesced. "You can get a good clear look at it from the lawn, out here in front." He took hold of him by the other arm, supported him on the opposite side from her.

"No," Reid said. "There's a rise over that way. To the back of the house, way over in that direction. Remember it, Jean? If we go up on that, that would make it last longer. You can see down around you on all sides from there."

"But that's pretty far out, isn't it? That's pretty far away from the house. Are you sure you—?"

"Let me go," Reid whimpered abjectly. "Let me go over there and see it. I can make it if the two of you will help me. Don't take this away from me."

Again she gave Shawn that signal of poignant indulgence.

"All right," he said.

They took him and trundled him between them diagonally across the close-cut plushy sward, until that had ended and the house lay well behind them, a bonfire in every window. Then over rougher ground, and beginning to tilt upward, they moiled. And he, of the three of them, strained farthest forward, his legs pistoning abortively, often, without gaining ground of their own efforts. Like a caterpillar without a very good grip.

"Hurry," he urged. "It's getting redder all the time. It goes fast, once it gets this far down."

"We'll get there in time," she soothed.

They skirted the belt of trees that Shawn didn't like, trees that seemed lifeless. You couldn't have told that anyone was in there. Just black tines of shadow, like pitchforks, all over the ground.

But it was gaining on them, it was going down faster than they were going up. The perfect roundness of its lower rim blunted, then flattened out, like a balloon that hits the ground, and then sits on it heavier and heavier.

It became a severed hemisphere, bloodying everything around it with its own flow of life fluid; their hands and their faces, and the ground under them, and even the sky immediately around it. It was like a solar hemorrhage.

Then the effusion began to coagulate, drain off into nowhere. The upper rim was all that showed now, like a scimitar peering over the crest up which they were toiling.

"It's not really gone yet," Reid panted, as though his life depended on it. "It's the hill cuts it off. When we get up on top of that, it'll last a little longer."

He writhed forward between them, as though his bodily contortions and not their footwork could accelerate their climb.

They reached the top at last. It wasn't very high. But it was high enough at sunset to blot out an earthbound sun. The smothered globe was disinterred, came clear again, intact in its roundness. It sent a coppery-gold blast full in their faces that all but blinded them for a few moments.

Shawn, squinting painfully away from it, saw Reid tilt his

face blissfully toward it, eyes closed; as if breathing it in, as if bathing his face in it; as if what it exuded was the essence of life itself. As in fact it was, Shawn had to admit.

"Its lower rim is still clear," Reid exulted. "There's a sliver of sky left under it. It's still whole."

It touched. It was so light, so furiously gaseous, almost they expected to see it bounce slightly, rebound, before settling finally against the earth's surface.

"It rushes downward so fast," he mourned. "Right while you look at it it moves."

He shrugged off their double grip on him, freed his arms. He held out his hands toward it, making a circle of them that did not quite join, as if trying to hold it fast between them, get it to stay, keep it up. It must have slipped through his fingers, though their eyes couldn't focus it where his did, between his curved hands; for to each of them it was in a different place: directly before himself. It must have slipped through his grasp, little by little, escaping irretrievably downward; for they saw him convulsively expand and contract his hands several times, the way a clumsy person would fumble trying to hold onto a slippery ball that has just been thrown to him. Then they came together, palm to palm, over emptiness, and he let them drop, frustrated.

"Good-bye," he sobbed softly. "Good-bye."

Shawn stole at look at Jean. Her face was impassive, peach-flushed in the reflection. A shiny thread, like a metallic wire, lay flat on her motionless face, from eye corner to mouth corner.

He looked away again. He hadn't meant to spy on her reaction. He thought, There is no consolation for what he is feeling, nothing to be said, nothing to be done. For if I thought that was my last sun, I'd be as he is now—and maybe worse.

It was gone now. The emanation it had left behind was like an open fan, with luminous ribs striking up the evening sky. And as if the fan were being closed by a submerged hand, the ribs shortened, drew downward into a common focal point just under the joining line of earth and sky. Only a little aftershine was left now, holding its own a moment, then finally swallowed by the merging tides of blue and chilly gray.

He shivered. "It gets so cold the minute it's gone. Do you feel that wind? That's night breathing on us."

He stole a glance behind him. "There's one of them out already. See it over there? Hurry up, let's get back. Quick, before any more—"

They turned and started down the rise, face forward into the dark tide flushing from the east. He strained forward between them, as though he were off balance and pulling them after him in a long, stumbling fall, head apprehensively low to keep from looking upward at the first stab of cold brilliance knifing through the darkening sky as if ready to plunge through full-blade and slash down at him.

And fast as they went, he careened faster still, legs at times almost seeming to paddle air without touching the ground they scurried over. They swerved from side to side, supporting him between them, in triple headlong flight.

"Faster," he panted. "Faster. Hurry up inside, where they can't follow us. More of them are starting to come out every minute. Don't look at them, don't look. Keep your eyes away."

They tottered across the level space of the lawn, and around to the foot of the paved walk, and sped up that to the sanctuary of the waiting entrance. One leg now was trailing out uselessly behind him, as they bore him forward. They vanished.

His voice sounded strangledly somewhere just inside.

"Close it! Close it tight!"

Someone reached out and slammed the door.

Behind them it was night.

12

Police Procedure: Molloy

"INSPECTOR? MOLLOY, INSPECTOR."

(staccato) "What've you got? Got something? What is it?"

"I'm on lions, you know. You gave me sort of a blanket—"

(irritably) "I know what I gave you. And when I gave it to you—two days ago! What you're giving me is what I want to hear."

"Yes, sir. Well, first I made sure of all the usual lions we know about. Then I got onto this. There's a small traveling tent show, sort of a peanut carnival, been working its way slowly across state up here. It was at Hampton when word reached me about it. That was about three yesterday afternoon. I started for there right away, but by the time I got there, what with engine trouble and a couple of flat shoes one right after the other, I was too late—"

The soles of the sheriff's shoes made a V atop his desk. This

237

split at Molloy's entrance and his face came through inquiringly. It was raw-looking, as though it had been freshly peeled.

"Do for you?" he said somewhat curtly, as one who has a position in authority to uphold.

The curtness disappeared at sight of Molloy's credentials, and what was intended for amiability, though it bore an equal resemblance to mere lethargy, succeeded it. "Don't often get you fellows up here," he said with slothlike pace of utterance. "Have a chair. Take a load off your—"

Molloy's question punched a hole in the fabric of unhurried sociability he was trying to spin. He looked slightly rueful for a minute at such haste between fellow police officials, then answered it.

"Yes, we had a traveling ruckus with us last night. I took my two kids and the missus. We let them pitch in that big lot next to the Methodis' church. They paid the usual fee for it, of course." He chewed something, probably something that was nonexistent, over to one side of his mouth. "In advance," he added.

"That big open place—? It's empty now, I just came by there."

"Oh, sure. They pulled up stakes right after the last customer was out, 'bout midnight. By one o'clock this morning they was already on the move. See, we told them, the way we run things, they would have had to pay for a second day's use of the lot, starting in at midnight, if they was still on the ground."

Molloy brushed this rather inhospitable local ordinance aside. "I was told they had some wild animals with them."

"Had a few. No great shakes," the sheriff said, with the pursed expression of one who has seen better in his time. "They sure smelled strong. Made up in smell for what they lacked in—"

Molloy dusted his knuckles across the desktop. "Any lions? That's what I want to know."

"Yeah, two. A pair. Both in the same cage. Male and female, I guess. One of 'em had one of these ruffs around its neck, one of 'em didn't. Dunno what good they were; didn't perform or anything. They were just shown off in the cage. Just slept there, chins to floor, through the whole show. They had a little trained zebra, now, that earned his keep. Took the kids for a ride, two at a time—"

Molloy swerved, so that from the shoulders down he was already facing the door, though from the shoulders up he continued to face his slow-spoken informant. "Where was their next pitch to be?"

"I don't rightly recall that they told anyone. Just picked up quietly and left."

Molloy was at the door now, as one who realizes that the only way to conclude a current conversation is to move bodily away from it, until the sound can no longer reach him and therefore it automatically expires. "Well, which way'd they go, which road' they take?"

"Well, there's only one," the sheriff had to admit. "It comes in from the direction of Fairfield and goes out again in the direction of Hanoveria. I know they didn't pass my house on the way out, because we was up; one of the kids had a belly-ache from too much—"

"They wouldn't go back and rework pitches they already worked," Molloy told him. "Which way'd they come in from?"

"Fairfield," the sheriff told him.

"What's along it going the other way? What's the first place you hit they'd be likely to make a stop?"

"That's Hanoveria, like I told you."

Molloy returned to the desk again, conversational obstacle notwithstanding. "Can I use your phone?" He picked it up without waiting. The sheriff looked slightly worried. He even batted his eyes off at a directional angle a couple of times, as though calculating rates.

Molloy hung up again presently. "Hanoveria says they passed through there about dawn this morning, without stopping. Traveling slow. What's the next—?"

The sheriff this time looked positively alarmed. He even edged the phone a little farther over on the desk. Away from Molloy. "Maybe you better— Did you come up by car?"

"It's outside. Yeah, maybe I better head after them myself," Molloy agreed. He started for the door.

The sheriff cleared his throat on a note that was almost physically arresting, there was such poignant anxiety in it.

"I don't like to mention it but—you know how it is—you might be up this way again and then again you mightn't."

"Oh," Molloy said, catching on. "*Oh.* How much was the phone call?" He was too taken aback even to be sore about it.

"Well, it's seventy-five from here to Hanoveria, on the first three minutes—

Molloy fumbled in his pants pocket, shied a bill toward the desk that fell short. "Keep the change. Nice business you've got here." The door closed after him.

The sheriff might have been a slow talker, but he was a fast mover. He was already crouched down below the gap in the middle of his desk, reaching forward through it on hands and knees, before Molloy's hand had even come away from the outside knob.

Molloy got back into the same car that had just brought him, still sweating at the seams from the trip up, and took the road to Hanoveria and parts beyond. A shift of the gears, a half turn on the tires—or so it seemed—and Hampton was already rearward of him, so small was it.

The road was dappled in the late-afternoon sunlight, and the landscape tranquil enough to have been a colored magazine layout advertising tractors or dairy products. Whipped-cream clouds were splashed up against the pottery-blue sky, and cows stood by fences and raised their heads at him as he whirred by. It was a shame to be carrying thoughts of danger through such a scene, even locked in your own head.

Hanoveria, when it came, was of no greater plottage than the place before. A half dozen house fronts set down here and there at varying angles and, *fft*, it was over. He passed through without halting. No need to stop and ask, it hadn't lingered here; there wouldn't have been enough audience to attract.

Somewhere beyond he was just in time to glimpse a roadside vignette that he couldn't quite make out as he streamed by. That is, he caught what it was, but he couldn't grasp the reason for it.

There was a lone farmhouse, back some distance, not at road's edge. Along the road there was a rail fence. It was scarcely knee-high, nothing at all. Over it was dangling and swinging a little girl. A woman came running out from the house, and hauled her off, and took her back, holding her clutched tightly underarm and lying sideward, in that peculiar way typical only of a badly frightened mother. And not anger nor preparation for punishment nor anything else.

But what he couldn't understand was the reason for her fear. It had nothing to do with the height of the fence, for even had the child toppled from it, she could not have hurt herself. It had nothing to do with him and his car. For she had already been well under way toward the child before he even came into sight. Nor was the fence close enough to the road to endanger the child from succeeding cars, of which there weren't any anyway. And the woman was tight-lipped and didn't scold, as though this were a fear she couldn't share with the child, too grave even to be broached to her. And last of all, the woman didn't look toward the car, nor after it, nor up and down the road at all. She looked toward a darkling line of trees off in the background.

Fear? wondered Molloy. Of what? But he didn't give it any further thought. It had just been a snapshot in passing. He'd taken it, but he didn't develop it.

Then another little nucleus of habitation came along. He didn't stop here either, didn't even get its name. You could see out of it in all directions, like a sieve, and it was obvious no traveling show was pitched there.

There was something a little strange-looking about it, he thought. He couldn't put his finger on what it was, because he kept going right on through. But there was an undercurrent of—well, heightened tension stirring through it. No one was doing anything, and yet that was the atmosphere it gave off. The men were in twos and threes standing around talking. They looked at him over shoulder as his car went by, but apathetically, as though their real interest lay in something else, and his passage through their midst was just an interruption to whatever it was that absorbed them. Nearly every house had at least one woman looking out of an upper window. And not downward into the lanes below, but leveled off into a distance. Toward the treelands on the outskirts. If you see a woman doing that at one house or two, Molloy told himself, it's just plain nosiness. But if you see them all doing it at once, it's something else.

And every time he caught sight of a child, he'd be just in time to see some woman making a bee line for it to haul it back indoors. This fear for the children, that seemed to have spread over the whole countryside like a strawfire, he wondered what it was.

He added a little speed to the respectable amount he was already making, and he didn't know he'd done it himself. It was only when he saw the speed gauge that he knew.

Dusk had fallen by the time he'd got to the next hamlet. It was bathed in purple sky glow, its crevices and seams shot with crapy black. The same small knots of men, but one among them had a shotgun this time; they were passing it from hand to hand judiciously looking it over. Another group had a dog on a rope and were gathered about that. The kids had vanished, there wasn't a sign of one. Where there were lights in upper windows, the shutters had been closed over them, and only frightened chinks got through.

He went on through, and he wasn't alone in the car any more. Disquiet sat there next to him on the matching seat to his own, and he thought the air was clammy and cool for this time of year.

After a while he saw some lights way off to the left, dim in the half-light before deep night set in, and he thought that must be Thackery, which was the next place he was to hit. He wondered what was the matter with the road, why it went off so wide of it. Then he saw them move peculiarly, and he knew those weren't the lights from houses. They palpitated, went up, down, up, down. Those were lights from men with blazing torches beating through the trees, looking for something, hunting something, in the woods.

Looking for what, hunting what? In the dark of the woods? They were like combustive sparks of danger, those lights, and as night fell he came into Thackery at a sizzling burst of speed, heads on full. They glared up the main street, with its two disjointed bends, and then came to a stop.

Thackery was at fever pitch all around him. The tent show was there, in the middle of it; he'd caught up with it at last. But it looked as if a windstorm had hit it. Several of the tents were down. Stands were over, and the jumbo peppermint-striped umbrellas that had shaded them were in tatters, dangling forlornly from their own ribs. One of the wagons had a wheel off and was down at a sodden lurch. The fill of popcorn bags streaked the ground in sticky swirls, spread about by countless stampeding feet, and crumpled bladders that had been toy balloons lay here and there. One of them, still blown up, had caught on the gable of a house nearby, and swayed there upright on the end of its taut string. There was even a man's straw hat on the ground in one place, trodden into shredded wheat.

He got out and walked around in the mess for a while. It was strangely deserted, as though everyone had sought refuge indoors. Finally he caught sight of someone loitering about as he was, went over, and sleeve-jerked him.

"What happened here, bud?"

The man kept his roving eyes on the ground. He acted as if that were a supremely gratuitous question. "Where were you?" was all he answered, on an ironic inflection.

"Not here. I wouldn't be asking if I had been."

The man was still interested in the ground. "Couple of them blame things busted out loose, right into the middle of the crowd."

"What blame things?"

The man's conversation slipped a notch. "I just had it repaired, too. Seventeen jewels. Imagine, torn right off my wrist. My whole sleeve was torn off with it, right off the coat." He picked up something. "Here's the sleeve. But no watch."

Molloy wanted the exact word. He wanted to hear it spoken aloud for the first time, like something that had been hanging formlessly over him for the past several hours now. He said in a slow-tempoed grating voice, "What were the things that busted out?"

"Lines," the man said. "What else d'you suppose would start a fright like that?"

Molloy let go his sleeve. In fact, flung it away from himself as though it were something detachable. "Lions," he said with soft fierceness. "That's my job."

The man went ahead using up stick matches over the ground. "Anyone hurt?"

"Plenty of bruises and black-and-blue—"

"By them."

"Only one guy, the fellow in charge of them. He was the only guy went *toward*'em. Everyone else had sense enough to go the other way, but fast."

"Who knows how it happened?"

The man shrugged elaborately. "Who knows is right," he agreed.

"Well, where is this keeper or whatever he is?"

"Laid up over at the minister's house. They took him there soon after it happened. We got no reg'lar hospital here. They're sending for him sometime tonight to take him over to—"

"Show me where the minister's house is."

"Get somebody else to show you," the man said ungraciously. "I got a watch to find."

"Well, take a good look for it," Molloy said brusquely. He left the man sitting down on the ground, legs spread wide.

Molloy's impression of the keeper was that he was much more bandaged than critically injured, and much more disconsolate than either. They had him on a cot in the reverend's front parlor, with women of three generations in attendance, and bickering over the proper procedures in first aid.

"The trouble with your bandages, ma, is you never know when to stop them. That gash is up round his shoulder, and you ran the lint all the way down past his finger tips. You got to end 'em *sometime;* you can't just wait till you get to the end of the roll."

Molloy managed unobtrusively to get the disputants and the dispute to shift outside to the hall, temporarily if not permanently, and was left alone with his witness-to-be. The setting would have broken down an interior decorator, if not an animal trainer, even before the first question was asked or answered. An oil lamp with an hourglass shape cast a milk-white glare about the room. Violets, or perhaps they were forget-me-nots, painted all over the frosted chimney speckled both their faces, questioner and questioned alike, as though they were coming down with smallpox. They also made the walls seem to be crawling with purple moths in patterned lines.

The keeper was visibly harassed, kept shifting feverishly from side to side as well as his mummified arms would allow, but the cause was unquestionably not the chamber of horrors he found himself trapped in.

"They shot Emma," he whimpered, wrinkling his chin as though he were about to weep. "They shot her. They didn't need to. They coulda got her back some way without that."

"What'd you expect 'em to do, set out a saucer of milk? Those things are killers."

"They didn't need to *shoot* her," the man insisted. "She wouldn'a hurt anybody—"

"No?" queried Molloy dryly. "Where'd *you* get clawed up, then? From tripping over a rake?"

"She was frightened. All that screaming, all them people running in all directions. She was more frightened than they were. That's all it was."

"Any animal that attacks a man does it from fright," Molloy said. "That don't make 'em any the less dangerous. But that isn't what I came here to talk to you about. How'd it happen?"

"I dunno, mister, I dunno," the keeper said, wiping some of the forget-me-nots out of his eyes with the back of one gauze-mittened paw.

"You must know. You were in charge of them. They slept through your last pitch, didn't even lift their muzzles off the ground. I spoke to a man who saw them there. Why should they suddenly go on a rampage here? What happened here that didn't happen there? What time was it?"

"I dunno, mister. The afternoon show was almost over. I don't stay right by the cage every minute. I strolled over to chat for a minute with one of the other guys. I wasn't more than twenty yards away. I heard something bang, like a firecracker, but I didn't pay any 'tention to it. Plenty of kids was using them around. And we got a shooting booth, and that was sounding off every few minutes. Then I heard some woman scream, and by the time I looked they was already both out. They come out the side door, the one I use, and run down the ladder one behind the other. It's only three or four steps high. One run one way and one the other. I tried to head off Emma, and she swatted me a coupla times and keeled me over and lit out like a streak."

"When were you last in the cage?"

"I gave 'em water when we first pitched. I never feed 'em before shows. It makes them sleepy and short-changes the public. I do my feeding after."

"You locked it up again behind you, this side door?"

"I been going in and out for seven years, mister. I never left it open yet behind me. There's my keys over there, attached to my belt; see them, on that sofy."

"How does it work? What's the hold?"

"Chain and padlock looped around it. Never used anything else in all the years I been traveling with 'em. Never needed to."

"Until now," amended Molloy softly to himself. "Notice anybody hanging around the cage, or loitering near it, before it happened?"

"They all do that; that's what we're in business for, that's what we make our money offa."

"I don't mean just goggling, with the rest. I mean anybody by himself, hanging around a little too long."

"There *was* a guy, pestering 'em a little," the keeper admitted. "But that ain't anything. We get that pretty nearly every pitch.

Some halfwit'll try to get a rise out of them, poke a stick through or—"

"Is that what he was doing?"

"No. First I noticed, he'd been standing there rooted before it for some time. I didn't pay much attention at first; I thought he was just watching 'em fascinated, like. Then I noticed they were getting kind of restless about something. I went up close to him and I found he'd been teasing 'em with a piece of dress goods, a dirty looking rag torn from a woman's dress. He'd lay it on the edge of the cage floor, just between the bars, and then when they'd paw for it, or lower their muzzles to it, he'd snatch it back again. You keep doing that, that's like waving a red flag to a bull, you know; to any animal."

"What'd you do?"

"Nothing much. Like I say, we get them wise guys nearly every pitch. I stiff-armed him and sent him staggering, and told him 'On your way, bud.' He made himself scarce."

"What'd he look like?"

"Just another village pie-face. I couldn't tell you more than that, I hardly noticed him."

"Did you take a look at the fastening after that?"

"Nah, why should I? He wasn't around by there, he was in front."

Molloy took a sarcastic tuck in the corner of his mouth. "You're a pretty careful keeper, aren't you?" he told him.

"But who'd want to fool around with the fastening of a lions' cage," the man demanded plaintively, "to purposely let them out?"

"Just because you can't answer a thing don't mean it can't happen." Molloy was at the door by now. "I guess that's all, then, from you."

The man went back to his original lament, turning his grimacing face away like someone bereft by a personal loss.

"They shot my Emma," followed Molloy out into the hallway. "They didn't need to do that. They coulda got her back some other way—"

"—went inside the cage myself and looked it over, and here's what I found, lieutenant. The end link of the chain, the one that looped onto the clasp of the padlock, had been filed down until it was worn thin enough to be severed. Then the two prongs of the open link had been pried in opposite directions, evidently by a pair of pliers, so that there was a wide enough gap for it to drop off the padlock clasp. The links weren't very thick or strong anyway. The chain was tarnished and dull from age, but there were shiny bright tracks where the file had rubbed that one link. From the ground underneath I collected a paperful of metal filings."

"Go on."

"On the inside of the door, the cage side, there were fresh claw marks; it was a wooden door, or trap or whatever you want to call it. As though one of the animals had reared up against it frightened—just like the ordinary cat when it wants out. You've seen them."

"Keep going."

"Frightened by something, see? And on the floor of the cage, when I went over it, I found little scorched tatters of red paper. I have those for you too."

"What do they seem to you?"

"What they'd seem to anyone else. All that's left of a jumbo firecracker that must have been lighted and tossed into the cage when no one was watching."

(Whistle from McManus, over the wire.)

"They were being sold all afternoon, at a concession that the show carries right along with it. But not those jumbo-sized ones, mostly the baby kind. I checked, and only two of those were sold. One to a kid about seven or eight. And one to a grownup, who claimed he was buying it for his kid, but who *didn't have any kid along with him.*"

"Did you get a line on this grownup?"

"Only very superficially. But from two sources, the concessionnaire and the keeper. And although neither description amounts to much, neither one conflicts with the other at any given point. So as far as they go, they're that of one and the same man."

"Then the escape was not accidental."

(emphatically) "The escape was *not* accidental, beyond any possibility of a mistake."

"And one was shot."

"One was shot."

"But one is still at large."

"One, the larger of the two, is still at large."

(troubled pause) "I don't like the way this thing is shaping up. Now we've got an actual lion and an allegorical one as well, both to contend with at the same time. You stay up there where you are, Molloy, stay with it and keep me informed. I'm going to contact Shawn, right away, and let him know he may be up against the real thing from one minute to the next, and not just a metaphor any more."

13
The Wait:
The Last Supper

SHAWN DRIED THE RAZOR AND put it away. He locked the bath-
room cabinet unobtrusively, and the key wasn't there any more
when his hand came away. He picked up a bottle of witch hazel
from the shelf below, dribbled out a palmful, moistened his
opposite palm from the first, and applied them both to Reid's
face. A little awkwardly, losing some of it in transit. Then he
took a towel and patted the area.

"I did pretty good," he said cheerfully. "Considering. I never
shaved another man before. Not even a nick." He picked up a
canister questioningly. "Use talc?"

Reid turned his head aside in refusal. "I could have done it
myself," he said dryly. "But you were afraid to let me get at
the blade."

"Look at your hands," Shawn reproached him mildly.

251

The one that had been vibrating on the edge of the washstand slipped off, hid itself under the towel Shawn had hung from his subject's shoulders. But then the towel itself continued to throb, above the place where the hand had secreted itself, as though there were a live pulse concealed there.

"You weren't afraid they'd be too unsteady," Reid said. "You were afraid they'd be too swift and sure."

"Now—" Shawn drawled appeasingly.

"Why before, anyway?" Reid wanted to know. "I thought they always shaved corpses afterwards. You could have saved yourself the trouble. A mortician would have—"

Shawn pretended not to hear. His thumb on the light switch amputated the sentence, blacking it out.

He raised the other man from the low stool he'd occupied during the process, detached the towel, led him inside to the brightly lighted bedroom.

"I've got all your things spread out for you on the bed," he pointed out. "Think you can get into them yourself? I'll help you with the studs when I come back. I want to chase in and get dressed myself. We'll be going down soon."

"Dinner jacket?" Reid quavered. He made a peculiar sound that would have been a throb of laughter a year before. It wasn't now any more.

"We're having a little dinner party, just the three of us," Shawn said soothingly. "We want to look presentable, you and I. We want to show her that we men can put the dog on too, don't we? I'll stop in for you in ten minutes."

Reid clawed after him with two quickly pouncing hands as he left his side, and missed. "Is the window all right?" he whispered fearfully.

Shawn went over and prodded at the latch. "Tight as a drum," he said.

He went over to the door and opened it, turned his head inquiringly.

"I'll be right across the way in my own room. Want me to leave the two doors open, so you can see me from here?"

"No," Reid said reluctantly. "It's safe enough—this early yet, I guess."

"Now—" Shawn said, a trifle mechanically.

"It's only a little before seven, isn't it?"

"You mustn't ask me the time," Shawn said patiently. "You're going back on our agreement."

"What a lovely time seven is! If it would only stay seven all evening." He wrung his hands imploringly.

"You get to work on that boiled shirt," Shawn said with professional briskness. "I'll be back in ten minutes."

He closed the door, exerting effort almost as though there were something resistant to his pull on the other side of it. His face changed. It wasn't sanguine any more, nor amiably grinning. It looked tired all of a sudden, as though a zipper had been let out somewhere along the seams of it; and hopeless. And there was even a faint reflection of horror on it. Horror that comes from without and not from within; horror the beholder has been a witness to; somebody else's horror.

He even reached up and dragged at his mouth, as though long smiling had wearied its muscles.

In his own room he shaved himself hastily and objectively, almost sight unseen, hardly glancing at the mirror for corroboration. He dug a comb through his hair a few hasty times, sawed a towel across the back of his neck with his two hands, and began getting into the unaccustomed intricacies of a dinner jacket. He'd had one on only about twice before in his life.

He let the tie go, after a couple of halfhearted attempts, came out, crossed back to Reid's door and looked in. The smile reappeared along with the reflected light from within the room, like a shade going up.

"How's it coming?" he said. "I'm going to chase down a minute and see if Miss Reid'll help me with this. All right?"

Reid was seated soddenly on the edge of his bed, his shirt spread across his lap. He'd evidently finished inserting the studs some time before—they were all in place—but had forgotten or was postponing the next step: putting it on. He had been sunk in an abject torpor.

He looked up sharply now, with a little constrictive spasm. A ripple of fear coursed across his ravaged face. Every remark, any remark, bearing on withdrawal, the withdrawal of another away from himself, could do that. They were like pebbles dropped into an oversensitized pool.

"You're coming right back?"

Shawn had learned not to go too near, except when he was prepared to remain for an indefinite time; Reid would fasten on him, and it was difficult to break the grip without a certain amount of gratuitous cruelty. He remained where he was, body outside the door opening.

"I'm coming right back. I'll be right down there at the foot of the stairs."

"Leave the door open this time. You won't be so near."

"Sure, Mike." Shawn gave him a chipper grin. He thought: What good is a smile? A smile on *your* face doesn't make the other fellow brave. But I don't know any other way.

He pasted the door back against the wall. Gave it a little extra pat as if to seal it there.

"And how about something wet? I'll shake them up while I'm down there. What'll it be? Martini, Manhattan, Cuba Libre?"

Reid began to laugh. It was soundless, a pantomime, just the lips and gums and teeth. It wasn't very good pantomime.

It rapidly veered off into a tearful grimace, the accompanying mask for a whimpering sound that never came.

Shawn turned away abruptly, as though feeling himself unable to cope with it at the moment and hence taking refuge in pretending not to have seen it. He clattered down the stairs a little more noisily than was strictly necessary. Almighty God! exploded in his harassed mind, on the way down. This is going to be hell, tonight, and it's only just beginning.

He found her in the kitchen, after traversing the lighted and readied dining room and the corridorlike butler's pantry beyond. She was standing over a table energetically beating up something in a bowl. She must have dressed a good deal earlier than either Reid or himself. She was in evening dress. Some sort of silver fabric. He could only tell for sure from the back. She had on a voluminous smock coat over the front of it, that must have belonged to their cook and was far too big.

"How is he?" she asked.

"Bad," he said. "We're going to have to do plenty about it." He glanced around him. "Did you do all this?"

"They left all the basic material ready to go in. I told them I wanted to do most of it myself. And these ovens nowadays are wonderful. You set them like clocks. I did all the last-minute trimmings. Thank God for them, too; they took my mind up." She tasted something on the tip of her finger. "How did you like the table?"

"I didn't notice," he admitted.

"I worked over it for more than half an hour. I couldn't use either candles or flowers; I was afraid of—their connotations."

"I thought I'd run down ahead, a minute, and set the mood with you. We mayn't have a chance to compare notes for the rest of the evening. It's got to keep up like this." He snapped his fingers in crackling succession. "He mustn't have time to think. Giddy, featherbrained; wisecracks; everything snappy from you and me."

"I know, I know," she said, biting her lip in excruciation and letting her eyelids drop shut for a moment.

"Will you be able to go through with it? It's important. See, the thing's coming closer now. It's that much closer than it was at last night's dinner. By tomorrow, the curse'll be off. Let's hope we'll have him already on the mend. It's this meal tonight that counts. It can be horrible or it can be—"

"Are you sure we're not overreaching ourselves? Maybe by emphasizing it so much, we're pointing up the fact that it's the last meal before—"

"He'd remember that anyway, even if we kept it plain. If we can drive the thought out of his mind at all, it's only with the help of these trappings that we'll be able to do so. Don't forget, we're fighting death, fighting death itself. I don't mean what he thinks, but death *in* him, already in himself. Try, Jean, try. Will you try?"

She nodded mutely. He was afraid she was going to cry, her eyes looked suspiciously wet.

"I'm going in and mix some cocktails now, and I think we both ought to have a good stiff one by ourselves before I go up and get him. We're going to need it."

"And before you do, go down to the cellar a minute. Here's the key. I want you to bring up— Do you know anything about brands?"

"No," he admitted candidly.

"Well, memorize this, then. Look for it. You'll see a case that's already been opened. 'Veuve Clicquot. 1928. Fine champagne,' you'll see on it."

"Feen?"

"It's spelled the same as fine. Bring up about three bottles."

"Three? Isn't that kind of heavy?"

"No, it's buoyant. If gaiety's going to have any chance at all, it's only on this stuff that you can float it."

He stopped in the doorway, came back again. "What're his favorite records? I want to have them ready on the machine, so that—"

"He's been playing the 'Danse Macabre' by Saint-Saens a good deal lately, but I threw it away yesterday. Be careful. Just dance pieces, for you and me, is safer. Because anything that he likes too much brings up the thought that he'll never hear it again, that he's leaving it behind. And that'll undo what we're trying to accomplish."

After he'd filled the shaker, and brought up the champagne bottles and cradled them in an ice pail, he looked in on her again.

"All set? I'll go up and get him now."

"Your tie."

"Oh, I forgot. Never mind, that was just a stall. I'm one of those rare guys that can really tie a bow."

"I'll do it anyway."

Their faces were brought close for a moment.

She stepped back, looked at him approvingly. Then she asked, "And how about me? Do I look all right?" Without coquetry; with anxiety and poignancy.

"You look just the way you should for what we're trying to do. Here, drink this. It's practically straight. It'll steady you."

She looked at it. Then she sighted it toward the one he was holding. "To our job."

"To the job," he assented.

They put their glasses down.

Suddenly she said, "Tom, don't misunderstand. But kiss me a moment. I have to have someone kiss me a moment, before this begins. To give me courage. And I have no one. I can't ask him. I have to have the kiss of someone stronger than I am."

"I wish I were," he said softly.

Only their lips touched.

"To the job ahead," she murmured.

"To the job ahead of us."

She opened her eyes again. They were a little too bright. But she smiled confidently. "Now go up and get him," she said.

She was in the dining room waiting for them. The encumbering kitchen smock had been discarded now, and she was slim and dazzling in festive silver, a garnet velvet bowknot at her shoulder, a garnet velvet bowknot at her hip. She was smiling one of Shawn's smiles, but better than he could ever have hoped to smile it, and warmer, and truer.

She was nibbling a salted almond through her smile, as any frivolous woman might, waiting by a supper table for a party. The light bathed her, and she was lovely. She was bad for their intentions, for it would have wrung anyone's heart to think that he must leave behind the sight of her, would never see her again after tonight.

They came down the stairs slowly, a step at a time. Shawn was supporting him by one arm, holding it both at elbow and at wrist. He had the railing on the other side of him, to lend him its immovable support.

They lost her to view, then retraced their steps along the floor at base of stairs and had her back again.

She hadn't moved. She'd flooded the room with light; there wasn't a shadow left in it.

Shawn's breath tripped, and he caught himself thinking: I'd die too, if I could only look at you like this just once before I— Then he kicked it out of his mind, like something that has a nerve showing up in the first place.

She curtsied with mock elaborateness.

"Gentlemen," she said.

She came toward them. She kissed Reid on the cheek. "Good evening, you," she said. Then she pretended she was going to kiss Shawn likewise. "And good evening *you*, as well." She averted her face teasingly at the last moment. "Tchk, tchk," she lamented ironically. "How confusing."

"You look lovely," Reid said.

"And from the other you, any comment?"

"Bingo," Shawn said.

"I must look that up." She gave her father a little private wink. "Wouldn't it be disconcerting if some evening some gentleman were to come up to some sweet young thing beside just such a dinner table as this and blurt out: 'You look like the devil!'?"

"I bet many a husband has already," Shawn contributed. "And I also bet whoever it was got a black eye."

"Depending on whose party he found her at, don't you think?" she came back at him.

Reid's lips had stretched into a grin without his knowing it. A little wisp of disfigured laughter emerged from them.

The point of her shoe touched the point of Shawn's unobtrusively. He knew what she meant. Anyone else would know they were overdoing it, but it was good, so far. Keep it up. We're succeeding already.

"Shall we have our cocktails in here?" he asked.

"Yes, bring the shaker in. That way we won't have to walk out to the other room and back again." And as they broke up their grouping and shifted about, she managed to convey to him out of the side of her mouth, "There's a clock in there."

Shawn shook and poured them.

They stood grouped about the shaker now. She had one arm half around Reid's waist. Shawn was on the other side, hand resting on the slope of his shoulder. They were holding the tiny, triangular, pink-filled glasses.

She peered at the light through hers. "A toast, somebody?"

Shawn said: "Here's how!"

They clicked glasses. The pink went halfway down the triangles.

"How about another? I'll give it this time. I like just a speck of soot on my toasts. I'm telling you, I'm bad tonight."

"And when you're bad, you're good," Shawn quoted softly.

"But when I'm good, I'm lonely. All right, up she goes."

They clicked glasses again.

Something happened. Shawn and she were still holding the little pink-lined glasses. Reid was holding just the stem. Several small wisps of glass lay on the floor in a moist patch down by his feet.

A look of consternation, quickly obliterated, fled from her eyes to Shawn's, from his to hers.

She blurted out, so quickly that it stumbled in her throat and half of it was swallowed, "—'posed to be a good sign."

Shawn's thumb flexed, there was a twiglike snap, and he was holding only a denuded stem too. The bowl of his glass, however, lay intact on the floor; it hadn't shattered.

She gulped her drink, knocked hers deliberately against the rim of the buffet. It disintegrated. "Now we're all even."

Fear of fear possessed the two of them, Shawn and herself.

Shawn's foot slid out, executed a curving sweep. The crumbs of glass disappeared.

There was no expression on Reid's face. His eyes were like painted eyes on a canvas face; only the painter had made them too large. He turned to Shawn.

"You broke yours," he said quietly. "Mine broke itself."

She moved quickly away from them, turning with a sort of spin of her skirts, that sucked up attention, drew it after herself, as if by some kind of centripetal air current.

"Let's begin now. We've been standing long enough." She waltzed behind a chair, touched it in passing. "You here." She touched another. "And you in your regular place, father. Gretchen's going in to get the soup."

"I'll help you," Shawn offered.

Her eyes flicked him a quick signal not to leave the other man alone, scarcely executed yet somehow perfectly conveyed. Its gravity was adroitly veiled behind the frivolous smile brimming from her brightly reddened lips. "A dinner party at which everyone's a waiter is simply a bucket brigade. Someone has to stay on the receiving end." She made a face at him and flounced out backward through the swinging pantry door.

"I've been hit," Shawn complained to Reid, sitting down, "but I don't know where. Does anything show?"

She came in backward, just as she'd gone out, forcing the door behind her and carrying the soup before her.

"A bustle would be most convenient at this point."

"At which point, did you say?" Shawn wanted to know.

She drew herself up haughtily. "Really, Mr. Shawn, I don't follow you."

"I didn't go anywhere."

"Your mind did. And I'll thank you to keep it on a leash hereafter."

"That's the trouble; I can't get a collar small enough to fit it," Shawn admitted.

They both glanced at Reid, in an optical aside, as if to see what success they were having.

His eyes, for a moment, looked like real eyes. Sick but real ones. He was even shaking a little at the shoulders, as if with submerged laughter too weak to force itself out.

Shawn stood and guided her chair in.

"No, don't come near me," she said pettishly. "Particularly from behind."

Reid shook his head. A guttural sound of enjoyment pierced the silence of his constricted throat.

The lights were bright. There were no shadows on the table. It was like eating over an expanse of sun-drenched snow. Silver gleamed mirrorlike and crystal sparkled, and there was a pleasant flurry of white as they unfurled and flaunted napkins. A diamond on Jean's finger was like a solar focus, haloed with imaginary and fleeting sheets of green and red.

"Good soup," Shawn approved.

"It's called crème de la crème de la crème."

"There's one de la crème too many in there."

"As a matter of fact I abbreviated it. There's one too few, if you're so smart."

A brief silence fell. Such as there might be at any table; nothing ominous, nothing prolonged. Yet it treacherously allowed an outside sound to filter through, to become present before they had time to guard against it. It was very faint, inoffensive: the ticking of a heavy clock in another room. Perversely blown up to audibility and carried in when they least wanted it, by some momentary freak of acoustics, or perhaps because their ears were so acutely sensitized. Fearing to hear anything, they heard the thing they wanted most to avoid hearing.

Her toe touched Shawn's below table. "The door," she breathed. "Quick." And then made a noise with plate and cutlery, to dissemble.

He slipped from his chair, made an elongated half circle around behind, came back again on the opposite side, and the door was sleekly closed. The sound had been smothered.

She stood up in turn, addressing herself. "You may remove the plates now, Gretchen. Yes, ma'am, thank you, ma'am, that I will. And you're owing me a week's wages since last Friday, ma'am, so don't get guffy about it." She went out, sideward this time, using the point of her elbow.

Reid's smile was a flickering film accompanying the sound track of Shawn's resonant laughter.

The door flashed open and she looked in again, ruefully. "The pièce de résistance needs a tractor, I'm afraid. This time I think I will let you give me a hand."

Instantly Reid's hand flashed out toward Shawn's forearm, resting on the table; sought to pin it down there where it was. "Don't both get up at once. Don't leave me sitting alone in here."

"I won't go out there," Shawn promised. "I'll stand here just inside the door, see, where you can see me. You hand it to me here," he said to her. "I'll carry it in the rest of the way."

She came back to the table in his wake.

"How would you like to carve for us?" she asked Reid brightly.

Then both her eyes and Shawn's flicked to the sharp-edged carving knife.

"Oh, on second thought I'll do it myself," she said. And as she went to work, "You know, one big advantage of Weeks—er— taking the night off is by doing my own carving I can be sure of getting just the piece I want. He had me browbeaten."

"Weeks is not coming back," Reid said stonily.

"Why, certainly!" she said in bright amazement. "He simply asked me for the night off, and I let him have it. He'll be back the first thing—"

Shawn cleared his throat a little.

"You can bring in the champagne, Tom, and start working on it," she said quickly. "It goes with this."

Shawn turned a delighted face toward Reid. "Did you hear what she called me? Tom."

"And if I call you that before the champagne, you can imagine what I'll call you after it."

They were both talking a little too rapidly, as if in a sort of running competition. It would not have gone over with anyone not in Reid's condition.

He came in again with the champagne. She began to give him amused instructions, jogging Reid's arm intermittently to attract his attention while she did so. "Work the cork out gently. It's going to pop in a minute, you know that, don't you?"

"Don't they all?"

"Is *he* going to be surprised! You've never heard a cork pop until you've heard a champagne cork pop. Get your sleeve back out of the way, or you're going to have a nice soggy cuff."

"What is this," Shawn wanted to know, "opening a wine bottle, or a wrestling match?"

It thudded back from the opposite wall, and he jumped.

"Quick, catch it!" she shrieked.

Shawn ran headlong for the glasses, filled them.

"It's angry stuff, isn't it?" he said disconcertedly, flipping down his hand to get rid of some of the excess that had foamed over. He approached his glass warily, quirked his head at it suspiciously. "And now look how quiet it is."

"But don't let it fool you."

He sat down. "Is it going to do that every time?"

"No, just the first. What do you think it is, some kind of geyser that erupts every ten minutes?"

They avoided touching brims this time. That perhaps emphasized instead of effaced the previous incident.

"Well, here's to the three of us, anyway," she said vivaciously. "You're here, and I'm here, and— Wait a minute, I'd better find out about him." She reached over and felt insultingly of Shawn's upper arm. "Well, partly, anyway. Up to the neck. Above that, I don't guarantee."

"You let the boy alone," Reid said weakly. "He's all right." He even tried to drop one eyelid amiably in Shawn's direction.

Instantly her foot had nudged Shawn's again, in momentary triumph.

"Oh, the poor defenseless boy," she cooed. "He only weighs about—"

"Go ahead, finish it," Shawn challenged her.

She mumbled something about "mostly bone."

They drank in unison. Lovely lips curved to the champagne goblet, and thin firm ones, and quivering frightened ones that sought its support. The spangled dots piled upward through the golden liquid.

"They used to drink this out of women's slippers," she remarked reflectively.

Shawn, the practical-minded, revolved his glass, squinted at it dubiously from all sides.

"He doesn't believe me. They didn't have the open-toed kind in those days. The sides were built up. They were like little boats."

He said, "Oh," with lukewarm conviction.

She leaned forward engagingly, arms across table. Looking now at them, now at the glass held between the enclosure of her two hands. "I can remember the first drink of champagne I ever had. It was at a night club in Rome. It was brought on by emulation, and I was sixteen. You weren't with us that night," she said in an aside to Reid. "Louise and Tony Ordway had taken me out with them. And at the next table there was this stunning woman; a little—you know what I mean—demimonde, I'm afraid."

"What does that mean?" Shawn asked.

"A girl who gets a great many proposals. But none of marriage."

He nodded soberly, and that made her laugh.

"I was all eyes," she went on, "just as everyone else in the room was. Why is it that the demimonde always holds such a fatal fascination for children in their teens? She kept sipping it, and sipping it, and growing more composed, and more statuesque, and more dignified all the time. She must have had a hollow leg. So finally, at an unguarded moment when both the Ordways were visiting at a neighboring table, I ordered some for myself. And I started in. I didn't like it, it needled my tongue. But if that woman at the next table was going to drink it, I was going to drink it too. She played a dirty trick on me. She saw what I was doing, and she must have known why I was doing it. But instead of laughing at me, as she probably felt like doing, she was charming. And they can be charming, let me tell you. She raised her glass and gravely saluted me across tables, as one does an equal. That was all I needed. You can imagine the compliment. At sixteen. I saluted her back. And every time she filled and raised her glass, I filled and raised mine. I did see her mouth quiver treacherously once or twice, but she was too well-bred to let her feelings escape her, and that was my undoing. When the Ordways returned to the table, there was a horrified commotion, but I was only blurredly aware of it by that time. I do remember stopping and insisting on shaking hands good night with her before they could half carry and half walk me out of the place. And do you remember when they brought me home to you? Oh, you tried to be so severe and so disapproving in front of them—particularly *of* them— but as soon as we were alone together, you helped me undress, and you had to keep turning your head away every other moment. *I* knew you were laughing, I saw you, and I knew you thought I was cute, I wasn't too tipsy for that."

"My little girl," Reid said almost inaudibly. His eyes slowly fell closed.

She turned quickly to Shawn, almost too quickly, too abruptly. "Now you tell us about your first."

"It wasn't as glamorous as yours," he said, hunching confidentially toward them. "It wasn't in Rome, it was in Jackson Heights, New York. It wasn't champagne, it was gin. And there wasn't anyone involved but an old uncle of mine, rest his soul, a retired captain on the police force. He didn't live with us habitually, but he was visiting us for a few days at that time. The family had always suspected him of taking little nips on the side, but he was a bachelor and no one had ever been able to prove it. Oh, and the main factor was this: I had you beat by about two or three years. I was exactly thirteen at the time."

"No!" she marveled, and Reid chuckled.

"Anyway, I'd been out roller-skating around the streets and I came in all steamed up and parched for a drink. He must have been in the room there just ahead of me, and stepped out of it to get his specs or his paper or his stogie. There was this half glassful of colorless, refreshing-looking liquid standing there on the table right under my nose. Did you ever watch a thirsty boy that age drink water? They don't fool around with it, you know; gulp-gulp-gulp and it's gone. There was never any liquor around our flat, so how was I to know? First I thought all the plaster came down off the ceiling and beaned me. Then I thought I'd caught fire inside and was going to burn to death. Anyway, when they heard all this strange noise and came rushing in, they found me hugging my own stomach and doing an Indian war dance all around the room, complete with howls and whoops and foot stamps. For five whole minutes they chased me, they couldn't get me to stand still long enough to find out what happened. And chairs went over, and it was terrible. At the end of that time, I had the most perfect bun on you ever saw, complete with singing, staggering, and hiccuping. Then my mother smelled my breath, and she quit crying into her apron and calling on the saints. Quit cold. And the injustice of it was this: he never got blamed. They thought I'd gone looking for it and poured it for myself. They let me sleep it off that night, but the next day I got the whacking of my life."

"Well, why didn't you—"

"I was brought up that way; not to blame other people or pass the buck. And it was worth it, anyway, in more ways than one. When he left he slipped a five-dollar bill into my hand on the q.t. and gave me a wink to show what it was for. And I was so completely cured, before I'd even begun drinking, that even today I can't stand the smell or taste of the stuff, at least not gin. I'm a beer drinker, by inclination. It was like a Keeley cure taken ahead of time."

Reid's head had turned furtively, to glance behind him.

"That door, Jean."

"But it's the pantry door, darling, you know that. It's hinged, it can't be latched tight."

"But I saw it swing a little just now. It swung out a little, then back again."

"Some current of air, maybe. A little draft," Shawn tried to say reassuringly.

She got up and went over, and swung a chair out in front of it, blocking it. "There, now it won't move any more."

She came back to them, stood behind him. Her arms crept down his shoulders. He couldn't see her face for a moment, it was above him. Shawn could.

"Drink a little more champagne, darling. Before it goes flat. Here, we'll make a loving cup together, you and I." They linked their arms and drank.

"Does the gentleman on the other side of the table want me to drink a loving cup with him too? He has a sort of wistful expression, but he's stuck for words. Either that, or it's heartburn."

She reached out toward him, took the end of his bow tie and pulled it out, dissolving the knot. "That used to be an invitation, if I remember correctly."

"But to what?" asked Shawn.

"That's right, I never did find out," she admitted. "I never was taken up on it. Most likely to tie the tie up over again."

He suddenly struck out at her when she wasn't expecting it, seized the garnet velvet bowknot on her shoulder, tried to pull it undone. Nothing happened.

"Idiot," she said. "It's made that way."

"Yeah, I know that now," he said, looking at his own fingers ruefully.

She struck back in turn. Her hand raked through his hair, and it was left standing on end like a feather duster.

He folded his arms, eyed her with patronizing self-control. "You know, you're playing with dynamite. You're going to get in trouble before tonight's ov—" He quickly checked himself.

A sudden stab of chill air—or of loneliness—seemed to knife Reid. He hunched his shoulders together defensively. "You're both too far away. There's so much empty space around me. Move up closer," he pleaded. "Just a little closer."

"All right. I'll move right up to the very corner, on my side. You move up to the corner on yours, Tom."

"Move *around* it," Reid faltered. "Get in right next to me."

They shifted chairs.

"But that leaves that side opposite you awfully bare, doesn't it?" Shawn remonstrated with kindly intent.

"I have the table in front of me," Reid said simply.

"It *is* chummier this way," she seconded. "After the main course, it doesn't matter where you sit. In fact you get cleaner places that way." Her arm draped itself about Reid's opposite shoulder. Shawn raised his own and crossed it over from that side.

"Here, we'll all put our heads together close, like this," she said. "Anybody know any stories? This is the time for telling good stories, with our heads close together. They don't have to be pasteurized, just so long as you use euphemisms."

"I know one about a cop," Shawn said. "It's clean, but I don't know how good it is."

She reached toward the pack of cigarettes he'd put down before them. "I hate women who don't bring their own to a dinner party."

Shawn told his story. It wasn't very good. But it meant well. She overcomplimented it with her laughter.

"Now you."

She told one, of rapierlike wit and subtlety.

His face remained unchanged. "I didn't get it."

"He just wants me to say that word over again," she protested. "*Enceinte*. There, now are you satisfied?"

"On scent? But what was she driving at when she said that? It sounds like an expression about bloodhounds or some—"

She gave the back of his hand a pat of finality. "You and I will have to have a good long talk sometime real soon, my lad. I can see there are things that haven't been told you."

"Only French things," he said.

She rose, and as she did so, swept her hand insultingly past his face, with a defiant snap of the fingers. He bucked his head back, pretending it had frightened him.

She brought demitasses on a tray. "There's cognac in this coffee. Want to see a pretty blue flame? Give me a match and I'll show you."

He was genuinely startled, evidently never having seen lighted *café-cognacs* before. "But how d'ya get it down?" he demanded innocently.

She laughed. "I like you that way. I think men should be simple. God, how I hate sophisticates. You blow it out first, *chéri*."

"Then why d'ya light it in the first place?"

"I give up," she said. "It would take a lifeti—" Again she checked her phrase, as he had before. They seemed to be running into those tabus all the time. And each one of them registered on Reid's face, like a ripple on taut transparent silk.

"Let's have a little music!" she exclaimed, pounding the table commandingly. "I feel like dancing. Put something on the machine in there."

The music reached them first; then he rejoined them. He tapered the door, so that the music could be heard plainly enough, yet without leaving it entirely open.

She stood and thrust back her hands to shoulder height. "Come on," she invited. "You've been tapped."

Reid turned worriedly sideward in his chair, so that he could still have them in sight. "Not too far away," he whispered, looking up at her beseechingly.

"Right here behind you," she promised. "Right here back of your chair. We'll stay in one place, as if we were on a dime-sized night-club floor."

Shawn was rocking, as though not knowing when to begin. "What is it?" he asked.

She listened to the beat. "It's a tango. You must have put a tango on there without noticing. Come on, I'll show you how." She shook him slightly, from the hands upward. "All right, start. Break loose. What is it, are you glued fast?"

He drew her to him. "Now whaddye do?"

"You just break the handclasp open. Stretch it out to a point. Like this. Then you go toward it on the bias. That's it, you're doing it."

"But that gets you over to the wall."

She rolled her eyes ceilingward. "Look, we're dancing, not surveying. Then you reverse, go back the other way."

"And what happens to the handclasp?" he asked, glancing around at it over his shoulder.

"That trails after you, that's the caboose this time."

A nasal tenor began to sing the vocal refrain in the distance.

"Oh-oh." She stopped short as though something were wrong, gave him a surreptitious push away from her. "Go in quick and get rid of that one," she said in an undertone. "The Spanish lyric may sink in; we both speak it, you know."

"What's the matter with it?"

" 'Adios, Muchachos.' A song of farewell."

He hustled out. She clasped her father lovingly by the head, and as she did so managed to press her hands to his ears as if in a caressing gesture.

The thing stopped short with a reluctant snarl. Something in a livelier tempo began. Shawn came back again, blowing out his breath.

They sat down again, one on each side of him. They began to sing the accompaniment themselves, this time. She began it. Then Shawn joined her, in a willing but not very reliable voice.

"Come on, you too."

She draped an arm about Reid's shoulder. Shawn raised his, on the opposite side, and linked the three of them together in an intimate little close-harmony group.

Reid's parchmentlike lips began to move at last too; he began to falter the words after them.

They held their three heads close together. She swung a gay accompaniment with her free hand hoisted in air, wielding an imaginary baton. Shawn struck notes against the stem of the nearest champagne goblet with the edge of a fork.

They were nearer success than they had been all evening. The gap of a vacant smile held Reid's lips fixedly parted, like the crowing grimace of an infant who senses he has just done something extra-commendable in the eyes of his doting elders.

It had lifted for a moment. He seemed to have forgotten. The champagne, the music, the lovely girl's high spirits.

"I want to dance too!" he said suddenly. "I want to dance with my little girl!"

She gave Shawn a look of triumph, jumped to her feet overjoyed.

"*Now* we'll show them something. These young men are so slow."

They began to move slowly, uncertainly about in a tottering little half circle.

"Like in the old days, darling?" she crooned questioningly close to his ear. "Like in Rome, like in—"

Shawn, seated at table, started to light a cigarette, face beaming approvingly. Suddenly he stopped, it dropped from his mouth.

They were in difficulties of some kind. Something had happened. Reid was inert, limp against Jean, and his body starting to trail downward toward the floor, against her attempts to hold him in continued uprightness.

A heartbroken whisper wrenched itself free above the vivacious, heartless music.

"Jean, I'm going to die. Going to die—"

Shawn jumped upright at the table, to help her, and one of the champagne glasses went over.

Reid had reached his knees now, as if in slow futility, slow succumbing. He was still propped against her, and her eyes were stretched out at full width, holding his transversely.

There was the semblance of a crucifixion in their agonized posture.

Shawn saw her lips stir, and knew what they were saying rather than actually heard. "We've failed, Tom. We've failed. It was all for nothing."

On the table the last laggard drop rolled sluggishly across the rim of the downed champagne goblet, and was spent. As impossible to recapture, once it was gone, as life itself.

14
Police Procedure: Dobbs and Sokolsky

"SOKOLSKY, LIEUTENANT. SOMETHING CAME, ALL right. Like you said it would. I'm sorry to get you up at this unholy hour—"

"Never mind that. That's what I'm for. Cops aren't supposed to sleep, cops are so other people can sleep. What broke?"

"The whole thing. Wide open. All apart. It's like this. About forty minutes ago, around two-thirty, I was asleep on the bed, taking a relief, and Dobbs was at the set. He'd been in bed himself, our pigeon, since around about eleven. We'd heard the bedsprings sound off, and not another sound after that, so we knew. Well, about two-thirty, Dobbs edged over toward me, still keeping the head set on, and nudged me awake. 'You'd better get in on this,' he said. 'Somebody just came in down there—' "

"Hunh? What'd you say?"

Dobbs clamped a cautioning hand across his partner's loose-mumbling mouth, held it a minute.

"Get on base. He just opened the door. Somebody's standing there. Somebody's been knocking at it. Low, but for a long time."

Sokolsky adjusted the spare headgear, groped for notebook and pencil. The latter eluded him, fell to the floor with a slight tick. "Watch it, you damn fool," Dobbs hissed viciously.

They were both set now, alerted.

Silence.

"Must be just staring at each other," Dobbs mouthed. "Not a word. The door's open, I heard it creak."

"Maybe he doesn't know him."

"Then he'd say 'Who are you?' Sh! Here it comes."

(shorthand transcription, as entered in notebook)

Shift of feet on uncovered section of flooring. More than one pair. Door closes. Feet blur onto a rug.

Voice (not Tompkins): "I want to talk to you."

No answer.

Voice: "Come on, wake up, will you?"

Tompkins: "Take your hand off me, don't do that."

Voice: "Then get some wake-up into you."

Tompkins: "What time is it? Why do you have to come here at this hour?"

Voice: "Because I'm not taking any chances, I don't want to come near you in the daytime."

Tompkins: "It's no more safe and no less safe in the daytime than it is now."

Voice: "Whatever you mean by that. And don't bother explaining."

Sound of a chair creaking, as weight is put to it.

VOICE: "Look, I haven't very much time. Let's get down to brass tacks. Are you seeing Reid tomorrow?"

TOMPKINS: "No." *(slowly)* "No, I'm not." *(pause)* "I'm never seeing him again. He dies tomorrow night."

VOICE: "Yes, you are. Don't give me that bellywash. Save that for your kitchen-maid audience. We're talking facts now, not nonsense. Send a message tomorrow that you want to see him. He'll come flying, like an arrow out of a bow."

TOMPKINS: "He won't come here. He'll never come here again."

VOICE *(angrily)*: "Will you cut out that tripe? You've been spouting it so long, you're almost beginning to believe it yourself. Well, I don't! Now I'm telling you what you're going to do, so listen and get it into your head once and for all."

Sound of a match striking. Odor of expensive cigar smoke through floor boards.

VOICE: "Now *I'm* doing the talking. You just listen. You send word to him you want to see him tomorrow. Alone. Without the girl. She's not to know about it. You tell him, when you've got him here, that there's been a change in the—vibrations, constellations, what do you call them?"

TOMPKINS: "I don't call them anything."

VOICE *(arbitrarily)*: "You tell him there's been a change for the better. He's been given a breathing spell. It may still come, but it's not as positive as before. He has a fighting chance now; it's become partly a matter of free will once again. It depends on him. He'll ask what he has to do, he'll beg you to speak, he'll tell you he's willing to do anything; I know that much. You tell him, very indifferently, there are one or two things he could do, to put himself in a more favorable position. There are certain alterations in the will, for instance. Everything goes to the girl, as it stands now. That's all right, he doesn't need to change that. But here's where the change comes in. In case of her death, if she has no children, it's to go to *you,* you become the sole heir. Suggest to him that would be a good way for him to show his appreciation to you, if he's anxious to do so. Point out that it doesn't take anything from her. And if she marries and has children, of course, it's canceled out. It's just in case *she dies unmarried and without issue.* I don't think he'll need much urging. Tomorrow is his last day, and he'd better do it right tomorrow. Explain to him that if your own life line and his are united in that way—and, after all, that's the only practical way it can be done—the favorable aspects of your own have a far better chance of influencing the unfavorable ones of his. You enter into his house, or something like that; you know the tripe. You'll be able to deflect the prophecy, maybe even gain him total immunity."

TOMPKINS *(wearily)*: "But I can't. I haven't the power. It's not a prophecy. It's just something that's there. It's going to happen."

VOICE *(furiously)*: "Will you cut out that crap? What do you think I am? Now I've given it to you straight on the line. He'll do anything you say—right? And you do anything I say, or—"

TOMPKINS: "I don't want his money. I could have had any amount of it, long before now. He's come here to me and pleaded with me to take it. He's left checks behind; I don't bother sending them back any more—"

VOICE: "No, you don't want his money, you don't want his checks. Not much. You lifted one of them, though, from five hundred to five thousand dollars, didn't you? And turned it over to me. I'm holding it right now. With your endorsement on the back of it."

TOMPKINS: "You brought liquor here. You gave me drinks. I

didn't know what I was doing. I'm not used to drinking. I don't remember whether I did it or not. I think you did it."

VOICE: "You did it right under my very eyes. It's got your endorsement on it, not mine. And if I put it through, d'you know you'd go to jail for twenty years for doing a thing like that?"

TOMPKINS: "I'm going to jail anyway. But not because of that check."

VOICE: "Are you going to do like I tell you?"

Long pause.

TOMPKINS *(indifferently)*: "No."

Chair scrapes back violently.

VOICE: "Now, how about it? Are you?"

Another long pause.

TOMPKINS: "Put that away. That can't hurt me."

VOICE: "It can't, eh? All I've got to do is jerk my finger and you'll see. You fool. You poor mangy flea-bitten fool. You could be a rich man. I'm trying to help you. I'm trying to help us both."

TOMPKINS *(sadly)*: "*You're* the fool. *You* poor fool, *you*. You came here tonight, and you couldn't do anything different. But *you're* not going to get his money, if that's what you think. You're not going to live long enough to. Why, you're going to die even sooner than he is. His time is tomorrow night, *yours* is right tonight. You'll never even leave this house alive. On the stairs outside, in a few more minutes—"

VOICE: "Who's going to see to it, you?"

TOMPKINS: "There are two plain-clothes men in the room over us, at this very minute, listening to every word we say—" (Sudden backward heave from Dobbs.)

TOMPKINS: "I've known they were there all along. I couldn't have stopped you from coming here, I couldn't have stopped you from saying what you have. What was the good? Their names are Eddie Dobbs and Bill Sokolsky, and they've been there for two days—"

(Dismayed backward topple by Sokolsky, creating a thud on the floor.)

TOMPKINS: "There. Did you hear that? Now, do you believe me?"

(Sudden race of footsteps across the floor.)

TOMPKINS: "It's no use. You can't evade it. You're going *toward* it, not away. Death is rushing at you right now, I hear the beat of his swift wings. I feel it, I see it, it's on its way. You have only seconds left—"

VOICE *(ragingly)*: "And here's yours, you dirty double-crossing bastard! For framing me!"

Revolver shot.

Door is jarred open, and footsteps stampede wildly down the outside stairs.

Sokolsky tore the headset off himself, nearly taking his ears with it, flung it at the wall, wrenched his own gun out of the holster slung over the foot of the bed, burst out of the room, around the stairhead, and down.

There was a man a full flight and a half below him, careening down at top speed. Sokolsky bellowed: "Hold it! Stay where you are!" He stopped short, and sighted at the landing, two down and a half flight below the man. It gave him a patch of opening, where the rest of the stairs were telescoped together.

The figure came around the turn, and as it did so, fired up at him point-blank. The bullet made a stroke of air past his jaw-bone, without touching it.

Sokolsky didn't move. He held fire, lowered his sights to the landing below, the last one of all, taking a chance on getting him there. It was a tricky trajectory, almost straight downward, just over a little. He clamped his hand to his gun wrist to steady it.

The figure flickered across the landing turn and Sokolsky's gun crashed, at one and the same time.

The figure completed the turn on momentum alone. It took the first three of the next downward steps still upright. Then it went into a long sliding fall. It fell all the rest of the way to the bottom, slid out a considerable distance, as on a skating pond and stopped moving.

When Sokolsky got there the man was dead.

Dobbs came down to him a minute later, his face very white and papery-looking, and not because a man had been shot.

"Who is he?"

He was around fifty. It had gone right into his brain, from the side. His clothing was good quality. There were no marks of identification on him. It must have been a deliberate precaution, for purposes of this visit. His billfold had money in it, but all papers of a personal nature had been extracted. There was a place where the initials had been stamped in gold, and they had been scraped off. Even the stitched-in canvas identity label had been ripped off the lining of his inside coat pocket.

"It'll take time," Sokolsky said, squatting over him. "Better get up there and—"

There was a slight sound on the stairs, and he turned his head.

Tompkins was on them, coming down very slowly. Not stealthily, but so slowly that his descent made hardly any sound. He was already nearly at the bottom.

Sokolsky straightened slowly to his feet, on the far side of the corpse; grim-faced, gun in hand. Gun that had fired only one shot.

"You've saved us the trouble, Johnny," he said truculently. He thumbed with the gun point for an indicator. "Get over there by the wall and stand still, until I'm through here." He turned away, about to resume his inquisitorial crouched posture.

Dobbs seemed to have come down bare-handed. He was

standing there leaning against the opposite wall, across from where Sokolsky had indicated; looking a trifle shaky, as though his nervous system had received a shock from which it hadn't yet had time to recover.

Sokolsky suddenly snapped his head around once more to their hostage. He hadn't stopped as ordered. He'd continued moving forward. As slowly as on the stairs, but forward. Since the corpse, and Sokolsky, were in his way, he moved around one side of them. He even stepped over the corpse's out-stretched feet.

This was direct violation of a police order, given at gun point. Sokolsky was entitled to shoot him down without another word.

He stood steel-straight, gun muzzle maybe six inches from the man's retreating spine.

"I said get back there!" he bellowed. "Stand aside where I told you or I'll let you have one! Dobbs, go over there and take him."

"I can't move," Dobbs whispered strickenly. He seemed to be trying to peel his shoulder off the wall, as though it had adhered to flypaper, and failing. "Even my given name he knew—"

Tompkins took another slow step away, like a man in pensive withdrawal from a place that no longer holds his interest. The street door was just ahead of him.

Sokolsky scissored his legs over the corpse, planted one on the outside of it. That brought the gun that much nearer.

"You've had your warning, Jack," he said, voice vibrant with imminent commission of what he'd threatened. "You take one more step away, and it'll be your last one on this earth!"

Tompkins turned his grave face only partially toward him, to address him backward. "You can't do anything to me with that. It isn't my time yet." He took the one more step.

Sokolsky gave him the break of the dummy shot, that even fugitives in full flight usually get, whether they deserve it or not.

He was still so helplessly close to the gun, the detective could hardly have done otherwise.

He tilted it an inch and fired a warning shot just over the top of his head. It went into the door with a drumlike concussion.

"Now come backwards," Sokolsky said wrathfully, "or it'll not only be your time, it'll be thirty seconds past it!"

Tompkins turned, but only to draw a wing of the door open, inward. He was now full-face to the gun, lingering smoke clearing its bore as though it hated to leave.

Dobbs moaned a little, went a notch lower on his wall-gummed shoulder.

Tompkins looked at the gun. He wasn't smiling, wasn't derisive; there was no expression of bravado on his face. There was, rather, a sort of mild, detached interest, as of a man taking a final glance at some particular object, but an object of no great moment, before he leaves the house to take a walk.

Then he took his hand off the knob, and turned once more, outward to the open night now, and set one foot across the threshold.

Sokolsky altered the gun and fired at the back of his knee, just to bring him down, not to kill him.

The trigger clacked, and there was no detonation, the shot had misfired. He'd put six bullets in and he'd fired only twice, once on the stairs and once into the door.

Tompkins's second leg trailed the first, out past the threshold.

Crazed, the detective stamped forward after him a single leg span, but a lengthy one, and sighted point-blank at the back of his head. Four feet away; no one could have missed, and he was trained in firearms. It was the death shot, all else having failed, and he was justified.

The trigger clacked, and it had misfired again. And it had never misfired before in all the time he'd had it.

Tompkins's arm came in and around, rearward to his body, and he drew the door wing slowly to after him, to closure.

Sokolsky pumped the trigger maniacally, twice more, his face twisting like a sopping wet rag with a sort of panic he'd never known before, and twice more that barren tubular click came. And nothing else but a flatter echoing click, as the door latch tongue went back into place.

Dobbs moaned a little again.

Sokolsky ripped the door open and staggered out. There was just darkness on the other side, nothing moving, nothing to be seen.

He worked with the gun, raised it and fired wildly into that darkness, and four times it cracked out in full-bodied explosion, once for every bullet there was in it—now that there was nothing in front of it any more to be hit.

Then he let it drop to the ground, and leaned soddenly back against the side of the doorway, as if he were all in and couldn't have moved another inch. And he couldn't have.

15

The Wait: Mid-evening

THEY LOOKED SMALL IN THE middle of the room, the three of them. It should have been a snug box room, to hold so few people, and so close together as they were, and it wasn't. It was too stately, and too classically proportioned. The ceiling was too high over them, and even the brilliantly lighted chandelier of crystal prisms couldn't bring it down any closer, seemed rather to accentuate its height. The windows were too tall, and the burgundy damask draperies smothering them, interfolded at full length before them so that not a trace of an opening showed, only emphasized their formal height and width.

They were lost in there, as they were indeed lost in fact. Three small people, three very small people, about a little foursquare table. Their backs to the room, two in black cloth and one bare-shouldered, its contours rippling gracefully from time to time with muscular play.

She shuffled with neat economy of motion, and in the silence the cards made a little spitting sound.

Their battle against the silence was a losing one, for they could push it back each time only for so long as they spoke, and each time it came back again, and encompassed them once more, and they had it to do over again. And each time it crept back, the wall clock in the room with them got its chance, as it had inside in the supper room before, and the hissing of its pendulum was breathed malignantly into their ears, like some sort of lighted fuse over there by the wall, working ceaselessly toward its detonation point.

She placed the re-formed deck before Shawn. "Cut," she said quietly.

He halved it, and she took it up again.

The sound of dealing was even less than the sound of shuffling had been. They fell like ghost cards about the table. Occasionally one snapped a little with the pressure of her thumb on leaving it.

They picked three of the four hands up; they shifted them into order. "I pass," she said.

She spoke again. "You bid," she said to Reid. It was too short a thing, too small a thing, to utter in such a large room, and after so long a time.

They waited.

It was excruciating. Shawn's face was white with it. Her eyes were wide, and taut at their corners, with it.

Reid collapsed his hand, as though overcome by helplessness. And it was not helplessness of the game, for his eyes were not on the cards. They were over them, in sightless fixity.

She touched him on the arm, in tender reminder.

Then he spread the cards again, as if her touch had automatically told him what to do. But his eyes still failed to see them.

"Would you like to pass?"

He looked at her as though he didn't understand. As though he'd heard her speak but didn't know what it was she'd said He didn't say anything.

"All right, I'll make the first bid," Shawn said. "One—" He stopped again, and referred to his hand, as though only belatedly remembering after he was well into mid-speech that his cards should have something to do with what he was about to say. "One diamond."

"One heart," she said.

It couldn't pick up momentum. It had come back to Reid again, and it recoiled, dead. His hand was shielding his eyes now. He was still holding the disregarded fan-spread in his other. It was wilting toward the horizontal.

She tilted it up for him. "I can see your hand."

Shawn lifted a seltzer-bottle from the floor beside his chair, shot a spurt into a glass, started to offer it to him.

Her foot reached under the table and tapped a period to his. Her head swung an unnoticeable quarter of an inch each way.

Shawn set the glass down.

"Do you pass again?" she tried to rouse him softly. He looked at her again. Once more as though he could hear her voice but couldn't tell the meaning of the words.

"Two diamonds," Shawn said, to put an end to the steady, haunting look Reid was giving her.

"Two hearts," she said.

Shawn thumped the table with his knuckles. They shifted seats, each one moved one place to the left. She began to turn over the fourth hand, now opposite her on the table, arrange it in suits.

The clock had now veered around to Reid's right. It had been directly back of him until now. His head started to turn, as if drawn by fine invisible lead strings. She caught the motion, and her hand went out, gently turned his chin to where it had been before.

The hissing seemed to become stronger, as if infuriated by her interference.

Nearly a full set of pictures in diamonds was exposed, only the king missing, from the auxiliary hand on the table.

She gave Shawn a look. Not the look of reproach a fanatic bridge player gives. A private look between the two of them meaning: You're not making believe hard enough. Play the game.

He snapped his fingers contritely. "I knew they were somewhere," he said. Something twinkled on his forehead, caught in a seam of the contracted skin. Something moist, but not big enough to be called a drop.

"Your lead," she said to Reid.

They waited.

"Play to me," Shawn coached him gently. "I'm your partner now."

Reid put down a card.

"Don't you want to take that back? You're leading into an ace in the dummy."

Reid retrieved it. "It matters so," he said hollowly. "It matters so." He looked at the card curiously, spread his thumb along its glossy surface longingly. "It'll still be here, for another game, another night," he said wistfully, "but the player—"

The siphon droned angrily in Shawn's hand and drowned out the rest of it. Charged water fumed recklessly to the top of the glass, bleaching the base of Scotch it had held to invisibility. Then he clacked a piece of ice noisily around in it, knocking its head off.

Her underlip went sharply in, making a crevice of woe, then returned to its normal position again.

"Cigarette and drink," she pleaded hoarsely. "I'll take that one you've just built."

Shawn retinted it with a little additional Scotch, handed it

287

over. Her lips touched it, she put it down. Her lips drew once on the cigarette he lighted for her; she stamped it out beside her.

The clock pendulum seemed to lash itself in unholy glee; they could hear its quickened, breathless sibilance.

She extracted a card from Reid's sheaf and put it down for him. Three others fell quickly over it, blotting it out. She took in the trick, placed it at the table's edge before her.

Reid was suddenly squeezing his cards, as if to extract life-giving moisture from them that he could no longer find in himself. He exerted such pressure on them with both convulsively compressed hands that those not caught and hopelessly bent shot up into the air before his face, and came down all about him, on his shoulders, on his sleeves, on his shirt front, in his lap.

He was breathing open-mouthed, as though he couldn't get enough air. "You're torturing me," he panted. "I can't stand any more of it. Don't, I tell you. Stop it. Playing with pasteboards, adding up points on a score pad, while my life is draining aw— I don't want points in clubs and spades, I want grains of life, more minutes to breathe in!" His hands fell open on the table, turned upward in empty supplication. "Give them to me. Give them to me."

They'd leaped back from the table, the two of them, Shawn and she, as though it were in imminent danger of upsetting, though it was firm enough. Shawn was holding a glass to Reid's lips. His other hand was pressing down firmly on the top of his head, as if forcing calmness into him.

"That's it, old man," he said steadyingly. "Tha-at's it."

They left him for a moment, sodden in the chair. The paraphernalia of the game disappeared as if by magic; suddenly there wasn't a trace left. Their paths crossed, just out of earshot of him, as they hurried about, each intent on his own appointed task in the impromptu rearrangement the outburst had necessitated.

"It was the wrong game. Too quiet," she murmured.

"I was afraid of that."

"Wait, there's a roulette wheel; help me bring it out. In his younger days, he used to tell me, at Biarritz and Monte Carlo— He'd start in at nine, he'd look up, and it was suddenly light out, the whole night had gone—"

"It may work now."

They set it up on the table. Reid looked at it dully; his eyes showed no interest at first.

"We'll play for real stakes," she said. "This is no friendly parlor game."

"Everything is real tonight," Reid agreed sepulchrally.

Shawn was already spinning the wheel, testing it. The two colors blurred as it swam around, then separated again as it slowed to a stop.

"I'll be back in a second," she said cryptically. She sidled out to the door, in a way that struck Shawn as having a touch of the surreptitious to it, though this could only have had to do with her errand and not with the fact of her going itself.

She was gone far longer than the second she had set, and longer than a minute too. Then the door reopened, and she had sidled inward again, and again with that same touch of secrecy with which she had gone. She was holding in her hand a large-sized handkerchief knotted together by its four corners, like a vagrant's pack in miniature.

She opened this on the roulette table, and a sunburst of fuming brilliance flashed upward into the light. Rings, bracelets, clips, pendants.

"These are all I have. And what are you two putting up?"

They stood looking at it, as though stunned. Shawn tried to catch her eye, as if seeking to fathom whether she was in earnest or not. She refused to meet his gaze. She thumped her knuckles arbitrarily, to one side of the massed profusion of jewels, as if summoning them to meet her challenge.

Slowly a faint gleam kindled in Reid's eyes, as if reflected there by what lay on the table. His lips even curved in a macabre smile. He turned abruptly to Shawn, clenched him by the arm. "Come with me a moment. I want you to go inside with me. I'm afraid to go in there alone."

Shawn accompanied him uncertainly to the door, glancing back toward her a couple of times.

"Warm up the wheel a while," Reid said to her.

They went out into the hall, and down it as far as Reid's private study. They opened and went in there.

"Close it," Reid said softly. Then when Shawn had, "Turn on that strong light over there. No, that one by the mantel. That's it."

He opened two adjoining sections of wood paneling. "You know what this is, don't you?"

"I do now," Shawn said soberly. "I didn't until I saw that safe dial behind it." He watched Reid a moment, started to turn on his heel. "I shouldn't be in here with you."

Reid's hand darted out, caught him by the arm, held him there. "I want you to see it. What difference can it make now? One, and then nine, and then three, and then two. It's an easy combination to remember. 1932. The year of the depression. Think of being broke, and then automatically you know how to open this safe and stop being broke."

"You shouldn't do this," Shawn repeated stubbornly, looking down at the floor like a man trying to keep his eyes off something indecent.

Reid suddenly thrust something at him, something in each hand. "Here, put this in your pockets for me. Carry it in for me. There's twenty thousand in cash here, that's all I usually keep in it at one time."

"Did you close it again?" Shawn asked, when he tried to turn him away from it.

"No, somebody else'll have to do that for me—tomorrow. They'll probably want it open again, first; it'll save time."

Shawn reached for the dial, twirled it so that the opening point was lost, closed the two wood panels over it.

They went back to where she was waiting for them by the table. She didn't look up. She was watching the wheel. She must have known what they'd gone for, where they'd been. The flickering blur of the wheel was reflected in her eyes.

Shawn emptied his side coat pockets, which was where he'd carried the bank notes, onto the table. She didn't look at the money, nor up at them, even then.

Shawn brought up his own wallet, from over his hip. It contained, he knew even without consulting it, one lonely ten and a few singles.

"You can't play, with what you've got," Reid said brittlely. "Those small denominations'll slow us up. Here, I'll stake you." He pushed a taped packet almost contemptuously over toward him. "A thousand."

"I can't do that either," Shawn said a little sharply.

"Give me your I O U for it," Reid suggested impatiently. "It's not a present."

"This is on the level," she warned, braking the wheel and looking up tautly.

Shawn stared at her hard for a moment. "All right, I'm game; I'll take a chance," he said abruptly.

He unclipped a mechanical pencil from the lining of his pocket, walked aside to another table, jotted something on paper, came back with it. "This do?"

Reid didn't even look at it; took it and thrust it sight unseen underneath the bottommost of the packets of bank notes stacked one atop the other.

Shawn mopped his brow furtively, but she must have seen

him. "You've never played for such high stakes before," she murmured.

"I've never played at all before," he answered.

"I've never had so little to lose," Reid said. "Or so little to win."

"Are we ready?" She thrust still farther aside a chair that remained too close behind her, threatening to hamper her. "Who'll be croupier?"

They both turned to her simultaneously. "You."

"Then I'll have to spin and bet against the wheel as well. It'll be a little irregular, but the wheel is honest. We trust one another here."

"But who gets the forfeited bets?" her father wanted to know.

"Winner takes all. The winner takes the losers' bets, instead of the house taking them. In other words, we're betting directly against one another, instead of against the house. And since there are only the three of us playing, we'll have to eliminate the numbers entirely. Just bet on the colors, black or red, and even or odd. No exact numbers. See what I mean, Tom?"

Shawn nodded.

"I'll make the calls in English, for Tom's sake."

She stood facing the wheel. The two men ranged themselves on opposing sides of the table, their stakes offside.

"Place your bets."

She picked up a ring from the embedded mass in the handkerchief, scanned it appraisingly, discarded it. She picked up a flexible bracelet of diamonds, in five closely fastened strands, turned it about in her hand. "I remember this. Cartier's, one hundred thousand francs. Or was it two hundred and fifty? It looks like something you would use in your profession, Tom. On the red, even." She put it down on ten.

Reid sheared off the topmost of his packet of bills. "On the black, odd." He put it down on five.

They both looked at Shawn questioningly. He picked up his single packet of bills, hesitated, started to work his thumb in under the paper tape to burst it.

"Oh, no change," Reid protested pettishly, "or the game won't have speed. And I haven't much time, Shawn, always think of that; we'll have to play fast."

"Sh-h," she cautioned him softly.

"I'll take a chance," Shawn consented abruptly. "But I'm liable to leave the table quick and early." He stabbed the packet of bills down intact. "On the black, even."

"Nothing more goes."

The wheel flowed blurredly, sending up ghostly high lights into their downpeering faces. It disintegrated into its two colors again, stopped with that little click of finality.

No one said anything.

Reid put his packet atop Shawn's, edged their double layer slightly toward him.

Shawn drew it the rest of the way back, into sterile margin, with reluctant slowness.

But his hand made a sudden damlike barrier on the tabletop when she tried to shift the coruscating bracelet his way.

"Oh, no," she insisted, and stepping quickly around the table, pulled out the mouth of his coat pocket and dropped the object in. "We're not play-acting."

"There's a fourth variant we haven't made allowance for," Reid said, as if talking to cover up the detective's embarrassment. "What happens if that comes up, uncovered by anyone's bet?"

"The spin is canceled out. Bets are carried over where they are until the next spin. Make your bets."

"Black, odd," Reid said. "I've started on it. I'll stay on it."

"Red, odd. This diamond dog collar. I'll see if I can change my luck."

"Black, even," Shawn said. He pushed his whole stake forward.

"You don't have to do that this time," Reid said. "You have a backlog now."

"I'm not going to hide behind that," Shawn said stubbornly. "It stays."

"Nothing more goes."

Again that click, and then a silence.

Shawn lit a cigarette, so that his hands would have the excuse of being occupied.

"Oh, don't be coy; let out your shirttails," she said a little brusquely. "Isn't it enough that I lose? Do I have to *hand* my stakes to you too?" She wedged the neckpiece in on top of the bracelet.

"I'll feel like a walking hock shop in a couple more minutes."

"Here, if this'll make you feel any better," Reid said. He took out the penciled I O U, tore it to pieces, flung them floor-ward, and retracted the topmost of Shawn's now triple packets. "Now you're what is known as financially independent."

"That doesn't wipe out the original—"

"Make your plays," she interrupted.

They posted their bets in silence, they didn't call them out any more as they laid them; they let their choices of squares on the chart speak for themselves. A change was coming over them, scarcely noticeable at first, yet growing more all-pervasive with each progressive turn of the wheel. From Shawn's point of view, he could only observe it as it affected the other two. Her color was higher now, especially up over the cheekbones, and her eyes were brighter. Reid's face had come back toward a semblance of normality; it was taut and grim, but it was the face of the emaciated living.

Shawn's necktie bothered him, and he hooked fingers under it trying to give more slack to its constricting noose.

"Is it getting you yet, Tom?" she said, the pupils of her eyes flickering in time with the restless rippling of the wheel.

He widened his eyes at her in surprised confession, meaning it was in spite of himself. He could feel heat at the back of his neck, as if a burning glass were being mischievously focused on it. He pulled at his tie and it came loose. He snapped up one wing of his collar, let it stand out like a sort of epaulet upended over one shoulder.

She pushed back her hair. "Pour me a drink," she said to Shawn. "My mouth's dry." She scarcely tasted it, put it down again. "Oh, everything!" she exclaimed, pushing over the entire handkerchief cabbage and what was left in it. "I can't stand any more of this, it's like dying by in—" She checked herself quickly.

"Make your bets!" she said, in too loud, too hoarse a voice.

Suddenly, by afterthought, she wrenched the ring off her finger, pitched that in with the rest.

The ball trundled, socketed.

She drew in her breath, in a long cooling whisper.

"He hasn't lost once," Reid said hectically. "He hasn't gone off that color once since we began. It has to end, it has to break sometime! The record, I think, for consecutive number of—"

"The wheel's a fix," Shawn said surlily. "Somebody's ribbing me."

"The wheel's straight!" she flashed at him. "And if I'd intended manipulating it in anyone's favor—" He knew what she'd been about to say. She tasted her drink again, twisting her body offside. She spilled a little of it, her hands were fluttering like leaves.

"I'm through. Luck doesn't love ladies." She backed her hand to her forehead, held it there a moment. "I'll go ahead spinning for you—if I can calm down a little."

"Should we quit?" Shawn asked, reaching out to steady her, then pulling back again.

"Don't leave me stranded *now!*" Reid whinnied, almost beside himself. He had one packet left. "Wait a minute. Where's my checkbook? I have more on deposit in my account. And my securities."

"Don't," Shawn objected throatily.

Her foot quickly trod his undertable. "Look at his face," she breathed. "We're winning. Keep on."

A light-blue paper oblong fell on the table. "Here—blank," Reid said. "The entire amount, whatever it is. Fill it in yourself afterwards. If you get it."

"The entire amount," Shawn said quietly. And moved all the packets forward once more.

"There are just two of us left. We'll leave out the odd and even after this, just bet on color. Color against color."

"Your bet," Shawn nodded.

"I'll take red, the color of life. The other is the color of—"

"Bet's down!" she snapped.

The click of finality seemed never to come. On and on and on, slower and slower and slower. Reid was gripping the loose fold of skin at the front of his emaciated neck, pulling it out until it almost seemed made of rubber. She had her hand crosswise to her mouth, was biting the back of it. Shawn kept slapping lightly and incessantly at his own thigh, as if curbing extreme pain.

The ball dropped home.

Looking at them, and not at the stilled wheel, it would have been impossible to tell who was the loser and who the winner. They all three alike seemed the losers, the players as well as the nonplayer.

"I'm done," Reid said strangledly. "I haven't anything left."

Shawn made a move to push the terraced accumulation of currency back toward him.

"No, that can't undo it!" Reid said fiercely. "Don't you understand? This little wheel runs true to the other, bigger one. You think this is just a wooden gambling wheel. It isn't; it's my wheel of life. I've got to win just once, before it's too late. I want a sign from it; then that'll mean— I've got to keep on playing, keep on playing, until I get one!"

He glanced at the clock.

"Wait. The house here. The deed is downtown somewhere. My daughter is a witness. I can't put it on the table. Give me a piece of paper. Oh, anything, anything."

He drew a square of four lines. He put a chimney over it. He put a window in it. He signed his name under it.

"Witness this," he said, and handed the paper to her.

She wrote her own name underneath his.

He took it back, and put it on the table.

"This goes against everything you've got. On the red."

Shawn nodded.

She spun.

"Stand back, a foot back," he ordered her. "Fold your hands on top of your head, and keep them there. I want my sign, but I don't want it from you. I want it from—" His eyes flicked to the ceiling, then down again to the blurred whirlpool of the wheel, that never finished dissolving. You could hear their breathing over the faint rustle it made. Short and swift, and sanded with tension.

The ball plunged. Their breathing stopped. There was silence.

Reid smiled. It was an awful smile. "The house is yours now, too," he said. "The house and all the money."

Shawn didn't answer.

"I have nothing left." Again Reid eyed the clock, as he had before, "No, wait." He turned slowly, and his eyes rested on Jean.

Shawn's face whitened. "No, don't," he faltered. "Don't do anything like that." He recoiled a step. "I've humored you until now—"

"Humored me?" Reid said viciously. "I'm not betting against

you! I'm betting against life." He was still looking at Jean. "Is it agreeable with you, Jean?"

There was a look of sickish repugnance on Shawn's face. "You're going mad," he said. "It's time to stop. You don't know what you're doing—"

"I don't?" He answered Shawn, but it was Jean he kept looking at. "The eyes of death are clearer than yours will ever be, son. *You* don't know you love her, but I do. She doesn't know she loves you, but I do."

He kept looking at her.

"Is it agreeable to you, Jean?" he asked again.

Her eyes didn't waver. She didn't even glance at Shawn, as though he weren't there in the room with them at all.

She spoke low, but her answer was as distinct as a tap against thin crystal. "It's agreeable to me, father."

"I bet again against the wheel of life," Reid said. "My daughter."

He drew a forked figure on paper, all single lines, of a two-legged creature. Put a tiny circle over it for head. Put a little kilt around its middle.

He signed his name.

"Now you sign your consent under that."

Shawn's face had a slight greenish tinge to it. His tongue touched at his upper lip, and he swallowed, as though something gorged him. "But it's not a—not a transferable debt. You can't convey ownership in a—in a living being across a roulette board."

"It's not ownership. It's her hand in marriage. You can refuse."

Shawn spoke as low as she had. And as clear-voicedly. "I don't refuse." He kept his hands off the table. "But I have nothing worth that."

Reid palmed the cartoon to the board. "The stake is down. Bet with what you have."

Shawn still refused to touch the money.

"You're on the black, then, by default. You're the wheel. You're life."

Her arm suddenly swept scythelike across the table, elbow down, pushed all his accumulated winnings into betting range.

"I refuse to go by default," she said quietly. "That would be worse."

The wheel flowed, seeming by optical illusion to go in the opposite direction to that which it actually traveled. Then suddenly, as it neared stopping point, reversing and only then actually reflecting its own direction of course. Then the faltering, castanetlike progress of the pellet, then its final pebblelike drop.

She had turned her back. She had moved several feet away. Their silence must have told her, before she turned and looked. When she turned, she turned slowly, on the side toward Shawn rather than on the side toward her father, still clasping her own arms, as she had held them clasped while standing there. A little tightly, as if in stress; not laxly. As if she needed a tourniquet, to check the flow of some emotion coursing through her. But what it was her face didn't say; welcome or unwelcome.

"That was your betrothal of marriage, just then," Reid said to her.

He waited. She didn't answer. "Do you accept?"

"I did before. Your daughter doesn't welsh."

"Do *you?*"

Shawn worked a commonplace seal ring off his finger, went over to her.

She offered her hand unasked. He slipped it on the middle finger, and it hung slack, even at the base. She tore off a tiny morsel of her handkerchief and wedged it in under the band, to hold it in place.

"I'm sorry," he breathed contritely.

She looked steadily into his eyes. "The winner can refuse his takings. The loser mustn't refuse to pay up. That's the rule of honor." Then she added softly, "The loser doesn't want to, anyway. My own wishes go with the pledge."

"I have one thing left," they heard Reid say. They both turned back to him.

He was fumbling in an inside pocket with palsied hands. He extracted at last an ancient Manila envelope, that he must have removed from the safe along with the currency, unnoticed by Shawn. From this in turn he withdrew a yellowed document, folded in quadruplicate, veined with cracks along its seams, so that it threatened to disintegrate at any further molestation. He effected its opening with cautiously manipulating fingers so that its context, or at least the upper panel of this, lay flat upon the table and could be deciphered. At top, in intricate steel-cut engraving, was the municipal coat of arms. Below, in heavy, shadow-raised nineteenth century capitals, the heading: "Certificate of Birth." Under that, in vanishing brown ink, in spidery antique penmanship, a namespace was filled: "Reid, William Harlan"; a date space was filled: "August the Twenty-third, Eighteen Hundred and Seventy-nine." The rest was lost to view beneath the continuing folds that had remained undisturbed.

"On the red to win," he said in a cackling voice. "On the last try of all."

Fetishism.

Shawn stood there, knuckles idly curved against the tabletop. "What do you expect me to do?" he said quietly.

"You refuse to bet? You know it's worthless?" Reid shrilled.

"What'll I meet it with? It's a hypothetical bet. This wheel can't affect it. If I win, how can I take it? If I lose, how can I give it up to you—when I haven't got it in the first place?"

"I want my sign," Reid insisted. "This wheel can give it to me.

This wheel can save me. There's still time. If I win, I've saved it. If I lose—"

"And what do I bet against it? This?" Shawn swept the accumulated winnings off the table edge onto the floor.

"Haven't you anything that you value? There must be something. Every man has something. Something that you want to lose as little as I want to lose—what I am staking."

She didn't say anything; she didn't help Shawn out. Her father wasn't to be denied, perhaps she knew that. Perhaps she felt by now as he did, that the symbol could influence the reality. Or perhaps she wanted to learn what the highest thing in life to Shawn was; or if he had any such thing at all.

"Well?" Reid nagged. "Isn't there anything? If there isn't, I feel sorry for you. Almost as sorry for you as for myself."

"There is something," Shawn said slowly. "But I don't go around putting it down on gambling tables." He took out a small black case, opened it, holding the raised wing so that what was in it was hidden from them.

"But I'm dying," Reid whispered fearfully. "That's my life, there, on the red."

Shawn put his badge down, on the black.

The symbol was complete.

"My dream, the other night," she murmured half audibly. "I saw it, and it looked just like that, and it was the only thing that could have saved us—

"Don't!" she said to the two of them aloud. "Don't do it. We shouldn't have begun this. Oh, for God's sake, don't make this bet!"

"The bet is down," Reid said, waving her back.

"The bet is down," Shawn agreed inflexibly. "Spin the wheel."

She did it with both hands this time, not as she'd done it before. Pressing them flat, palm to palm, over it, then slicing them apart, one forward, one back, and drawing them away from it as quickly as if it were hot, and to touch it for too long was to be burned.

Reid's face was a mask of elastic, pulled so tight at the back of his head that only a flattened suggestion of former features was recognizable any more.

Shawn's knuckles made five double white ellipses, like eyelids, across the back of his tightly packed fist. A fist that seemed to grow smaller, tighter, with every turn the wheel made, until it was like a knob of solid bone, there at the end of his arm.

And she, she kept watching his face, more than the wheel, more than her father even, with a sort of pensive, carefully concealed admiration. As you do someone who, dimly perceived though he may have been until now, has suddenly become fully known to you for the first time.

It stopped more quickly this time, it scarcely rolled at all, as if activated by a malign intelligence of its own, in a hurry to strike without sparing, to cut short even the slightest merciful delay its indecision might have given them. Their eyes were still swimming around in the orbit it had set for them to watch, after the wheel itself had already stilled and was at rest. Like something that throws its pursuers off the track by stopping short while they go on past it.

Their rigidity melted; a flux of limpness ran through all three.

Shawn took the badge back slowly, covered it with both his hands. Held it thus in a sort of cherished contrition for a moment.

"Hold him," he said suddenly. He grabbed at a chair and drew it up behind the tottering figure that she was trying to keep erect on its feet.

They sat him down in it between them, limp as an overcoat stripped off someone's back. His head went back over the chair, and Shawn had to hold it with his hand below it, to give it the support that its own neck couldn't give it.

"It's just a game," she was saying into his ear, in a frantic smothered voice. "It's just a wooden wheel, made in a factory, a workshop, somewhere. You could make one yourself. It doesn't *know*. It doesn't feel. The ball stops here, the ball stops there—"

"Here," Shawn said. "Here. Look. Take it." And crushed the desiccated birth certificate into the nerveless hand.

"You're giving me back a piece of paper."

"That's all you put down on the table, nothing else."

"I put my life down there." His hand twitched, and a part of the brittle paper, caught within it, was ground into particles that sifted downward to the floor like confetti. "See? There it is. There it goes."

His head, righted by Shawn's supporting hand at the base of its skull, overbalanced the opposite way, came forward now. It dropped inert on the table, cushioned by one arm. The other hung down straight to the floor, swinging a little at first, loose in its socket. Then at last it stopped, like the pendulum of a clock that has run down.

Jean's hand trailed reluctantly across his bowed back, as she moved away from him, powerless to help. She moved around the table, and as she passed the wheel, she spun it, in despairing valedictory, in idle finality.

It whirred and coursed and stopped again, unwatched behind her, as it had so many times before; its board sterile now.

She saw something on Shawn's face, and that made her turn and look around at it.

For the first time all evening, now that the game was over, now that the player was destroyed, it had stopped on red.

16

Police Procedure: Molloy

THEY FOUND HIM LYING THERE bestially mangled, along a footpath that led through clumps of trees down into the village. It was a short cut, a sort of branch trail, that left the main highway out at about the Hughes farm and rejoined it again at mid-village. The main highway took a slight bend getting in, and this little trail ran straight. It was the string to the highway's bow. It was tree-walled and bramble-blind and not very good, but it was the shortest line between two points.

The thing must have lurked around in the trees along there, after clearing the screaming carnival ground, and then he'd come along all unwitting, and—the condition of the ground told the rest of the story.

Even the locals could read that part of it fairly accurately. Anyone could have. He'd been coming along alone. That was obvious. And he'd been coming along *toward* the village, and not out *from* it. That was equally obvious. Because everyone in the village knew what was at large somewhere out there, and no one would have been dumb enough to strike out alone along such a trail. He obviously hadn't known; so he hadn't heard yet; so he hadn't been in the village, he'd been heading for it.

Word spread like wildfire, and Molloy got out there, to where they'd found him, within ten minutes of the time they'd first found him. So did most of Thackery; the adult male part, anyway.

The torches made it bright as day, around there where he was lying. A little too bright, in fact, for what they had to show. It was pretty bad. Those that crowded in closest to take a first look backed out fastest to take a good deep breath.

You could see he'd been a man, and you could tell what color his hair had been. You couldn't tell much else about him with any definitiveness. He was tarred and feathered with leaves. He'd bled a great deal, and that had acted as the tar. Leaves and twigs were papered all over him, from threshing and struggling on the ground, and they played the part of the feathers. In many places his actual outlines were fuzzy.

The fight must have gone around in a circle. It had flattened the shrubs and things, and churned up the ground, like a great flat wheel, with him as the axle of it.

People were spitting all over, into the bushes, in the background, and some of them trying to keep from doing even worse.

They found the piece of dress goods a considerable distance away, as though it had caught onto something moving, a claw perhaps, and been dragged, and then finally been shaken loose. It was stiffened with dried blood. Not his. Far older blood, far browner.

Somebody finally recognized him. There wasn't much to go by, but somebody did.

"That's Rob Hughes," they said. "I know him by that tooth with the gold cap, on the side there. See it wink when you pass the torch close over his face. He was always showing it around last year when he first got it put in. I used to see it glint like that when he'd open his mouth to puff out a match after lighting up his pipe. Do it again, move it past his face." The mouth was wide open already, in an arrested death scream; there was no need to pry it wider. "See it glimmer? Catch it?"

Other heads nodded. "Yeah, that's Hughes."

"That's enough," Molloy said. "Cut it out." They wanted to keep on doing it indefinitely.

They made up a party to go and break the news to his wife. Molloy went along, for purely professional reasons. At this end, there wasn't enough left of the man to tell very much about him; there was bound to be more at the other end, there couldn't very well be less.

"They've been fighting like cats and dogs for ten years," somebody said on the way over.

"The quiet kind of fighting, behind closed doors," somebody else added.

"Then how did anybody else know about it?" Molloy asked not unreasonably.

"You could see the marks on her afterwards, each time. She was always having 'accidents' around the house. Never saw a woman have more things fall on her, or trip over more buckets and get lamed—"

"Sh-h," somebody cautioned softly. Not out of respect for the dead, but out of proximity to the living. There was a light in the window.

She came to the door, and the four of them—there were three others besides Molloy—pushed into the room, took off and swiveled their hats, and suffered a momentary attack of group tongue-tiedness. Not Molloy, perhaps; he wasn't trying to talk, he was just trying to watch.

She was past fifty, and tall and thin and steely-looking. As though she'd been fused in a crucible of hate, and all the soft parts smelted away.

She had to speak first, as women often do in tragedies. "Something's happened," she said impassively. They nodded.

"To Rob," she said. She bit off a thread she'd been working into some cloth when the summons at the door interrupted her. Then she added, "I reckon. Or else you wouldn't be here in a parcel like this. Without him with you." She berthed the needle in a scrap of chamois or felt that already held several others, and waited.

"That lion, that lion that escaped, got him," they said falteringly.

She took it with strange calm. She didn't scream or cry, and several of them that were at the ready to hold her up if she started to go down found they didn't have to. She stayed up.

"Did't get him pretty bad?" she said.

"He's dead, Hannah."

"I know," she said, as if that wasn't what she'd asked. "But did it get him pretty bad?"

"It got him pretty bad, Hannah. Pretty bad."

Some of them said—said afterwards—she smiled at that; bitterly. Some of them said she couldn't have, the others must have just imagined it, it was a trick of the light. But some of them still said, even after that, they were pretty sure they'd seen her smile. Molloy didn't say whether he had one way or the other.

Presently she reseated herself in the rocker she had been occupying when they first knocked. But not from weakness or from grief, apparently more as an indication that the interview was about over. To do so, she displaced a mass of material, a dress of flowered pattern, white upon a blue ground, that she had been working upon, and placed this on her lap once more in readiness to continue.

Molloy's eyes hadn't left it the whole time he'd been in the room. He'd brought the scrap of bloodied goods along with him. He took it out and unpapered it now, in full sight of her. There was scarcely enough of it left unbloodied to indicate what the original pattern or colors had been. It was oblong in shape, however, and a faulty oblong, growing narrower at one end than at the other.

She glanced at it with perfect unblinking composure; even, one might say, with lukewarm interest. "That's from this dress I'm working on now," she said. "My Sunday dress. I found a piece scissored out of it. I wasn't aiming to wear it tonight, but I just happened to take it down and look at it. Then I decided to stay home and fix it." She held open the folds to expose a mutilation. Oblong in shape, a faulty oblong, growing narrower at one end than at the other. "I was just patching it up, with the closest match I could get."

No one said anything. She answered the unheard question. "Early today I killed a chicken for supper. He might have used that to mop up after me—kind of messy, you know—and then kept it with him."

Some of their faces were a little white. She went on sewing. She was the only one doing any talking. The only one able to.

"He was going to take me down to see that tent show tonight. He'd been in town this afternoon and seemed to think I'd like it. I didn't want to go, but he coaxed me real bad. Seemed to have his heart set on it." She smoothed her work tidily. "But then he got fidgety, said he'd go down ahead, and I could follow. He told me where to find him. He told me to meet him by the lions' cage. Said there'd be a lot of folks there, and I should wait for him right smack in that one place, and not stir away." One of the men began to reach backhand for the doorknob, as though he wanted to get out of the room, didn't like it in there any more.

She went on talking. Dutifully taking stitches, and talking.

"I saw him take something from the tool chest before he left this afternoon. We got a tool chest, you know, out in back. Didn't see what it was, but I went out and looked after he left. There was a pair of pliers missing and a rasp. Guess that must have been what he took. Dunno what he'd want them for, I'm sure. Especially to take down to town with him."

And those that said she'd smiled the first time said that now she smiled again. But those that said she hadn't then still said she hadn't now.

"Let's go," one of the men said thickly, as though he were gagging.

"But then he did curious things every now and then. About six months ago I found an ax lying on the floor under our bed one night. I picked it up and handed it to him handle first, told him he must have mislaid it. He allowed he must have, and took and put it back where it belonged. I never found it out of place from that day on."

Molloy spoke for the first time since he'd been in the place. "Did you own the farm, Mrs. Hughes?"

"Yep," she snapped. "I certainly did. It was in my name. I saw to that years ago."

"You're a very brave woman," he remarked half under his breath.

"It's not that most womenfolks are so brave," she contradicted. "It's just that most menfolks are such cowards."

That was about all she said.

"Good night," she concluded as they were filing out. "Thanks for coming around to tell me. I'll ask you to excuse me now. I've got to finish mending this dress he took a chunk out of. Then I've got to get it dyed soon's I can. It's the only thing I've got fit to wear to the funeral."

17

The Wait: Moments Before Eternity

THE ROOM DOOR WAS LOCKED now, on the inside. The key had been withdrawn from the lock.

(11:46) Reid was huddled in a big overstuffed chair; so thin, so shriveled, he resembled one of those elongated rag dolls, left propped there in a sitting position by someone, head to chair back, feet to floor. He was staring wide-eyed at nothing. His eyes gave out no impression of life, took back none. They were like inserts of agate peering out through almond-shaped ridges of hard, corrugated flesh. A hand could have sliced past them an inch away, and they would not have flickered.

The chest rose and fell; if you looked intently you could see it. That was the only indication of life in the whole stringy frame.

Shawn was perched slantwise on the broad rounded arm of

that same chair, making a protective screen for its occupant on that side. Reid was gripping his near arm tightly with both hands, fingers lashed in a tourniquet just above the elbow; as if in that one arm lay his whole salvation. Shawn's other arm, the outside one to the chair, ended within the tautly stretched outside pocket of his coat. But the impression that came through the cloth was not the rounded one of a hand but the semi-squared one of a sharply defined, angular piece of metal.

She was across the room, her back to the two of them, head inclined to a small table on which had been placed a basin of water. There was a slight rippling sound, cautiously checked as though she was not anxious to attract attention to what she was doing; then she turned and came back toward the chair, holding extended between her hands a freshly steeped bandage or application, made of a man's flat-folded handkerchief.

(11:47) She bent over Reid. His eyes never moved, even at the imminence of the bandage.

"Here, cover them awhile," she pleaded.

She placed it gently across his burning rock-hard eyes, smoothing it, softly pressing it down with her finger tips. Over and over stroking it, shutting out horror.

Then cautiously she withdrew her hands at last, allowing it to remain adhered of its own wetness.

His head moved weakly, as though he were only now becoming belatedly aware that sight had been shut off. He tried to shake it in refusal. "No, no—" he protested. One hand relinquished Shawn's arm, tried to go up to it and peel it off. She caught it gently and stopped it, led it back to where it had been. "Rest them, just for a while. Don't look at it. Stop looking for a minute."

"It goes faster when I can't see it. It cheats on me."

"I'm here beside you, he's here beside you." She perched on

the opposite arm of the chair to Shawn, that presumably she had already been occupying until a moment or two before.

Reid was now walled in on both sides. Their upper bodies, inclining somewhat toward each other, even formed a sheltering arch above him, though not quite a closed one. It was to Shawn's arm, however, he continued to cling tenaciously, and not to hers. Her hand stroked his hair soothingly, over and over. Until the gossamer sweeps became lighter and lighter, then stopped altogether.

(11:48) They watched him cautiously for a moment, both looking down on him from above in mutually conspiring silence.

Then their eyes sought each other, by common accord. She pointed toward the clock. Then made a twisting motion with her hand, counterclockwise. Meaning, turning it back.

He pointed downward, using his head for indicator, to the tight grip on his arm that held him immovable.

She nodded slightly, turned a finger toward herself in alternative, meaning she would be the one to go.

He withdrew his hand from the gun-weighted pocket, stayed her with a slight cutting motion, pointed toward himself after all. Then he started to withdraw his body little by little across the chair back, first to the strictly perpendicular, then outward to gain the clear floor space beyond the chair, upon which to arise.

Reid felt him stir, instantly clove to him with redoubled intensity, that almost held a shudder in it.

"My foot's asleep. Just let me change it a minute."

He unlocked the terror-welded hands, pried them off one at a time, passed them to her to take into her keeping. She had to hold them back against their almost reflex attempt to swing back to where they had been.

Shawn was already erect and free of the chair.

(11:49) "No—don't get up," the blindfolded face grimaced.

"I'm standing here right beside you." He gave a heavy stamp

to the floor, in feigned attempt to restore his circulation. "Just let me stand up on it a minute."

She gave her head a sideward cast toward the clock, telling him to be quick.

He moved fast but carefully, elongating his strides but picking his way so that his steps fell soundlessly, moving wide around objects of furniture to avoid the risk of brushing against them. When he reached the clock he placed hands to it, while continuing to stare watchfully back over his shoulder, to make sure Reid had not detected his withdrawal.

The half-blanked-out face remained immobile. It was hers that was aquiver with agonizing expectancy.

He turned his head to what he was doing. He covered the latch controlling the rimmed face pane with his palm, trying to smother the sound it would make, even while he tweaked it open with his other hand. The click came through blurred but hollowly audible.

Reid didn't move.

He had the circular glass casing standing out at right angles now. There was a wire-thin squeak from the recalcitrant hinges, at the very instant the motion of opening had already stopped.

Suddenly Reid began to writhe violently in the chair. One of his hands escaped her, flew up to his face, clawed off the hampering blind. His eyes suddenly appeared, not as though they had been covered over until now, but as though they had only just that moment emerged into his face again, after some freakish physiological disappearance beneath its surface.

(11:50) Shawn's hand was at the nub of the two indicators on the clock face, about to stretch them into a wider angle. He dropped it as though their touch had burned him.

They were silent, all three of them. Even from Reid there

were no outcries. There didn't need to be; his dilated, accusing eyes spoke for him.

"Come back, Shawn," she sighed at last in resignation. "Come back."

Shawn moved slowly away from the clock, back toward the chair. He sank back onto the arm of it which he'd originally occupied.

Reid's eyes were burning questioningly up toward him, unseen behind the turn of his shoulder. "You didn't do it yet? You didn't touch it?"

"I didn't do it," Shawn said listlessly.

"Swear you didn't. Swear."

"He didn't, father. I watched."

Reid's fingers wriggled around the curve of Shawn's forearm, like white worms. "Have you still got the key there? The key to this room?"

"It's still there."

(11:51) "Show me, make it sound. Let me hear it."

Shawn touched his pocket, and something jangled restlessly.

Five more white worms crept up the other side of the arm, to commingle with the first five. "Is your gun still loaded? Are you sure it's loaded?"

"I showed you only a couple of minutes ago."

"Break it, look again, make sure."

Shawn took it out, held it with both hands, wrenched it open. Vacantly, without looking at it himself. The worms crept over it and gropingly felt of the chambers one by one.

Shawn forced it closed again, still without looking at it himself. "The room around us is locked," he said tonelessly. "The house around the room is locked. The grounds around the house are being watched." His eyes contracted into a squint at something that he alone was staring at and he alone could see; some thought, some emotion. "Nothing; nothing can get through."

(11:52) Reid took a deep breath. "You hate me, son. You hated me just then for a minute. I could feel it go through you just then. I could feel your body harden for a minute."

Shawn said, with no emotion in his voice whatever, "Don't call me son, sir. I had a father of my own. He wasn't afraid to die."

"But, then, he didn't know when it would be."

"My mother, then. She wasn't afraid to, either. She did know. She had cancer. And they couldn't use anesthetics, because her heart was weak. She smiled feebly up at me, at the end. The last thing she said was, 'I'm sorry, Tom, to be giving so much trouble.'" He fell silent.

The wriggling fingers slipped from his arm; they mangled together, in the semblance of an afflicted handclasp. Then they crept up over Reid's face, covering it for a moment. As if trying to brush the fear off it.

"I'll try not to give you any more trouble," he said through them. "I'll try not to—" He swallowed hard, dropped his hands, folded them manfully one atop the other. "See, Shawn? I'll sit here very quiet—like this—and I'll just wait."

The detective smiled a little, with a sort of pensive ruefulness. He reached around backhand, and he gripped Reid's shoulder and pressed it encouragingly for a long moment.

(11:52) "Call me son," he said softly.

18

Hue and Cry

IT WAS THE TYPE OF lunchroom that stays open all night. It was almost clinically white. The tops of all the tables were white; the walls were faced with white tiling to a point halfway to the ceiling. Their remainder, and the ceiling itself, were daubed with a hasty coat of white, rent and peeling now in places. Down the center of the ceiling from front to back ran a row of milky-white light bowls, alternating with spare-ribbed electric fans, at rest now. Even the jacket of the attendant behind the order counter was white, but this designation was by courtesy only.

On the wall a sign said, "Watch your hat and coat. Not responsible," and then ran into smaller lettering.

A middle-aged male cashier drowsed behind a desk flanking the entrance. The counterman, back at the rear of the room, pored over a newspaper for lack of other duties.

316

In between there was nobody. Nobody but one man. He sat slumped at one of the white-topped tables, hat brim low protecting his eyes against the overbearing, two-way play of snowy dazzle, coming down from the light bowls and up from the vitreous tabletops.

He was not in there to eat. He was in there to rest, perhaps. Or perhaps he was in there because he had no other place to be. A long-neglected mug of coffee stood before him. It had cooled to a point where the milk in it had separated from the coffee, drifted to the sides, forming a hollow white ring. In the middle of it the coffee was back almost to its original blackness. A spoon handle thrust up through the center of this like a submerged spar. There was also on the table before him a pasteboard ticket bearing numbers up to 100, with the 5 punched out of it. And nothing else.

He sat there inert, in the somnolent silence of the place, in a sort of comatose consciousness. He had an air of not having moved for a long time past, a full half hour perhaps. Even the cashier moved more than he, though his eyes were closed. His head kept nodding lower, then correcting itself at intervals, remaining erect for a brief while, then beginning its nodding-lower all over again. Even the counterman moved more than he. He turned a newspaper page every now and then, moistening his thumb each time preparatory to doing so. He didn't move at all. He sat there inert, lost in forgetfulness or reverie, one arm spineless across his lap, the other unstirring at full length drop from his shoulder, as though there were no muscular mechanism in it to lift or bend it. Only his mind, perhaps, was not at a dead halt.

Thus for half an hour past, and thus in all likelihood for half an hour yet to come.

And then suddenly he had ignited into full, over-all motion. It wasn't just a stirring, a shift. From the static, without transition, he was amove all over. For no apparent reason, at no apparent cause.

Not a sound came in from outside, not a sight. He moved quickly, as though the impulse, the mental detonation that had set him off, were an urgent one. His chair scraped back, he was standing fully erect, he was looking toward the door. There was no one in it, no one beyond it on the outside, no indication of anyone approaching even at a distance, no sign of life whatever, within, without.

Yet he moved. He made haste away from table and chair, leaving untouched coffee and unpaid marker behind, and bore down toward the door, as if about to make his way hurriedly through it to the outside.

Halfway there, he checked himself, as though a counter-warning to the first one had overtaken him. He looked about behind him, as if in search for a substitute to the aperture he'd been about to hasten through, and which was now useless to him for some invisible reason. There were two telephone booths against the wall, toward the back. He veered over that way, cutting through a subsidiary lane between tables, followed the wall, and entered the rearmost of the two. He sat down within it, and the impulse seemed to flow all out of him, and he was quiescent again. He didn't disconnect the instrument, he didn't immediately close the door. He sat there as if waiting for a briefly allotted space of time to pass.

It passed. It was about two minutes in length, not less.

The first full minute, nothing happened. Then the ascending whine of rubbered wheels rounding a corner could be heard. Very faint, hardly anything. Then brakes gripping, somewhere just outside. Still almost as faint, still easy to miss. Then a heavy shoe striking open sidewalk.

The two minutes was up. The revolving door fluxed and two men entered one behind the other. One was Dobbs, one was Sokolsky. Their faces looked tired and harassed. They weren't speaking to each other, acted as though they'd grown tired of that, come to the end of that, a full hour ago. Dobbs pushed his hat farther back on his head, in a sort of limp acquiescence of failure.

They each plucked a pasteboard from the round rubber mat on the counter in front of the cashier.

When they were halfway toward the back, halfway toward where he sat ensconced, and not until then, the man in the booth drew the slide closed. Dobbs, in the lead, glanced momentarily at his projecting hand as it did so, then indifferently away again.

A light went on over him, making the whole interior of the booth glow a dull yellow. It powdered the crown of his hat and his shoulders like sprinkled corn meal. He looked up at it but he let it alone. He turned his head a little, so that the back of his neck was to the outside room. As though the blank wall he was now facing wearied him with its monotony, he took a stub of yellow pencil from his pocket and busied himself tracing an abstract geometrical design on it, with minute draftsmanlike attentiveness to each shading stroke. It had no meaning, it was purely hypothetical in outline. He continued it industriously, nevertheless. At times he would break off, and look at it critically, as though deciding whether it suited him or not. Then he would resume again. His unfeigned absorption in it was the epitome of enforced idleness; but of an idleness experienced in surroundings of perfect security. He was utterly relaxed; he did not once look around. It was as though he knew ahead of time that interruption was not to occur, was a guaranteed impossibility, and therefore had no concern about it.

Dobbs and Sokolsky were carrying mugs of steaming coffee away from the counter now, still one behind the other. Dobbs, in the lead, came to the table where the man now in the booth had sat, and stopped at it, about to sit down there in turn. It may have been the fact that the chair before it was already partly withdrawn and therefore offered less effort in seating oneself upon it than the matching chairs at surrounding tables, which were thrust closely in under them and would have had to be pulled all the way back. But then seeing the discarded mug of coffee, he hesitated, continuing to hold his own aloft. Next he picked up the cardboard ticket left lying there beside it, held it for an instant to show Sokolsky, as if confirming the fact that someone else had a prior claim upon this table, put it down again where he'd found it. They went on one table more, sat down at the immediate next one.

They took seats on opposite sides of it, facing each other, but they still didn't speak to each other, they didn't look at each other. They had the expressions of men who are sick of the whole world and everyone in it.

Dobbs looked down at his brown-streaked coffee mug, Sokolsky looked up at one of the milky light bowls studding the ceiling. The trajectories of their looks missed each other by a mile. But they also missed what they hit, didn't take in anything.

They sugared their coffees, copiously and dejectedly, from the patented container, that simply had to be reversed and shaken. They lifted and partly drank them, Sokolsky still looking upward, Dobbs downward. Then they set the mugs down again heavily, still partly filled. The coffee was too hot to be drunk all at once. Sokolsky wiped his lips with the side of his hand. Dobbs took out a battered cigarette package, shook it upward so that the single cigarette it still held jumped through the gap torn in it at one side of the top.

He mouthed it, but then he didn't bother lighting it after all, as though to do so would give him no real pleasure. He took it out and looked at it as though there was something very disappointing about it. Then he dropped it into the moat running around his saucer, and it turned brown and wet half the way up, like a siphon.

The man in the booth was correcting some of his own handi-work now. He had reversed the pencil stub, was conscientiously erasing a marginal detail of his design. Then he leaned close, blew at the place he'd just been frictioning, to remove any particles of eraser that might conceivably have adhered. The surface he had chosen to work upon now restored, he resumed sketching. He seemed to have forgotten the existence of the outside room.

Sokolsky had got to the bottom of his coffee now. He wiped his lips again, but with a gesture more of apprehension than of fastidiousness. He spoke for the first time since they had entered.

"You want to do it?" he said. "Or you want me to?"

Dobbs seemed to require no explanatory preamble to understand the remark.

"I'll do it," he said glumly. "One of us has to."

He got up from the table, turned, went back toward the booths. He didn't look directly at them as he neared them; he'd seen before that they were there, and that sufficed him apparently. Then, too, there was a colored porter, now, mopping the floor in that section of the room. He had shoved some of the tables aside to make clearance. The crouched figure, the bucket that it was necessary to avoid overturning, the moist area that had to be traversed watchfully to avoid slipping upon, may have all combined to deflect his eye as he arrived before the booths.

He reached for the door grip of the one that was occupied, the one that was lighted, and swung that back in lieu of its neighbor. Then the back of a neck, almost against his blundering shirt front, confronted him as he raised foot to step in.

The man in it didn't turn his head. All he did was desist for a moment, hold his pencil point back from its handiwork, as if passively waiting for the intrusion to be discontinued.

"Sorry," Dobbs blurted, and recoiled. He swung the door closed on him again, and entered the one alongside.

The pencil point rejoined the wall, resumed its meticulous tracings of the same lines over and over, to give them body, to give them firmness.

Through the thin lateral partition came the jangle of a

deposited coin, and then the ricocheting of a dial. One long swift stroke. Then a voice, guardedly: "Headquarters, please." After that it was audible only at intermittent intervals, not only because it was pitched so low, but because of the frequent, halting pauses it seemed to be constrained to, due perhaps to incessant interruption.

"Not a sign of him—

"Been trying our best—

"Been running our heads off—

"I know, lieutenant, but we're doing the best we can—

"Yes, sir—

"Yes, sir—

"Yes, sir, lieutenant—

"Yes, sir—"

Sokolsky was standing outside the booth now. He put the flat of his hand out, at one point, as a brief support to his uneasiness of posture, and it rested against the glass paneling of the second booth, not the first one, the one Dobbs was in. Then he withdrew it again, and a steamy smear remained behind, inflicted by the nervous moisture of his skin. The man within turned his face briefly outward to look, and the evanescent print that had remained dimmed the lower part of his features, like a filmy transparent mask over which his eyes peered unobstructed. Then he turned his face wallward again, and the stigma evaporated.

Dobbs stepped out, and they stood there for a moment outside the two booths. "He gave me hell. I wish you could've heard."

Sokolsky mangled his own lower lip worriedly.

"He's going to break every one of us," Dobbs went on. "It's bring him in or else."

A throttled gulp of dismay percolated from Sokolsky's throat. "What does he think, we're holding out on him?"

"Let's get going," Dobbs concluded. "It's not going to do us any good lousing around here."

The profile and its satellite rind of cuticle swept from the glass, and a pair of shadow-blobs glanced fanwise across it, after a momentary time lag.

They made their way down the side of the room toward the doorway ahead, still in the same order in which they'd entered, Sokolsky at heel.

"Don't forget the checks," Sokolsky said. Dobbs digressed toward where they had been sitting.

Again he came first to the table that had been occupied before their entrance, picked up that ownerless check by mistake. Then, noting, cast it down, this time with a fillip of impatience; went on, picked up the two rightful ones, and rejoined his teammate at the cashier's desk. A register cymbaled, and they had gone.

The man in the booth was fumbling in his pocket. He brought out two dimes, a quarter, several pennies, scanned them in the palm of his hand. Then he returned them, stood up.

He opened the door of the booth and came outside. He went up front to the cashier's desk.

"Give me a couple of nickels, please," he said meekly, and put one of the dimes down.

The cashier made change for him with an ungracious scowl. He picked the nickels up and went back toward the booth again.

The door swirled once more and Dobbs had come in again. He palmed down change in front of the cashier. "Give me a pack of cigarettes," he said impatiently. "I forgot to get 'em when I was in here just now."

The other man's shoulder, elbow, hip were just receding into the gap of the booth. The slide shuttled closed over them.

Dobbs snatched up the cigarettes and bolted out again. The tormented door spun once more, came around empty.

In the booth a deposited coin clanged. Then a dial rustled. One long swift stroke. "Headquarters, please," a submissive voice said.

19

End of Police Procedure

TEN-FIFTY-ONE. MCMANUS IS in his office, alone. The same one in which he had them all lined up before him—was it two days or was it two months ago?—and gave them their assignments and instructions. He's by himself now, under a cone-light making a great white triangle, its base flat on his desk. He's poring over a report. On his left are two more he's just finished poring over. On his right are three, maybe four, he hasn't come to yet. All the men have reported. All about the same thing.

His coat is off, and his tie is off, and he's made a bird's nest of his hair, still plentiful for a man his age. On the desk is his pocket watch, sitting open, lid reared. His eyes keep going from report in hand to it, and back to report in hand again.

McManus is time-harassed, too; as time-harassed as anyone

else in this affair. And he hates it. He's not used to working against a deadline. He's never had to before.

He finishes the report. He punctuates it by a heavy, frustrated clout of his fist to the desktop. He did that with the first two, too. No good, don't lead anywhere. He discards it, takes up the next one.

The phone rings. It's been doing that on an average of every four or five minutes, for hours, and now its beginning to pick up speed if anything. It's only from the desk sergeant outside, though, this time. "No," he says, "I'm up to my neck in here. Switch it to somebody else."

He takes up the new report, starts reading. But his mind is still on the one before, something has lingered. He drops the new one, goes back to the old, reshuffles his hair in the meantime.

Then he drops the old, after a refresher glance, picks up the phone. "Go out and bring in that rummage-shop owner. Spitzer. I want to talk to him myself. You can't tell me he didn't know those shoes were in the window. No, never mind. It's too late."

And even if he did, he thinks, how much further are we? The point is, how did Tompkins? Always that same stone wall. In all these reports. No matter which direction you start out in, you always end up in the same place.

He finishes the next report; punctuates it with the same pummel of thwarted dissatisfaction.

Ten-fifty-three. Call from Molloy, upstate. More details on the escaped-lion episode. "The mother of a kid of about eight or nine just brought him in by the back of the neck to the local constable's office. I was present. He was still squalling from the lambasting he'd been given at home. He admitted lighting a firecracker, throwing it into the lions' cage, and running for his life."

"Then what's the score?"

"It stinks from paradox. Two of them were sold, see, I told you that. One to Hughes, one to this kid. Hughes had murder in his heart, the kid just mischief. The kid just happened to pick on the selfsame thing that Hughes himself intended to do. Only the kid beat him to it. Hughes had the chain around the side trap filed through, all in readiness and waiting; left loosely draped to look like it was still intact. But he didn't have his wife standing there in position yet, in front of the cage, waiting for him 'to show up.' The lion came to meet him halfway, instead of waiting for him to get there. Just a little too soon, that's all. But the method was his identically, firecracker and all. Stinks with paradox, like I said."

"It has nothing to do with our case, anyway."

"Except that the lion's still at large. And slowly working closer to Shawn's base of operations. A report came in just now before I picked up the phone that a couple petting in a car had the daylights scared out of them by what they took to be an enormous tawny dog, running out at them, then diving back into cover again. The spot they indicated is only about five miles from the northern boundary of the Reid estate."

"Do something about it, will ya!" McManus exclaims shrilly. "Aren't there any State Police up that way? Head it off!"

He hangs up, and no sooner does than it rings right back again. Desk sergeant outside again. "How many times do I have to tell you, Hogan? I'm busy!"

Ten-fifty-seven. Call from Dobbs, this time. Breathless, anxious to redeem himself. "I think we've nailed him, lieutenant. Somebody answering his description was just seen entering a house at Fourteen Dexter Street. It's just two blocks over from where we lost him earlier today. No, we didn't see him ourselves, but we're not taking any chances, we've got the place sealed up tight, back and front."

"Don't do anything until I get there. Sit tight. I'm going to take charge of it myself. I'm leaving right now."

He jumps up, sidesweeps all the reports, finished and

unfinished alike, together into the discard, grabs for his hat, grabs for his coat, and starts for the door. He comes back and grabs for his watch. Two to eleven. Sixty-two minutes to go. He snaps the lid shut, shoves it into his coat, which still isn't on his back. His tie he lets go altogether.

It rings again before he can get away from the desk. The desk sergeant, for about the third time in a row. He kills it quick, without listening. "Not now, Hogan. I'm on my way out."

He goes out fast. It starts to ring again no sooner has he closed the door, but this time he keeps going, wrestling into his coat along the way.

The desk sergeant tries to stop him as he flits past the vestibule outside, still struggling with his coat.

"Lieutenant—"

"Some other time, Hogan. Can't you see I'm in a hurry?"

"What'll I do about this guy, lieutenant?" the sergeant calls after him in a stage whisper, shielding his mouth with the edge of his hand. "He says he's been phoning you all day and now he's pestering me to get in to see you—"

A forlorn-looking figure that has been slumped patiently on a bench against the far wall straightens up a little inquiringly. "Is that him—?"

McManus flicks a brief look that way in transit, keeps going. "Find out what he wants. Sick him on somebody else."

"He won't say. I tried that. He won't see anyone but you."

"Then throw him out," McManus concludes, and by that time is already out himself.

A moment later, on the steps outside, someone comes after him, touches him placatingly on the sleeve.

"Beat it," McManus growls, swinging his arm free. "You heard what I just told the sergeant, didn't you?" He goes on down the steps.

The supplicant follows at an abashed distance. Again that hesitant touch on the arm, as McManus stops once more, crouches, about to step into a squad car at the curb.

This time McManus whirls on him exasperatedly. "Get outa here!" he roars savagely. "What d'ya want? Who are you anyway?"

"Jeremiah Tompkins," is the disclaiming answer. "And I've—I've been trying to give myself over to you."

20

End of the Wait

IT WAS THE AWFUL SILENCE that was so hard to bear. They couldn't get him to say anything any more, he was past speech. Almost, he was past life itself. If there was any spark of it left, it was sunk so deep within the cold, accumulated ash of fear that not a glimmer of it peered through. Technically, he was still alive. His heart was going, his breath was going. His eyes were open, though whether they saw anything any more was problematical. But spiritually, he was dead already. As completely, as irreparably dead as a cadaver on a mortician's table.

They weren't as lucky. They were both still alive enough to feel. They were without speech, too, but not from the same cause. They still had use of their voices. But there wasn't anything to say, so they quit trying after a while.

The girl's face was the color of talcum. Shawn's was the

darker color of granite, with glistening lines of sweat pinpointed along it here and there. But his—Reid's—wasn't a face any more. It was just that puckered part of the corpse where the eyes and mouth and nose used to be.

Shawn knew they'd never forget this night, the two of them, no matter what else happened for the rest of their lives. It would never be altogether over, either. It would never completely fade into daylight again. It had grown *too* dark this one night. Some of the darkness would always be left behind. They were getting scars on their souls, the sort of scars people got in the Dark Ages, when they believed in devils and black magic. Scars that would never completely heal. Pain would leave, the stiffness would leave, some day, but the scars would always be there, if you kneaded real hard and close. When it got dark, when other nights came, when other fears came, there would be twinges.

The clock was there in the room with them yet. It was far better to have it than not to have it, far less torment to see it than not to see it. That problem had decided itself long ago. Not for his sake any longer, for their own now as well. He wouldn't have badgered and asked them any more, he was past even that now. It was they who had to know now, had to watch. The pendulum, like a harried gold planet, kept flashing back and forth behind the glass that trapped it. A thin splinter of white remained between the two black hands. It was two minutes to twelve.

It was like drops of water falling onto a hollowed wood surface. Clop, clop, clop, clop.

Jean kept manipulating her two solacing hands over his temples, stroking them gently, soothing them. Like a masseuse. But like an absent-minded masseuse, who has been massaging for so long that she has forgotten she is doing it, has forgotten to stop.

Shawn thought rebelliously, Damn! Why doesn't it happen? Something, anything! Big, noisy, the works; I don't care what it is. Why doesn't a lion bust headfirst through the window over there and send glass showering all over the room? Now, this very minute! Why doesn't a stream of bullets come spitting in from the dark out there? Let him get killed! Let me get killed, too! Yes, even let her get killed! Only, get it over; let something happen! Anything would be better than this nothing. He began to swivel the muzzle of his gun restlessly in and out atop his thigh, turned flat on its side. I'm going to shoot pretty soon, he warned himself. I'm going to have to. And I only hope there's something there to shoot at, because I'm going to shoot whether there is or not. I'm going to go gun-happy, I feel it coming on. He lowered his head, and pinched it tight across the forehead for a minute with his other hand.

Then he remembered that she was there, and that pulled him out of it again, for another minute or so.

It was one to, now. The white splinter had been pared to a thread. If you had very good eyes you could still see it. If not, you could just see the two double-width hands. Clop, clop, clop, clop; the horses of death were trotting to the post.

Suddenly the figure in the chair was holding out a hand toward each of them. They'd already thought him incapable of further motion, but this must have been the final flicker.

A scratchy sound that was no longer a voice came from him.

"I'm going to say good-bye now. Take my hand, son. Thank you for—for staying with me to the end. Jean, darling, come around in front of me, kiss me good-bye. I can't turn my head."

She hid his face with hers for a moment. The warm, living mass of her hair took the place of the taut, bone-stretched dead skin.

The two hands were single-width now. They had blended perfectly, one atop the other. The clock had only one hand. The time was *now*. The time was death.

A bell, a pair of them with a flickering hammer in between, began to jingle, febrile, flutelike, puling. It was like a lowering mountain of menace spewing forth a squeaky toy mouse on wheels.

They jumped as though the filament of a live wire had been put to their skins; the two living did, at least. Shawn's gun nearly went off by reflex action. They couldn't orient their faculties for a moment; everything had been centered on the clock for so long.

The sound interrupted itself, then resumed. Its rhythm told what it was, that break that kept recurring. It was a telephone ringing; the one outside in the main hall, up from this room, over against the stair base.

Shawn was on his feet, arrested, half crouched.

Bong! the clock went, mellowly, majestically. The hour was sounding. It was almost anticlimactic to the other, the lesser noise. There was a needling immediacy to that, it tattooed their nerves.

Shawn had the key out. He was over at the door now, looking back at the two of them, head inclined, as if trying to analyze what the sound boded by its very timbre.

Reid's incised lips kept fluttering. Words finally came, hoarsely. "No, don't— It may be a trick, a trap to get you away from us—"

Bong! the clock went a second time. It seemed to send out waves of jarred air, as though the room were a still pool and something heavy had been dropped into the middle of it.

It resumed again, as though touched off by the greater sound. There was a different rhythm now, its tempo was faster.

Jean's hand caught in her hair. "Go out and stop it," she choked. "I can't stand it any more."

"Wait a minute," he said. "That's a police call. Three short rings at a time— They told me they'd use that if they wanted to get me."

His wrist flicked and the door was open. He widened it behind him.

"I'll be right out here in full sight of the door," he said. "Nothing can get past me."

He saw her crouch protectively over Reid, enfold him, draw him to her with both her arms.

He stepped quickly down to the phone, stopped, lifted it, gun hand watchfully fanning the empty air around him as he stood there. Shadow-boxing the emptiness.

Bong! welled out to him from the distance, like a mucous tide. It was McManus. "Are you all right?"

"Yes," Shawn bit out, eyes roving the walls, the stairs over him, the securely locked main door down at the end of the hall.

"It's over. We've beaten the rap. The guy's saved. Tompkins just committed suicide in his cell. Took everything away from him, and he found a way to do it anyway. Broke one of the large flat buttons he had on his clothing, and used the jagged edge to open his throat. Didn't find him in time."

Bong! vibrated in Shawn's eardrum.

"Just before that I had a call from Molloy. A large lion that was on the loose ever since this afternoon was shot and killed. Only about twenty miles up from where you are. Tell him. Tell him it's over, nothing more to worry about. No time to tell you any more now. I'll be out there quick as I can myself, starting right now--"

Bong! cut across it, fourth stroke of the hour.

Her frenzied scream blended in with it, searing through him like cauterization. He dropped the phone like a red-hot rivet.

Reid flashed through the open room door, like an inanimate projectile fired by some detonation within. He shot straight down the long hall toward the entrance door at the far end, darting with a swiftness that could not have been rational physical motion any longer, that was rather an integral spasmodic symptom of death throes already well in progress.

"Hold him! He's gone out of his mind!" she screamed from the room.

"Door's locked, he can't get out!" he shouted. He sprinted after him, sure to overtake him within a matter of seconds as the immovable door blocked the insane flight. He had a glimpse of her, as he passed the open doorway, lying semiprone upon the floor within the room, either flung there by Reid as he burst free with final superhuman strength or dragged there after him until her hold was exhausted and she dropped from him.

The door was directly before Reid now. "I'm coming!" he keened wildly, "I'm coming!" as though racing toward an invisible appointment.

He turned suddenly, leftward, almost at contact point with the door, and disappeared into the darkness of the conservatory, on that side. "I'm coming!" came once more from the darkness.

There was a sudden crackling crash, and then silence.

"The lights! For God's sake, the lights! I can't see a thing in here!" Shawn beat both hands wildly up and down the inside facing of the doorway. She was uphall, staggering down after him, sobbing. With lack of breath rather than grief.

He found the switch just before she reached him, tripped it.

The lights glowed on behind those beautiful cathedrallike panels, ruby, emerald, amber, sapphire. Reid was standing upright, motionless, close up against one of them. Shoulders and head bent forward, as though he were peering closely at it, myopically close.

For a second Shawn couldn't understand what was holding him there. Then he saw that he was headless, or seemed to be; he ended at the neck. Jagged teeth of thick, splintered glass held his craned neck in a vise, formed a collar, had pierced his jugular. His head was on the other side, had been rammed through the leaded pane to the space where the lights were. You could see the dark shadow that was his life blood running down the inside of the lighted pane in uneven sprayed tendrils, pacing one another, dimming its magnificent coloring.

He was gone.

And the panel he'd chosen, he'd aimed himself unerringly at, in his blind headlong flight, with the room pitch-black around him, out of all the many others, was that of the lion rampant. Its mane and rabid eyes and flat feline nostrils still showed unde-stroyed above his gashed neck, as though it were swallowing him bodily. And for fangs now, instead of painted ones it had those jagged incisors of glass, thrusting into his flesh from all sides of the orifice he himself had created.

Death by the jaws of a lion.

Bong! the clock went for the twelfth time, and the hour was past. All was silence.

21
End of Night

THE TENSION WAS GONE FROM the room now. It was like a place where the air has been cleared by a violent electrical discharge. It was tinctured with past fear, but fear in the present, in the actuality, was no longer in it. Just a shadowy awe remained behind, clinging to its walls, as in a place where death has been.

The girl was gone. Someone else was gone too. Someone it was better not to think about. (Shawn tried not to think about him; failed each time; tried again.) Gone for good, gone forever; beyond pain, beyond fear, beyond time, the enemy.

The clock was still there. The golden planet still swung. The hollow-hoofed horses still galloped, clop, clop, clop, clop, for someone else now. For the next one. The hands were at four and at six. Half past four in the morning.

The house was quiet. The door had closed long before on the

trundling stretcher bearers; and it seemed as though that was the last sound there had been. And it seemed as though that had been a long, long time ago.

Shawn and McManus were alone in there. McManus picked up his hat, looked at it, put it on; in the slow way of a man who has been contemplating departure for some time past, and now has brought himself at last to the point of carrying it out.

"What was it?" he said. "What'll I say? I'm going back to town now. Tomorrow or the day after, I'll have to be making out a report on it. Oh, I'll have the report of the medical examiner. A severed jugular, he'll say; something like that. But what'll *I* say, what'll *I* put down, that's what I'm wondering. Death by accident. Death while of unsound mind. Murder by mental suggestion. Death by decree of—" He turned speculative eyes toward the windows, where the draperies were now thrown wide, and restless twinkles simmered across the face of the sky.

"Are you asking me, lieutenant?"

"No," McManus said. "I'm asking—myself." He moved on toward the door. "Oh, the report'll be made. And the word that I'll put down, that won't matter much. Because no hand touched him. And that's all we, the police, are for. To see that no hand's raised." He shook his head. "But there are so many things I'll never know for sure." Then he added abruptly, "Will you?"

Shawn didn't answer. He put out one of the lamps, and as though the same switch controlled them, the glimmering outside the windows grew that much brighter, came that much closer.

They went out into the hall one behind the other, Shawn behind his chief.

"We have all the answers," McManus said. "I mean I have, down at my office. But the answers don't really answer anything. There's a 'why' in this too big to go down on any report. It seems to slip away each time you think you've got it pinned down. The man who was shot dead the other night on the stairs of Tompkins' rooming house—well, we've identified him. He was Walter Myers, and he was Reid's broker. He handled all Reid's financial affairs, all his investments, for years past. It's the same old story, as old as the first brokerage office, as old as the first share of stock ever floated on a stock market. Temptation, too much funds to manipulate, too much carelessness on the part of a wealthy client. Reid didn't go near him for years at a time, left everything in his hands."

He put out his hand to the doorknob, and then left it there, without turning it.

"It'll take years to uncover all his activities, check through all his accounts. Years and a brigade of auditors. Anyway, I can tell you this much right now, before going any further. That girl upstairs will be poor. Maybe not poor as you and I go, but poor to what she was until now."

"Good," said Shawn softly, fervently; so low that the other man didn't even catch it.

"Well, he got himself into a great big hole, somewhere along the way. And he kept trying to shore up the bottom by dumping in Reid's funds and securities. Only, there was no bottom to shore up; it got deeper all the time, the way those things do. Eventually, some day, there was bound to be a cave-in, and he knew that as well as anyone else. It was staring him in the face as surely as—"

He thumbed toward the room they had just come from, and Shawn knew what he meant.

"The only thing in his favor was, there was no hard and fast deadline on it, he could still string it out a while, he had a few months' time. But there were just two possible outcomes: either a crash, and exposure, or flight without waiting for the crash, and exposure. Maybe he didn't have the stomach for flight. Or maybe the way his affairs were fixed, he wouldn't have been able to flee wealthy, he would have had to flee broke. So he had to sit tight and wait, shaking in his shoes.

"And then something happened that must have seemed a godsend to him at the time.

"Among his other clients—he didn't have very many—there was a wealthy old woman. You know the type. Not as juicy as Reid, and a lot more stingy, so he seems to have had sense enough to let her alone. But he noticed she was having uncanny luck with her amateurish, shoestring investments, while he himself kept going down in quicksand. I don't know how he broke her down, but he had a way with him, and he finally got to the bottom of it. He learned she was getting tips from her housemaid. And the housemaid in turn was getting them, especially for her, from some unrevealed source.

"This particular woman has died since, and the maid herself took her own life. But we have enough evidence to reconstruct the thing. We have records showing that an Eileen McGuire was employed as maid by such-and-such a woman at such-and-such a time, and also records that that same woman was a client of Walter Myers. It's a pretty logical reconstruction, isn't it?"

Shawn nodded.

"Anyway, Myers finally ferreted out the source of the information, and, his curiosity aroused, he went there to investigate. From there on, there's a very great blank to be filled in. This part is purely supposition. Neither one of them is alive any more to tell us just what went on; we have to fill it in as best we can, with the little we have.

"Myers didn't do any better in his transactions and frantic jugglings, so it's safe to assume Tompkins didn't help him as he had the woman. Either that, or else Myers was already in such a mess by that time that a few tips on the market were no longer enough to pull him out of it. He needed to come into outright control of the balance of Reid's fortune, be no longer subject to an accounting, in order to cover up the previous defalcations. You can misuse your own money, and not be held accountable; misuse somebody else's and you go to jail.

"Here's what set the fuse to the bombshell. Tompkins had his room practically papered with unsolicited and uncashed checks that Reid had thrust on him at various times. Myers came across one of these, and that gave him the idea for the whole setup. Tompkins wouldn't co-operate knowingly, he didn't want anything from anybody, so Myers deliberately framed him, to get something on him. We can only guess at what it was, and if our guess is right, it was pretty crude. But Tompkins was a simple man, a rustic, and Myers was a glib talker, so he seems to have got away with it. One of Reid's checks turned up in Myers' office, we found it there. It had been endorsed over to Myers by Tompkins, to whom it was originally made out. It had been lifted from five hundred to five thousand dollars. And in such a sloppy way that it wouldn't have passed any bank teller in the world, not even one who was stone-blind. But the important thing about it is this: it had never been presented for payment at any bank. Myers was just keeping it as something to hold over Tompkins' head. I don't think Tompkins was the one who endorsed it, and I don't think he was the one who lifted its face value. He could have got a genuine five-thousand-dollar check from Reid any time he wanted to, just by crooking his little finger. I think Myers did both those things, and then threatened him with the consequences."

"Then the prediction was Myers' suggestion, to break down Reid, drive him to his death?"

"I wish I could say it was. That would be simple. No, the

prediction came by itself. Myers was an outsider to it; he tried to cash in on it, to twist it around to serve his own purposes, when he heard it had been made. He was trying to maneuver Tompkins into inducing Reid to change his will, so that Tompkins himself would be the beneficiary once-removed, after the daughter. Tompkins would have been putty in his hands; for all practical purposes, the estate would have been turned over to Myers, with Tompkins just a figurehead, not knowing what it was all about. And that way, his own name, Myers', would have safely stayed off paper."

"What about Jean? You said 'after her.'"

"I don't think she would have lived very long after her father. I think she would have been put out of the way within a very few days, or maybe right along with her father tonight, if Myers had remained alive. I don't think Myers believed in the prediction himself. I'm pretty sure he would have tried to give it a hand, in one way or another, to make sure it was carried out; maybe tried to talk the two of them, Reid and the girl, into a suicide pact as the time approached. He didn't know we'd been sailed into it. Well, anyway, one of the fellows got him on the stairs, so we'll never know just what he would have done about it."

"And then Tompkins did away with himself, and then the prediction—"

"—came off anyway," McManus finished it for him. "Leaving that big 'why,' leaving us just about where we were before. Myers wasn't the villain in the center, pulling all the strings. Myers was just a pint-sized villain on the outside, trying to muscle into something that was already in progress without any activation from him."

"Tompkins wasn't the villain either, I guess," Shawn suggested.

"Far from it. He was just a poor tormented soul, cursed from the day he was born; caught in the middle of something, crushed by something that he probably couldn't understand himself. Wriggling all the time to get free, like a blind worm under a stone. A farm boy, with a flash of searing fire between his eyes."

"There were prophets in the Bible," Shawn reminded him.

McManus flung open the door.

The stars were like silver hailstones beating into their faces; hailstones without sound, without feeling.

They both dropped their eyes, uncomfortably, warily.

"I don't feel good," McManus muttered rebelliously. "There *was* something there. Something I can't get down on a report, so it'll stick there, fast; it keeps slipping away. That actress and the diamond wrist watch. That kid that nearly got run over. The way Dobbs' gun misfired on the stairs. He even knew their *names*, Tom, their Christian names, from the floor below—" His voice meshed with what sounded curiously like a sob, though his face was grim enough. "There *was* something there, and I don't *want* to know what it was! I tell you, I don't feel good. I feel just like I do when I'm coming down with a cold, and I'm not coming down with a cold! I'm going home to my old lady, and drink a stiff hot toddy." He sounded argumentative, as though Shawn were trying to stop him, and Shawn wasn't.

"Are you coming in with me?" he demanded. "Give you a lift?"

Shawn glanced inside, along the hallway to the stairs. "I guess I'll stay out here. Tonight anyway. She's alone up there."

"Isn't there anyone with her at all?"

"Yes, but—you know what I mean. We sort of went through the whole thing together from first to last. I'll walk you down to the car."

They walked down the path heads inclined, watching the ground as they walked over it; like men deep in thought do.

McManus suddenly gave vent to an irritable thought. "I wish you'd never brought that girl to me! I wish I'd never seen her, never heard the whole thing." After a moment, he added, "I bet you wish you'd never walked along the river that night."

"I had to," Shawn answered simply. "That was where I was to walk, there wasn't any other place."

McManus glanced at him with a sort of furtive curiosity.

"See you tomorrow, Tom. Take it easy, come in whenever you want."

He watched the car go down the driveway, its red tail-light making a corkscrew twist until it had straightened out to take the public highway.

Then he turned and trudged back toward the house. A little blue rivulet of shadow rippled before him in the palish starlight. It was cool and quiet and dark. He wasn't afraid, but he felt very small, very unimportant. He felt as though there were no longer any need to worry about what happened to him, whether for good or for ill; that was all taken care of from now on, that was all out of his hands. It was a strange feeling, a light feeling, as though something heavy had dropped off your back.

There was a dim light upstairs, in the window of the room where she slept and the nurse kept vigil. He wondered if she felt that way too.

And when you felt that way, you needed your complement. You couldn't go on alone, you were too small, too helpless. Two helpless children in the dark.

He didn't want to sleep. Who could have slept? He lit a cigarette and stood around out there on the gravel, waiting. Waiting for it to be light, for when he'd see her again. Suddenly he threw the cigarette away. The door had moved a little. Something white, the edge of a face, was peering through at him.

"Who is it? Is it you?"

The door slipped open a little wider, the face nodded.

"Come out. Come out here to me."

343

She stood poised there. He saw her eyes go up overhead, then quickly drop.

"Don't be afraid. It's just a few steps, and I'm standing here. My arms are out to you."

Suddenly they were together, pressed close.

"You should be resting."

"*She* fell asleep, and *I* stayed awake. I knew you were down here somewhere. I knew you wouldn't go away. Wherever you were, that was where I wanted to be, that was where it was best to be. Even out here, in the open."

She squinted defensively, and averted her face.

"Open your coat, let me cover my face."

She burrowed her face against his chest, as though she couldn't get in close enough. He covered almost her entire head with the flaps of his coat. She snuggled against him as in a cocoon of safety.

You couldn't hear them from a foot away, they breathed their confidences so low to each other, *for* each other alone. Two children in the night.

"Lie still, don't tremble so. You're in my arms. I'll be your husband in a few more days, and you'll never be alone again. Lie still, beloved, the stars are going, one by one. Morning is on its way."

But his eyes went uneasily upward past his own shoulder, studying those distant inscrutable pin points of brilliance.